Also by Jane Wenham-Jones

Raising The Roof

Perfect Alibis

One Glass Is Never Enough

Wannabe A Writer?

Wannabe A Writer We've Heard Of?

Praise for Jane Wenham-Jones

"The irrepressible Wenham-Jones has a sense of humour as well as a complete lack of inhibition..." *Daily Mail*

"Great fun." *Heat*

"A perfect read for bored gossips." *OK*

"A great read." *Best*

"Deliciously different" *The Bookseller*

"Thoroughly enjoyable and full of deft, sparky humour." Jill Mansell

"Brilliant" Sue Cook

Acknowledgements

Some novelists spend years on their research, involving long hours poking through dusty archives, months holed up in The British Library and weeks of background reading.

My own approach is generally to hit Google or ask a friend/colleague/bloke in the pub, who might know.

This time those kind souls have included:

Anne Catchpole, Domenic De Paolis, Joanne Derrick, Lyn-Marie Fabes, Sally Forgette, Helen French, Bill Harris, Lorna Marchant, Trevor McCallum, Catherine Pool, Lynda Wenham-Jones, Tom Wenham-Jones and the person I've forgotten (there is always one).

I am also grateful to Dr Mark J Hudson-Peacock FRCP (a whiz with the Botox) and Laurence Shaw FRCOG (if *your* hormones arc in uproar – he's the best) for sharing their professional expertise; Heather Leatt for being my gym buddy (and task-mistress!); Lynne Barrett-Lee for my first taste of Daytime TV; Jacqui Cook for the inclusion of Greens Wine Bar and Tony Mulliken for being such a pal when I was losing heart.

Thanks too to my agent The Fearsome One, Hazel and Bob Cushion, Peter Newsom, Sarah Davies, Alison Stokes, Della Galton, Liz Coldwell, Peter Brookesmith, Felicity Brookesmith and Judith Haire. We got there in the end, eh? ☺

www.janewenham-jones.com

Chapter One

Recent research has shown that the kind of male face a woman finds attractive can differ depending on where she is in her menstrual cycle. For instance, if she is ovulating she is drawn to men with rugged, masculine features. Whereas if she is menstruating she is more prone to be attracted to a man with a heavy pair of scissors shoved in his forehead ...

HO BLOODY HO. I sit on my hands so I can't punch the computer screen. Hilarious, these Internet jokes. Or they might be if not so close to the truth. I quite often imagine Daniel cowering in a corner, whimpering while I take a blunt instrument to him. Or the way he might look if I wiped away that supercilious expression by treading on it. Especially on Day 19. Day 19 of my menstrual cycle is when I am at my most malevolent and think my darkest thoughts. Then I write vitriolic letters in my head and fantasise about wreaking revenge on everyone who has ever done me wrong. It is when I smash crockery, forget things, scream, shout and eat four KitKats without drawing breath. It is Day 19 today and already I am ...

'Am I going to Dad's tonight?'

Stanley appeared in the doorway in his school shirt and boxers. His hair, as usual, stood up in tufts. He yawned and wrinkled his freckled nose. 'Do you know where my tie is?'

I gripped the edge of the keyboard. 'No, I do not know where your tie is. It is wherever you left it, the same as it is every morning when you ask me, and yes, you are going to your father's. We've been talking about it for five days. Since the last time you went, in fact. Which was last Sunday. When your father said he would pick you up this Friday, which is today, and you could stay the night with him and he would take you to the football match. You *know* you are going to your bloody father's ...' I clapped a hand to my mouth and bit it.

Stanley's face, which had lit up at the thought of 22 blokes kicking a bag of air, clouded again. 'I hope *She* isn't there.'

'She will be,' I said grimly, suffused with shame at swearing and giving my son's future therapist even more material to work with. 'She lives there.'

She is Emily, Daniel's new girlfriend, who is totally welcome to him because I wouldn't have him back if his was the last paunch on earth. She has set up home with him which I don't care about at all. I do think, however, it smacks of indecent haste as far as Stanley, who has to visit them, is concerned. Them and their laminate floors and low black coffee tables and single lilies in tall glass tubes (I didn't press Stanley for these details – he gave them up quite readily under cross-examination).

Stanley wrinkled his nose even more. 'I can't find my trousers either.'

'Boiler!' I got up from my desk in our tiny spare bedroom and stomped to the door in two paces. 'They were muddy, remember? I washed them. I told you they were on the boiler to dry. I knew you weren't listening ... And why weren't you dressed ages ago? I've got to get this lot finished today,' I shrieked, jabbing a finger at the pile of paper teetering on the top of the ancient filing cabinet. 'And how can I do that with you constantly interrupting me?'

'All right. Take a chill-pill.' Stanley sighed and plodded across the landing. He knows when it is *that* time of the month.

'Keep it on,' he called from the safety of the stairs while I kicked the waste bin. 'Will you make me some toast?'

One, two, three, four, five. Breathe in and out. Adopt sing-song voice to disguise the fact I want to throttle him. 'Yes darling,' I trilled through gritted teeth. 'I will make you toast even though you are 11 and a half and quite old enough to make it yourself. Even if I am right in the middle of a paragraph.'

'You were doing emails.'

'Work ones. When I was 11 …'

'You got up at dawn to scrub all the floors, made breakfast for the whole family, did all the washing and walked through fire and flood 20 miles to school …' Stanley poked his head back round the door and grinned.

I glared. 'Just get ready!'

The bloody toaster has a mind of its own. It knows when I am tense and uptight and in a hurry and it quite deliberately sends the bread out pale and flaccid, then, when you push the lever back down for just ten more seconds, burns it to a cinder.

I hurled four blackened slices out of the back door, where a squawking herring gull immediately pounced. 'Bugger off, you vulture,' I snarled. It ignored me and swallowed down the first slice whole. It stuck out in a ridge from the creature's fat white neck as the bird salivated, pop-eyed.

'Peanut butter or Marmite?' I leapt on to the toaster to stop it cremating the third lot. 'Juice or milk?'

Stanley heaved a rucksack through the kitchen door. 'Can I have hot chocolate?'

Hot chocolate, yes, yes. If we've got enough milk which we probably haven't. It's all feast or famine in our house. There's either six pints in the fridge door, in various stages of becoming cheese, or there's half an inch which the whole world wants.

I got out two more slices of bread for me. I was going to start the Atkins again but who's got time to start buggering about with eggs first thing in the morning? And anyway carbs release serotonin which is supposed to keep you sane (fat bloody chance) and Marmite is full of B vitamins – ditto. The peanut butter jar was empty. Carefully scraped out, lid screwed tightly back on, replaced on the shelf. The hot chocolate drum was bereft of hot chocolate.

I waved it at Stanley. 'What is the bloody point of putting it back like this? Why don't you write it on the shopping list instead? I am not psychic, Stanley. I can't mind-read or see through cardboard.' I poured milk into a mug and plonked it down in front of him. It slopped and sent white drops across the table. 'Damn it.'

Stanley picked up the mug and began to drink with maddening slowness. He chewed on a corner of toast and flicked open his PlayStation magazine.

'*Stop doing that, you bastard ...*' Stanley's head shot up as I hurled myself at the toaster that was belching out black smoke. 'I don't eat carbohydrates anyway!' I yelled, chucking more burnt offerings through the door and restraining myself from ripping the plug from the wall and hurling the toaster after them.

'Stop shouting!' Stanley yelled back.

I picked up a J Cloth and scrunched it into a hard ball. 'I'm talking to the toaster,' I shrieked. 'Not you ...'

Stanley sighed.

'Sorry,' I said.

'It's OK.'

I ran a hand through his spiky hair, leaning over to pick up the crust he'd left. 'Look at the time – we're going to be really late now,' I said, with my mouth full. 'You must go and clean your teeth. Have you checked whether you've got enough money? Is your phone charged? I want you to text me when you get to your father's. I want to know you've been picked up safely ...'

'I will.' Stanley shook his head at me. 'Don't stress.'

'I'm not stressing. I just worry about you.' All of a sudden I felt my chin trembling and I turned away quickly and looked in the sink for some crockery to break when he'd gone to school. *Get a bloody grip, stop bloody bursting into tears over nothing. Be nice ...*

I got one of my secret supply of plain chocolate Bounty bars out of the tin hidden behind the teabags. 'Take one of these for break.'

Stanley smiled. 'I did yesterday.'

How it takes Stanley 20 minutes to brush his teeth I don't know, but it does. Another five minutes goes on putting his shoes on. He ambled his way to the front door as I squawked my way through the daily check-list. 'Money? Food? Drinks? Phone?' (Here there was a short interlude while we discovered it was still upstairs and needing charging) 'Homework? Games kit?' Stanley's rucksack was a solid block I could barely lift.

'Yes, yes, yes,' he said wearily.

'Overnight stuff?'

'*Yes.*'

'Let's go then,' I cried brightly. The quiet night in on my own I'd been looking forward to all week suddenly seemed a rather dismal prospect.

I picked up my car keys and strode to the front door.

'Mum!' Stanley shrieked. 'You're still in your dressing gown!'

So I was. It wouldn't bother me driving like that but Stanley still hasn't recovered from the day when the head of Year Seven came across the road to reprimand me about stopping on the zigzag lines and I was wearing a nightie and slippers (I've never recovered either – he's really quite attractive and I hadn't even had a shower).

I ran upstairs for some tracksuit bottoms and a T-shirt. 'Don't worry,' I called heroically. 'I'll get you there ...'

It takes twelve minutes to drive to Highcourt House Grammar, nine and a half if I break the speed limit and the lollipop lady at the top of the hill nips out of the way. Today she was on the pavement, deep in conversation, and only three of the five sets of traffic lights we encountered were red. My china might be safe after all. We pulled up outside school, at exactly 8.35 – I could hear the first bell clanging. 'There you go!' I said triumphantly. 'You have got clean socks, haven't you?'

'Yes, Mum.' Stanley got out of the car.

'Your bag!'

Stanley shook his head at me and heaved the rucksack out after him.

'That bag's so heavy – I do worry about your back.'

'It's OK, Mum, don't fuss.'

'I'll see you tomorrow night.'

'Yep.'

'I'll get us something nice to eat.'

'OK.'

'I'm sorry for being such an old dragon and for shouting so much this morning.'

'It's OK.'

Stanley got out of the car and hoisted the rucksack on to his back, frowning with concentration as he struggled to get his arms through the straps. As he shut the door, my solar plexus went into spasm. I jumped out of the car, leaving the engine running, and ran round it after him.

'Stanley,' I said, as he began to wander off, 'I really love you. You're a lovely, kind boy and gorgeous and I'm so proud of you ...'

He stopped, rolled his eyes and looked nervously at three passing girls. 'Do not,' he hissed, through gritted teeth, 'kiss me.'

'Coffee, hurry, urgent!'

By the time I got back, Charlotte was already on the doorstep, hopping with impatience.

'I think we're out of milk.' I growled, sticking my key in the lock.

She followed me into the hall. 'Hello Charlotte,' she intoned. 'And how are you today? How lovely to see you, oh best friend of mine ...'

'Shouldn't you be at work?'

'I am. I'm doing a viewing round the corner.' Charlotte is Wainwright & Co Estate Agents' top negotiator and, despite the ailing state of the economy, still earns herself a small fortune in commission, though how she ever sells anything by spending her entire working week in my kitchen is a mystery.

'Looks to me like you're here, holding me up ...'

'Laura Meredith, you are a terrible old bag,' said Charlotte, shooing Boris, my large tabby cat, off the work surface and putting the kettle on.

I sat down at the table and put my head in my hands. 'Yes, I know. I was gruesome to Stanley this morning. Chalked up a whole load more WIT points. Referred to Daniel as 'your

6

bloody father' – not something they recommend in the "how to handle your separation so your child's not damaged" handbook – and then mortified him by hugging him outside school.'

'It's one's job to embarrass one's children,' said Charlotte. 'it'll toughen him up for when he's got a wife.' She ran her hands through her frizzy blonde hair. 'I called Becky a little bitch last night – more WIT points for her too.'

WIT stands for When-in-Therapy. It goes without saying that with a mother like me (and a traitorous, philandering father who can't keep it in his trousers) Stanley will probably succumb to treatment at about 22. So far he has enough material to keep him going, at two sessions a week, until he's past 30. I keep a mental tally of my wrongdoings to supply to him when the time comes. So the shrink can cut straight to the chase.

'I hope that bloody Emily woman doesn't make any more comments to upset him,' I said. 'I don't want him to have low self-esteem – and you know what she's like.'

Emily is blonde and perfect. Pin thin, given to wearing sharp little suits and spiky heels. Daniel is smitten. As well he might be he probably can't believe his luck. There he is, 47, with a receding hairline and a beer gut and there she is, 28 years old (a whole decade younger than me – bitch), perched in their minimalist flat on her pert little buttocks, while I sit here on my droopy ones. Actually there is more than a decade between us. I might pretend I'm 39 but really I'm 42. All my 40th birthday cards – apart from the ones full of witticisms about being over the hill and one's teeth falling out – were at pains to point out that I was now entering my prime. It doesn't feel that way to me. Though *She* is, undoubtedly, in hers.

'Wait till she has his baby,' said Charlotte, in what she clearly imagined was a comforting manner. 'Remember Karina being all distraught because Mark's new bird was all blonde and willowy and made her feel like an elephant? Until they started producing. Now she's put on about three stone and looks a right mess. Karina calls them Mark and Stretch-Mark.'

I laughed, although the thought of Daniel with a new baby had sent a shaft of pain right through me.

'She's as thick as two short planks too,' said Charlotte.

'Emily isn't,' I said gloomily.

Emily is very clever with a degree in Food Science and a lucrative job being a food "stylist". She spends her days arranging beautiful, inedible displays – waxing fruit or spraying pork pies with varnish so they shine for the camera. Making food look pretty before it's thrown away – that's her speciality. We wouldn't actually want to eat anything, would we?

'She had the bloody cheek to tell Stanley the fat content of his pizza!' I said.

Charlotte tutted disapprovingly. 'You haven't got any biscuits,' she said, plaintively shaking the tin.

'I ate those last night – but there's more.'

Charlotte got up and opened the door above the bread bin. Because I live a short walk from her office and she likes lots of tea breaks, she knows the inside of my cupboards as well as her own. Her hand hovered over the packets. 'Digestives or custard creams?'

'Both.'

I wouldn't mind but he only met Emily because of me. I was the one writing the brochure copy for the presentation of Happy Pig Pies to all the supermarket chains. It was me who'd done such a totally brilliant stayed-up-all-night-to-bloody-finish-it job on the captions for the display boards that Mike, Creative Director of A & G Design & Advertising and my one-time boss till I gave birth, dropped out of the rat race and went freelance from home (a somewhat hit and miss affair. Note for other mothers considering same: do not leave the stills for your company's newest account on the floor when potty-training), suggested I come along and swell the numbers and quaff the free champagne.

It was *me* who asked if Daniel could come too, since he'd been complaining that he'd hardly seen anything of me all week and I thought we could have a nice evening out afterwards.

And there she was – Emily – putting the finishing touches

to her Pie Tower, a massive golden structure of interlocking pastry mounds, a veritable triumph of cold-water crust, doing creative things with highly polished tomatoes and sprigs of colour-enhanced parsley.

Daniel walked over there and I heard him quite distinctly giving that deep-throated chuckle someone once told him was sexy (it might have been me – bastard!) and saying what a turn-on it was to see a woman in a pinny and high heels. And she – instead of slapping him, like any self-respecting post-feminist – simpered. She shouldn't have been wearing heels anyway. What about Health and Safety?

'You're not listening!' said Charlotte loudly.

'I am,' I said, guiltily, realising I was holding two custard creams.

'What did I say then?'

'I have no idea.'

'What are you doing tonight?

'Sleeping.'

'No, you're not – you're coming out for a drink.'

'I've got too much work on.'

That's what Daniel said, from then on. Too much work on to go out with me, or come home on time. So much work on that he suddenly had a whole lot of calls on his mobile that necessitated him going into another room, and texts like you wouldn't believe! Every time I looked at him he was fiddling with that phone – I picked it up once, when it beeped, just to see what he'd do. Haven't seen him move so fast since we went to Egypt and he insisted on eating the salad.

'Work,' he said, 'so much damn work.' Did he think I was totally stupid? Daniel is an inspector at the tax office in Maidstone. In 14 years of marriage I've never known him work past six. It's nine to five with an occasional bit of report-writing in the evenings, so he can knock off at four instead. The whole point of the civil service is that they work to rule.

I did enquire, of course. He looked furtive. 'A big inspection coming up,' he said vaguely. 'An investigation to prepare. A seminar on evaluating assets ...' Turned out the sort of assets he was evaluating were spread-eagled in a flat in

Tunbridge Wells being willingly given up to an in-depth inspection during his flexi-time.

'He's old enough to be her father,' I said indignantly, reaching for another biscuit.

'Becky's on a sleepover,' Charlotte said, ignoring me. 'Though God knows why they call it that. The last time she had one at our place they were still on Facebook at 4 a.m. And Roger and Joe will be glued to the football. So I've told them I'm hitting the town. With you.'

I shook my head. 'I really don't fancy going out. I'm uptight, bloated, fat, ugly, and bad-tempered with deadlines coming out of my ears and the washing to do.'

'You're always like that.'

'And I've got to get some shopping in tonight – those biscuits are the only food in the house.'

'We'll eat in the wine bar.'

'There's something on TV.'

'Video it. I'll see you at Greens at 8 p.m.'

'I'm tired.'

Charlotte stood up. ''You're boring me now, love.'

I am boring myself.

Chapter Two

CHARLOTTE LIKES GREENS WINE Bar because it's "happening". As far as I can see, it's happening to someone else. We've been drinking in Greens for years, seen it through a variety of different owners, menus, and internal décor. Some things have never changed. I've stood at that oak bar with its rows of wine glasses overhead and its floor-to-ceiling wine racks and scrubbed wooden floorboards on and off since I was 18 and champing at the bit to get to London and begin my glittering career.

In those days, I thought London was happening and didn't realise I would one day crave to be back at the seaside where the water didn't run grey when you washed your hair and the woman in the post office not only knew your name but remembered your mother had just had her varicose veins done.

If I popped down for the weekend I always came in for a drink, even when it went through its grubby dive-like times or once, horrifically, its short-lived fruit machine, plastic stool, and karaoke phase. I've been in lots of pubs in Broadstairs at various stages of my life but it's this bar that evokes the memories, that always makes me think of being young or happy or in love or up the duff …

We finally moved back to Broadstairs when I was pregnant and thought it would be nice to be near my mother (you live and learn). Daniel was taken with the property prices and how much more we could get for our money if we lived down here and he transferred to a Kent office. I think that's where the shock lies, really. He was supposed to be the boring, stable one, who thought about capital growth and pension yields, and I was the bohemian wild child. Now look at us.

I'm walking around in big knickers and a pair of old slippers, nagging Stanley to death and he's buying trendy new trainers (they are quite cool, reported Stanley in surprise) and finding all sorts of uses for a mashed avocado (they apparently have a huge, pear-filled bowl on their granite worktop and I can't imagine her eating them – too many calories).

Now I am thoroughly over Daniel, I would quite like to have a bit of a fling involving a few vegetables myself but where do I find the men? Once I would have come here to Greens. Now, if there are any fanciable blokes in here, I'm old enough to be their mother. And if I'm not, and they're even vaguely good-looking, then they're gay. This does not deter Charlotte.

'Ooh, look! Clive!' She shot off across the bar the moment we got in there. In a town where "man falls from bicycle" is front page news, Clive enjoys near-celebrity status. He has a TV production company, a weekend cottage in Broadstairs, and a Bollinger habit that keeps him pretty popular with the girls who own Greens.

He was sitting at a round table in the window, wearing Armani and a delicious aftershave I could pick up at ten paces, champagne bucket before him. Charlotte wedged herself down on the window seat next to him. Even though she knows it's Jack behind the bar who Clive hankers after, Charlotte enjoys what she sees as their flirtation.

'Darlings!' Clive swept back his glossy brown hair with a toss of his head and kissed each of us on both cheeks. 'How are we doing?'

Charlotte viewed him through lowered lashes. 'Laura's got shocking PMT so we're here for medicinal purposes.'

'Have you really?' Clive looked concerned.

'Oh, it's nothing.' I shook my head, embarrassed, and glared at Charlotte.

She laughed, unabashed. 'Once we get a few drinks down her throat, her fangs will subside.'

I glared some more. Clive leant out and took my hand. 'You must come and sit down here. I'll get two more glasses.'

'I'm quite interested in the whole female hormonal issue,'

he said when he had poured us each a glass of fizz and I had drunk most of mine in one gulp. 'I've been working on a documentary for Channel Four – and they've done some research which suggests that more than half of all women are governed emotionally by their menstrual cycle. We're planning on doing it as a topic for *Rise Up With Randolph*: are women at the mercy of their hormones?'

'*Rise Up With Randolph*? That oily creep?' snorted Charlotte. 'I didn't know you did that.'

'Actually he's very caring,' said Clive. 'It's been a huge success – the ratings are going up all the time and it's really putting Yellow Door Productions on the map. We've been tackling some really key issues – child abuse, drug addiction, as well as the usual infidelity/he slept with my sister type shows. They always go down well. Now for this PMT programme, we've got a woman who threw her husband down the stairs and another who got six months for threatening to stab the ...'

'I'm not that bad!' I said hotly, pushing the incident with Daniel and the bag of frozen chops to the back of my mind.

'Of course not, poppet,' Clive patted my hand. 'Irritability?' he asked soothingly. 'Short temper? Weight gain, bloating, feelings of low self-worth ...?'

I scowled.

'She's got all of them,' said Charlotte.

'Not all the time,' I explained crossly. 'On Day Two I feel a deep sense of calm and on Days Three and Four I'm really quite sane and energised – give or take that I'm carrying around four pounds of extra fluid and look like a hippo. Then Days Six to Nine, I feel terrific – get loads done, am perfectly normal and positive, then there's a bit of a wobble on Day Ten and then ...'

'This is fascinating,' Clive was gazing into my eyes. 'You are so in touch with it all – so precise ...' He stared at the ceiling, hand outstretched before him as if about to make a great pronouncement, and then looked back at me again. 'How is that?'

I shrugged. 'I went to a nutritionist. She got me to keep a

13

diary. How I felt, what I ate –' I paused, thinking I would spare Clive the details of the in-depth analysis of bodily functions and girth measurements I had also undergone. 'And there was a clear pattern.'

'How fascinating,' said Clive again, still gazing at me with something close to rapture.

'Yes, my husband thought so too,' I said waspishly. 'It was his idea.'

Because, having jogged along quite happily for a decade with me being gruesome for several days a month, he suddenly decided that he couldn't stand it. And then, having spent six months shagging himself stupid with another woman and barely speaking to me, he had the barefaced cheek to blame the break-up of our marriage on my mood swings.

'And has it helped?' Clive asked eagerly.

'Yes – he left me.'

Charlotte smiled brightly. 'But she's much better off without him and we're going to find her someone else lovely.' She gave me a kick under the table. 'So it's all for the best.'

'It's all terrific,' I growled. 'I am ecstatic.'

It was probably Emily who suggested the nutritionist. Emily is a vegetarian who eats no dairy and only does organic. Her moods are totally stable and she probably takes the pill all year round. I should imagine periods are much too messy for her to contemplate.

'Have you tried any supplements?' enquired Clive, looking from one to the other of us with a slightly desperate smile. 'One of the researchers was talking about oil of evening primrose ...'

'Yeah, and starflower oil and B vitamins and magnesium and zinc ... I've got them all at home.'

'I think you're supposed to take them,' said Charlotte.

I pulled a face at her.

'I believe a lot of it is down to diet,' said Clive, hurriedly refilling glasses.

'Yes this nutritionist – Kristin – she's a friend of Charlotte's, actually -'

'She's boring,' Charlotte added. 'Doesn't drink ...'

'She said to cut out wheat, sugar, and alcohol,' I continued.

'And has that helped?' Clive asked earnestly.

Charlotte raised her eyebrows at me.

I took another swallow of champagne. 'Er – not really.'

The bar had filled up with a lot of young girls who I noticed were, each and every one of them, very thin. I studied the one nearest to me who was about 25. She was wearing a cropped T-shirt and revealing a band of perfectly flat, brown stomach. Her upper arms were beautifully toned, her thighs enviably slim.

When did young people start getting so attractive? When I was in my twenties, I was a slightly less blobby version of how I am now, with fewer wrinkles and probably a smaller bum. But I didn't look like that. Now everyone under 30 is totally gorgeous. There was a song playing that I didn't know the name of but I remembered it was one Stanley liked. I felt like everyone's grandmother and wished I could go home.

But Clive had ordered another bottle of Bolly and Charlotte, somewhat uncharacteristically, seemed to have forgotten we were going to eat. So I was also getting light-headed. 'Crisps, anyone?' I asked.

'Not for me, darling.' Clive got a packet of cigarettes out of his pocket and gazed at them longingly.

Charlotte looked apologetic. 'Oh, sorry, I was so starving I had to have a sandwich before I came out.'

'Thanks,' I muttered. 'I thought we were eating here.'

Charlotte shrugged. 'OK then, I'll have some cheese and onion. But aren't you supposed to be eating lots of vegetables?' she added.

I hate her sometimes.

'I can do you some crudités and hummus,' said Sarah, one of the owners of Greens, from behind the bar. 'Are you OK?' she said peering closer. I looked over to the open door and beyond, where Clive and Charlotte were puffing away on the pavement outside. Charlotte suddenly threw back her head and laughed and nodded vigorously in my direction, clearly agreeing I was a mad old bag.

'Just tired, old, fat, and hormonal.'

'Sounds like me,' Sarah said cheerfully (and wildly inaccurately – since she is a slim and attractive redhead who is younger than me). She deftly opened a bottle of red wine and reached up for glasses. 'I've eaten four packets of Maltesers today, screamed at the kids, and threatened Richard with divorce at least twice.'

'Hmm,' I said, 'I must get on to that ...'

Sarah had turned to ring something up on the till. 'Don't rush into anything,' she said over her shoulder.

Sarah was lovely when I told her about Daniel. Her first marriage had broken up a couple of years back, leaving her with three kids to look after on her own. 'It's hard, I know,' was all she'd said, but she'd poured me a large glass of wine on the house and been full of concern and sympathy ever since.

'How's Stanley?' she asked now, coming back to stand opposite me.

I shook my head, feeling suddenly miserable. 'I don't know really. It's all very difficult for him, it must be. Father clears off, new school, me all stressed out ...'

'It gets easier,' said Sarah. 'Charlie went through a bad patch when Paul and I split up but he came out of it – he's really happy now, gets on well with Richard, has adjusted to the new situation. You look after yourself,' she continued. 'If you're OK, he'll be OK.'

'I'm starving,' I said, 'and not for raw carrot.'

'Stodge is what's needed,' said Sarah, picking up a notepad. 'What about a plate of nachos and some chips?'

'So,' said Charlotte, tucking into the chips with gusto, 'these programmes are going well, then?' She looked meaningfully at Clive.

'Ah, yes,' he said. 'The hardest bit is finding audience participants who are intelligent and articulate.' He shone a smile in my direction. 'For example, this programme on PMT and things ...' He touched my arm sympathetically. 'We're still looking for some more ...'

'Ooh,' said Charlotte, in a dismal attempt to sound surprised, as if they hadn't just spent the last ten minutes discussing it.

'You've got to be joking,' I said.

'I think you'd be terrific,' Clive said seriously, refilling my glass. 'You're bright and eloquent and you'd bring a lot to the debate.' He leant across the table. 'A lot of women would really appreciate hearing what you go through.'

'She is such a cow when she's got it,' put in Charlotte. 'And clumsy! You're always dropping things, aren't you? Remember when you smashed that milk jug and you were so cross you threw the sugar bowl across the room too? And when Daniel asked you if you'd put on weight and you got hold of him by the throat and –'

'Perfect!' cried Clive, clapping his hands.

'I'm not discussing all that on breakfast television,' I said heatedly, grabbing a handful of nachos before Charlotte could swallow them all.

'Well of course you wouldn't be expected to do anything you didn't feel comfortable with,' soothed Clive. 'That's not what it's about at all. It would just be a group of people – mostly women – discussing their feelings. You can say as much or as little as you want.'

Charlotte grinned. 'You could tell the nation Daniel's got smelly feet and a vinyl fetish …'

Clive winced. 'It's a lovely day out,' he said firmly. 'We'd send a car for you, give you lunch, you'd have your hair and make-up done –'

I picked at a strand of melted cheese and dug a chip into the sour cream. 'I'd feel completely stupid.'

'You'd be really helping other women not to feel so alone.'

Charlotte nodded, trying to look serious. 'You owe it to others, really – it needs somebody to speak out.' She pulled the plate back toward her.

I snorted. 'You do it then.'

'I don't get it.'

'Well that's debatable. What about when you –'

'Now don't fall out, ladies!' Clive swung the bottle of champagne about with affected jollity.

'Imagine,' said Charlotte forcefully. 'Television – it will be fun! What an experience. People would give their right arm –'

'I've got too much work to do.'

'It's only one day – you can catch up at the weekend.'

'What about Stanley?'

'He can come to us after school – Roger can leave work a bit early and hold the fort till we get back.'

'We?'

'I'm coming to watch.'

'You don't have to go alone,' sang Clive.

I glared at Charlotte. 'You're not coming because I'm not going. I am too busy, too bad-tempered, too fat, and I haven't got anything to wear. That's the end of it.'

Charlotte was unfazed. 'You've got stacks of stuff – we only went shopping last week. And we can go again this weekend. Stop making excuses. You're boring me.'

'Who'll feed the cat?'

'You'll be back in the evening.'

'I'm camera shy!'

Charlotte folded her arms. 'You're *really* boring me now ...'

'I don't care. No!'

'You'll love it when you get there.'

'I'm *not* doing it.'

Chapter Three

'WHY DO YOU HAVE to do it?' Stanley looked at me in disgust. 'And why Becky's house? She's completely horrible – she always laughs at me.'

'Girls are like that, darling.' I held yet another ghastly garment up against me and looked at it from several angles in the full-length mirror. 'Just ignore her. Play with Joe.'

'Joe is seven,' said Stanley wearily.

I threw the dress on the bed and picked up the flouncy grey skirt I'd started with. 'Well, Roger says you can go on the PlayStation. It's only for a couple of hours, I'll be back by six.'

'I'll be starving,' said Stanley plaintively.

'Charlotte's leaving snacks for you all and we'll have something fabulous for dinner.' I looked at the fabric in my hands. Maybe I could wear this skirt with a black T-shirt and my wide studded belt? No, damn it, they said no black.

'Pizza?'

'OK. Pizza.'

I could wear a red T-shirt, but then red can sometimes make my hair look a funny colour. Depending on what colour my hair is. At the moment, it is grape. Well, the box said "grape" – it started out burgundy and is now a faded shade of prune …

'Delivered, not a frozen one.'

'OK.'

The girl on the phone – Toni – said to wear anything I felt comfortable in, as long as it wasn't black or white, or boldly patterned or had stripes. That left one pink dress that would look OK if I lost ten pounds (unlikely in the next three hours), one brown suit I've always hated (bought on Day 23 when judgement impaired), one pair of green trousers that make my

arse look huge (a fact kindly brought to my attention by Daniel
after I'd been wearing them for several weeks of ignorant bliss)
and the aforementioned long, flouncy grey skirt that didn't
have a top to go with it.

'Stuffed crust.'

'What?'

'Stuffed crust pizzas delivered.'

'Delivered? They cost a fortune.'

'You just promised.'

'Did I?'

'And I can stay up late.'

'Don't push it. Oh, Stanley,' I wailed. 'What am I going to
wear?'

Stanley screwed up his nose. 'I dunno. Why are you doing
this anyway? It's stupid you going on TV. You're not even
going to win anything.'

'I'm doing it because my friend Clive really needs my help
and - it's a bit of an experience and ... Charlotte nagged me
into it.'

Stanley, who has known Charlotte all his life, nodded.

I didn't tell him it was what Charlotte had said about Daniel
that had swung it. I was trying not to talk about his father
unless he did – I only chalked up WIT points galore and
deepened my scowl lines.

'Daniel thinks,' she'd explained, 'that you're an out-of-
control harridan and we know you're not. This is your chance
to prove it. You will be sitting there, perfectly poised, looking
stunning, speaking intelligently about PMT and how simply
everyone who's anyone gets it and it will be very obvious that
he is the one who's a total tosser for being so out of step as to
not understand ...'

I love the word "tosser" – it so perfectly conjures up an
image of Daniel's ridiculous face when he's gazing like a love-
sick bovine at that silly blonde stick-person.

'And you can,' Charlotte had said, warming to her theme,
'talk about supportive partners being important and how, while
men who are insecure – probably because they have
unnaturally small genitalia – might use it as an excuse to go off

shagging others, the modern, sensitive man – which Daniel is pretending to be now – will realise it is all part of the raw, primitive passion of woman ...'

I wasn't instantly converted. 'What *are* you talking about?' I said crossly. 'He won't be watching daytime TV, will he? He'll be at the office.'

'Stanley can show him the video.'

'Stanley won't go anywhere near the video. Stanley doesn't approve. And can you blame him? What boy wants to watch his mother discussing periods?'

'Well, anyway,' said Charlotte, changing tack, 'the papers will pick up on it – you'll probably be asked to write a think-piece for the *Guardian*. Daniel will jolly well see it then.'

I laughed sourly. 'The *Guardian*? Come off it. What I should be writing is 14 pages of scintillating copy extolling the properties of the new toughened-glass Grow-Bright range of greenhouses and conservatories. Wanted by tomorrow! How come you're not working again?'

Charlotte looked at the clock 'Because I've got half an hour ... Shit! No I haven't – I'm supposed to be in Waldron Avenue now. See you later!'

When she'd dashed off, hair and handbag flying, I thought about what she'd said. There was something oddly seductive about her vision of me being interviewed on TV about PMT. Of being a kind of expert. Of my collection of symptoms being acknowledged as a proper syndrome. Of being listened to, my intelligent observations on its devastating effects being taken seriously by millions of daytime viewers.

I didn't know of course, if there were millions. I personally had never even seen this Randolph Kendall and his 9 a.m. show – who gets to watch television then? But presumably someone must do or it wouldn't be on. Charlotte said she'd seen it and he looked a bit smarmy but they'd had a good female psychologist on saying weight was all about what felt good to you and that if you felt sexy at size 16, then by definition you were.

Charlotte is a firm believer in such philosophies – when Daniel moved out she brought round three chocolate cakes, a crate of Kettle Chips and a wine-box. 'At least there's no one to mention the size of your arse now,' she said, before tucking in. 'All that trying to be thin is so bloody tedious.'

Instead of the psychologist, presumably there would be me. I would be able to provide astute insights into the role of progesterone and the function of the pituitary gland (I had already mugged up on Google so I had the facts to hand), the delicate balance of the reproductive hormones and their effect on the female both psychologically and physiologically, leading to a possible fall in the brain chemical serotonin which controls mood …

Daniel had summed this up in his own way. 'You're mad,' he'd said.

'It's quite an honour to be asked,' I said now to Stanley. 'Imagine – your mother on TV.'

'I am imagining,' he said gloomily.

'We must get you to school. You'd better clean your teeth if you can't be useful on the clothes front.'

Stanley surveyed the heap on my bed. 'That's too pink,' he said. 'That one makes you look horrible like Connor's mum and I don't think you should wear those trousers.' He looked at me doubtfully. 'The skirt,' he advised. 'You wore that when we went to Grandma's birthday and it didn't look too bad.'

'Thank you, darling,' I said, overwhelmed by such sartorial endorsement. 'But what top?'

'Ask Charlotte,' said Stanley, now clearly exhausted by his efforts. 'She,' he added sagely, 'will tell you what to do.'

'I don't think so, love.' Charlotte frowned critically as I put on an olive green scoop-necked number. 'Whole effect is a bit too Sunday school teacher for my liking. Hmmm, let's think, what would Joan Bakewell wear?'

'What's she got to do with it?'

'I'm thinking erudite,' said Charlotte, 'though –' she paused to look me up and down '– perhaps we're on to a loser there. Here, what about this orange one?'

'Isn't it a bit bright?' I picked the T-shirt up and held it beneath my chin. 'I only got it because they were doing three for the price of two and I'd already got a black and a white one.'

'It's going to have to do,' she said, looking out of the window. 'The car's here.'

'Oh my God, oh my God.' I ran up and down the bedroom. 'I'm not ready!'

'Well, hurry up.'

Charlotte opened the window and began gesticulating at whoever was at the front gate as I scurried about in a panic.

'I haven't sorted out a handbag.'

'You won't have a handbag on TV!'

'Why not?'

'They never do. Do you ever see Kaddy with a handbag?'

'She's doing the weather. Margaret Thatcher used to have one.'

'She was running the country. Just bring your usual.'

She ran down the stairs and opened the front door. 'Hello, yes, she's just coming!'

'I haven't got my make-up on,' I said, running down after her.

'They'll do it.'

'But I don't want them seeing what I look like without any.'

'Come and get in the car.'

'I'm not sure I've left Boris enough food.'

'He's got enough to feed every cat in the street – no wonder he's obese.'

'He is not – he is naturally large. Do you know the vet said he had excellent muscle tone?'

'What, round his jaw?'

'Shall I put my hair up or leave it down?'

'Just get in the bloody car!'

'Ah that's what I like to see – a vehicle befitting my style and status …' Charlotte smiled graciously as she dragged me down the path. 'Good morning, again!' she called to the driver, a large handsome guy of about 30 with dreadlocks, dressed in a shirt and tie, who was standing next to the big white Mercedes having a fag. He ground out the end on the pavement and turned a huge grin on us, his teeth matching his dazzling white shirt.

'Morning girls. I'm Kevin – but you can call me Kev.' He winked. 'Got your knickers on now?'

'I'm Charlotte,' said Charlotte. 'And this is Laura, the soon-to-be-star.'

Kev guffawed in a way that did not sound entirely complimentary. 'In you jump,' he said holding the door open.

'Ooh look, a drinks cabinet,' said Charlotte when we were settled back in the leather interior and Kevin had started the engine. 'What have you got in here then, Kev?'

'No alcohol allowed before filming,' he said. 'My instructions are to get everyone there sober. There's orange juice and water. I'll see what I can find you for the way back,' he added. 'You'll probably need it by then.'

I looked anxiously at Charlotte. She grinned as she snapped the ring pull from a small can of juice. 'We always need it,' she said.

I looked out of the window as we drove up Broadstairs High Street. At the last minute I'd put on a pair of black trousers with the orange T-shirt, on the basis that they could hardly send me back to change and nobody would see much of them if I was sitting down and if they did, at least black was slimming.

Because an outfit that your 11-year-old thought looked OK when you were out with your mother hardly screamed sexy sophistication. Now, however, I was thinking longingly of the grey skirt after all, since the black trousers were already digging into me round the waist where a roll of flab was clearly visible beneath the orange top. Which I still had my doubts about, but which Charlotte had insisted on, saying it would be bright enough to distract the eye from anything else.

'So,' said Kev, as we stopped at the traffic lights at the Broadway. 'Going on with Randolph, eh?' He looked at me in the rear mirror. 'Into the lion's den, huh? Ha ha …'

'It's not that bad, surely,' I said, frowning at Charlotte.

'A right punch-up last week,' Kev continued. 'Bloke on there says his third kid ain't his: he'd always reckoned his missus was up to no good with the next-door neighbour. She's sitting next to him, like, and the next thing, she's got up and landed him one. He goes to thump her back and the bloke sitting in the row behind leaps over the seats and smashes him in the face. Turns out he *is* the next-door neighbour and he's got his wife with him too, so she's none too pleased. Bedlam it was – all of 'em screaming and crying. Old Randolph thought all his Christmases had come at once. Ratings went right up.'

Charlotte laughed. I didn't. 'This programme's about female hormone issues,' I said stiffly. 'It will just be women discussing their feelings, there won't be anything like that.'

'I wouldn't bet on it,' said Kevin confidently. 'Randolph likes to get a bit of confrontation going. You divorced, are you?'

'No, I'm not.'

'What's he like, this Randolph?' asked Charlotte hastily. 'Always looks a bit of a creep to me,' she added cheerily.

'He's all right.' Kevin turned left at the roundabout and took the main road out of town. 'I don't see much of him these days. My mate Jerry's the one who drives him mostly. Says he's always on the phone and they have quite a few stop-offs. Likes a bit of extra-curricular himself, if you know what I mean.'

'Don't they all,' said Charlotte. To me, she added conversationally, 'I've told Roger if he ever even thinks about it, I'll castrate him with the bread knife.'

'He wouldn't,' I said. 'He loves you too much and you terrify him.'

Charlotte nodded, satisfied.

She and Kev kept up a conversation for the rest of the journey, while I did what I could with concealer and a tube of "photogenic" foundation I'd got free when I bought that new lip-plumping balm. By the time we were turning off at Teddington, I looked marginally less raddled and we'd heard all about Kev's girlfriend, Cindy, their forthcoming wedding, and the problems they were having with her mother, which were in sufficient quantity to last the entire stretch of the M25.

I stared out of the window and began to feel nervous. Suppose I dried up, suppose I forgot whether it was too much oestrogen or progesterone that caused all the problems and why, exactly, taking fatty acids were such a good idea. I took a swig of water and worried that I might have forgotten to put a drink in Stanley's packed lunch, rendering him dehydrated and unable to concentrate and achieve his potential, leading in turn to feelings of inadequacy, extra WIT points and probably three more years on the couch.

I was just wondering whether I should phone the school and ask them to remind him to buy a bottle of something from the cafeteria if I had forgotten, or to use the water fountain, when I suddenly realised we had pulled up at a barrier and Kev was exchanging witticisms with a couple of security guards.

'More lambs to the slaughter,' he said. They all laughed. 'Here we are,' he added over his shoulder.

He pulled up by some steps. 'Go through those doors. And someone will meet you in reception.'

'I don't want to do this,' I muttered, as Charlotte jumped out of the car and strode ahead of me.

'Don't be daft,' she said, marching through the automatic doors and up to the large, curved, shiny yellow desk where a blonde girl was on the phone and several people in jeans and white T-shirts stood around looking at each other. Framed stills from Yellow Door Productions' TV shows covered the wall behind the desk; a huge poster of a suspiciously raven-haired, tanned man in his fifties with a wide smile full of American-looking teeth filled a display panel in the corner. *Rise Up With Randolph. Every weekday at 9 a.m. Always There For You.*

Charlotte coughed. The receptionist cupped her hand over the receiver and raised her eyebrows. 'I'll get Toni,' she said without enthusiasm, when Charlotte had explained who we were.

We sat on a yellow leatherette sofa in front of a glass-topped table piled with copies of *Hello*. Charlotte began to flick through one of them while I stared at the lemon carpet. I was even more nervous now. I glanced at my friend. Charlotte was wearing a new beaded, bottle green top with plunging neckline. She'd obviously been topping up her tan on the sun bed (did the woman ever go to work?) and looked voluptuous and terrific. I could see myself reflected in the smoked glass wall opposite. I looked like an overweight wasp.

'I don't want to do this,' I said again.

'Shut up,' replied Charlotte. 'Hello!' She smiled at the girl who had just come through a side door. The girl smiled back.

'Hi, I'm Toni. Are you Laura? Cool!'

Toni looked about 14 and said "cool" a lot. She had on a tight black T-shirt and torn jeans, her brown hair scraped back in a pony tail and a nose-stud. I felt like an ancient aunt.

If it wasn't cool, it was wicked. 'I spoke to you on the phone didn't I? Cool. Did you have a good journey? Wicked. Come through to the waiting area – cool. Would you like a cup of tea? Cool. This way, wicked, sit over there, cool. Shane will see you in a minute. Cool. He'll run through everything. Cool, wicked, cool, cool, cool.'

She led us into a large, noisy room filled with tables with people around them. We sat on two plastic chairs in the corner where I stared at a blue carpet this time, until Shane, who made Clive look seriously macho, danced over to meet us.

'Now, ladies, who's our guest today? Ah, you're the lovely Laura – wonderful. Now let's see ...' He consulted his clipboard, ticking something off with a flourish. 'Ooh, you're an A guest, my darling, which means Randolph will definitely be coming to *you*!' He beamed. I looked blank. Shane settled himself on a chair in front of us.

'Row A are our prime guests – the major contributors with the key storylines; Row B, secondaries – we'll come to them next when we open it up to general discussion; Row C we'll call on if there's time; Rows D and E, you can put your hands up but we'll only come in an emergency.' He lowered his voice. 'F and G – coach trip from Oldham. Clapping and hissing only.'

'They won't be hissing about PMT, surely?' I said.

Shane giggled. 'No, I shouldn't think so.'

'And I'll be asked questions?' I said nervously.

'Yes, you will, my darling. Now, we're never quite sure exactly what Randolph's going to say because he's a bit of a naughty boy about going off script, but then that's what makes it such exciting television. We never know *what* will happen …' He giggled again and twirled his pink Biro in his fingers.

'The thing to remember, my darling, is be yourself and let it all out, no holds barred. Just be honest – imagine it's just you and Randolph at home in your kitchen having a cuppa and tell him everything, my darling.' He lowered his voice to a cosy whisper. 'Ever been violent?' he asked, hopefully.

'I'm really not at all sure about this now,' I said urgently to Charlotte, when Shane had finally skipped off to prime somebody else. 'No, listen. I feel pretty good today – Day Ten – I feel positively positive. Who cares about Daniel?' I shrugged. 'Who gives a fuck about any of it?'

'Thought you said Day Ten was when you often went bonkers out of the blue,' said Charlotte. 'Anyway, can't you just pretend? Just get all ratty when you're asked a question. You usually manage it OK. Shall we get something to eat?'

There was a table along the back piled with food and a lot of old women shoving each other in front of it. 'Looks like a bit of a bun fight,' I said. 'I wish they had some wine.'

'We should have brought you a hip flask,' said Charlotte. 'I'll go and investigate what else they've got.'

I took off my bracelet and fiddled with it. I did care about Daniel. Well not about him, himself, per se, of course. He was just a middle-aged saddo loser who was trying to pretend he was still a stud (here I took a brief moment to imagine kicking him hard in the shins). But I cared about the grief and wretchedness he'd caused me. I cared about what he had done to our son.

'Why?' Stanley had asked bleakly when he'd heard Daniel was moving out. Just the one word, delivered round-eyed, bewildered. Daniel couldn't answer him. It was left to me to try to explain. 'But why?' he said again, miserably, when I'd finished.

I did give a fuck about that and the whole way Daniel had done it. The way he had tried to make it all my fault, my moods, my hormones. And when Charlotte had spoken before about me doing this to put my view, to have my say, it had felt right. A chance to redress the balance. But now …

She came back proffering a plate of bendy-looking sandwiches and sausage rolls.

'I couldn't,' I said. 'I want to go home.'

'Shut up,' said Charlotte. 'The grannies over there are all very excited. Left home at six this morning to be here. And I got talking to an old boy called Wilf whose wife used to go bonkers every time there was a full moon. She died on the operating table in 1988 when she was having her prolapse sorted.'

'For God's sake,' I said, pushing the plate away from me, 'I'll be sick in a minute.'

A cross-looking girl in her twenties came up. 'I'm Sharon – I'm going to mike you up.' She tugged at the bottom of my T-shirt. 'That should be OK. Can you stand up and turn round? Hmm,' she said, apparently examining the size of my bottom. 'OK then, this clips on here –' she attached a small black plastic box to my waistband. 'Try not to sit back too hard, and then this –' She lifted my T-shirt again and began to feed a length of wire up under it. 'Can you put your hand down and get this?'

I fished about down my cleavage and grabbed a little microphone which Sharon clipped on to the neck of my top. 'You'll be called when we need you,' she said before walking off.

Toni reappeared with polystyrene cups of something that could have been coffee. 'Oh good, you've been miked up, cool. Oh – here comes Randolph.'

There was a stir over to our right as the doors opened and the suited man from the poster swept in with several people scuttling along in his wake. He paused and addressed the room. 'Good morning!' Somewhere in the corner came the sound of clapping. In the flesh, Randolph's teeth were even whiter and his face distinctly orange.

'Don't call him Perma-tan for nothing,' said Charlotte.

'Rows D, E and F,' called a young man from the middle of the room. Several groups of pensioners stood up. 'That's you,' said Toni to Charlotte. She put the cups on the table next to me. 'You wait here, Laura and I'll be back for you.' She led Charlotte off. 'Looking forward to it? Cool.'

The room had gone quiet. There were probably a dozen of us still dotted about at tables, and a few of the ubiquitous young people in white T-shirts and jeans holding clipboards clustered around the doors at the back. Randolph had disappeared.

I smiled awkwardly at a middle-aged woman on the next table. She looked at me dubiously. My stomach was a sick mass of butterflies. I couldn't remember a single thing about the causes of PMT.

'Ready?' said Toni, reappearing. 'Wicked.' We walked down a corridor and through a set of double doors into a large, warehouse-type place with lots of cameras and a set in the corner of it. Circular rows of red leather seats were placed around a small platform – the oldies from Oldham were already seated around the back. Charlotte waved from the middle of them.

A long sign Rise Up With Randolph in neon letters – was suspended from the ceiling. I was suddenly aware of my knees knocking together and a huge urge for a pee. My God, what was I doing …

Shane rushed up, clipboard flapping. 'Now come along As and Bs.' He shepherded me to the front row. 'And you sit over there, Alicia darling. This is Laura – you're both As together.'

Alicia was mid-twenties with jet black hair streaked vibrant red and blonde, part braided with gold and silver beads jingling at the end of each plait and some lime-green hair extensions. She wore a bright pink pair of dungarees, purple boots, a lot of black eyeliner, and huge silver hoops in her ears. She was positioned further round the circle so she was almost opposite me.

I smiled at her.

'Hi,' she said sullenly.

Sharon, the sound girl, arrived and fiddled with the black box bumping against my bottom. My trousers were now cutting me in half. She checked Alicia's mike too and spoke to us both.

'Once we start, this will pick everything up – so no whispering to the person next to you,' she said sternly, as if addressing a class of infants. Three other women were brought in and sat in the seats between us. On my other side, an older man in a grey suit sat down.

Cameras wcrc wheeled about, lights turned up and down and shone in our faces. Randolph came in with his entourage and frowned up at the auto-cue screen in front of the platform. My mouth was all dry. I cleared my throat. Sharon glared.

I suddenly realised nobody had done anything with my hair or make-up. I still looked the same washed-out old bag I'd been all morning. Oh my God, again.

Shane was standing in front of us now, giving instructions. No bad language, no interrupting, no shouting out unless invited to do so by Randolph. No looking at the camera. Keep our eyes on Randolph or whoever is speaking at the time. No fidgeting or fiddling with jewellery. My hand went instinctively to my left earring. I was dying to cough and already had pins and needles …

Music began to play. Someone began counting down. 'Five, four, three, two, one.' Sharon and Shane disappeared into the shadows. Randolph stepped forward. Lights, camera, action!

I think I am going to faint.

Chapter Four

'SOMETHING JUST SNAPPED,' MAUREEN was explaining. 'I just turned round and I shoved him.'

Randolph was crouched beside her, a hand on her arm. 'Tell us how many flights it was, Maureen. Were you afraid he'd broken his neck?'

Maureen was a small, tired-looking woman with faded red hair. You couldn't imagine her throwing anyone down the stairs, let alone battering him with an umbrella afterwards. 'I thought I'd end up in Holloway,' she said mournfully. 'Lucky he left me, really.'

I could feel my heart thumping in my chest. I had sat glazed and frozen with terror while the woman next to me, Jean, gave an impassioned account of how she had driven her car through the front window of the local newsagent's when it was "the wrong time of the month" and her husband, Brian, who looked as petrified as I felt, haltingly explained how he used to lock himself and the children in the cellar when she "had the painters in".

Every time Randolph moved, my stomach lurched in case he came to me. The woman next to me was breathing so heavily I wondered if she was in the midst of some sort of heart failure. At least they'd have to stop filming.

'And your husband left you too, didn't he, Laura?' Suddenly Randolph was perched on the step in front of me, his microphone almost touching my nose. 'Was that because of your violence?' he asked silkily.

'No!' It came out too loudly. How did they know about Daniel, I thought wildly. Nobody had told me he'd be mentioned. 'I just get very bad moods,' I said hastily. 'I've never hit anyone.'

Randolph brought his orange face closer to mine. 'Tell us how you feel, Laura. What happens when you get angry?'

'Well, I sort of get very impatient,' I said, flustered. My voice sounded higher than usual. Randolph nodded encouragingly. 'I find I shout at my son a lot. I get clumsy and drop things, I feel very fat …' My hand moved protectively over the half-yard of stomach that was trying to escape my waistband. 'Things make me cry and once I threw a shepherd's pie against the wall …'

Randolph turned and smiled into the largest camera. 'And yet Laura looks quite normal. With us today, we have Dr Steven Barrington, consultant gynaecologist at St Saviours Hospital …'

I sat and squirmed as Grey Suit on my left went through all the scientific stuff I'd prepared and forgotten. What on earth had possessed me to say that about the shepherd's pie? It was years ago. I'd never given it a thought since and suddenly, here, in a TV studio when I was supposed to be sounding sophisticated, it had just popped out of my mouth. Now the whole country would think I was totally bonkers and it wasn't even true. It was lasagne.

Grey Suit had finished and Randolph was standing in front of us all again, sounding sincere.

'We've heard all sorts of stories this morning, of violence and domestic mayhem, of lives being ruined, of relationships in the balance. Ordinary-looking women going about their lives with a terrible secret …' He gazed around the audience. His eyes were beginning to get a strange light in them. 'They are filled with pent-up, barely suppressed rage just waiting to boil over …'

I jumped as he suddenly swung the microphone back toward me. 'Would you say, Laura, that PMS was the single most contributory factor to the breakdown of your marriage?'

I opened my mouth and nothing came out. My brain whirred, searching for the right thing to say. 'The single most contributory factor to the breakdown of my marriage,' I might have replied, 'was my husband having a mid-life crisis and getting his leg over the first available female that came along. Lying to me was most definitely a contributory factor, as was trying to pretend I had developed paranoiac-personality-disorder for assuming that finding a packet of three extra-long-lasting melon-and-passion-fruit flavoured condoms and a carton of chocolate body paint in your husband's briefcase when he was supposed to be meeting up with the district auditor (male, 57, shocking case of halitosis) was a fair indication that he was up to no good. For let me tell you, Randolph, Daniel may have liked to pretend he only left me because I was difficult to live with but smashing crockery against the kitchen tiles was the least of it. I had been hurling the dinner about for *years* ...'

Randolph's eyebrows were raised enquiringly. He leant forward and opened his own mouth a couple of times as if to demonstrate what I should be doing. I swallowed. 'I don't know,' I said, lamely.

Randolph sprang to his feet and went leaping up the tiers of seats. 'How old are you, Doris?'

'I'm 88.'

We all twisted round to look. My microphone pack had slipped and I put a hand back to pull it into a better position. Randolph was bending over a white-haired old lady.

'Are you really? You don't look it,' he said gallantly.

Doris cackled. 'Get on with you.'

Randolph crouched down beside her. 'So what do you think about what we've heard this morning, Doris? Did you suffer from PMS when you were younger?'

Doris made an impressive snorting noise that went on for several seconds.

'Never heard anything so ridiculous in all my life,' she retorted. 'In my day we just got on with it. We didn't have time for any of this malarkey. And another thing, we didn't speak about things like that. Downright disgusting, if you ask me. We kept ourselves to ourselves. Talking about private women's things on the television for everyone to hear? It's a disgrace!' She folded her lips inwards until they disappeared.

'But what about period pains?' asked Randolph, moving in

a bit closer.

Doris glared. 'We didn't have those neither. A bit of proper housework that's what you need –' Her eyes fixed on me. 'If you got yourself down on your knees and scrubbed the floor you wouldn't have pains. It's the same with these girls today and all that nonsense when they have a baby. Epidurals, is it? What's wrong with them? Nothing in my day at all. You gritted your teeth and you pushed when you were told to. I boiled the water myself when the midwife got the forceps out.'

Some of the back row had opened their eyes and were sitting up in interest. 'You tell him, Doris,' croaked one excitably.

'It's like these disposable nappies. More money than sense that's your trouble.' She was really glaring at me now. 'Too much trouble to wash a few terries, through, is it? And I bet you've got a washing machine too, haven't you?' She jabbed a gnarled finger in my direction. 'Haven't you?' she cried.

'Well, yes,' I found myself saying, 'But ...'

'Four lots of nappies I had,' shouted Doris, 'and the whitest in the street too ...'

The oldies from Oldham were now beside themselves. One of them cheered.

'I haven't even got a baby ...' I protested.

'Well perhaps you should have,' yelled Doris in triumph. I caught a glimpse of Charlotte behind her, wide-eyed. 'That would sort you out!'

'Thank you, Doris!' Randolph patted her shoulder as the crones all pointed at me and muttered to each other. I was trembling. None of this was how it was meant to be. I could feel the sweat running down my back where the microphone pack was digging into my spine.

Randolph had now settled himself beside the brightly coiffured Alicia. He brought the mike up between them.

'Now you're 17,' he drawled. What? She was much older than that, surely? Alicia was nodding. 'And how old were you when your periods started?' He gave her a slow smile.

Alicia stared at him. 'Twelve,' she said flatly.

'Twelve!' cried Randolph, as if this were an achievement of

note. 'And do you get any of these symptoms, Alicia?' he asked smoothly. Alicia brought her head up high and stared boldly around the studio.

'No, I do not,' she said loudly. 'And if you ask me,' she said, her voice rising further. 'It's all a load of rubbish. This is just an excuse for middle-aged women to behave like witches and make other people's lives a misery.' She pointed at me. 'My mother was like her,' she snarled, almost spitting the last word. 'Always shouting and screaming and blaming everything on the fact that she had a bad period. Made us all miserable and gave my poor dad hell. She thought nothing of throwing a carving knife across the kitchen but it was never her fault. When I think what we went through –'

I clenched my fists in frustration, feeling hot and angry. The sense of hurt and disappointment and raw injustice that had begun rising when Doris was speaking rose further.

'I shouldn't think she wanted to be like that,' I said tightly. 'None of us do. Do you think anyone chooses to feel bad? Do you?'

Alicia shrugged. 'Probably,' she said, aggressively.

'Oh yes, I'm sure.' I scowled at her. 'Would you want to spend half the month with bloating and poor concentration?' I asked, suddenly miraculously remembering the list of symptoms I'd memorised from the Internet. 'Would you want to feel depressed and worthless? Would you want water retention and swollen ankles? Would you?'

Alicia rolled her eyes as the oldies began murmuring again. 'Look at you. Just like her, always feeling sorry for yourself. Always blaming something else.'

'What do you know about my life or how I behave?' I shouted. I realised I was waving both arms.

Alicia looked at me, eyebrows slightly raised, a sarcastic half-smile on her face. The mutterings from the back grew to a crescendo.

'We all know the trouble with you!' Doris yelled. The row behind her began to bay.

'Screaming the place down,' said Alicia. 'You're all the same.'

'I do not scream!' I shrieked.

I saw Randolph smiling as he turned back to face the camera. Horror struck as I realised my tirade would go out all over the country. 'Fuck,' I muttered, forgetting what Sharon had said about the mike picking everything up. 'Fuck it, fuck it,' I added, as I remembered.

'Why should we all put up with it?' Alicia was calling. 'Why should we be your victims?'

Furious with her, furious with myself, I struggled for something dignified to come back with, but the sight of her smug, triumphant smile was too much.

'You don't know what you're talking about,' I exploded. I leant forward and jabbed a finger at her. 'The woman with PMT,' I yelled, 'is a victim herself!'

There was uproar at the back. Three of Doris's cronies got to their feet and appeared to be trying to climb over the seats in front.

Alicia leant forward to give me the full benefit of her evil eyes. 'Well if it's that bad,' she said nastily, 'get a hysterectomy. But it would probably be more useful for everyone,' she ended victoriously, 'if you got a *life* ...'

'My God,' said Charlotte, appearing at my side looking visibly shaken as Sharon, the sound girl, rummaged around in the back of my trousers to retrieve the microphone pack. 'What a load of old harridans.

'You were very good,' she added doubtfully. 'Well, until the end anyway ...'

I shuddered. 'Did I sound like a fishwife?'

'Yeah, you did a bit, love.'

Terrific. So much for being poised and serene then. 'What happened to my hair and make-up?' I said crossly. 'And where's bloody Clive anyway? Shouldn't he be here?'

'You were totally marvellous, darling,' said Shane, bustling up. 'As I just knew you would be. Now let me just check my little list – have we got all your details?' He consulted his clipboard and then looked at me coyly. 'Just in case we need you again. Just in case you make *Randolph's Round-up*.' He lowered his voice huskily, 'Which I think, my darling, you just might ...'

'Randolph's what?'

'Round-up,' said Toni, who had appeared by my side, holding my jacket and handbag. 'We do it at the end of the series – a re-run of the best moments. It's totally wicked.'

'We get the really good guests back to watch themselves,' added Shane. 'You know, sitting on the sofa, smiling at how upset they got – a sort of where are they now?' He gave me a little nudge. 'Maybe you'll have cured yourself by then by taking dried loganberry leaf or something ...' He winked. 'Or you can pretend you have ...'

'That's cool. You were wicked,' Toni said, as Shane waltzed off. 'If Shane's saying that, I'm sure we will call you again ...'

'Really?' I preened a little. 'Did you hear that Charlotte? I may get called back as one of the best ...'

'Hmm,' said Charlotte. 'They probably say that to everyone just to stop them suing for damage to their reputation. Bloody hell. Look out!'

I turned to see Alicia striding toward us, arms swinging, face determined.

'I think she's going to hit you,' murmured Charlotte.

Afterwards, I couldn't really quite recall how it happened – I saw her arms come up and I remember bracing myself, thinking it's probably best to stand quite still and just let her do it, hoping all the while that Charlotte would land her one hard, decisive blow and knock her out, in the manner with which she had once dealt with Janine Jackson when we were at school, and thus save me having to get involved in an undignified brawl. As Alicia bore down on me, hand outstretched, I closed my eyes.

And then opened them again when I felt a pair of arms wrapped round me.

'You were brilliant,' someone said in my ear.

'What?' I looked into Alicia's face. She was grinning. 'Your face was a picture,' she said. 'But you were so good – I loved that bit when you screamed back at me.'

'Yes, well,' I said, uneasily. 'Of course I'm sorry for what you went through with your mum and I can see how you'd feel upset for your father in those circumstances but really, I do feel that some of us, in certain cases ...'

Alicia threw back her head and laughed. 'My dad pissed off when I was three and Mum and her boyfriend are totally cool,' she said. 'If anyone starts throwing the cutlery about, it's me!' She laughed again. 'I made it all up,' she giggled. 'They had dozens of mad cows already – no offence – so they needed someone to put the other side. I was just doing it to be on TV. And you know – it's a day out and a few quid, isn't it?'

I looked at her in shock. 'Is it? Do we get paid?' I raised my eyebrows at Charlotte. Nobody had mentioned money to me.

'Yeah, they don't advertise it but if you tell them you've got to miss a day's work to be here, you can usually pick up a couple of hundred. You should have done it beforehand, really – last night or first thing this morning when it would be really inconvenient for them to find someone else. That's the way.'

'Right,' I said faintly, marvelling at her acumen and my lack of it.

'I'm trying a get a tape together,' she explained. 'I really want to become an actress. I've got myself an agent and he said get as much variety as possible. So I'm going on *Hang Out with Hannah* next week to talk about marital abuse.'

'Are you married?' asked Charlotte.

'Not likely.'

'And how old are you?' I enquired.

'Twenty-four.' She grinned. 'Tell you what,' she said, linking her arm through mine, 'I'm looking for someone to go on *Cook Around the Clock* with me. Fancy that?'

Charlotte snorted with laughter.

'What?' I said.

'It sounds brilliant,' said Alicia. 'My friend, Shirley, went on it and they had loads of champagne and got put up in a really posh hotel. You could be my mum.'

'Thanks.'

'No, seriously, that's what they want. You go on as a pair – sisters, married couple, friends, or whatever. I phoned up and they said that, right now, they're looking for mothers and daughters. Haven't you ever seen it?'

'No.'

'Yes,' said Charlotte. 'And you're kidding. You've never seen Lu in a kitchen.'

'It's great,' said Alicia to me. 'One of you can cook and one can't. The one who can't cook gets a chef to help them and they have a race to cook something with the one that can. They have a chef too but he just watches and says whether they're any good or not. So I could be all hopeless and you can be a yummy mummy type who makes cakes all the time and is trying to encourage me.'

I shook my head. 'But I can't cook either.'

Alicia waved her hand dismissively as if this were a minor detail. 'It's supposed to be fabulous and you get to meet two famous chefs – we could get Jamie or Gordon Ramsay or anyone –'

'Mmm,' I said, 'I like him but I really don't do cookery. Well, not apart from pizza and chicken nuggets and things you just put in the oven. I made a beef casserole once and left it in the oven all day and it was still like leather ...'

Alicia shrugged. 'We can work something out.'

'No thank you,' I continued. 'I don't want to do anything like this ever again. I mean you may have been pretending but some of those up there ...' I nodded toward the now-empty back row of the set.

Charlotte nudged me. 'I thought you'd had it when that old dear started on about the housework. What a dragon she was.'

'Oh God yes,' I shuddered. 'She scared me rigid. Terry bloody nappies. Doris, wasn't it? Where the hell did they get her from?'

Alicia grinned again. 'That's my gran.'

Chapter Five

'SO HOW'S THE STAR?' Charlotte's husband, Roger, kissed her on the mouth and turned to grin at me. 'Hollywood called yet?'

'It was hilarious,' said Charlotte. 'We thought Laura was going to get lynched.' She smiled happily, clearly cheered by the bottle of wine she'd managed to procure from Kevin on the drive back.

'It was ghastly,' I corrected, having drunk less of it than she had. 'Has Stanley been OK?'

'Fine. He's upstairs on the PlayStation with Joe.' Roger put his arm round Charlotte's shoulders and squeezed. 'And Becky's flouncing about somewhere. Don't suppose you've thought about dinner?'

Charlotte waved a hand airily. 'Not really. Have you thought about a bottle of wine? Laura and I have had a very arduous day.'

Roger rolled his eyes indulgently. 'There's one in the fridge. Shall I go and get us all fish and chips?' He looked at me. 'Are you and Stanley staying?'

I pulled a face. 'I promised Stanley a delivered pizza apparently.'

'Oh, well we'll all have that,' said Charlotte briskly. 'There's a leaflet in the kitchen dresser.' She headed purposefully across the hall. 'Roger, give the kids a shout and we'll phone up!'

Before Roger had a chance to draw breath she'd thrown back her head and yelled herself. 'Beckeeee!'

I followed her into her bright kitchen with the vast scrubbed pine table I'd spent many a wine-soaked night round. The assortment of empty cups and glasses on it, along with the discarded crisp packets and biscuit wrappers, suggested that the kids hadn't exactly starved in our absence.

Charlotte opened the huge fridge and pulled out the bottle of wine. 'Didn't strain themselves clearing up, I see! Ah, there you are,' she went on, as her daughter Becky appeared in the doorway. 'Go and ask the boys what pizzas they want, Bex.'

Becky pushed back her long, dark hair and scowled. 'Why do I have to do it?'

'Because I just asked you to,' said Charlotte sweetly. 'And say hello to Laura, please – don't be so rude.'

Becky shone a smile on me. 'Hello, Laura,' she said in exaggerated tones, and then in her ordinary voice, 'what was it like?'

'Wait till you see it!' said Charlotte with glee. She crossed the room to the doorway. '*Boys*!'

'You'd have loved it,' she told Becky. 'If Laura has to go back and you're not at school, we'll take you next time.'

'I want to go on *The X Factor*,' said Becky.

'You're too young,' Charlotte replied in a tone that suggested they'd had this conversation before. 'You have to be sixteen.'

'I can look sixteen,' said Becky. 'In fact,' she added with quiet relish, 'one of the sixth-formers at Highcourt saw me on Facebook and said he'd have thought I was eighteen.'

'Well you're not,' said Charlotte, wagging the corkscrew. 'You're thirteen and you remember it. Which reminds me, you can put my new lip gloss back where you found it. And my eyelash curlers. Now go and get your brother.'

Becky pulled a face, sighed loudly and moved off.

'Little moo,' Charlotte said, handing me the corkscrew and rummaging in a drawer. 'I'd better get on that damn Facebook page and check it again. You should see the photos she and her mates put up. All this pouting and finger-sucking stuff – total jail bait.' She shook her head. 'I've told her Roger would have a fit.'

'What about?' said Roger, coming up behind her.

Charlotte held up a pizza menu. 'Found it! Nothing – just Miss 13 Going On 26 up there.' She frowned. 'Get that wine open, Laura, for God's sake.'

Joe burst into the room, wearing a red football kit, with Benson, the family's black Labrador, bounding along beside him. Stanley trailed behind in his socks. My son had taken off his tie and his shirt was untucked, with a large smear of mud down the front. The bottoms of his trousers, still much too long despite my torturous attempts to take them up, were scrunched around his feet and had already began to fray from constantly being walked on. There was another smear of mud on his face and his hair was more than usually unkempt.

'Good day at school?' I asked, holding out my arms to him.

'OK.' He looked sideways at Joe and frowned.

'Both come and give me a kiss,' instructed Charlotte, hugging Joe and reaching out an arm to Stanley. 'And you, young man!' Stanley blushed, smiled and allowed himself to be embraced. 'Now go and give your mother a smacker.'

Stanley smiled sheepishly and came over to me, looking me up and down.

'Is that what you wore on television?' he asked disapprovingly. 'What did you say?'

'She was very good,' said Charlotte firmly. 'As we'll see when it comes out. I must write it down.' She crossed the room to where a big desk diary lay open on the work surface and picked up a pen with a flourish. 'Weds, 9 a.m. Set video, Laura!' She gave one of her raucous laughs. 'Ooh, I can't bloody wait.'

Stanley pulled a face at me. 'I hope none of my friends see it.'

'They'll all be at school. And nobody we know watches that sort of thing anyway.'

Charlotte raised her eyebrows at me.

I hope.

By the time we'd finally established who was having what size pizza with which extra toppings and how many free side-orders we'd earned, it was nearly 8.00 p.m. and I was starving.

'Where's that damn phone gone now?' said Charlotte, lifting up tea towels and moving school books. 'Becky, have you taken it upstairs again? I've told you before, it stays in the kitchen.'

'I'll go and get them,' said Roger.

'There's no need – we can have them delivered.' Charlotte was still moving things around. 'It drives me mad the way they do this. The idea of a cordless phone was to make things easier – now I can't find the bloody thing. Whoops – sorry Joe, naughty Mummy,' she added hastily as her son came back into the kitchen. 'I'll go and use the phone upstairs.'

Roger shook his head. 'Really – I don't mind going at all.'

'What's the point? Delivery's free if you spend over 15 quid.'

'But will they bring wine too? We've only got the one bottle and by the look of that ...'

Charlotte smiled. 'Good thinking! What would I do without you?'

Roger picked his car keys up from the table. 'OK, I'll see you in a bit.'

'Take the dog with you,' said Charlotte.

'I'll come too, Dad.' Becky got up from the table.

'I thought you had homework to do.'

'Oh, it's not much, I can do it later.'

Roger shook his head 'You get it finished now.'

Becky stuck out her bottom lip and sighed. 'It doesn't even have to be handed in until next week.'

'You'll have more by then. Do it now, please.'

Becky gave another huge sigh and flounced toward the door. 'Whatever.'

'I won't be long.' Roger kissed Charlotte briefly on the cheek and went out into the hall. We heard the front door open and close.

Charlotte shook her head. 'She doesn't give him half the lip she gives me. If I'd said that, there'd have been a half-hour debate.'

'Have you got homework, Stanley?' I suddenly realised my son was very quiet beside me.

'I've done it.'

'Sure?'

'*Yes*!'

Charlotte topped up both our wine glasses and handed me mine. 'I'm just going to hustle Joe into a quick bath before Rog gets back. Make yourself at home.'

I always did feel at home at Charlotte's. It was usually noisy, often chaotic, with assorted extra children around and people coming in and out, but it always felt welcoming and warm.

Charlotte paused at the door and looked back. 'What do you want to do, Stanley love? You can go and put the TV on if you like – or go back on the PlayStation.'

'Thank you.' Stanley nodded. He seemed subdued. But before I could ask him anything, he followed Charlotte out of the room.

'I'm going to finish my game,' he said over his shoulder. I looked at his spiky hair. Maybe he was tired – or hungry. At home, we'd have long eaten by now and he'd be having a bath himself. Or perhaps Becky had been teasing him – he could be quite sensitive. No brothers or sisters to knock off the edges – as my mother was fond of reminding me with thinly veiled disapproval. I'd have a chat to him later.

Upstairs, I could hear the sound of running water. I sat down at the table and pulled the paper toward me, skip-reading the dreary stuff about the economy and the problem of house prices and flicking to where a survey had found most high-flying women agreed that what they needed more than anything was a wife. Someone, as one top female banker explained, to look after all the domestic minutiae, keep the house organised, and have the dinner cooked when they got home.

Hmm. Daniel wouldn't agree with that definition. In one of his tirades about what a dreadful partner I'd been for the entire 16 years we'd been together – silly him, for not spotting it sooner – he had turned purple and spluttered that I was completely "incompetent".

'You,' he'd spluttered, grasping at clichés, 'couldn't organise a piss-up in a brewery.'

'Unlike Emily,' I'd yelled back, 'who knows how to get a

shag from one!' A reference to the fact that the peroxide lollipop had been hired to artfully arrange barrow-loads of hops and piles of malt for a photo-shoot in a brewery in Faversham and had invited Daniel along to "watch". He'd tried to pretend he was doing an undercover on-the-spot tax check of off-licence sales but even I wasn't stupid enough to fall for that one.

Really, I thought now, that was what galled me most about the whole business. It wasn't him deciding that, after all, he'd prefer to get his leg over a simpering blonde 20-something instead of his increasingly grouchy and greying 42-year-old wife – given the choice between Daniel and, say, Cristiano Ronaldo or that lovely young man who'd just joined *EastEnders*, I'd have been tempted too – or even that he'd lied and connived and tried to have the best of both worlds and would still be stringing us both along now if I hadn't found out and thrown all his clothes in the garden. No.

It was the way he obviously had no respect for my intellect at all. He really, genuinely thought I was brainless enough to believe all his silly stories. Like the time when he came home and announced …

I was jolted out of my reverie as somewhere in the corner of the room a phone began to ring. I looked round trying to work out where the sound was coming from.

I started picking up random items of school uniform piled on the end of the work surface, wondering if Charlotte would answer it upstairs. But the phone was still flashing away as I finally located it beneath what looked like Becky's games shirt. Maybe it was Roger with a query on the pizza order. It was a withheld number, but perhaps he had his phone set like that.

I carried the handset to the doorway. I could hear the sound of a hairdryer going upstairs. 'Shall I get it?' I called. There was no reply. The phone rang on. I pressed the green button. 'Hello?'

It was a female voice, speaking hurriedly, almost breathlessly. 'Can't you see what's under your nose?'

'Sorry?'

'Your husband – can't you see what's going on?' Daniel? I

thought stupidly. Was this old news or was he having yet another affair? These weren't Emily's cool tones. 'It's me he wants to be with. He's just left me ...'

Then I realised with a sick start – of course it wasn't Daniel. This was Charlotte's phone. This woman, whoever she was, was talking about ...

I heard Charlotte's feet on the stairs and slammed the phone down.

'Who was that?' Charlotte crossed to the fridge.

'Double glazing.' I realised my hands were shaking.

'Urgh. Get them all the bloody time. Hope you gave 'em short shrift.'

'Yes, I did.'

Charlotte, wine bottle in hand, turned to look. 'Are you all right?'

'Yeah, I'm just – I don't know–' I tried to laugh. 'Bit dopy. Think I need something to eat.'

'Yeah, me too. Where's Roger? He's been ages. I bet he's sneaked off to the pub on the way back. No wonder he was so keen to go!'

She pulled open a drawer and got a handful of cutlery out. 'Here, chuck these round the table. I'll give him a ring.'

I began to lay out knives and forks, heart still pounding. Charlotte pressed numbers out on the phone.

'Oh, are you?' I heard her say. Then she laughed. 'Thought you'd buggered off to the boozer. OK!' She put the phone back down on the work surface. 'He's outside – long queue, apparently. Not run off with the barmaid yet!'

I forced a smile back but my stomach was churning. Not Roger; not big, smiling, affectionate, dependable Roger. I found myself staring at him as he came in.

He was smiling in the perfectly ordinary way I'd seen him smile a hundred times before – plonking the wine on the table, unpacking the pizza boxes, sorting slices onto Joe's and Stanley's plates. I swallowed.

'You OK?' He looked directly at me.

'She's all sugar-depleted and doo-lally,' said Charlotte, before I could answer. 'You know what she's like.' A large

47

slice of American Hot with extra peppers landed on my plate. 'Get that down your neck and have another drink.'

'Thanks. And thanks for going to get them.' I held Roger's eyes for a fraction longer than usual but he didn't appear to notice, grinning easily at me as he always did.

'No problem.'

Charlotte sat down opposite me. 'Yes, most impressive. Without even having to be asked too. There's hope for you yet, my love.' She grinned at Roger and raised her glass. 'My hero!'

Stanley was monosyllabic in the cab on the way home and once indoors went upstairs without speaking at all.

'What's the matter?' I said, when I went into his bedroom to say goodnight. He was sitting on the edge of bed in his Batman pyjamas, looking very young. He gazed at me miserably.

'I hate school.'

'No you don't, darling – you're just tired. You know what you're like – you always hate things when you stay up too late.'

Stanley shook his head. 'It's horrible. I wish I'd never gone there. I wish I was still at St Katherine's.'

I sat down beside him and patted his arm. 'But you're all grown up now. And incredibly clever. And I'm so proud of you.' I gave him a kiss.

Stanley wrinkled his nose. 'But I don't like it at Highcourt.'

'You said you loved it the first week.'

'No, I didn't.'

'Yes, you did. And you like your teachers.'

Stanley's voice rose. 'I don't. Mr Jenkins hates me and I haven't got any friends.'

'You've got Connor.'

'He's not in my class, is he?'

I recognised the stubborn negativity Stanley always displayed when overtired. I used to like to think he got it from Daniel, but if I was honest I saw shades of my mother and knew it was a behaviour pattern that had my genes stamped all

48

over it. I took a deep breath.

'Look, darling – it's always difficult at first, at a new school. You'll make friends soon. Come on, get into bed.'

'I won't. The only ones I like are all friends already. They all go on the bus together in the mornings.'

'Do you want to go on the bus?'

'No. I don't know.'

It was clear we weren't going to get anywhere much tonight. I pulled back the duvet and prodded him. 'Move.'

He sighed and lay down. I made a fuss of tucking him up.

'We'll talk about it tomorrow.' I turned the light off. 'Go to sleep now.'

'I'm fat.' Stanley's voice was small in the darkness.

I stopped in the doorway. 'You're gorgeous. And not at all fat. Has somebody said something to you?'

'No – but I am.'

'You're not.'

'Well, I'm not skinny, am I? Not like Jonathan.'

I pictured the boy from Stanley's primary school who was now at Highcourt with him too. 'Jonathan looks like a famine victim – some children are just like that.'

'And he eats much more than I do.'

'Well, there you are, then.'

'Do you think I have too many pizzas?'

I turned the light back on. 'Has Emily said something to you?'

Stanley turned away from me and faced the wall.

'Not really.'

'Stanley, has she?'

'I just feel worried about everything.'

'Oh darling.' I sat down on the edge of his bed and stroked his hair. 'Everything will be OK, I promise,' I said softly. 'There's nothing to be anxious about.' I patted his shoulder, trying to be reassuring, hoping he couldn't sense what I was really feeling. I was worried too …

Chapter Six

IT FELT VERY STRANGE having a problem I couldn't tell Charlotte about. Charlotte knew everything. She'd been through every step of Daniel's treachery with me. It was to Charlotte I'd given a blow-by-blow of each new depth he'd sunk to, and to her I'd turned to during every stage of the inevitable, unremitting disintegration of my marriage. Up until now, there was nothing I wouldn't have shared.

And up until now, I'd always envied Charlotte's marriage to Roger. Not because he was particularly good-looking or sexy but he was always the same.

Charlotte might complain that he was unromantic and quite capable of sitting on his backside watching football for a nine-hour stretch while she ran herself ragged and how she had to prime the kids to remind him a) when her birthday and their anniversary was and b) that it would be a nice idea to buy flowers, but when it came down to the important things he was kind and dependable.

And he clearly loved Charlotte and would listen to what she had to say about things and she could tell him anything. He wasn't sarcastic or defensive, like Daniel. He didn't try to make everything her fault. He drove her mad by leaving his teabags in a little wet puddle on the side instead of putting them in the compost pot and she was always complaining that he took more looking after than both kids put together. But still –

'Pain in the arse at times,' as she once succinctly put it, 'but my best friend. Best male friend,' she'd corrected herself, grinning at me. 'Not much good to go shopping with, though.'

Now it looked as though he might not be too hot at keeping

his marriage vows either and the very thought made me feel sick to my boots.

Obviously I would have to tell him about the call I'd taken and I wondered how best to go about it. I could drive to his offices in Canterbury – where he was a senior partner in a highly respected firm of solicitors – and accost him on his way home, insisting that he tell me what the hell was going on and who the hell he thought he was, to be shagging a mad-sounding woman with adenoids, but I didn't even know he was shagging her.

She could have called the wrong number. Though somehow, much as I wanted to, I couldn't believe that. After all, she had called to say Roger had just seen her shortly after Roger had been late home with the pizza. That was too much of a coincidence even for me.

Or I could call Roger, except somehow, despite knowing him for decades, I had never needed to have his mobile number and if I called the house Charlotte might answer. If I called him at work, I might put him in an awkward spot, especially if he had clients or colleagues with him. So I'd have to say, 'Let's meet for a drink – I have something important to say to you.'

But then he would think I was mad too, and he might just say to Charlotte, 'Hey, I had a weird call from Laura – do you think she's all right?' Or he might think I was menopausal (as I have been horribly suspecting myself – please God, no) and feel a frisson of fear the way men do when faced with a tidal wave of uncontrollable hormones and bring Charlotte along too. *Then* what would I say?

I would have to pretend I was reminding him about her birthday – even though that is Becky's job – and it would look pretty damn odd at the end of September when the birthday in question wasn't till April.

What I really needed was to bump into him face to face and tell him straight about the phone call and demand an explanation. Alternatively I could get him followed. Trouble was private detectives cost a fortune. I knew this from doing some basic research on the Internet the night Daniel first came home smelling of banana and passion fruit massage oil when

51

he was supposed to be at a seminar entitled *Tax Breaks for All – Can You Have Your Cake and Eat It?* (obviously, at that point, he was hopeful), from which I discovered you were talking four figures to even get started on any sort of surveillance and that was plus expenses.

None of which was very conclusive. So, after a largely fruitless day worrying about Roger interspersed with trying to espouse the virtues of a range of wrought-iron garden furniture about which I'd been told nothing except it was on sale in John Lewis and the ad copy had to be in by 5 p.m., I decided the only thing to do was keep turning up at Charlotte's until I could get Roger on his own and tell him about the call and see how he reacted.

In the meantime, I had the joys of my own philandering husband to contemplate, as somehow it was already one of those Fridays again and I had requested that Daniel pick up Stanley at home rather than straight from school, so I could make a few things clear.

I had finally emailed the copy off at 4.32 p.m. to the surprise of my old boss, Mike, who knows me and deadlines of old, and was just telling him how delighted I'd be to write an entire brochure on the full range of artefacts and garden installations – he gives me all the exciting jobs – when the bell rang.

'Got to go,' I sang gaily into the phone. 'The worm's at the door.'

Daniel stood in the hallway with that self-conscious, half-ingratiating, half-defensive expression he always wore whenever he saw me.

'How are you?' he asked, warily.

'I am fine,' I said. 'Stanley is very upset.'

Daniel sighed. 'Why's that?'

I folded my arms. 'Why do you think? He is 11 years old and maybe a little chunky but at a perfectly normal weight for his height. He does not need a problem with his body image; he does not need low self-esteem; he does not need to be fretting over calories and the GI index.'

I took another breath. 'He especially does not need some

half-starved bimbo telling him how much hydrogenated fat there is in a sausage roll or what he can and cannot eat. In other words, tell your *girlfriend -*' I put particular emphasis on the word '- to keep her comments to herself.'

'She didn't ...' began Daniel uneasily.

'She did,' I said firmly, inwardly congratulating myself on sounding calm, reasonable and very clearly in possession of the moral high ground, despite it being Day 21. 'She made comments about what he wanted to eat. Again. And implied he had a weight problem. Don't you think he's got enough on his plate as it is? A new school, hitting puberty – coming from a broken home ...'

Daniel's face hardened. 'You never miss a chance do you? Is this your main ambition now, Laura – to make me feel guilty? To remind me that everything is *my fault*?'

I tried one of those sneers Pauline Fowler from *EastEnders* used to deliver with such devastating effect (that programme's never been the same since they killed her off).

'If the cap fits, wear it,' I said nastily. 'I was simply stating facts. Stanley has lived in a single-parent family ever since you decided you wanted to explore -' I gave a delicate pause '- pastures new, and he needs lots of extra support. Not a lecture on what trans fats do to you.'

'Emily was just trying to help,' said Daniel. 'And certain fats *are* bad for you.' He looked accusingly at my hips. 'You should be glad someone is thinking about his health.'

'I think about his health,' I said hotly. 'It was his health I was thinking about through all the weeks you were lying to me and conniving to dump your son for that stupid woman.'

I was aware that my voice had risen several octaves. Daniel visibly relaxed. 'Here we go again!' He gave a superior smile. 'That time of the month again, is it?'

I clenched both fists. 'Look,' I said, trying for an icy tone while longing to pick up the hall table and batter him with it. 'The fact is that Stanley is now anxious, worrying about his weight and feeling unattractive. So would you please ask Emily –' I deliberately made her name sound like an unpleasant viral disease '– to desist with her nutritional advice and personal comments and leave the care of Stanley's body mass index to his mother.'

'I'm his father,' said Daniel, stonily. 'I care about him too. And he can't eat pizzas all day long.'

'He doesn't! But 11-year-old boys – as anyone with two brain cells to rub together knows – do not like living on sushi. And there was a time,' I added triumphantly, 'when I remember you turning your nose up at it too!'

'Well, I've changed,' said Daniel. 'I've started looking after myself.' He looked down at his stomach. 'It's the only body I've got.'

'Yes, unfortunate that, isn't it? Well, why don't you do something useful with it, like playing football in the park with your son – if you can manage it – instead of making him miserable by telling him how many calories he can eat. That would make him happy and do him good.'

I was pleased to find that not only had I calmed down again but – judging from the two rather unattractive red blotches on Daniel's cheeks – I had regained the upper hand too.

'What's she cooking him tonight?' I enquired breezily.

'I'm taking him out to eat,' Daniel said sullenly. 'Emily will be at her tai chi class.'

'Of course she will,' I said silkily. 'Well, that's excellent. Make sure you let him have exactly what he wants and tell him how proud you are of him. That might undo a little of the damage you've both done. You may be basking in domestic bliss, Daniel, with a girl young enough to be your daughter, but just remember what he's going through.'

'I do,' said Daniel crossly. 'You know, Laura – you are turning into a really unpleasant person. I think you ought to get out more.'

'It's a bit difficult now I'm a single mother.'

Daniel glared. 'Well I've got him tonight, haven't I? Go and hit the town, why don't you? Probably because you haven't got any friends left to go out with because you're such a dried-up old shrew.'

The rage came over me like a hot flush. For a moment I was close to lunging at him and had I had a long, cold drink in my hand it would undoubtedly have landed right between his eyes. But the bang of the front gate brought me up short. 'Shut up,' I hissed furiously as Stanley came along the path. Our son wriggled out of his rucksack and looked from one to the other of us.

'Everything all right?' he said glumly.

'Of course, darling.' I smiled as brightly as I could with my teeth locked together in fury, and kissed Stanley on the cheek. 'You go and get changed – I've already put some things in a bag for you.'

Daniel clapped him heartily on the shoulder. 'All right, old chap?'

Stanley nodded.

I pulled a face at Daniel over the back of our son's head. 'You tosser,' I muttered out of the side of my mouth as Stanley clumped upstairs.

Daniel gave a patronising smile. 'Perhaps,' he said, 'you should think about what you eat, yourself. Emily says a lot of hormone imbalance is caused by diet. She is a professional and knows about these things.'

I took a deep breath and spoke in a low tone. 'We are not talking about me, we are talking about Stanley – and his body image.'

'Are we?' Daniel was now looking thoroughly pleased with himself again. 'Are you sure, Laura, you're not really talking about yourself?'

Chapter Seven

'CHRIST, I HATE HIM,' I said furiously, pacing up and down Charlotte's kitchen. 'I would like to wipe that self-satisfied smirk right off his face. He deliberately winds me up – deliberately. Do you think he really believes he is in the right and this is all my fault? And what is it with him and all this psychobabble? Talking about myself – bastard.

'I could kill him,' I concluded with venom, suddenly realising I had picked up a potato masher and was pounding it up and down in front of me.

'Let's have a drink now and go to the wine bar later,' said Charlotte decisively. 'I've had a crap day and it is, after all, nearly five thirty. Roger's going to be late back – they've got a partners' meeting –' I looked at her sharply, but she seemed perfectly relaxed. 'So why don't you hang around and eat something with me and the kids and we'll pop out for a late one once he's back.'

'How late will he be, then?' I asked, making my voice sound casual.

Charlotte shrugged. 'Oh, I don't know. He said they'd be having a drink – maybe even get some food in – they've got a lot to get through, apparently.'

Is this usual? I wanted to ask but I couldn't. I would have to wait until I could get Roger on his own, as I'd planned. And if I hung around this evening I could probably do that later tonight.

Charlotte was lighting a cigarette. 'You've just got to keep very calm with Daniel. Don't rise to his stupid comments and don't start waving your arms and squawking – that's never a good look.' She opened the back door and blew smoke toward it – her idea of not smoking in the house, which was, apparently, the first phase in her giving it up altogether, something Becky had been nagging her about for as long as I could remember.

'He implied it was me with the weight problem.'

'What did you say?'

'Nothing. I just looked really hard at his beer gut and then said that Stanley needed a new pair of trainers.'

'That's the spirit,' said Charlotte. 'If Roger upsets me I don't say anything any more. I just take it out on his credit card.'

She stood up and leant in the doorway, blowing another lungful of smoke out on to her patio. 'Don't listen to Daniel – there's nothing wrong with your weight.'

I smiled gratefully at her, but I knew that it wasn't about whether I needed to lose a few pounds, which we both knew I did. It was the "old" that had got me. "A dried-up old shrew" he'd called me. And that was what had stung. Because I was beginning to feel my age.

I was all right before Daniel met Emily. I'd had the usual traumas over my 40th – spending the day lying in a darkened room, refusing to speak to anyone – but that is only to be expected.

Once I'd got over the shock of the F-word – and had learnt to lie though my teeth and keep smiling – I didn't really feel, or look, that different. I felt I could still scrub up well, that all the hype about 60 being the new 40 or 40 being the new 29, or whatever it was, was not so far wrong. I still on balance felt *young*.

Or at least young-ish. Perhaps it was going to happen anyway, but ever since Daniel had removed himself for a woman 14 years younger than me I felt as if I had aged enormously.

Suddenly, no amount of concealer quite did it for the shadows beneath my eyes, hand cream had to be applied hourly or the backs of my hands shrivelled and there was a definite sag about my knees that I had never noticed before. I had, for the first time, found myself picking up clothes in trendy high street chains and hastily putting them down again, because I just couldn't wear that sort of thing any more.

I couldn't decide what was worse: the days when I felt a weariness inside me that said *you're past it*, or the days when I still had a spring in my step and felt the same as I always had done and then would catch sight of myself in the mirror and be startled to see a middle-aged woman scowling back. A slightly unkempt, mad-looking woman, having a bad hair day.

Grooming, said the magazines. Grooming, instructed the bossy article on how to make the most of each decade. Grooming was apparently paramount once you were in your forties.

Forget grunge, the glossies exhorted. And short skirts and messy curls. Eschew cheap jewellery, "fun" handbags, T-shirts with slogans and coloured tights. Basically I had to empty out my entire wardrobe or I would end up resembling a bag lady. I looked in the mirror again and realised just what I'd been reminding myself of.

I was a past master at witticisms about getting old but I'd never really meant them before. Now, after a warm-up decade of self-deprecating jokes about crow's feet and sagging flesh, it suddenly wasn't funny any more.

'I look old,' I said to Charlotte now.

She didn't turn round.

'Shut up and get the wine open.'

'Seriously,' I said, after our second glass, 'I am finding the ageing process difficult. Aren't you?'

'Not at all.' Charlotte waved a cigarette. 'Anyway, you should worry. I've got a lot more lines than you.'

'That's because you smoke,' said Becky, coming into the kitchen. 'It's very ageing. So is drinking,' she added, looking pointedly at the glass in Charlotte's other hand.

'Go and tell someone who cares,' said Charlotte cheerfully. 'I've had my days as a gorgeous dolly bird,' she went on. 'Now I'm a middle-aged wife, mother and *drudge* –' She raised her voice to yell after Becky's retreating back. 'Do you know how long it took me to pick up all the clothes off your bedroom floor this morning?'

Charlotte looked back at me and smiled. 'And actually you know, I quite like it. I've spent years trying to hold my bloody stomach in. Now I'm looking forward to buying elasticated trousers and letting it all hang out.'

'Ugh' Becky stopped in the doorway and looked back at her in disgust. 'You're revolting.'

'I'm not ready for it,' I said. 'I'm not a wife any more and I don't want to feel it's all over.' For a horrible moment I felt my chin quiver.

Charlotte grabbed the wine bottle and leant across the table. 'Come on, don't get maudlin. You've got a few years left in you yet.'

An hour later, Charlotte, who has a useful talent for still being able to produce food while three sheets to the wind (unlike me, who only manages to burst into tears and then go to bed), surveyed the remains of the lasagne and salad she'd managed to knock up at the same time as climbing down the Pinot Grigio.

She balanced the tray with the last of the garlic bread on top of the Aga and looked ruefully at the empty bottle. 'Sorry, love, think that's it. The Forbes cellar is empty.'

I picked up my handbag. 'I'll go and get some more.' Charlotte very handily has an off-licence cum general store on the corner of her street – it was one of the main reasons she bought the house ("I can't be doing with running out of fags, love") and is on first-name terms with the Turkish family who run it.

'Get me some more ciggies while you're there.' She waved a ten-pound note at me. 'I'd text Roger but he deliberately forgets.'

'He just worries about your health, that's all. As I do. You know I read an article about degeneration of the retina due to smoking and how if you're over 40 and smoking more than 20 a day then your sight –'

Charlotte yawned loudly. 'Do shut up. Nothing wrong with my eyes except that they haven't caught sight of a new bottle of wine recently. So stop being boring and get your arse down the road.'

'Ah,' said Mustafa, when I put two bottles of Soave on the counter and asked for 20 Rothmans. 'How is Mrs Fobbs?'

After a pleasant little discussion about what a fine woman and good customer Charlotte was, and how very kind she'd been when Mustafa's son, Emin, had broken his arm, I walked back along the pavement, warm and fuggy from all the wine we'd had already, thinking how much I loved Charlotte and how it must be quite nice to be her, unworried by the prospect of double chins and wrinkles, secure in one's role as wife and mother and occasional estate agent, when a familiar car went past.

It was pretty dark but I recognised the car instantly from the distinctive number plate, ROG 58. Charlotte had bought it for Roger for his 46th birthday, telling him that since it had cost her a small fortune, it had to last for the next 12 birthdays too.

I increased my pace, thinking that I might catch him while he was still on the driveway and have a quick word before we went into his house. But as I watched his rear lights go on down the road, he slowed up and pulled in outside a house a few doors along from his own. Oh my God. Surely he wasn't knocking off a neighbour? As I stopped in surprise, the car lights faded.

I stood still for a moment, waiting to see if he would get out. When he didn't, I hurried toward the car. As I walked up beside it, I could see Roger in the light of the street lamp – obviously on the phone, nodding away. It must be her! Why else stop along the road? He had a Bluetooth ear phone so why not pull into his drive as usual and, if necessary, walk straight on into the house still talking as I'd seen him do plenty of times before?

I hesitated, then, emboldened by alcohol and a burning sense of injustice, I stepped forward and tapped smartly on the passenger window.

Roger looked up, saw me, said something into the receiver and snapped the phone shut. Then he re-started the engine. The electric window nearest to me whirred down and he grinned at me, a trifle manically, I thought.

'Hi – how are you?'

'Sorry. I didn't realise you were on the phone,' I lied. 'Hope it wasn't important.' I looked hard at him but he kept smiling.

'Only someone from work.' He leant across and pushed open the door. 'Get in.'

'It's only three doors down,' I said pointedly, getting in anyway. 'I wondered what you were doing skulking up the road.'

'I stopped to get a bit of paper I needed out of my briefcase,' he said. 'Office problem.' Was his tone a touch defensive now? He was already turning into his drive.

'Oh yes, Charlotte said you'd had a late meeting.' I gave him my most searching stare again but he didn't appear to notice.

'Yes,' he said, getting out of the car and opening the back door, 'it went on a bit.' He leant in and pulled out his briefcase and jacket. 'Have you just arrived?'

'No, I've been here all evening. Stanley's off with Daniel. I just got sent out for more supplies.' I held up the carrier bag with the wine and cigarettes.

Roger laughed. 'Jolly good. I could only have one – it's a pain having to drive.'

He was striding toward the front door. It was now or never. I hurried after him.

'Roger –'

'Yes?'

I hesitated as he stopped and turned toward me. We were almost at the door and I could hardly blurt out, 'Are you having an affair?'

'Last week,' I began instead. He looked at me questioningly. 'I was in your kitchen –'

The front door opened. 'Ah, there you are!' Charlotte filled the doorway against an oblong of light. 'I thought I heard the car. Glad you're back, Rog – Laura and I want to go out.'

Roger walked toward her and kissed her. 'Sure.'

'We don't have to,' I said quickly. 'I mean, Roger's only just got in – I expect he wants to talk to you.'

'He's got all weekend to talk to me,' said Charlotte. 'Anyway, I expect he wants to veg in front of the football if I know him. There's lasagne in the oven if you want it, love. The kids are upstairs somewhere. Joe wants you to help him with his model – apparently, the wings keep falling off.'

Roger nodded. 'OK. I'll just have a beer and get changed and I'll have a look.' He opened the fridge, pulled out a can, and wandered out into the hallway.

My stomach had gone into a knot. It all seemed completely normal, yet why had Roger been sitting outside in the dark talking on his phone? Why not just drive on a few metres and come in?

And nothing could take away the fact that the woman had called last week.

Was that why Roger was so happy for Charlotte to go out? So he could call her back in peace? Although in fairness, he'd always been pretty easy-going about whatever Charlotte wanted to do. Did this mean he'd been at it for years?

'What's the matter?' Charlotte was looking at me quizzically. 'You've got a very odd expression on your face.'

I shook my head. 'Sorry. I was just thinking –'

'Yes?' Charlotte was still watching me.

'Just what a nice marriage you two have,' I said feebly. 'Daniel would have moaned if I'd gone out the moment he came in.'

Charlotte laughed. 'He wants to watch TV without me interrupting,' she said. 'Right, I'll just go and put a top on that hasn't got pasta sauce down the front and kiss my lovely children and we'll get going. You call a cab.'

She and Roger crossed in the doorway. She put a hand on his waist and gave him a little squeeze as she went past. He smiled at her. I sat down at her table and took a deep breath. Roger had come back in and was opening cupboards and drawers, getting out a plate and cutlery. Charlotte would only be a couple of minutes. Should I say anything or leave it till another time?

I took a swallow of wine.

When I looked up, Roger was gazing at me with an

expression I couldn't place. 'Are you OK, Laura? What were you saying out there?'

I could hear Charlotte's footsteps coming back down the stairs already and I suddenly felt a lump in my throat. I shook my head. 'It doesn't matter,' I said.

By the time Charlotte was back in the room, Roger had got me the tissues and was hovering kindly. 'What's up? Has something happened to upset you?'

'She's all hormonal – you know what she gets like.' Charlotte was moving round the kitchen lifting up bits of paper. 'Where are my bloody keys?'

Roger patted me on the shoulder. 'Anything we can do?'

Charlotte was brisk. 'I'm going to take her out, get a few more drinks down her, and if she's still a misery after that I'll bring her back here for the night.'

Roger grinned. 'Jolly good – there's always a much better breakfast when we've got guests.'

'You should count yourself lucky you get breakfast at all,' said Charlotte, digging in her handbag. 'Can't find my damn lighter now either.'

'It's on the microwave – with your keys.' Roger crossed the kitchen and picked up both. 'Are you sure you're not hormonal too?'

'You'd be wearing the frying pan if I was.' Charlotte took the items from him and kissed his cheek. 'Thank you, love.'

She turned and looked at me. 'Come on, you get some slap on and let's get out of here. She's feeling old and ugly,' she added to Roger.

'You look fine to me,' said Roger gallantly.

'Not that he'd know,' said Charlotte. 'He fancies the most peculiar women. Have you called that cab yet?'

'What did you mean?' I asked, when we were settled at a table in Greens, a bottle of Frascati in the cooler in front of us. 'That Roger fancies peculiar women?' I made my voice light and cheery. 'He doesn't fancy anyone but you, does he?'

Charlotte laughed. 'Oh, it's an old joke. I've told you before about the girl he was going out with before he met me. Very odd-looking woman. And you know that weather girl on the local news – the one with the weird eyebrows? He thinks she's pretty – always going on about her. He's got no taste whatsoever.' She grinned. 'Except in marrying me, of course.'

'He's a lovely bloke,' I said, taking another mouthful of wine. 'Oh God, am I slurring? How undignified. Don't you think we are getting a bit old to drink this much?'

'What's age got to do with it? You're getting obsessed. Roger's all right, yes. I'm pretty lucky. Bloody infuriating at times, but aren't they all? Though, you know,' she said, suddenly thoughtful, 'he's been a bit funny lately.'

'Has he?' I could feel my heart beating harder. 'In what way?' What was I going to say if she said he'd started buying lots of new clothes and slapping on the aftershave. If he'd got a gold medallion or was waxing his chest …

Charlotte swirled her wine about and considered. 'I don't know, really. Sort of very nice.'

'He always seems nice to me,' I said carefully, wishing I hadn't had so much to drink and praying I wouldn't seem over-interested. 'What's so different?'

'I'm not sure. He's a bit distracted, yet unusually helpful and accommodating. I mean, Roger's usually so useless around the house. Yet he's suddenly started putting things in the dishwasher and he brought me tea in bed the other morning. Quite unnerving, really!'

I looked at her in alarm. Was this Roger's guilty conscience manifesting itself? Was she going to come to that very conclusion any second? Would she want to know what I thought?

But she was laughing. 'I should capitalise on it while I can and get a new handbag out of him. And Becky could do with some jeans. We'll probably have a massive row tomorrow and it will all be back to normal.'

'Perhaps he's just appreciating you more. Perhaps a colleague at work is going through a divorce or something,' I said wildly, 'and he has suddenly realised how lucky he is to be happily married.'

Charlotte looked sceptical. 'No, I think it's more likely he's trying to butter me up for something. He's in line for a really big bonus at work if nothing changes between now and Christmas. He's probably wondering how he can go about buying himself a new Jag instead of taking me on the holiday to St Kitts I've set my heart on.' She frowned. 'What is odd, though, is —'

She stopped as a familiar figure floated across the floor toward us.

'Darlings!'

Charlotte smoothed back her hair. 'Clive!'

Clive posed for a second in front of us, to allow us to take in his pink silk shirt, skinny black Armani jeans and Italian leather shoes. As usual, a cloud of expensive scent wafted around him. Then he bent down and kissed Charlotte on both cheeks before twirling toward me and taking my face in his hands. He rolled his eyes heavenward and sighed happily.

'I hear that you, my sweet, were a triumph ...'

Chapter Eight

IN ALL THE WORRY about Roger I'd forgotten about the programme. But if I'd thought about it at all, the idea had been for me to watch it on my own – possibly with a cushion over my face – and then, if it was fit for public consumption and I was able to bear it, to have a second viewing of the video later with Stanley and Charlotte and her kids, so we could get all the jokes over in one go and then put it behind us.

But thanks to Clive, Charlotte was having none of it. She was waiting on the doorstep when I got back from the school run armed with a bag of croissants and a blank tape. 'I've set the kids' machine at home of course and Roger has programmed the hard drive, so we should have it twice but, just in case, we'll record it here too. I said I'd take it to the next PTA meeting – Carole was in hysterics when I told her what had happened.'

'Thanks,' I said crossly. 'I didn't want anyone to know, really.'

'Come off it – in a town like this?' Charlotte laughed. 'All those yummy mummies like to pretend they spend their lives whisking up fairy cakes and arranging Baby Princess manicures and extra maths lessons but really it's wall to wall daytime TV. They start with Randolph and go straight through to *Bargain Hunt.* Everyone was bound to find out.'

I scowled at her. 'That's not what you said when you were persuading me to do it – you said only about thirty people watched it in the whole country and they included nobody we knew.'

'I lied,' said Charlotte cheerfully, switching my TV on and squatting down in front of the video recorder. 'Get the bloody

66

kettle on, for God's sake.'

She was on her second croissant by the time I brought the mugs in. I handed her one and flopped down on the sofa beside her. 'This is going to be horrendous,' I said.

'Clive reckons you went down a storm,' Charlotte pushed the bag of pastries toward me. 'He says you look a bit frightened at first, but they all loved the bit where you started screeching.'

'What about my make-up? I meant to ask him that the other night. The cheapskates. Didn't he promise me …?'

'He says he didn't realise they'd stopped doing it. It wasn't cuts – they're going for the more natural look. They like to see when people go all red and blotchy.'

'Well, that's bloody great,' I began, clapping a hand to my mouth as I saw the graphics that had just appeared on the screen. 'Oh my God!' I sunk into the sofa as the opening music began and Randolph Kendall loomed large in front of us. 'They used it all up on him, more like!'

Though actually he looked less orange on screen. Unlike me. I recoiled as I spotted myself hunched in my front row seat – body like a misshapen Satsuma, face positively ashen, and looking as though I'd just been told I had three days to live.

'Why did I do this?' I wailed to Charlotte, who wasn't listening.

'There I am!' She jabbed a gleeful finger at the screen. 'And there's Doris. Look, you can see her grinning her teeth already. Ha! There I am again. That was a terrible blouse that girl next to me had on …'

She kept up a joyful commentary all through Maureen and Jean and Brian, while I cringed inside, waiting for the moment when I would start speaking.

'Ah! Here you are,' yelled Charlotte as the camera panned in so horribly close you could see the hairs up my nose. My voice sounded strange and my hands were flapping about all over the place but I looked calmer than I remember feeling.

'I had no idea I pulled all those faces when I speak,' I said in wonder.

'Oh yes,' said Charlotte airily. 'You've always looked

freaky as soon as you get excited about anything. Hey, look at you now,' she shrieked. 'Oh my God, Lu – look, *look*!'

My face was contorted into the sort of "snarl like a wolf" expression recommended on the *Save-Yourself-Surgery* video of facial exercises that had been Charlotte's idea of a witty birthday present, and I was waving both arms now.

I turned away and groaned.

'You tell 'em, love,' said Charlotte, grinning. I looked back briefly as the camera panned into my open mouth, while my voice rose in a crescendo. Back on my own sofa, I blocked my ears and firmly shut my eyes …

The phone rang almost as soon as the credits began to roll.

'Oh Lord, I hope that's not my mother,' I said. 'If she's seen it there'll be hell to pay. She'll be saying I should have sat up straighter and why wasn't I wearing a nice navy suit with my hair set?'

But it was Alicia.

'Did you see it?' she cried, the moment I picked up the receiver. 'I'm sitting here with Gran – we've been pissing ourselves laughing.'

'I'm sitting here groaning,' I told her. 'I can't believe how awful I looked.'

'You looked cool,' said Alicia dismissively, 'and I reckon we made a jolly good team. Now, I've downloaded the form for this cookery programme, and filled in most of it. All you have to do is answer your questions and get them back to me – what's your email address?'

'Oh no, I really don't think –'

'Yes – go on. They definitely do your make-up on this one – I told you my friend Shirley's been on. And one of you wins five hundred quid – we can split it, whoever it is. Come on Laura – £250 for a few hours and a bit of a laugh.'

'I don't even know what I have to do.'

'Well, watch it at 5.30 p.m. – it's funny. I'll phone back this evening.'

'No, listen. Alicia …'

'Oh, and Gran says hi. Catch you later.'

'Where did she get my number from anyway?' I asked Charlotte, as I put the phone down.

'I gave it to her. Oh bloody hell – look at the time. I'm supposed to be showing someone round a house at North Foreland in five minutes – must scoot.'

She gave me a hug. 'You TV star, you. Want to come round tonight and we'll watch it with all the kids?'

'No, not really. I'd rather sit here with my head in a bucket.'

'I'll see you about six. I'll do spaghetti.'

When she'd gone, I went upstairs to consider the delights the day held. Namely finishing the copy for a double-glazing brochure filled with plastic-looking men in suits pointing at equally plastic-looking white windows while a suitably thrilled-looking family of four stood arm in arm surveying their new heating bills, slashed to a fraction of their normal size, by the installation of Glow-Glass Windows and Doors …

I thought about Alicia as I waited for my computer to whirr into life and yesterday's page to come up on the screen. I didn't want to do any more TV, that was for sure, but there was something attractive about being around young people who still had some drive. I liked Alicia's energy – the way she was bent on success. I remembered Daniel saying it about Emily. With his usual tact and sensitivity, he'd thought nothing of listing his new girlfriend's latest achievements. Telling me how well she'd done, all the top clients she'd had. 'She's very ambitious,' he'd finished with pride.

Was that the must-have quality now? To be ambitious? To make something of yourself, as Daniel had put it.

Once, it had been enough to earn sufficient funds to pay the mortgage. To have a child. Daniel had been promoted every few years since his initial days of filing and form-filling in the civil service but he'd always just accepted this as the natural order of things. He'd never shown any particular excitement or hunger to be elevated up the ranks. He'd take the odd exam, come home and tell me he'd been put up a grade. I'd say well done, and we'd both agree the extra money would be useful and we'd turn on *EastEnders*. There was no talk of ambition then.

In fact, when Stanley was a few months old and I still couldn't stop crying and had sat at my computer trying to write an ad campaign for Mike, tears dripping, feeling as though the copy was in a language I couldn't understand, it was Daniel who'd phoned Mike and said I wasn't ready to be back at work.

'We'll manage,' he'd said to me. 'The money isn't worth you putting yourself through this. You're looking after our baby – that's more important than any sort of paid job.' No mention of ambition then either.

But now, he was impressed with career, money, status ... fame?

'She's made something of her life,' he'd said accusingly. The implication being that I hadn't. I had sat back and done the same job writing brochure copy for the same clients for ten years, driven back and forth down the same roads on the same school runs, gone to the same supermarkets and now I was 42, with the same face looking ever more ravaged, and nobody would employ me now even if I did want to get on a ladder. It was all rather too late ...

'Why are you watching this?' asked Stanley in surprise, coming into the sitting room at 5 p.m. to find me in front of the TV.

'One of the women I was on the other programme with wants me to go on it with her.'

Stanley raised his eyebrows. 'Cooking?'

'I might win some money.'

'Can I have the new iPhone if you do?' Stanley looked hopeful.

'It might not be *that* much money,' I said hastily. 'But who knows,' I added, giving him a small wink as his face fell again. 'We've got a couple of months till your birthday.'

I smiled at him, thinking that if I could make the £250 I could offer to pay for the handset and Daniel could provide the swingeing monthly payments for the contract they'd make us have. After all, Stanley did need a better phone now he was at secondary school; the old one of Daniel's he carried in case of emergency was on its last legs, and why shouldn't he have the latest gadget for once?

Maybe it would give him a bit more street cred with the other kids –make them treat him like one of the gang. The more I thought about it, the more the idea took hold. If I went on the TV programme I could try to win the money for my son. It would only take a few hours, after all, and he deserved something nice. I'd do it for him. For Stanley ...

'Come off it,' said Charlotte that evening as she strained the pasta. 'You've got the TV bug. Stars in your eyes! You just fancy yourself on the box again.'

'It might be a bit of fun.'

'Can I come?'

'I don't know, Alicia is sorting it. But in the meantime, I've got to fill in all these bloody forms.'

Charlotte put a large, steaming bowl on the table and picked them up.

'An amusing anecdote? The shepherd's pie against the wall again?'

'It was lasagne, and no thank you. Something funny, it says.' I looked at her desperately. 'What's happened to me that's funny?'

'What about that time you fell asleep with your head in the trifle?'

'*No.*'

'Or when you got locked in the loo at Janice's hen night. Now that *was* funny–'

'Not for me it wasn't – I was in there hours.'

Charlotte waved a hand. 'Just make something up.'

'Like what? And, oh God, look at this one: What is your greatest achievement?'

Charlotte considered. 'Forcing someone to marry you?'

'Getting rid of him again,' I corrected sourly.

'Look,' said Charlotte, putting a pot of parmesan cheese and a pile of cutlery in front of me, 'you just need to make yourself sound as though you can say something witty when asked. If you sound like a dreary old divorced housewife they won't touch you with a barge pole.'

She sat down opposite me and picked up the pen. 'I'll fill it in – you lay the table and get the wine open. I always find a glass of vino inspiring in these situations.' She looked at the paper in front of her. 'Who would you love to have dinner with?'

'You. That gorgeous young bloke who's on *Strictly Come Dancing*. I don't know.'

'We'll say Jeremy Paxman – they won't be expecting that. Say you go weak at the knees when the *Newsnight* theme tune comes on.'

'But I don't …'

'What would you spend a million pounds on?

'Um, er, I'm not sure. Maybe a bigger house. Stanley's bedroom is a bit small …'

Charlotte wrote rapidly. 'Diamonds, fast cars, loose men, and a boob job. What is your favourite party trick?'

'You can't talk about boobs and I haven't got one.'

She thought for a moment and then bent over the paper once more. 'Playing – the – spoons.'

'Charlotte!' I squeaked. 'Come on – I can't do that.'

Charlotte looked up and sighed. 'It's a *joke*,' she said wearily. 'Remember jokes?'

Chapter Nine

NOPE. I CAN'T SAY I did. Some things just weren't funny.

The rubbish bag splitting as I dragged it from kitchen bin to front door wasn't at all amusing, for example. Particularly when an empty tin of spaghetti hoops bounced out of it and left tomato sauce drips all along the hall carpet. The house being in a mess didn't make me laugh either, nor did discovering Stanley's school trousers were totally covered in mud while the other pair were still in the washing machine, or him wailing that he would get detention if he went to school without his tie again and he'd looked everywhere and still didn't know where it was (it eventually turned up beneath Boris).

I didn't smile once when I dropped a cup of coffee and the china not only smashed into a thousand pieces on the quarry tiles but the dregs managed to splash all over the front of every kitchen cupboard and half way up the wall. (How does that *happen*? How does a mere inch of liquid left in a cup manage to drench an entire room?)

By the time Stanley and I had finished yelling at each other and I'd driven him to the bus stop as it was pouring with rain, and given in to his request to pull up round the corner so his friends wouldn't see me in my dressing gown if the bus happened to arrive at the same time as we did, and had narrowly avoided driving into the back of a rubbish truck while I did it, I was at screaming point.

I let myself back into the house and took seven Oil of Evening Primrose capsules – and some vitamin B which is supposed to be good for one's nerves. Mine were shredded – it being Day 24, which is only one step down from Day 19. I still felt ready to explode.

'I wish I had your life,' I told Boris, who was laid out on the floor with the length of his body pressed against the radiator, sleeping peacefully. I could have done with being comatose myself.

Instead, there was the joy of another catalogue of garden artefacts and water features for Mike's newest client, and some ad copy for a series of uninspiring-looking shelving units.

I'd already had three emails from Mike and it was only a matter of time before he started phoning as well. In a moment of weakness, I'd promised him some slogans by lunchtime for a presentation he was making at 2 p.m. so I averted my eyes from the washing up and trudged upstairs to get going.

If I could get a load of work done this morning, I could catch up on other things this afternoon. I still needed to get hold of Roger. I'd come up with the cunning plan of phoning him up at work but giving a false name until I actually got him on the line – so that if he wasn't there and didn't have time to ring me back, there'd be no danger of him doing so from home and/or saying to Charlotte, as he was bound to, Laura called me today.

I'd pretend I was a client, with something private to say and avoid giving any details since I wasn't entirely sure exactly what sort of solicitor Roger was. Saying it was strictly confidential and I could only speak directly to Roger seemed foolproof enough.

As soon as my thousand words of dullness had safely disappeared down the line to Mike and I figured Roger would be back after lunch, I got the number from the Internet and dialled. A female voice answered at once.

'Hammond and Barnes.'

'Roger Forbes, please.'

'Who shall I say is calling?'

'Lucille Hamilton.'

'Just putting you through.'

There was a pause and then another voice came on the line.

'Mr Forbes' office.'

Must be the secretary. I adopted a chummy tone. 'Is Roger there, please?'

'I'm afraid he's in a meeting. How can I help you?' Her tone was cool. She probably thought I was being over-familiar. But I was pretty sure it wasn't the same voice I'd heard before.

'Thank you but I need to speak to him personally, really.'

'If you'd like to give me your number, I'll pass the message on.'

Unless, of course, this was her professional telephone voice and she only went into the breathy one when she was being a stalker out of hours.

'No, don't worry, I'll call back later.' If I gave my mobile number and he wrote it down and took it home, Charlotte would recognise it at once and how would I explain that? 'When will he be free?'

'Perhaps after three. I'll tell Mr Forbes you called, Mrs Hamilton.'

Damn it. Now he'll say he doesn't know me and it will be even more difficult next time.

'Thank you.'

Sure enough, he wasn't there after three either. The secretary was chilly and polite. 'If you could tell me what it's concerning, maybe one of the other partners could help you?'

'No, thank you. I'll phone back again.'

But not today. In the meantime I'd realised that not only were we almost out of cat food and there was no milk for Stanley's cereal in the morning, but I only had about £2.50 in my purse.

Fortunately I had thought to look at the calendar on the kitchen wall which had revealed it was parents' evening. That started at five and went on till God knows when, so I needed something I could cook quickly for dinner once we got back. I looked at the clock. There was just time to get to the cash point and the small Tesco in the High Street before Stanley got home.

Or there would have been if Mike hadn't phoned to drone on about his presentation and how marvellous everyone thought it had been and how I'd be pleased to know they loved my ideas for the ads and wanted me to do their next brochure as well.

'Great, great,' I said with forced jollity, one eye on my watch.

'So I'm emailing the brief and can we be looking at the end of the month?'

'Yes, yes, that's fine,' I said, thinking I'd worry about the fact it was already the 23rd later. 'Must go now, Mike. Got to dash – need to pick up Stanley.'

It was raining again by the time I'd run into Tesco for some free-range chicken Kievs and salad, so since I knew Stanley would be getting off the bus soon, I found a space on a double yellow line just up the road from the bus stop and waited.

I answered a text from Charlotte, demanding to know where I was, just when she needed a coffee, and despatched another to Sarah from Greens Wine Bar who'd sent one days ago saying she'd seen me on TV (thanks Clive!) and to whom I kept forgetting to reply.

I was just contemplating a quick game of Mine Sweeper to pass the time when I looked up and saw Stanley trudging up the hill toward me. He looked rather red in the face. A group of boys trailed behind him. I saw Stanley look back as if someone had called out to him. I wound the window down and waved.

Stanley looked behind him once more and then hurried over to the car and got in. 'What are you doing here?' he said crossly.

'I was shopping – I thought I'd save you getting wet.'

'Oh. Thanks,' he said shortly without looking at me.

I started the engine. 'Were those boys being horrible?'

'No.'

'I thought some of your friends got that bus with you. Were they the ones behind you?'

'No – they weren't there today.'

I glanced sideways at him as we made our way down the High Street. 'Stanley – is everything all right?'

'Yes.'

'You would tell me if it wasn't, wouldn't you?'

'Just leave it, mum.'

I changed the subject on to cheerier matters. 'Have you

76

remembered it's parents' evening?'

'Yes, said Stanley glumly.

'We have to be there at five. I'm not sure how it works, but –'

'I've got you some appointments.' Beside me, Stanley rummaged in his rucksack and pulled out a crumpled piece of paper. 'We had to fill in these times when you could see the teachers. I didn't do all of them but Mr Lazlett said if we didn't have a time, we could just wait about till one of them's free. He said sometimes it's a bit of a bun fight.'

I smiled. 'Did he? Oh well, at least we've been warned. I've got us some of that chicken you like for later. Do you want a baked potato with it or oven chips?

'Don't mind.'

'We'll have baked potatoes,' I decided, as we pulled up outside our house. 'Then I can put them in now on low. Are you staying in your school uniform? We're going to have to leave as soon as I've put the oven on.'

I started to get out of the car but Stanley didn't move. 'Mum?'

'Yes?'

'Do we have to go?'

'Yes, of course we do. I want to hear how you're getting on. What are you worried about?'

'Nothing. I'd just rather watch TV.'

'Well, I don't want to leave you at home on your own and–' I smiled at him '–I'll probably get lost without you to show me where to go.'

He didn't smile back. Just looked at his feet.

'Why don't you bring a book or something,' I offered. 'Then you can sit in a corner while I talk to the teachers if you're going to feel embarrassed.'

'It's not that.'

'What's the problem then?'

'Nothing.'

Stanley was quiet all the way there and I began to think perhaps I should have dropped him off at Charlotte's or my mother's after all, instead of dragging him along with me, so that I could get to speak to the teachers privately. But it was too late now – we were turning into the school gates.

'It's such a lovely setting, isn't it?' I said, looking at the old red brick building, the green fields sloping down toward thc church beyond. Stanley nodded doubtfully. Some boys, ties discarded, shirts hanging out, were on the grass playing football, rolled-up blazers doubling as goal posts.

'Yeeesssssss!' yelled one, careering past us as a ball narrowly missed Stanley's head.

Perhaps joining them would prove a suitable distraction while I quizzed Stanley's form tutor.

'Are any of those your friends?' I asked my son as we walked on past.

'No,' he said.

I stopped by the main entrance to the school, consulting my piece of paper. 'We have to go to the main hall –'

Beside me, Stanley was pointing. 'There's Dad.' I looked round, an unpleasant feeling rising in my stomach at the sight of a familiar, dark-suited figure standing a few yards away, and besidc him, in a short red coat, blonde hair clipped back from her face …

I scowled as Daniel came toward us. 'What's she doing here?'

Daniel looked instantly defensive. 'She's come with me. Because of course I want to come to parents' evening, and it's lucky,' he added nastily, 'that I thought to give the school my address and request a copy of all the correspondence because you obviously weren't going to tell me about it.'

I glanced sideways at Stanley, then pulled crossly at Daniel's arm before striding ten metres away and jerking my head for him to follow me.

'I didn't think you'd be interested since I don't recall you ever attending a single school meeting in the whole of Stanley's life,' I said, when he reached my side.

'Don't be so unfair, Laura,' Daniel did that thing with his lips that was half sneer, half smirk. 'That's only because you always said you'd go and I stayed at home to look after him.'

'Not last time, I countered triumphantly. 'When we came for the new parents' introduction, you said you had to work late

– again – and I came on my own with Stanley.'

'I did have to work late.'

I raised my eyebrows and glanced over my shoulder to where Emily was inspecting her handbag next to Stanley. 'Is that what you call it?'

'Don't start,' said Daniel. 'The fact is that I'm here now. I want to be involved with Stanley's schooling and I want to hear what his teachers have to say and so does Emily.'

I snorted. 'What for?'

'Because she is my partner and she takes an interest. There's no easy way of saying this,' he went on pompously, 'but we're getting married. Emily is going to be my wife.'

I glared. 'I'm your wife, in case you'd forgotten. Unfortunately,' I added quickly, in case he thought I cared what he did, even though the news had sent a sickening jolt through my solar plexus.

'I'm going to talk to you about that,' said Daniel.

'Not now, you're not.' I looked back to where Stanley was watching us anxiously. 'Look,' I said, in a low voice. 'Please can I just do this on my own tonight? I need to talk to his form tutor privately. I'll tell you everything afterwards but right now why don't you take Stanley off somewhere and let me see the teachers alone? I want to check how he's settling in and they might not tell me as honestly if he's sitting next to me. I'm worried about him.'

I could see Daniel hesitating and I looked at him hard. 'And, quite honestly, I think he's going to find it stressful with all three of us dragging around and so,' I said, in a sudden moment of honesty, 'am I. I do not want to do this with Emily there too and I don't think it's the right thing for Stanley – so soon.'

I looked at him, feeling suddenly upset and hoping I wouldn't cry.

Daniel looked back at me, as if deciding. 'I don't want the staff thinking I don't care,' he said peevishly.

I sighed, exasperated. 'It's always about what other people think of you, isn't it? It's not about Stanley at all – just bloody appearances. Look, there's the headmaster – go and shake his hand and say how thrilled you are with the school but that you can't stay because you and your wife –' I gave a small derisory sniff '– are a little concerned about how he is settling down and Stanley's mother is going to raise these issues in confidence with the teachers while you take care of our son. Then he will think you are a jolly splendid chap and you can leave me to it.'

Daniel put back his shoulders and flicked something from his sleeve. 'Good idea,' he said stiffly.

'Tosser,' I muttered, as he strode away. I looked over to where Emily was still standing next to Stanley, fiddling with the strap of her bag, and gave Stanley a small wave. I watched Daniel shaking hands with the head and nodding vigorously at whatever was being said, and then plastered a bright smile across my face and walked back toward my son and The Twiglet.

'Right, darling,' I said brightly to Stanley. 'Daddy is going to take you for a burger or something –' I flicked my eyes toward Emily, who looked pained '– and I'm going to see the teachers on my own. So you don't have to stay after all. You can go and eat chips instead,' I added, as Daniel came up behind us.

'There's a nice little Mediterranean place in Harbour Street,' he said hastily to Emily. 'You can have a Greek salad.'

'Feta cheese?' I said, in shocked tones. 'Packed full of calories …'

Daniel frowned and put a protective hand on Emily's arm.

Stanley looked at me uneasily. 'I think I'm supposed to come with you.'

'It's optional, I've checked,' I said firmly. 'It's only if I want you to come. And of course that would be fine, but I really think you'll get bored and we'll be a bit of a crowd, all four of us going round and since Dad's here … I'll text you when I'm finished,' I said to Daniel.

As they walked away, Stanley a little behind, shuffling his feet slightly, Daniel taking long strides, Emily little short ones as though her tight black skirt wouldn't allow anything else, I stood transfixed. As I watched the back of Emily's red coat, spindly red heels tap-tapping along beside Daniel, I saw him reach out and take her hand. She moved in closer, their forearms close together, the side of his body touching hers as the three of them walked toward the school gates.

My son, my soon-to-be ex-husband and the woman who

would be his new wife. I had stopped Daniel saying the D-word – in that instinctive, self-protecting way the squeamish stop someone telling them the details of a gory operation. Oddly, although I'd quipped about it to Sarah, I hadn't seriously thought about divorce.

I wasn't in denial – I knew he wasn't coming back. I didn't even want him back, did I, not now, not after all he'd said and done. But I hadn't thought beyond that. Panic gripped me. Surely he wouldn't make us sell the house? Not while Stanley was still young. I would have to find out my rights. Get a solicitor. As the three of them disappeared from view I sat down sharply on a low wall, my stomach knotted in a sick spasm of foreboding. I felt hot and suddenly tearful.

'Have you got a list?'

'Sorry?'

A boy of about 15 was proffering a sheet of paper. 'It tells you where all the teachers are.'

'Oh – thank you.'

Another boy with round glasses and an acne problem stepped forward. 'What's the name of your son?' he asked politely.

I swallowed, suddenly unbearably moved by having to say his name out loud.

'Um. Stanley Meredith'

The second boy ran a finger down his list and ticked something.

'Most teachers are in the hall,' he said gravely. 'But some are in the gym and the music teachers are in the music department. The metalwork room and art rooms are open if you would like to see a display of Year Seven and Eight work.' He stopped and looked at his list again. 'And welcome to parents' evening,' he finished.

The other boy nudged him. 'You were supposed to say that first.'

'You go in there,' he said helpfully, pointing to some open double doors. 'That's where the hall is.'

I saw them exchange glances, obviously wondering why the mad old bat was still just sitting there. I got up and forced a smile, swallowing hard. 'Thank you very much.'

Chapter Ten

THE HALL SMELLED OF school – that warm, airless mixture of past dinners and socks and cleaning fluid and the odour of hamster cage that emanates from six hundred over-heated boys. Tables were dotted about, with teachers sitting one side of them, parents and boys on chairs opposite. More parents stood about in clumps.

I stood for a moment, breathing deeply, letting my ears adjust to the clamour of voices, and then skirted the room, making my way through the groups of parents, consulting my list, looking at the names on the tables. Most of the staff already had a small queue forming. Eventually I found a small, bald man who was apparently Stanley's chemistry teacher and sat down opposite him.

'Laura Meredith,' I said. 'Stanley's mother.'

He looked down a long list of names. 'Ah, yes.'

'This term,' he intoned robotically, 'we have looked at the periodic table …'

Five minutes later I had a full breakdown of the syllabus but was none the wiser about Stanley's progress, learning only that he was quiet, "no trouble" and had, so far, always handed his homework in on time. I moved on and joined another queue.

Mr Geography evidently had trouble visualising which boy Stanley was, but also offered the view that he did his homework, most of the time, and the French teacher – Madame Lavisse, a well-preserved 50-year-old with bright red lipstick and a particularly nice handbag – said he was a "good boy" who needed to learn his verb endings.

There was a large crowd of parents jostling to see Mr Crawford the maths teacher; the noise was deafening and I was beginning to feel rather hot and in need of some fresh air, so I made my way over to the door out to the playground.

I looked at my list again and the piece of paper Stanley had given me. He'd got me down to see Mr Lazlett, his form teacher and head of Year Seven, at 5.45 p.m. and it was nearly that now, so I took one last gulp of the cold air and re-entered the fug of the hall.

I found him in the corner, a dark-haired man in his forties, who looked vaguely familiar, wearing a blue sweater. Another family – a sharp-faced woman with one of those mouths that went down at the corners, a morose-looking husband and their lanky son – were already waiting.

'And try and look a bit intelligent,' the mother was instructing the boy. 'Anyone would think you weren't all there.'

The boy rolled his eyes. I heard him mutter, 'Get a life,' and she swung round again.

'What did you say?' she demanded.

'Just leave him, Jan,' said the father. 'It's up to him.'

The boy pulled another face and our eyes met. I smiled and he gave me a self-conscious grin. He had a nice face – I wondered if he knew Stanley. I wondered too how Stanley was getting on. I hoped Daniel had bought him something decent to eat and was making a fuss of him, rather than mooning over The Twiglet. At the thought of Emily, I got that sick feeling again. I thought of her small hand tucking itself into Daniel's, her petite, stylish little feet tripping along beside him …

The couple at the table had got up and the family in front were settling themselves in front of Mr Lazlett. 'Sit up straight,' I heard "Jan" instructing her son.

I moved back a bit and studied the notices on the wall without seeing them. I really didn't want Daniel back – he was a stranger to me now – but it felt weird seeing him with someone else. Particularly someone who made me look like an ageing hippo.

I wished he'd emigrate or at least move to Scunthorpe or somewhere. I just didn't want him in my face. Particularly with her hanging off him. I was going to have to talk to him. Make it very clear I was staying in the house until Stanley had left school. I couldn't put him through any more upheaval …

My mind drifted off, thinking about my son. It seemed amazing he was at secondary school – it felt like only last week that I'd dropped him off at nursery for the first time, feeling sick like this all morning in case he was bereft without me. I still thought we might have another child then. Perhaps the way things had turned out, it was just as well it had never happened …

'Are you waiting for me?'

I came out of my reverie to find the family with the lanky boy filing past me. I smiled at him again. Mr Lazlett was standing up. 'Would you like to come and sit down?'

'Er - yes, thank you.'

He held out his hand. 'Andrew Lazlett.'

'Hi.'

As I sat down I suddenly realised where I'd seen him before. He was the one who'd taken me to task for stopping on the zigzag lines outside school. When I'd been wearing my nightie. And hadn't brushed my hair.

He'd had a suit and overcoat on then and looked tall and imposing. He looked a bit tired now and slightly crumpled but it was definitely the same bloke. I felt myself blush as I wondered if he remembered. If he did, he showed no sign of it. He smiled and said in a friendly voice: 'And you are?'

'Oh, er – I'm Laura Meredith. Mother of Stanley.'

He nodded. 'Ah, yes. Stanley.'

He shuffled some papers on the desk in front of him and then looked at me directly. 'Nice, polite boy.' He smiled again. 'Seems to be settling in – a bit quiet at first but seems fine now. Very co-operative, not one of the raucous ones. How do you feel he's finding everything?'

'He's …' I paused, thinking how to put it. 'I'm not sure how he is. He won't say much about it. He did tell me he was being teased, but then again I suppose that's normal with a lot of boys together, isn't it? It's just that he was very happy at his primary school, had good friends … and now,' I faltered, not sure what I was trying to say, 'he doesn't seem so happy.'

'In what way?'

'Well, he's quiet – I mean, he's always been quiet but now he's –' I struggled to find the right word. 'Unforthcoming.'

Mr Lazlett didn't speak but just nodded as if I should go on.

'At his old school, I'd ask him about his day and he'd tell me. And I always heard about what his friend, Connor, had been up to as well. What the teacher had said, that sort of thing. Now all I get out of him is that it's OK and I hardly hear about Connor at all although he's here too. Perhaps they've fallen out? I mean, he is in a different form, but I would have thought they'd see each other at breaks …'

I stopped – a sudden image of Stanley, on his own in the playground with nobody to talk to, giving me a lump in my throat. I swallowed hard and spoke a little more briskly.

'I've asked him, of course, but he won't really say. He just seems – different.'

There was a small silence. Andrew Lazlett still didn't say anything – just continued to look at me as though listening intently.

'But then again,' I went on, 'I can't really be sure if that's school or other things. He's been through rather a lot since he started here. My husband and I separated during the summer holidays and so Stanley now only has me at home …'

As I said it, I was suddenly overwhelmed and felt, to my horror, my chin begin to quiver and my nose tingle. *Oh Christ*. I looked away across the room, biting my lip. More parents had gathered around us, waiting.

'We do find,' Andrew Lazlett said quietly, 'that the boys often form new friendships when they get here and they tend to congregate with the others in their form. Has he mentioned any of the other boys at all?'

'Um, I'm not sure really –'

'Are you all right?'

'Sorry,' I said, mortified, 'it's all been a bit …' I stopped, feeling the tears well in my eyes and spill over, helpless to stop them running down my face and wishing I could shrink away to nothing. 'I'm sorry.' I scrabbled in my pocket for tissues. 'I'm so sorry.'

'Would you like a glass of water?'

I felt the parents standing behind me begin to shuffle their feet.

Mr Lazlett stood up. 'We'll be a little longer yet, I'm afraid,' he said pleasantly. 'Sorry for the wait but perhaps you'd like to go and see another member of staff in the meantime or you could sit over there.'

I heard muttering and the sound of steps moving away. I sat hot-faced, head low, my hands over my eyes. A few minutes later, a glass was put down in front of me.

Andrew Lazlett sat down opposite me again and began speaking, still in the same quiet voice. 'A lot of the boys take a while to adjust. It's a big change – moving from primary school to here – all the different teachers, having to move about the school for the different lessons. The noise, the sheer numbers of pupils, having to remember which books to take where.'

I took a mouthful of water, too embarrassed to look up and meet his eyes. He was still talking.

'It takes a few months for some, but they get there in the end. I haven't seen anything to make me worried about Stanley but I'll keep a special eye on him and if you have any concerns you can always phone me. If I'm not able to speak right then, leave a message with the school office and I'll call you back ...'

His voice was low and soothing. 'And I'd like you to tell Stanley that he can always come and speak to me at any time too. If there's anything he's unhappy about.'

'Thank you,' I mumbled, still feeling like sinking into a hole.

'And I will make a point of having a chat with Stanley myself. Not in any heavy way that will draw attention to him, but when the opportunity arises. I'll make sure that happens quite soon.'

He was looking at the papers in front of him again. 'He seems to be doing fine work-wise. No concerns from any of the staff. No detentions. I take him for English, as you know, and there are certainly no problems there.'

'That's good. He was always quite good at English at primary school,' I said lamely, forcing myself to glance up. 'I'm not really worried about the work, more whether he's happy or not. I think it's all been very hard on him since ...' I felt my voice begin to break again and stopped.

Andrew Lazlett went calmly on. 'I don't know the details of your situation, of course, just that it's always difficult when a marriage breaks up. But kids are surprisingly resilient, you know. My wife has children from her first marriage and it hasn't always been easy – my stepsons were going through a hard time when I first met them.' His tone was reassuring. 'But they came out the other side and, if anything, are stronger for it. I'm not in any way minimising the situation, but I'm sure Stanley will be fine.'

I nodded and sniffed and blew my nose. I opened my mouth to say something – to thank him and tell him that I knew I was probably being over-anxious but that Stanley was sensitive and not given to talking much and that it hadn't really been very long since Daniel left – but I knew if I actually attempted to put any of this into words, I would cry all over again. So I just kept my head down and nodded a bit more and took another sip of my water.

'We do our best to look after the boys here,' Andrew Lazlett was saying. 'I'll have that chat with him as soon as I can.'

There was the sound of more feet around the table. 'Could you just give us five minutes?' I heard him say. His voice dropped again. 'I know a bit about what you're going through.' There was another small silence. Then I felt his hand briefly touch my arm. 'It will get better.'

Chapter Eleven

'AND NOW,' SAID THE young man in the suit, who was walking ahead of me, 'it gets even better.'

Oh gosh, I can hardly wait.

'Here is our range of gnomes ...'

Yee-ha!

I had now spent two hours trailing around the Ashford yards and warehouses of Paradise Gardens – Bespoke Iron Furniture and Quality Garden Installations – and was beginning to feel slightly deranged. I stopped and surveyed the army of small, garish, bearded folk.

'Do people really buy these?' I enquired.

The young man – Martin – raised his eyebrows. 'They're ironic,' he told me loftily. 'I was told you were being sent down as you were the person best suited to conveying the unique wit of our own original hunting and fishing range.'

Yes, that definitely had Mike's brand of bullshit all over it.

'Of course,' I said wearily. 'Talk me through them.'

I followed him along the line of green-jacketed gnomes with red hats and red-jacketed gnomes with green hats and cross-legged yellow gnomes with fishing rods and blue gnomes holding something that looked like a shovel.

Martin stopped proudly before a stripy-hatted gnome standing in the middle of a pond grasping a small – "note the quality of the distressed iron" – watering can from which a fountain cascaded around the legs of several metallic storks. Or they might have been herons.

I fixed on a bright smile. 'Wow,' I said. 'That's quite something. Now, tell me about your target market ...'

By the time I got back in the car half an hour later, I was

gnomed out. I looked at the clock on the dashboard as I started the engine. It was coming up to five. Stanley was being picked up by Daniel straight from school. He'd made mutterings about having to leave work early but I'd insisted, not being able to bear to see his smug face again quite so soon.

He'd ended up bringing Stanley back two hours after I'd got home from parents' evening – by which time, unable to fancy the wrinkled, over-baked potatoes that resembled a couple of large walnuts, I had climbed down half a bottle of Pinot Grigio (never a great idea when the hormones are raging) and was having a nourishing supper of tortilla chips topped with melted cheese. I came to the door holding several in one hand which Daniel immediately looked at pointedly.

'Still on a diet, are we?' he said.

'Find yourself some nice alfalfa shoots, did you?' I replied sweetly, adding, in an undertone once Stanley was safely upstairs, 'You pompous wanker.'

He'd still insisted on coming into the kitchen for the "feedback" on what the staff had had to say about our son, and had then been so condescending and objectionable, implying that if Stanley hadn't settled in properly it was down to having a mother who didn't feed him enough nutrients or have the wits to ask him the right questions, that I'd ended up only managing to avoid battering him with the cheese grater by digging my nails into my palms and silently visualising him with a shrunken baked potato rammed up each nostril.

'He probably feels you're nagging if you go on all the time,' he finished self-righteously. 'I'll have a man-to-man with him on Friday night and get to the bottom of what's upsetting him.' He stood up a bit straighter. 'I've been a boy of that age myself, remember.'

Clearly thinking this gave him very much the upper hand, he finally stalked out, leaving me kicking the swing bin and resolving to avoid any further conversation with him until at least Day Five in case I ended up in Holloway.

So Stanley was going straight there and staying overnight and wouldn't be back till Saturday afternoon. Maybe I could leave the door on the latch – Stanley was sure to have forgotten his key – and manage to avoid seeing the wanker then too.

But in the meantime, there was no rush to get home and I'd resolved if it was at all possible I would try to catch Roger at his office. I'd explain I was on the way back from a meeting and just needed a quick word. We could go for a drink and I'd tell him calmly about the phone call and see what he said.

I was beginning to think that maybe I was making too much of it – perhaps it had been a wrong number, after all, or it was some mad woman who just liked phoning numbers at random and wreaking havoc.

Or perhaps it was someone with that complex where you fall in love with someone in authority – perhaps Roger had handled her company takeover or whatever it was he did, while she was also going through a divorce and was a bit unbalanced – and she was now in love with him and convincing herself they were having an affair, whereas really he was just being his usual, smiling, professional self.

(I had read an article about this once where a woman had got a fixation about her GP and used to sit on the wall outside his house for hours and ring his wife up to tell her they were going to elope together, until one day the wife got so fed up with it she came out to sweep the front step and ended up hitting the woman with the dustpan brush and was done for assault, which seemed a little unfair. I'm not sure you can do much damage with a plastic brush and if the woman was that barking, she probably wouldn't feel it anyway.)

Anyhow, after the usual delights of being stuck in the traffic on every roundabout on the ring road, I eventually made my way toward Canterbury city centre. Roger's offices were in a couple of bow-fronted terraces knocked into one, in a little back street behind one of the main car parks near the bus station. I'd been there once before with Charlotte when we'd been perusing wrinkle creams in Fenwicks.

By the time I'd parked it was nearly 6.00 p.m. I walked down the dark street, hoping I'd remembered it right and that Roger would still be there and hadn't left promptly at five just for once.

I peered at the house numbers, shop fronts and brass

plaques until I found Hammond and Barnes. It appeared to be closed. The solid green front door was shut tight and the blinds were down.

Pressing my face against the glass, I could see through the slats a tidy, empty desk in reception, the lights turned down low. Stepping back across the road, I could see full lights on upstairs. Perhaps Roger was still up there. Dammit – I'd brought their number with me but it was back in the car. No doubt even if I called reception it would go straight to answerphone as it was out of hours. I went back over to the door, found a buzzer and pressed it. No-one came. I stood in the street again and tried hollering, 'Roger!' A passing couple looked at me pityingly but nobody appeared.

It was cold. I pulled my coat more tightly around me as I walked back down the road, thinking I'd get the number, try calling just once and then give up and drive home.

I'd almost reached my car and was just wondering, whether, if I put a note through his office door marked "Roger Forbes – Personal", it would actually be left for him to deal with or some nosy secretary would rip it open anyway, and cursing the fact that I didn't carry envelopes in the car with all the other junk, and was fumbling with my keys, when I looked up and saw him. He was with a woman.

I jumped in alarm. They were coming into the car park from the other entrance. Instinctively, I found myself ducking down behind a car, heart thumping. It suddenly seemed terribly important he didn't see me. I peered round the back of the bumper of a grey Ford.

It was difficult to see her that clearly in the street light but she seemed to be about 35, thinnish, light-brown hair, mid-length skirt, short jacket, boots. She appeared to be talking fast and be slightly agitated, she was waving her hands around and pushing her hair back. But it was Roger I was fixated on.

He was walking close by her, head on one side, listening intently in a way Daniel had never listened to me or – come to that – I had never seen Roger listen to Charlotte. I looked at his face coming toward me, oblivious to anything around him, deep in concentration, his body curved toward hers, and I got a nasty sick feeling. This was serious.

Roger did listen to Charlotte, of course he did. She would allow nothing less. But not in that way men do when you're new. When they're still behaving as if you're the most fascinating creature on the planet, as if what you said really mattered. As if they cared ...

I swallowed.

Should I just breeze over there? Say, '*Hi*, Roger! I was just passing – wondered if you fancied a drink?' Force him to introduce us?

But then he could say anything and I could hardly interrogate him in front of her. He could say she was a client. Maybe she *was* a client. Maybe all that attention was just Roger doing his job. I wished I could get close enough to hear her voice and see if she had the same breathy, bunny-boiler tones I'd heard on the phone. But they were coming closer and instead I ducked down again, hugging my knees until they'd passed ten metres or so in front of me.

Where were they were going? For a drink? Maybe they went for a drink together every night. And there was Charlotte saying how he seemed to be working ever harder and longer these days.

I would have to get hold of him and get hold of him soon. I'd have to have a scout around Charlotte's kitchen and see if his mobile phone number was written up anywhere. Or grab her phone when she wasn't looking and get it out of there. Bloody Roger – what the hell was he playing at?

Please let it be nothing, I thought. Let it be my fevered imagination working overtime. It was one thing Daniel being a snake in the grass. I really couldn't bear it if Roger was doing it to Charlotte as well ...

I still felt upset when I got home. My plan to have a long bath, watch *EastEnders* and cram some junk food didn't seem right when there could be a marital crisis looming a mile and a half away. I looked at the phone. Should I just phone Charlotte and ask to go round? See if I could get Roger on his own, or at least procure his mobile number?

She wouldn't mind – she never minded. On the other hand, I'd been round there a lot lately. She always seemed to be feeding me and Stanley and all she ever got from here was a few biscuits when she called in between appointments. It was really my turn to invite *her* round for the evening – maybe cook them all dinner. She probably just wanted to chill out herself in front of the TV without listening to me going on …

She answered on the first ring. 'Hello, you.'

'You OK?'

'Marvellous. Just contemplating a couple of mountains of washing and wondering how this kitchen manages to look totally trashed by the time Friday comes. As well as being overwhelmed, as ever, by the eager offers of help from the rest of the family –'

'It's all a bit of a mess here too,' I said, surveying Stanley's breakfast things congealing on the table. 'But I was phoning to tell you I've got another form to fill in for this cookery programme. Alicia says that means we're definitely getting an audition. And one of the questions is how would your best friend describe you?'

Charlotte laughed. I could hear the flick of her lighter as she lit up a cigarette. 'A right bloody nightmare.'

'And there's a load of other stuff to write as well. I'm beginning to regret ever starting this.'

'Don't give me that – the fame from being on with Randolph has got to you. Did I tell you what Sandra said? She said she couldn't imagine you throwing shepherd's pie around, 'cos you always look so demure. I said, "Oh, that's a front love, she's as mad as a fish. I could tell you tales of her hurling the food about that would make your hair stand on end –"'

'Thanks. What would I do without you?'

Charlotte chuckled again. 'You coming round? Roger's going to be late back – got a meeting or something.'

My heart gave a little lurch. 'Has he? Um, well …' I could hear myself stuttering but Charlotte carried on in her usual tones.

'I know that's all you were phoning up for. Stanley's away and you'd rather have my sparkling company than sit there on your own. I can totally understand it.'

I gave a feeble laugh. 'Something like that.'

'You'll need to bring some wine – I've drunk the only thimbleful we had left.'

'I will.'

'And I could do with some nibbles to sustain me too.'

'No problem.'

'What you waiting for then, girlfriend? Get your arse round here now.'

I decided to drive, thinking I'd leave the car there and cab it home – it would be good for me to walk and collect it in the morning. Perhaps if Daniel got Stanley home at a decent time, we could both walk.

I'd been up to my eyes in gnomes and distressed iron fountains all week and Stanley had been glued to his Nintendo – only grunting if I asked about school. We could walk along the beach to Kingsgate, where Charlotte lived, and have a proper conversation. I could have a mother-to-son with him and see if I, too, could find out how he was really doing.

I stopped off at Charlotte's corner store and bought two bottles of Pinot Grigio, a large pack of Kettle Chips, some peanuts and a pot of hummus.

'Ah, you go see Mrs Fobbs,' said Mustafa. 'You need cigarettes too?'

I shook my head. 'I don't want to encourage her.'

Mustafa shrugged and held out his hands in a gesture that said whatever I did, it wouldn't make the slightest difference to Charlotte's nicotine intake. I shrugged back. 'Yeah. Go on then.'

I kept an eye out for Roger's car as I drove slowly down her road. It would be good if I could give him the third degree out of Charlotte's earshot – but there was no sign of him.

Tucked up in pub somewhere with *her*? I did hope not.

'Ooh, you angel – thanks, darling!' Charlotte pounced on the fags and gave me a hug. 'How did you know I was getting low? I sent Roger a text asking him to bring me some but we know he won't.'

'That's because he doesn't want you to die of cancer.' Becky strode into the kitchen in her dressing gown, scowling.

Charlotte pulled a face. 'Shut up,' she said in a good-natured tone.

I gave Becky a kiss. 'How are you, sweetheart?'

'She's a moody cow,' said Charlotte. 'She's even worse than you.'

We settled companionably at the kitchen table with a glass of wine each and my forms. I picked up a pen and looked at the first one.

'Right. How would you describe me, really?'

Charlotte adopted a studious expression. 'Well, the way to look at it is this,' she said gravely. 'They don't really care what I think – they just want you to entertain the punters. So we'll keep quiet about my inside knowledge and write "good for a laugh" or "always up for a party" or "never says no to a drink". If we start going into your mood swings and your talent for smashing the crockery, they'll run a mile.'

'You make me sound bonkers,' I said grumpily.

'And your point is?'

We were on the second bottle and giggling in a juvenile fashion over the section on likes and dislikes

(Likes: Chocolate
Charlotte
Tadpoles
People who tell me I've lost weight.

Dislikes: Slimy ex-husbands
Blondes of eight stone
Liver
Squashed sandwiches
Tax inspectors – see above)

when Roger arrived home. 'What are you two snorting about?' he asked, getting a beer from the fridge and reaching into the cupboard for a tall glass.

'Miss *Britain's Got Talent* here,' said Charlotte. 'On your screens *soon*.' Roger threw his jacket over the back of a chair, leant down and kissed the side of her forehead. 'Had a good day?'

'Very wild and exciting,' said Charlotte, reaching for her cigarettes. 'You?'

'Oh, about the same.' Roger opened the swing-top bin and squashed his empty beer can into it.

Charlotte got up from the table. 'Don't do that, you lazy sod. It needs emptying, not just more and more stuff forcing into it. I'm the only one,' she said, looking at me, 'who ever empties the bins. They'd go on cramming stuff in for ever – no matter how bad it started to smell. Couldn't possibly walk ten paces to the wheelie bin, now could we!'

She put a cigarette in her mouth and heaved at the black liner. 'I'll put it out while I'm having a ciggie.' She picked up her lighter with her free hand and went out through the back door. Roger sat down in her empty chair.

'What's your mobile phone number?' I hissed.

Roger looked startled. 'What?'

'I need to speak to you privately and I don't have your number.'

'Oh!' He stared at me. 'Umm, OK.' He looked around and pulled the newspaper toward him, tearing off the top corner and reaching for a pen from his jacket pocket. 'What's the matter, then?'

'Just write it,' I said, thinking I'd better at least get that before I said anything as Charlotte could come back any minute. 'And don't tell Charlotte.'

He wrote quickly and pushed the piece of paper across the table. I shoved it hurriedly in my jeans pocket.

He looked at me quizzically. 'You OK?'

'No, I'm very worried about you,' I said in a low voice.

He frowned as Charlotte came back to the doorway and lounged in it, puffing smoke. 'What are you looking so miserable about?' she demanded of her husband. 'That bloody wheelie bin's nearly full already and it's only Friday,' she added, without waiting for an answer. 'Have you eaten?'

'Had some sandwiches in the meeting earlier,' said Roger. 'I'll make another one in a minute.' He swallowed the last mouthful of beer. 'I'll just go and get changed and say hi to the kids.' He didn't look at me as he went out of the room.

'Hmm, I think I'm a bit peckish myself,' said Charlotte, surveying the empty hummus pot. 'Shall we have some cheese on toast? Or there's a bit of the fish pie I made the kids earlier.' She opened the oven. 'Ah – no there isn't. Joe's got his friend, Ryan, staying and they must have come back for seconds. His mother says he's a fussy eater ... Not when he comes round here he isn't – eats more than the rest of us put together ...'

I was barely listening. Roger was obviously bemused by my wanting his number. Did that mean he was innocent or had it just not occurred to him that I could possibly be on his trail? He probably thought he was safe seeing her in Canterbury – he wouldn't expect me to be hanging about there and of course he didn't know about the phone call ...

'Actually,' Charlotte was saying, 'I'd better just go and check on them. They've been awfully quiet for ages ...'

Come back, Roger, I willed him silently as I heard her feet go up the stairs. *Quickly – get in here now!* It was like a bloody farce, all this coming in and out of doors and trying to get a sentence out before the wrong person reappeared. But, with perfect timing, as in the best comedies, Roger strolled back into the room in jeans and a Ralph Lauren polo shirt.

'Now tell me what's going on?' He gave me his usual friendly smile.

'Come here,' I said. 'We mustn't let Charlotte hear.' He sat down opposite me and leant forward expectantly. I leant forward too.

'You know when you went to get the pizza the other week – after we'd been to the TV thing?'

Roger nodded, his mouth twitching as if trying not to laugh.

'Well, a woman phoned up,' I said sharply, feeling cross now that he wasn't taking me seriously, 'and implied you were having an affair.' I saw he was taken aback though he looked at me calmly and his voice was even.

'What did she say exactly?' he asked.

I tried to remember. 'Something about couldn't I see – she obviously thought I was Charlotte – what was going on? She said "your husband" and then Charlotte came back in so I put the phone down and pretended it was double glazing.'

Roger sat back and shook his head. I couldn't decide if there was a tinge of relief there or I was imagining it. 'It was probably a wrong number.'

'I wanted to think that too,' I said boldly. 'But she also said you'd just seen her and you had been a long time getting the pizza and then you parked up the road on the phone–'

'That was work,' said Roger firmly.

'OK,' I said. 'So who was that woman I saw you with in Canterbury? Was she work too?'

For a moment he looked stricken, then leant forward again, his voice sounding urgent now. 'What do you mean? When did you …'

He sat up straight as Charlotte walked rapidly back into the room. I felt myself blush but she'd already started to laugh at the sight of our heads bent together.

'What are you two whispering about?'

Chapter Twelve

I WONDERED WHAT ROGER would do now he knew I knew. Would he phone me on the QT with an explanation? Demand to know what else I'd got hold of? Or would he just pretend the exchange had never happened and hope I'd keep my mouth shut as far as Charlotte was concerned? I didn't have to wait long to find out.

The following afternoon, as I was making my seventeenth coffee while thinking how to best make *Gnome with Watering Can* sound like this season's must-have, the doorbell rang and there he was – in his business suit on the doorstep – looking decidedly twitchy. He glanced around him as he stepped inside. 'Are you on your own?'

'Just me and Roderick.' I waved a hand down the hall to where a blue and yellow-jacketed gnome sat on my kitchen floor, clutching a bucket. 'He is staying with me while I sum up his attributes,' I explained.

Roger looked perplexed. 'I wanted to finish our conversation,' he said.

'I thought you might.' I pulled another mug from the cupboard. 'So what are you playing at?' I continued without preamble. 'If you're up to no good and Charlotte finds out –'

'I am not having an affair,' he interrupted.

I took the lid off the coffee jar and waited.

'I don't know who the phone call can have been from and I don't know what you mean about a woman in Canterbury.'

I kept my back to him as I stirred. 'Are you sure?'

'Yes, there's nothing going on.'

I turned round and put the mug in front of him. 'I saw you, Roger. I came to your offices, hoping to catch you and tell you

99

about the phone call. And I saw you walking across the car park with a woman. So close you were almost touching. You both looked pretty cosy.' I could hear the agitation in my voice.

Roger looked uncomfortable. 'That was a colleague. She was a bit upset and was talking to me, that's all.'

'What's her name?'

Roger hesitated. 'Hannah.'

'And was it Hannah you were talking to parked up your road in the dark? Hannah you had a drink with last night before you came home?'

I saw from his face I'd got that bit right.

'She's split up with her boyfriend,' he said heavily. 'I'm just a shoulder to cry on, that's all. It's not sexual.'

My heart sank. 'What you mean is – it's not sexual yet. Men always say that when they've started fantasising about getting their leg over but haven't managed it so far. For God's sake, Roger, what on earth are you –'

'I'm not! Just listen to me for a moment. She's one of our staff. She's having a very hard time and I'm just trying to be helpful and supportive as I would be to any of my colleagues. We've been for a couple of drinks, and that's all.'

'And have you told Charlotte?'

'No, because it's not important. She's not interested in my colleagues' personal problems.'

'She might be if she knew this one just happened to be 35 and single and adoring.'

'She's 36,' Roger said stiffly, 'and she's not adoring at all. She just needs a friend right now, that's all.'

'Hasn't she got any, then? Roger, if she was the one who made the phone call then she's bad news.'

'I'm sure it wasn't her. That must have been a wrong number.'

'Or someone at work who thinks you and Hannah are an item and wants to warn your wife. I should let someone else counsel her if I were you, and steer well clear.'

Roger looked troubled. 'I will when she's feeling a bit better. She sort of needs me at the moment …'

My heart sank deeper. 'Roger – I know that sort of woman.

She's trying to make you feel all protective – being all helpless and needy. Men are so gullible. The next thing you know, she'll be trying to get you into bed with her and then –'

Roger shook his head. 'Look, Laura, I know you're thinking about Daniel but this is me. I wouldn't do that to Charlotte. I'm not gullible. Hannah's a very genuine person actually who's been really badly treated and I'm just –'

I shook my head. My stomach had that feeling it gets when it detects impending doom. 'Had you seen her that night when you went to get the pizza?'

'No.'

'Had you phoned her?'

'I can't remember.'

I raised my eyebrows and looked at him hard.

'Yes, maybe – I was worried about her, I think.'

I sighed, exasperated. 'I don't even have to meet Hannah to know just what she's like. She's playing on your sympathy, she's –'

'No!' Roger was emphatic. 'She isn't and what are you doing pre-judging someone like this? You know nothing about her. This is all about you, Laura. Just because Daniel behaved badly doesn't mean we're all going to. I am being a friend to a colleague and that is all.'

I could see he was getting irritated.

'OK, OK. I'm only thinking of you,' I said in a more conciliatory tone. 'I'd just hate anything to be – misconstrued.'

'Well, so far,' he said, smiling at me again, 'the only person misconstruing anything is you.'

'Yes – so far,' I said darkly. 'Roger, please be careful! I know you think I'm overreacting but I think you should ask her about that phone call and watch her face very carefully. It's too much of a coincidence not to be her …'

'She's a professional woman –'

'What's that got to do with it? So was Glenn Close in *Fatal Attraction*.'

'Oh, for goodness' sake, Laura.' Roger gave a hearty and totally unconvincing laugh.

'What does she do anyway? Is she a solicitor?'

'One of the senior secretaries. Not mine,' he added.

'Well then, why are you involved? Why can't her boss listen to her tales of woe?'

'We're not like that, we all help each other.' He took a mouthful of coffee.

I stared at him, unable to decide whether he was really being naïve or spinning me a line, and hating the thought of the latter. Nothing changed the fact that he hadn't told his wife and if it was all that matey and innocent, surely he would have done? Just in passing at least, just as part of his day's work …

I opened my mouth to make this very point and had got as far as, 'Well I can't help thinking …' when the doorbell rang and we both froze.

'Oh my God,' I squeaked. 'Suppose it's Charlotte!'

Roger leapt to his feet alarmed. 'Could it be?' He stared wildly at the clock. 'Does she often come in at this time?'

'She comes in any time – if she's got an appointment nearby. I'm her coffee stop.' I glared at him. 'Quick! What are we going to say?'

Roger looked blank. 'Um – I left work early and popped in to borrow something?'

'What?'

'Er – an electric drill? I'll say mine's broken and I want to put a shelf up.'

'Does she know anything about this shelf? Have you got the wood?'

'No.'

'Well, it won't work then, will it, you pillock? She's not bloody stupid.'

My heart was beating faster than usual. The doorbell rang again. Roger was pacing around the room. 'Come on!' I urged him.

'We'll say I needed to use your computer because our one at home froze this morning.'

'Didn't you leave before her?'

'Yes – but she won't remember if I was on the computer first or not.'

'It doesn't sound right. You could be checking with me

what size she is because you want to buy her a dress.' Even as I said it, I knew it was hopeless.

He shook his head. 'She'll never believe that.'

The doorbell rang for a third time. This time we could hear knocking on the glass too. Taking decisive action, I hurled his coffee mug into the sink, opened the back door and shoved him through it. 'Go and hide in the shed!'

'But my car's outside.'

'I'll think of something.'

My brain was in overdrive as I made my way up the hall, heart still pounding. I'd act surprised – say I hadn't seen him. Buy us some time to think of a plausible reason why Roger might have parked outside my house and then pissed off somewhere. Bloody Roger! Jesus Christ – here I was, locked in lies and subterfuge against my best friend, all so Roger could play Samaritans.

'I'm coming,' I called gaily, knowing she'd take one look at my face and know I was hiding something. 'Sorry – I was in the loo,' I cried, flinging the door open. It was Stanley, who'd left his front door key at home again. I leant weakly against the wall.

He frowned, his face slightly red in the afternoon sun, his hair stuck up on end. 'You were ages,' he said.

'Sorry, darling,' I said, pulling him into a large, motherly embrace in my relief. He wriggled away from me. I moved backward, blocking his path to the kitchen. 'Would you like a drink – you look hot. Something to eat? A sandwich?' I smiled brightly. 'I'll do it – you get out of that uniform first. And don't forget to hang your trousers up. Oh, and make your bed if you didn't do it this morning. And maybe get your books sorted for tomorrow,' I added, wondering what else I could add to the list that would give me time to get our visitor out of the shed and send him packing before Stanley reappeared. 'I'll be getting your food. Cheese and ham OK?'

Stanley sighed and began to plod wearily up the stairs. As I reached the kitchen door I heard him pause by the window on the landing.

'Mum,' he called. 'Why's Uncle Roger in the garden?'

Chapter Thirteen

MY MOTHER SNIFFED AS only my mother can.

'What on earth do you want to do that for? I would have thought,' she continued, without waiting for an answer, 'that you had enough to be getting on with here, what with the house to keep clean –' here she paused to look in the corners for dust '– and your son to look after, now you are on your own.' The last three words were weighted with disapproval.

I breathed deeply. My mother spent the entire eighteen years Daniel and I were together delivering regular, if veiled, criticisms of him, our marriage, and our lifestyle. But since he left, she has switched tack and makes it very plain that I was careless to lose him, because he is, after all, a man, which affords him a far greater status than I will ever have, even if he does happen to be a very poor example of the species.

Any man is better than no man, her warped thinking goes, which is why she spent 40 years complaining bitterly about my father's shortcomings yet refused to let him out of her sight. I sometimes wonder if he died of sheer desperation.

I spoke as cheerily as I could. 'Because it will be interesting and a bit of fun and I might win some money to buy Stanley the new mobile phone he wants for his birthday.'

'Hmm,' said my mother, crossly, knowing I had got her on that one because Stanley, being her only grandchild *and* a male, could do no wrong.

My brother, Anthony, the other light of her life, had so far failed to produce any offspring, being too busy drinking and chasing unsuitable women – a fact my mother resolutely refused to acknowledge — and had very sensibly gone to live 200 miles away in Nottingham.

So, in the absence of either him or a second generation of geniuses sprung from *his* loins, all her love – grandmotherly and otherwise – was lavished on Stanley.

'I think he's looking a bit peaky,' she said now. 'Are you feeding him properly?'

'Don't you start,' I said. 'I've had Daniel on at me about too many pizzas and not enough vegetables.'

'Well *he* can talk,' my mother said. 'I can't ever remember a Christmas when he finished his sprouts.' Here she paused again to see if there were any other festive misdemeanours she could dredge up and relive for the enjoyment of us both. Clearly disappointed that there weren't, she continued briskly, 'I'll make sure he has something proper while I'm in charge.'

"Something proper" was an expression she had brought Stanley up on without realising that, for him, it had become synonymous with all he didn't like. As in "please don't make me have something proper, I want chicken nuggets". Or "Connor's mum is cool. She doesn't make us have anything proper – we had ice-cream and crisps".

'So you'll do it then,' I said quickly, before she could start going through menus. She'd been here for half an hour so far and not yet taken off her coat but I could feel we were in for a long haul. 'Charlotte would have him but he gets a bit fed up going round there too often and there's Boris to think of.'

I eyed the sprawled form of my slumbering cat, who always seemed to look even larger by the time he'd been under my mother's tender care for 24 hours. 'I don't know what time I'll be back.'

'I'll get him some chopped liver,' said my mother decisively. 'All this tinned rubbish isn't any good for him either. Our cats always had proper scraps from the butcher's.' She looked me up and down and gave one of her sudden laughs. 'Do they know you can't cook?'

It is always a double-edged sword asking my mother to do anything. On the one hand she'll clean the entire house, weed the garden, and rediscover the carpet in Stanley's bedroom but, on the other, will then provide a full catalogue of undusted ornaments, unmatched socks, and rose bushes inexpertly pruned, as well as her personal insights into where I am going wrong on the mothering front, which can last for several weeks.

Which is why I hesitated before asking her to step into the breach while I went for the *Cook Around the Clock* audition with Alicia. But Stanley hadn't seen much of his grandmother lately and I felt oddly uncomfortable about the idea of asking Charlotte.

Quite aside from the fact I knew Stanley would moan about having to share airspace with Becky again so soon, I was feeling guilty about keeping secrets from my best friend and didn't want my son saying anything unfortunate about having spotted Roger emerging from our shed.

He'd seemed perfectly satisfied with my explanation that there was a large, hairy spider in there, preventing my reaching the secateurs unscathed – a result, no doubt, of having witnessed me screaming over many an arachnid over the years – and accepted my good fortune in spotting Roger driving past at exactly the right moment to rescue me with equanimity. But I couldn't be sure that Charlotte would be quite so convinced.

I'd sent Roger a long, fervent text, detailing the cover story should we be forced to provide one – he having hastily returned Stanley's wave and then scuttled down the side path before you could say "squashed it" – while reminding him that comforting strange single women when you had a wife like Charlotte was *a very bad idea* and urging him to keep this Hannah at arm's length.

I'd heard nothing from him since and had barely seen Charlotte. She'd dashed in once between appointments, had half a cup of coffee, talked non-stop about the problems of trying to sell a two-bedroomed maisonette that housed 27 parrots and reeked to high heaven, and shot off again, but we hadn't had any sort of proper conversation and I felt awkward at the thought of one.

I wondered what she would have done if she'd seen Daniel in action with The Twiglet before I'd got wind of it and I couldn't help feeling that yes, she'd have got him by the short and curlies and demanded to know what was going on, but she'd probably also have told me. This made me feel bad.

On the other hand, what, so far, was there to say? It wasn't a crime to listen to a colleague's boyfriend problems and even if this Hannah was a bunny-boiler flake and had made that phone call, it didn't mean Roger had done anything wrong. Charlotte might be upset and furious with me for even suggesting it. I just had to hope that Roger had taken my words of wisdom to heart and was now giving Hannah a wide berth instead of one-to-one therapy on a nightly basis.

I decided that I would get myself round there once I'd been to London and try to have a quiet word with him to find out the latest.

In the meantime, my mother had agreed to be in the house to greet Stanley after school. She was insisting on staying the night too – "you know I don't like going home in the dark" – so, on the downside, she'd be there for breakfast but, on the upside, I wouldn't have to worry about what time I got back and she'd do the hoovering and very probably defrost the fridge.

'I'll put you on a diet when I get back,' I told Boris when she'd finally gone. He purred loudly as I looked ruefully over my shoulder and viewed my backside in the hall mirror.

I'd put myself on one too.

Chapter Fourteen

THE AUDITIONS WERE TO be held in a hotel in Cricklewood at 2.30 p.m. and I was meeting Alicia at Willesden Green tube station at midday.

'We can have lunch first and get our stories straight,' she'd said cheerily.

'What shall I wear?' I'd asked.

'Oh, anything,' she said airily. 'Something bright's best – so you stand out.'

After another hour spent staring hopelessly at a wardrobe of unrelenting grey, brown and black, I'd decided on a pair of jeans with butterflies embroidered on them, and a bright pink T-shirt I'd found in TK Maxx which would have apparently cost such a fortune before it was marked down to £9.99 that I couldn't not buy it even if it was a size too small.

I wore it over the top of a longer vest top so there was no danger of any stomach hoving into view and a pair of very high pink heels – another knock-down bargain — hoping for an illusion of slimness and elegance.

Since the shopping trip had put me even further behind on my latest exciting project from Mike – a 24-page brochure on a unique water-cooling system for home and office – I spent the train journey staring at his almost incomprehensible notes on the subject and trying to work out which way up the diagrams of the filter system went. By the time I was on the tube I felt ready for a lie-down.

I also felt quite nervous. As I tottered out of the station, trying not to break an ankle, I almost hoped Alicia wouldn't be there and I could turn round and go home again. But she was waiting right next to the entrance.

She looked different, younger somehow, from the last time I'd seen her. Her hair was in a thick plait down her back this time and she had almost no make-up on. She was wearing a short, flowery dress over jeans and green mules with glittery bits on them. She gave me a hug and then looked me up and down and grinned. 'OK, Mum?'

'I thought I'd be 19 and you could be 35,' she said, as I followed her along the road. 'That's about what you are anyway, isn't it?' she asked innocently. 'Or are you a lot younger?'

I laughed. 'Come off it! I'm over 40. Why don't I say 40 and you say 20 – otherwise I'd have been very young to have a baby.'

'Say you're 39 – sounds better.'

It did indeed. 'Am I still with your father?' I enquired, once we were sitting on the pavement outside a little Italian café and had ordered paninis and mineral water. ('Better not have wine till afterwards,' Alicia had instructed. 'If they smell it on you, they might think you're a lush.')

Alicia considered my question. 'Nah – he left us both when I was three months old. That's why we've got this extraordinary closeness. And I was thinking – this will give it a nice twist – I'm the one who can cook and you've never really got to grips with it. You've been working too hard holding down three jobs to support us both, so now I look after you.' She beamed.

'I've already put down that I make a mean lasagne,' I told her.

'Well, say that's all you can do. Tell them I do everything else – all the creative stuff.'

'Can you cook really?'

Alicia shrugged. 'Yeah, sort of. It's not that difficult, is it? And they're hardly going to check.'

'They might as it's a cookery programme,' I said, marvelling at her nerve.

Alicia gave a dismissive snort. 'I'll learn a couple of recipes. My mate, Shirley, carried on for about 20 minutes on how to knock up the perfect paella and she's never so much as made a bacon sandwich.'

'So what happens when we get there?' I asked, sipping my water.

'Shirl said there's a load more forms, then they'll film us talking about ourselves and then film us pretending to be playing the game and talking about our ingredients – what were your favourites?'

I shook my head in alarm. 'Oh God, I can't remember!'

Alicia shrugged again. 'Doesn't matter – just make it up. Everyone always brings chicken breasts. I put down pig's trotters just to be different.'

'Ugh! Yuck!' I said as the waiter put a mozzarella and basil panini in front of me. He picked it up again, looking affronted.

'Sorry,' I said, flustered. 'I was talking about something else.'

Alicia laughed, pulled the top from her lunch and gave the contents – some sort of ham – a prod. 'In Portugal,' she said gleefully, 'I went to a restaurant where they had pig's face.'

I began to feel even more nervous as, an hour later, we approached the Majestic Hotel.

'How many people do we have to speak in front of?' I asked as I hobbled through the big glass doors. The balls of my feet were already burning.

'Not many,' said Alicia brightly. 'Now don't forget to call me darling.' She tucked her arm through mine. 'OK, Mum?'

We followed the signs in reception and went up to the fourth floor where we were directed to a huge room filled with people sitting about on chairs. There was a table at the back with pots of coffee and tea and orange juice. I went and got some water, trying to stop my stomach doing that jumping thing.

The usual young-man-in-black-T-shirt brought us some forms to fill in and said he'd be back to see us in a while. Alicia and I sat at a small table in the corner with the orange *Cook Around the Clock* pens we'd been given and perused the questions.

Have you ever been on television before?
Yes! I ticked proudly.
If yes, give names of programmes with dates.
Easy enough so far.
Who is your chosen partner for Cook Around the Clock*?*
'Haven't we done all this already?' I asked Alicia, who was chewing her pen and looking bored.
'Yes,' she said.
Relationship to you.
I stole a sideways glance at Alicia who was now thoughtfully sucking her ball point. She couldn't look less like my daughter – she was an olive-skinned, Mediterranean-looking exotic with glossy black hair, huge brown eyes, and a snub nose whereas I was pale and a bit blotchy with the ill-advised plum hair that would otherwise be a sort of mid-brown/blonde (I refused to think of small rodents) and a nose that at best could be described as substantial.

She scrawled something on the bottom of her paper and looked up at me. 'I'm whizzing out for a cig,' she said. 'Have you finished yet?'

'Nearly,' I said, glancing back at the two pages of unanswered questions in front of me before watching her stride across the floor dropping her forms into the waiting hands of the young man who'd spoken to us earlier.

'Are you done?' He appeared at my elbow moments later.

'Almost.'

I rushed through the rest, putting the first thing that came to mind while he hovered.

Anything you'd be afraid to cook?
Well, yes, most things really …

By the time Alicia came back, several of the frighteningly young people from the TV company had been examining my form for some time.

As Alicia plonked herself down beside me, a very skinny girl with spiky black hair, black jeans and the regulation tight black top pointed across at us with a long purple nail and went into another huddle with a couple of the guys.

111

'What do you think they're talking about?' I whispered.

'Just saying how we're just what they're looking for,' said Alicia confidently. 'They'll call us in to do our stuff in a minute.'

'What did you write for your guilty pleasure?' I asked her.

Alicia grinned. 'The same as my obsession ...'

'I put tuna mayo as my favourite sandwich,' I mused. 'But really, you know – it's egg mayo with tomato and raw onion ...'

'They don't care,' said Alicia. 'All they're interested in is whether –' She broke off as a beautiful young man with floppy brown hair with a single blond streak across the middle and dark brown eyes, walked over to us.

I saw Alicia look him over appreciatively but he fixed his gaze on me and said pleasantly, 'You're not really her mother, are you?'

Alicia sat up straighter. 'Of course she is!'

I looked up into his eyes – he had incredibly thick, glossy eyelashes – and hesitated.

He gave me a slow smile. 'Are you?'

'No.' I said.

Beside me, Alicia gave an audible hiss of exasperation. 'But I think of her as my mother,' she said, 'because my real mother died when I was a baby and Laura practically brought me up ...'

The young man ignored her and held out his hand to me.

'I'm Cal,' he said. 'I'm the assistant director.' He looked down at the form in his hand. 'You've been on *Rise Up With Randolph*, I see ...'

Alicia rolled her eyes and shook her head in disgust. Cal was still looking at me. 'I think I saw it,' he said thoughtfully. 'You were very good.'

I laughed self-consciously. 'Not really – I squawked like a fishwife.'

He laughed. 'PMT, wasn't it?'

'I don't know, really. It shouldn't have been because it was only Day 10 but, mind you, I do go a bit funny then sometimes – it's quite odd – though Day 19 is the time when I really – oh, I see,' I said, flustered, as Cal grinned and Alicia rolled her eyes some more. 'You mean the subject of the programme? Yes, yes, it was.'

Cal was still smiling as I blushed. 'I must have another look at it,' he said. 'You could be just what we're looking for – for something else.'

'What about this one?' put in Alicia, sounding cross. 'What about *Cook Around the Clock?*'

'I'm just coming to that,' said Cal pleasantly. He looked at her. 'Weren't you on that programme with Randolph too?' he asked, one eyebrow raised.

'Yes,' said Alicia reluctantly.

'But not as Laura's daughter – so we can't use you for this. I'm afraid you can't go on television and pretend to be something you're not.'

Alicia shrugged. 'This is a different production company,' she said boldly. 'Why not?'

'Because,' said Cal patiently, 'it may still be watched by a lot of the same people. Our programme is on at 4.45 p.m., which still counts as daytime TV, so we'll be getting a lot of the viewers who watched at 10 a.m. on other channels. They tend to be the same group who are at home all day. Housewives – and house husbands, of course –' He suddenly flicked a smile at me and I felt a funny little frisson run down my spine. 'We can't risk –'

'Why can't we be friends, then?' interrupted Alicia. 'We could have made it up on the set afterwards and been inseparable ever since. We could even tell the story on air –'

Cal smiled again. 'And promote a rival channel? I don't think so!'

'OK, well, then we'll –'

'I'm sure we can sort something.' Cal spoke over her, his voice firmer. Then he looked back at me. 'You have a really interesting face. I'd like to use you ...'

Alicia scowled. 'So we can audition, yes?'

'Laura and Alicia!'

We were called into a small room where there was a bloke

113

behind a camera, the skinny girl who we'd been introduced to as Tanya, holding a clipboard, and a sound man carrying one of those big microphones covered in black furry stuff.

At the front of the room was a table with various objects arranged on a cloth. Alicia and I were directed to stand behind it.

Cal was at the back of the room. 'Laura – could you just talk about yourself for a minute or two? Just tell us who you are and what you do.'

I cleared my throat. 'Er, I'm Laura and I'm a sort of copywriter. Well, I am a copywriter but I have worked from home since I had my son.' I stopped. Cal nodded encouragingly. 'Um, my son is called Stanley and my cat is called Boris.'

I stopped again. Tanya was looking at me with undisguised disdain, Alicia was frowning. Cal smiled. 'That's great – a bit more? What do you do when you're not working? Are you married?'

'I am separated,' I said. 'I have an odious ex-husband called Daniel who has shacked up with someone else and when I am not working I make little Plasticine models of them both to stick pins in.'

It was meant to be funny but it came out of my mouth sounding bitter. I saw Tanya's eyebrows go up, but Cal laughed.

'Go on,' he called.

'I have a good friend called Charlotte,' I continued desperately, 'who I also drink too much wine with when I'm not working. She spends most of her time in my kitchen even when she is working and then we eat biscuits ...'

Tanya had put her clipboard down and was wandering about the room, looking bored. Alicia had closed her eyes. The cameraman didn't appear to be filming me but was looking out of the window.

Cal clapped his hands together. 'Fantastic,' he called brightly. 'Now can you pick up some of the objects in front of you as though they were your ingredients and talk us through them?' I looked at the table. There was a stapler, a couple of marker pens, a notebook, someone's mobile phone and a roll of Sellotape. I held the latter aloft.

'Today,' I said, lamely, 'I have brought a tin of tuna.' I grabbed the marker pens too. 'And some tomatoes ...'

Why ever did I let Alicia talk me into this? I thought, as I sank into a chair, hot-faced, while Alicia beamed at the camera and held forth wittily about her dreams of becoming an actress and the time she'd burned a turkey curry so badly that the neighbours called the fire brigade.

All I had managed, when asked for some kitchen anecdotes, was a lot of drivel about the best way to make scrambled eggs, which left everyone looking rather glazed. But Cal was still smiling as he came over.

'That was terrific, both of you,' he said easily. 'We'll be in touch, see what we can do.' He had his eyes on me. 'I think you'd be good. Maybe we can pair you up separately with other people.' He pushed back the floppy bit of hair over his eyes. 'Though this won't be my baby much longer, thankfully.' He nodded over toward the skinny girl. 'Tanya and I are leaving to work on something else.'

'Well, then,' said Alicia at once. 'Put us forward as mother and daughter and say you didn't know anything about the Randolph show.'

Cal shook his head. 'I have my reputation to think of,' he said. 'Some of us have principles and ethics. We don't knowingly mislead our viewers. Can you hold on a moment?'

Alicia pulled a face at his back as he walked away. 'Wanker!'

'He's got a point,' I said, thinking how nice it was that he cared so much about the integrity of the programme. 'If someone saw us who'd watched *Rise Up With Randolph* they'd know we were pretending and he could get into terrible trouble.'

Alicia's face was pitying. 'So?'

'I've just had a word with Tanya,' Cal told me when he came back. He looked again at the skinny girl, who glowered. 'And I think we might be able to use you for the next thing we've got on.'

I shifted self-consciously under his gaze.

'You're smart and funny and sexy,' he continued. 'And we've got some projects coming up that might really work with you involved ...'

I stared back at him in disbelief. 'Really?' I felt all fluttery inside. *Me? Projects?*

'Look,' he was saying, 'do you have a card or something?'

'I could – um ...' I began to scrabble in my handbag, feeling around in the murky depths for something pen-shaped. My fingers closed round a tampon that had come out of its wrapper. 'I might have some paper. Or the back of an envelope or something ... I'll just ... I've got rather a lot of things in here.'

I laughed awkwardly as I saw Alicia over his shoulder, shaking her head wonderingly at my ineptitude. I dug about a bit more. He moved a bit closer and appeared to be having a look too.

'Er – no,' I said brightly, abandoning the search and trying not to feel flustered by his undeniable beauty at such close proximity. 'I've never really needed ... I don't have a card.'

'Well, here's mine ...' He pressed a small piece of cardboard into my hand, his skin brushing mine for a tiny moment, and pulled a silver pen from the back pocket of his jeans. 'I can write your number down for now, but –' He looked up and gave me a long, slow smile. 'I think it's time you got one ...'

Chapter Fifteen

'I THINK IT'S TIME you did something about that bath.'

My mother opened the door wearing blue gingham overalls and brandishing the Dettox. 'What on earth's happened to it?'

'It's only hair colour,' I said, plonking my handbag onto the hall table and throwing my jacket over the newel post. 'Is Stanley OK?'

'Hmm,' she said. 'Good thing I was here, that's all I can say. He's had some proper food and we've tidied up his bedroom – there were clothes on that floor that don't even fit him any more. He says you never give him vegetables – he's had carrots, swede, and broccoli tonight.' My mother breathed deeply and looked me up and down.

I smiled. Was she about to finally enquire how I'd got on? If I'd had a nice time? Whether I had passed the audition I'd told her about? It seemed not.

'All very well for you gadding off, getting yourself on television,' she finished. 'What about him?'

'It's only been one day after school, Mum, and it sounds as if Stanley's had a really lovely time with you –'

'Hmm.'

She turned and walked down the hall to the kitchen. I followed her.

'He's all right, isn't he?'

She picked up the kettle. 'Bit quiet, I thought. Not his usual bubbly self at all.'

'Mum, he's never been bubbly.'

'Well he's not himself,' she said darkly. 'Is something going on at that school?'

'I don't think so,' I said uneasily. 'Like what?'

'I don't know. Sounds like it's full of riff-raff to me. Shame you couldn't have got him into somewhere decent like the sort of place Conway Hall used to be. It's gone downhill, of course, since your brother left ...'

'Highcourt is decent. It's one of the best schools in Kent.'

My mother sniffed. 'If you say so. But they don't do so well if there's girls there – puts them off. I remember the headmaster saying to me about Anthony. That boy could go to Oxford ...'

I reached into the fridge for a bottle of wine, pouring myself a large glass and forbearing to point out that my brother spent most of his education behind the bike sheds at the girls' school up the road, where, far from ever wishing to go to a redbrick university, he'd been rather more interested in getting into the nearest bar.

'They're only mixed in the sixth form,' I said. 'And Stanley's doing very well. I'll just go and say goodnight.'

My mother peered into the teapot. 'He'll be asleep now. I sent him up early – it being a school night,' she added, as if I would have been too feckless to consider such things.

'I'll pop up and check.'

As I suspected, Stanley was sitting up, gripping a games console, a deep frown of concentration on his face. He looked up and gave me a brief smile. I perched on the edge on his bed and waited. After a few minutes of intense grunting and swatting of buttons, he let out a sigh of satisfaction and put the PSP down. 'Are you going to be on TV?' he asked.

'Maybe, yes. Not on the cookery programme, I don't think, but maybe something else. Or perhaps on the cookery programme, but not with Alicia the way we thought. Someone's going to phone me.'

I felt a little flare of excitement at the thought of Cal writing down my number.

'Well done,' said Stanley doubtfully.

'Have you had a nice time with Grandma?'

'Yeah, it was fine.'

'Good day at school?'

'It was OK.'

118

'Much homework?'

'Not really.'

'Well, you'd better go to sleep, darling. School tomorrow. Grandma,' I said, lowering my voice, 'was expecting you to be asleep already.'

'OK.'

I kissed the top of his spiky head.

'Love you,' I said, switching out the lamp and moving toward the door.

'You too. Mum –'

'Yes?'

'Why did you call me Stanley?'

I turned back and frowned. 'You know why.'

'It's a stupid name.'

It felt like a little stab in my stomach. 'It's a great name – why are you saying that?'

'Why couldn't you call me something normal like Jack or Connor?'

'You know why,' I repeated. 'It's after your granddad. Stanley Edward Meredith – hasn't it got a lovely ring to it? I can just see that on a brass plaque when you're a mega-famous lawyer or top surgeon keeping your old mother in the style she longs to become accustomed to.'

I laughed. Stanley didn't.

'It's stupid,' he said again. 'And I hate it.'

'Well,' I said calmly, although my intestines were now fluttering anxiously, 'don't say that to Grandma.'

'She agreed with me,' said Stanley. 'She said, "I don't know why your mother called you that." She said she wanted you to make it my second name – so I was Edward Stanley. That would have been much better. I could have been Eddie then – Eddie's quite cool. But she said you wouldn't listen.'

I felt a flush of rage go through me. *How dare she?*

'Well you can change it when you're older,' I said, trying to keep my voice reasonable. 'Tell everyone you want to be called Eddie instead.'

Stanley shook his head. 'I want to change it now.'

'It would be a bit difficult now with school and everything.'

119

I sat back down on the bed and reached out a hand to pat his dark form. 'Has somebody been teasing you?'

'No.' His voice was muffled.

I switched the lamp back on.

'Really?'

'A bit.'

'What have they been saying?'

Stanley rolled over to face the wall. 'Just, you know, "Ooh, Stan-ley". He put on a sing-song voice, stretching out the two syllables, but kept his head turned away from me.

'Well,' I said, trying to keep my voice light. 'Boys are like that sometimes. They're just being silly. I expect some of the others get teased too, don't they?'

'Not about their names.'

'But other things, eh?'

'Sometimes.'

I stroked his shoulder. 'When I was at school, people were always calling each other names. Charlotte used to be called Concorde because she had a big nose.'

Stanley turned on to his back and looked at me. 'I've never noticed.'

'Exactly. It doesn't seem big at all now – I think she sort of grew into it.' I gave his arm a squeeze. 'And I had funny thick hair that used to stick up in all the wrong places,' I said.

'Which you've now given to me,' said Stanley gloomily. 'Thanks, Mum.'

'Your hair's lovely,' I said. 'It's one of my favourite things about you. And if they're making silly comments about your name it's because they can't think of anything else to say.'

'They call Danny Four-eyes.'

'There you go, then.'

'And Billy's Ginger-carrot 'cos he's got ginger hair.'

I nodded. 'They used to call people that sort of thing when I was at school, too'

'Michael's Tank,' Stanley continued, warming to his theme. 'Alex is Rug Head 'cos his hair is like all over everywhere and Tyrone's Drainpipe 'cos he's so skinny ...' He gave a sudden giggle. 'And Kieron's called Burger Lips ...'

I smiled at him. 'You see? They look for something to call everyone. In a way,' I said, 'it's a sort of affection.'

'I don't think it is, Mum.'

'It's similar,' I said firmly. 'Just try to remember that, and also that it's not only you. Try to ignore it. People only tease to get a reaction and if you don't react they'll lose interest. The trick is to smile as if you don't care.'

Which is what I would have to do. I settled him back under the duvet and kissed him for a second time. Then I took a deep breath as I went back into the kitchen.

'Do you want a glass of wine, Mum?'

My mother was sitting reading the paper, a cup of tea in front of her. She didn't look up. 'No. Oh all right, go on then.'

'You were up there a long time,' she said, as I put the glass in front of her. 'I hope you didn't wake him up.'

'He wasn't asleep.' I took a mouthful of wine. 'We were talking about his name. He seems to be suddenly quite upset.' I looked at her, wondering if she'd admit to her part in it.

My mother nodded, matter-of-factly. 'Well, why *did* you call him Stanley? Edward's much nicer and it's not as if he even knew his grandfather!'

This sent such an unexpected pain through my solar plexus that for a horrible moment I could feel my chin wobbling. Why was I feeling everything so very intensely? What time of the month was it?

'I know,' I said tightly. 'That's why I wanted to give Stanley his name – you know that, Mum – you were there. God,' I went on, suddenly realising. 'I can't believe that was more than 11 years ago.'

'Twelve soon,' said my mother briskly. 'It was 12th December.'

'I know when it was.' I could still see it clearly. My father propped up on pillows, his limbs like sticks, striped pyjamas hanging off his bone-thin frame. Face yellow-grey and exhausted. Nothing like the tall, strong, capable man he'd always been but still the same eyes fixed on mine. Trying to jolly me along.

'Tell him to get a move on,' he'd said.

And I'd sat there huge and bloated, my baby wriggling round inside me, showing no sign of wanting to leave his comfortable home. 'I'm doing my best,' I'd joked, though I was desperately close to tears. 'Curry, hot baths, I've tried the lot …'

I didn't tell Dad that I'd even asked the consultant to induce me but he wouldn't. Said nature would take its course when nature was ready.

It did. Dad died 12 hours before Stanley was born. He tried to wait but he couldn't hang on any longer.

'I really wanted to put my baby in his arms,' I said, my voice full of emotion, my throat tight even after all these years. 'I just wanted him to see.'

My mother made a fuss of taking her teacup to the sink and rinsing it noisily. 'That was him all over,' she said, 'wasn't it? Always did have a rotten sense of timing.' She gave one of her sudden barks of brittle laughter, as if that might soften her words.

I swallowed hard, trying to get a grip. 'I don't want you saying anything negative about Dad to Stanley,' I said. 'I want Stanley to be proud of his name and who he was named after. He was a good father and he would have made a wonderful grandfather.'

My mother sat back down opposite me and pressed her lips together. 'Hmm,' she said, as if she didn't believe it.

I gritted my teeth. 'He would have loved Stanley and Stanley would have loved him.'

'He was always difficult with your brother,' she said stubbornly. 'Anthony was always such a good boy and your father could never say anything nice. Jealousy, that's what it was, because your brother went to university and is far cleverer than your father ever was – and he just couldn't stand it.'

Here we go again. There was never any mileage in pointing out that my father was only trying to provide a bit of balance. Trying to temper the canonisation of my sainted brother by occasionally asking him to remove his head from his back passage. It was futile to say that his was simply a vain attempt to prevent my mother making the poor boy even more insufferable than he already was. But still I couldn't help the familiar rush of anger and frustration that ran through me whenever we had this conversation.

'He was very proud of Anthony,' I said, as calmly as I could manage, considering that from the way I would have liked to tip the contents of the washing up bowl over her head, we must definitely have hit Day 21 again. 'He just had a different way of showing it from you.'

In other words, I added silently, he saw no reason to wait on his son hand and foot when that son was well into his twenties, nor bore all the neighbours with regular bulletins on his achievements.

'Humph,' said my mother loudly.

I was only just starting my second glass but the wine had hit my bloodstream with a vengeance and I knew I was in that slightly pissed, slightly reckless state where I opened my mouth first and considered the wisdom of what I was about to say at some point in the early hours when I woke up sweating about it.

I might regret it later, but it suddenly seemed a fine opportunity to bridge some gaps and to say something that had been bugging me for years, to perhaps reach some sort of new understanding with the difficult woman in front of me. I took another deep breath and topped up her wine glass too.

'Mum,' I began in my friendliest tones, noting the way her head immediately jerked up in suspicion. 'I know you and Dad had your problems and in families we all experience each other differently because of the varying dynamics and obviously Anthony did not have quite the same childhood experiences as me –' I stopped and breathed again.

'And Dad may have been a slightly different father to him than he was to me – but then again, you had varying styles of mothering and you were not quite the same sort of mother to me as you were to Anthony –' I saw her eyebrows shoot up and swept resolutely on. 'But I can only talk about how Dad was to me, and to me –'

I paused for a moment, feeling my treacherous chin beginning to quiver once more and thinking that I really must start taking Oil of Evening Primrose again and trying to remember whether it was Agnus Castus or the hormone balancing mix they sold in the health shop that really had seemed to stop me bursting into tears and smashing things for a while.

'To me, he was the best father I could imagine. And even after all this time I miss him and wish I could talk to him because he always made things seem better.'

I took a gulp of wine. She didn't speak.

'And you are, of course,' I added inconsequentially, 'a fantastic grandmother to Stanley.'

'Yes, well,' she said, picking up her wine glass too, clearly mollified by this but still looking as if she'd got something unpleasant in her mouth. 'I know what boys need.'

But not much about daughters, I added in my head, saying out loud only, 'And I loved Dad very much.'

My mother's lips immediately went into what my brother describes as "a cat's arse" but I ploughed on anyway. 'And so it hurts me when you run him down, and you've done it for years. Can't you stop now? Especially if it's going to affect Stanley.' I looked at her hard, but she was gazing at the wall tiles above the hob.

'Because if Stanley is being teased about what he's called, then he needs our support, not you suggesting it's a daft name too. Couldn't you just say something nice about his grandfather for once?' I said, pushing down my rising emotions with another enormous swallow. 'If you can't do it for me, then do it for Stanley.'

As I said it, I was suddenly acutely aware of my own shortcomings in this department. I had started off making a token effort to present Daniel as a father to be proud of (even if he had rotten taste in women and a tenuous relationship with the truth) and had made a point of regularly reminding Stanley that Daniel still loved him to pieces, but I'd soon slipped into the habit of speaking about him as if – as if I were my mother!

I felt hot at the thought. It wasn't as if I specifically listed Daniel's faults and crimes, but I knew I had a tendency to refer to him in that disparaging, dismissive tone as if he were someone who deserved little consideration or respect – at times positively screwing up my face as if my ex-husband were one of the half-chewed mice that Boris brought home.

I must stop it now. Here I was, in my forties, bleating to my mother about how hurtful it was when she did it and all the time I was doing it to Stanley, who was only 11. How many WIT points he had accrued from me so far was anyone's guess but if I didn't want him to be in therapy a single year longer than necessary, things had to change right now.

'I know,' I said to my mother, in an heroic effort to be fair and honest, 'that it is easily done. I make unfortunate comments about Daniel sometimes. But, as far as Dad is concerned, I'm just saying ...'

I trailed off as she turned and met my eyes at last. Her face was impassive. For a strange moment I thought about putting my hand over hers but I knew she'd stiffen and we'd both be embarrassed.

So I just gave her a small smile and said, 'It was really hard for me, you know, when Dad died. And Mum – whatever you say about him, I know it was hard for you too. I know you missed him for a long time. Maybe you still do?'

She continued to look back at me and now there was something different in her expression. I couldn't decide if she was moved or angry but as she raised her eyebrows a little and her mouth opened, I realised I was holding my breath.

She was getting to her feet. 'Do you use that downstairs lavatory much?' she said as she passed me. 'I cleaned the hand basin while you were away. Never seen taps like it.'

Chapter Sixteen

BLOODY TAPS, BLOODY WATER cooling systems, bloody biodegradable filters that only need changing once every six bloody months ...

I sat and stared at my screen – at the set of diagrams and specifications and small paragraphs of mumbo jumbo I was supposed to convert into something guaranteed to top everyone's Christmas List.

'I need you to make this sound sexy,' were Mike's exact words in his third call of the morning. 'This could be a big account for us. It's only the brochure for now but they've got a huge budget there. We're talking corporate videos, we're talking exhibitions, we could even be talking –' here my illustrious boss paused for a fraction of a second so I could brace myself for the full excitement '- a TV ad campaign. You do know they were on *Dragons' Den*,' he said for the umpteenth time. 'We are talking some seriously big backers ...'

'I will do my best,' I'd said tightly, thinking that a clear ten minutes without him ringing up would go a long way to helping. 'It's just that, you know, water coolers – I mean it's all very well, but why not keep a bottle of Evian in the fridge?'

I heard Mike's hiss of impatience at the other end. 'It's not just about cold water, Laura – it's about cutting edge technology. It's about the touch of a button. It's a lifestyle thing,' he added, as if I were particularly dim.

'And this is only the beginning,' he went on, once I had grunted to show I was still alive. 'We are talking not just water but ice. Crushed ice, cubed ice, cracked ice. Everyone wants one of those big American fridges, right? But not everyone has room for one.' He waited until I'd grunted again.

'So – enter the Chill-Out Deluxe. Wall mounted and does all that at a fraction of the cost. You need to get this across, Laura; it's a lifestyle *choice*. So much more than a water cooler. Later models will do hot water, steam, and froth your cappuccino too. Imagine – no more boiling the kettle –'

This reminded me what I had been about to do before he started droning on. I carried the phone downstairs and got the coffee out of the cupboard while Mike was still talking. Tucking the phone under my chin, I held the kettle under the tap.

'Make a good job of this, Laura,' I could hear him saying tinnily halfway down my neck, 'and there'll be months' more work ...'

Can't bloody wait, I thought sourly. My perfect career plan just around the corner – writing about sodding water systems for ever more. Eventually he rang off, promising to email yet more photos to stimulate my creative juices, and I carried my mug back upstairs.

Crystal clear, chilled water at the touch of a button ... I typed half-heartedly. *Always on tap* ... I sighed and hit the delete button. *Cold, pure, and ready when you are* ... Beside me the phone burst into life again. How the hell did he expect me to ever get anything written if he never left me alone?

I picked up the receiver. 'What now?' I snarled.

'Laura – it's Cal from *Cook Around The Clock*. Is this a bad time?'

He sounded amused when I told him I had my boss on my back. 'Well here's something to take your mind off him,' he said warmly.

I wondered how old he was. His voice was very self-assured. – if I hadn't met him, I'd have put him in his thirties – possibly even his forties. Voices could be deceptive though – he'd looked more like 25 ...

'As I said on Thursday,' he was saying, 'we can't have you and Alicia on as mother and daughter. We have to be honest and ethical – we have a code of practice that precludes anything else–' His voice was quite Sloaney in a deep, sexy sort of way – and he was obviously well-educated. Perhaps he'd been to Oxford ? I'd have to tell my mother. She *would* be pleased. Not that she'd consider him a patch on my exalted brother, of course …

'But there is a spot on the programme you might be interested in. You've seen the *Beat the Chef* slot we do at the end?'

I didn't like to admit I hadn't seen the programme at all bar the few minutes I'd caught before Stanley interrupted me. This had consisted of a couple of chefs furiously whisking things in bowls while a middle-aged woman in a pinny held up a cake she'd made and another middle-aged woman in a contrasting pinny – introduced as Barb, her next door neighbour – clapped.

'Er – sort of,' I said.

'Well, it's a fun segment where you bring along some ingredients for a quick dessert and you make it for us and at the same time the chef is given the same ingredients – blind, without any preparation – and we see what he can come up with in the same time. It's very popular. Gets high marks on our viewer satisfaction surveys.'

'Well I don't know – I'm not really that good at puddings …' *Or any cooking at all, in fact …*

'We're not looking for any immense culinary skills. We have people doing things with ready-made ice-cream, or tinned peaches and sponge cake – that sort of thing.'

'Well I'd have to think –'

'We think you'd be fabulous.'

'Oh!' There was a pause.

'The thing is, Laura,' he went on, 'I'd really like you to do this so we can get to see you on camera a bit more. Because I've got something else in mind that I feel you'd be just perfect for. I've been looking for one more woman for a new programme we're making and I think –' his voice seemed to drop to a new, low huskiness and I felt a little shiver go down my spine '– that you could be the one …'

'Really?' My own voice sounded rather high and squeaky.

'Obviously we need to sit down together so that I can

discuss it in detail with you and see what you think, but basically it's a documentary about women entering their prime in their forties. You know how 40 is the new 20 and these days 40-somethings are considered to be sexy and happening – they're a huge consumer group and recent research has shown that it is considered to be a really great age because now you're more confident, more in control ...'

'I don't know about that,' I chortled, remembering the way I'd hurled the empty cornflake packet onto the kitchen floor that morning and then stamped on it.

He laughed. 'I do. I was watching you at the audition and I've been watching the tape with Randolph Kendall – I think you could be great.'

'I shouted and waved my arms about.'

'You showed passion and energy.'

'Yes, but I'm ...'

'You're just what I'm looking for.' The way he said it sent another small frisson up my arms. Get a grip, I told myself. He does this smooth-talking job on all the middle-aged women he wants to film screaming the place down.

'I don't know ...'

'Look,' he said persuasively. 'Come up and do *Beat the Chef*. It will be a great day out, we'll do your hair and make-up ...'

'They said that last time and they didn't. I looked ghastly.'

Cal gave a deep chuckle. 'Laura, I promise we'll do your make-up and your hair, you will look fantastic and you will have a lovely day – everyone does. And then we'll talk about the other programme. Over a drink. Or dinner ...'

'Well, I'll have to get back. My son ...'

'I'll organise a car if it gets too late. Look,' he said again, this time more decisively, 'let me sort out the schedule and come up with some times and dates – we could be looking at next Wednesday for the filming and then ...'

After he'd gone, I went back downstairs for more coffee, my mind even less engaged with water cooling systems, now. It all seemed deeply unreal – taking phone calls from beautiful young men about filming next Wednesday. It didn't feel as if it should be happening to me. Cookery programmes, being fabulous at 40 …

I looked in the mirror. 'You don't look very fab from here,' I said out loud, peering at my messy hair and make-up less face. Boris leapt up on to the work surface, meowing loudly as I shooed him off.

'You cannot be hungry again!'

He wound himself round my legs and prepared to yell until I got the tin opener out. I stroked his head as he munched. Did I really want to go on TV again? Part of me felt silly and apprehensive but I had to admit the attention was nice and if this time I was definitely going to get my hair and make-up done …

I phoned Alicia's mobile to see what she thought. It went straight through to her voice mail. She sounded bright and sexy. *Hi, this is Alicia – leave me a message and I'll be right back to you, I promise* ...

I put the phone back down …I didn't need to ask to know what she'd say. She'd be in there like a shot.

The afternoon passed in a frenzy of water-cooling excitement and by the time I had manhandled the last paragraph of techno-speak into something vaguely readable – using all the words I knew Mike would love, like 'cutting-edge' and 'hi-tech' and 'state of the art' (a particular favourite) – and emailed it to him, I was wrung out and in need of biscuits.

Charlotte hadn't been in today so my calorie count was definitely down and although I'd have to think about losing weight if I was going on the cookery programme – Alicia had told me the reason I looked so gross on the Randolph show was because the camera puts on ten pounds – right now, I could probably manage two HobNobs.

I wondered how Stanley was today. He'd not mentioned his name or any other anxieties again since the other night and had seemed OK after school, but he still wasn't very forthcoming. I wondered if Mr Lazlett had had his chat with Stanley yet. I hadn't heard. I must ask Stanley about inviting Connor round too …

The phone broke into my thoughts. I walked into the hall. Mike no doubt had been through my copy and wanted a bit more blood out of this particular stone, or perhaps it was Alicia who'd seen my missed call.

It was Cal again, voice sounding even more dark brown chocolatey movie star-ish than it had that morning.

'Oh, *hi*,' I said, feeling all fluttery again. 'How are you?'

'I'm good,' he said warmly. 'Did you get all your work done?'

'Oh yes – well, no, not really, got some of it sorted, you know ... Oh, could you just hold on?'

Stanley was banging on the glass of the front door. I tucked the phone under my chin as I opened it and let him in. I pointed at the handset. *I'm on the phone,* I mouthed.

Stanley rolled his eyes.

'My son has just come in from school,' I said.

'That's nice,' said Cal. 'I hope he's had a good day too.'

We both laughed.

Stanley shook his head in the way that meant I was a very sad person and walked down the hall into the kitchen. I heard him opening cupboards.

'We're definitely on for Wednesday,' Cal was saying. 'Now we'd like you here by 11.30 a.m. – are you happy to come by train? We'd meet you from the station, of course. One of the girls has looked up times and will call you about tickets. We thought if you caught the 8.59 ...'

'Yes, OK, sure,' I said, writing this down on the back of an envelope that was on the hall table and checking my eyes for new crow's feet in the mirror as I listened a bit more. 'Sure, yes, yes, I shall look forward to it too. Thank you, yes, thank you, yes, bye, yes, you too.'

I put the phone down in a flush of excitement. Stanley surveyed me from the kitchen doorway. 'Who was *that*?'

'Just someone from the TV company,' I said airily. 'Just,' I added, as if it were an everyday occurrence, 'about some more filming they want me to do.' I beamed at my son.

'I thought it must be something like that,' said Stanley flatly. 'You put on that voice you get.'

'What voice?'

'The one that goes all high and squeaky when you're trying to be posh.'

I laughed a high, squeaky laugh. 'Don't be so silly.'

I phoned Charlotte so she could properly demonstrate the level of enthusiasm my son sorely lacked.

'Yes?' she snapped, sounding remarkably like me on Day 23.

'It's me!'

'Oh Lu,' she said in her normal voice. 'Sorry – some stupid bastard keeps phoning and then putting the phone down.'

'Really?' I said, on immediate alert. 'What do they say?'

'Nothing – they just hang up. It's happened about six times in the last hour. I've tried ringing 1471 but the number's always withheld, of course.'

'Probably a wrong number.'

'Too much for them to say that, is it? Anyway, it happened the other night too. Roger said it was probably one of those sales calls where the computer rings six numbers at once but they only connect to the first one that answers.'

'Oh right, well, that's that, then,' I said reassuringly, knowing it was much more likely to be Roger's mystery flake – Hannah.

'They're going to get jolly short shrift from me when they finally do speak, I can tell you. No, I do not want a new flaming kitchen, bathroom or Internet connection, thank you very much – even if you do throw in cable TV and a free holiday voucher.'

'Nuisance, aren't they?' I said lamely, feeling guilty for not telling her what I knew. But did I know anything? Perhaps it *was* just sales calls …

I told her about the TV but could hardly concentrate on her replies. I put the phone down, determined to get on to Roger again in no uncertain terms and make sure he'd got that Hannah woman under control. He'd have to tell Charlotte all about her and how he'd been trying to help but she'd turned out to be a loony and was now coming on strong etc. If she was.

But it must be her – who else would it be? Bit of a coincidence that I'd taken that call and now Charlotte was getting them at just the same time as Roger had decided to be an agony uncle.

I had a look in the fridge to see what I might conjure up for dinner and, finding it lacking in inspiration, decided there was no time like the present. His mobile rang for quite a long time before he answered.

'Roger Forbes.'

'It's Laura. Have you told Hannah to lay off yet?'

There was a long sigh at the other end of the phone. 'I'm rather busy now, Laura.'

'So am I,' I said shortly. 'Did you know someone keeps putting the phone down on Charlotte? She's had six calls this afternoon. Suppose Hannah speaks next time? Suppose the mad cow says the same thing to Charlotte as she said to me?'

'She won't,' said Roger, adding, a tad hastily I thought, 'it wasn't her – I asked her.'

'Well she's hardly likely to admit it, is she? What was her face like?'

'Look, Laura, I'm about to go into a meeting. I know you think you're being helpful but I really think you're getting carried away here. Daniel may have …'

'Stop going on about him. This is *your* marriage we're talking about. How long since she split up with her boyfriend?'

'Er – I don't know. A few months.'

'And you're still comforting her? Roger, she's obviously got you lined up as the replacement. You've either got to stop seeing her on your own or tell Charlotte about it.'

'There really is nothing to tell but, OK, I will if it makes you happy. But right now I really do have to …'

'It's not about making me happy, Roger, I'm looking out for you here. You're playing with fire, you're dicing with death, you're –'

'Laura, *I have to go!*'

'Has she got a breathy voice?'

'Goodbye!'

I banged the receiver down in frustration. Why were men so

blind sometimes? Roger couldn't really think he was just being a friend in need. Clearly this woman was all over him and it was massaging his ego no end. But it wouldn't be his ego he'd have to worry about if Charlotte got wind of it.

Or was Roger right? Was I just totally overreacting because of what Daniel had done? Maybe the phone calls Charlotte had were indeed a sales thing and maybe the woman I spoke to was a wrong number or someone at his office was trying to make trouble out of a totally innocent friendship.

But if it was so innocent, why wouldn't he tell Charlotte? I wished I could get hold of the woman myself to warn her off. *You cannot go round disrupting perfectly happy families just because your boyfriend's left you*, I imagined myself saying. She was listening and nodding. I could be kind and empathetic. *I know how you feel because my own shitbag of a husband did the same thing but that doesn't mean I can cry all over somebody else's ... Hannah*, I could offer in a huge sisterly gesture, *you can talk to me instead ...*

'Why've you got that funny look on your face?' Stanley appeared in the doorway in his socks. 'What's for dinner?'

I thought about the half a cucumber and packet of cheddar in the otherwise empty fridge. 'I haven't been shopping yet,' I said brightly. Shall we go now and choose something?'

Stanley sighed. 'OK.'

'Are you all right, Stanley? I enquired, as we drove in the direction of the supermarket. 'What sort of a day have you had?'

'OK.'

'How's Connor these days?

'OK.'

'Does he want to come round to eat some time? Have a sleepover?'

'Dunno.'

'Well, why don't you ask him?'

'Dunno.'

'Go on, he used to come round all the time when you were at St Katherine's. Shall I ask his mum?'

'No.'

'Stanley, is everything really OK, darling?'

Stanley sighed again. 'I just don't like school,' he said eventually.

'What don't you like about it?'

'It's horrible.'

'Does Connor like it?'

'I dunno.'

'Say "don't know",' I said, at a loss as to what else to say. 'Look, we're here. Let's have a talk about this later.'

'OK.'

I parked the car and Stanley jumped out and headed for the trolleys. 'I'll push it,' he called over his shoulder.

'As long as you do push it and don't ride it down the aisles the moment I'm not looking,' I lectured, when I'd caught up with him. 'Remember what happened with the eggs.'

'I was five then.' He kicked off with one foot and swung himself up on to the side of the trolley and careered off ahead of me with a grin.

I walked slowly behind him, picking up vegetables. He seemed cheery enough now. Perhaps he just didn't like being asked questions. I decided I would phone Michelle, Connor's mother, anyway, to see if Connor wanted to visit and whether he too had become monosyllabic since beginning at Highcourt. Maybe a few hours with Connor in front of a DVD, stuffing pizzas, would help Stanley unwind a bit. Deep in thought, I turned into the next aisle.

'Careful!' I almost crashed into Stanley as he came to an abrupt halt in front of me and started to turn the trolley round.

'Oh great,' he muttered.

'What's the matter?' I looked at my son, who was now intently examining his trainers.

Then I looked up and felt myself blush.

Stanley's form teacher, Andrew Lazlett, was standing in front of us. He looked a lot less tired than he had at the parents' evening and taller again now he was standing up. If he was remembering that the last time he saw me I was snivelling into a handkerchief, he kept it hidden and greeted us both warmly.

'How are you?' he asked me. 'Hello again, Stanley.'

'Hello, sir,' Stanley mumbled.

He smiled from one to the other of us. 'Don't suppose you can help me, can you? I've been wandering up and down here for ages,' he said, 'hoping to be rescued. My wife's told me to get –' He consulted his list. 'Low-fat halloumi. I don't even know what it is.'

'It's a cheese,' I told him helpfully. 'I didn't know they did a low-fat version though. Very nice grilled with pitta bread.'

'I don't think I'm allowed bread,' he said, looking mournful. 'I'm on a diet. I've put on a stone since I stopped smoking.'

I looked him up and down. He didn't look fat – just chunky. Which is always preferable – on a man – to being too skinny.

I nearly said this aloud and then thought better of it. 'You can lose it again though, eh? More important not to smoke.'

'Trouble is –' He glanced toward Stanley, who had moved some feet away from us and was deep in concentration over the fromage frais and lowered his voice. 'I'm still doing that too. Don't tell anyone. I only have the occasional one – when there's nobody looking. It's very difficult not eating and not smoking. I'm starving,' he finished plaintively.

'I know the feeling,' I said. 'I'm supposed to be on a diet too. Are you on the Atkins?'

He looked gloomy. 'I think so. Thing is I love sandwiches.'

'So do I,' I said. 'I gave up bread for a week and started dreaming about it. Egg and cress on granary…'

'Chicken and bacon,' said Andrew Lazlett with feeling.

'Tuna mayo,' I cried.

Stanley gave a shudder, muttered something about getting more cereal, and headed rapidly for the next aisle. When he'd disappeared, Andrew Lazlett lowered his voice again. 'How's he getting on now?'

'I'm not sure – he won't really tell me. Some days he says everything's OK; today he said he still doesn't like school.'

'Well, sometimes it's not cool to say anything else. He seems fine to me when he's there. I had a little word and he didn't mention any problems. But I'll keep an eye on him.'

'Thank you very much. I'll show you the halloumi.'

I led him along the aisle to the cheeses. 'Have it with basil leaves and tomato,' I suggested.

'I'd rather have oven chips.'

I laughed. 'So would I. It's terrible shopping when you're hungry. I ought to have a salad but I bet we end up with something fattening just as I must lose weight.'

'You look fine to me,' said Andrew, evidently feeling he should.

'So do you,' I said, thinking I'd better too.

'Well I'm not – I can't do my trousers up.' My eyes involuntarily went to his waistband. He looked down too. 'I've had to buy new ones,' he explained as I blushed again.

He gave a wry laugh. 'I think it would be easier to just light up …'

As soon as we'd gone our separate ways, Stanley reappeared, clutching a box of Frosties and a packet of chicken burgers. 'How embarrassing was that!' he said accusingly.

'Not at all for me,' I said firmly. 'He's a very nice man. You're lucky to have him as a teacher. He's very understanding.'

Stanley shook his head disbelievingly and pulled a face that implied he might shortly be sick. 'Ugh, Mum – you fancy him,' he said, voice laced with revulsion. 'That is *so* gross …'

Chapter Seventeen

I WONDERED WHAT STANLEY would think if he knew who I really had the hots for.

I sat in the green room at the TV studios in Wandsworth and surveyed the delicious-looking little pastries piled up next to the platter of fresh fruit. I'd already had a mini pain au chocolat, a lovely little apricot tartlet and a few grapes and was trying hard to avert my gaze from the shortbread.

Cal was leaning in the doorway, loose white shirt over jeans, talking into his mobile. 'Won't be long,' he mouthed at me.

'No problem,' I mouthed back, looking at his slender hands and long, artistic fingers that gestured as he talked. Mmm.

I looked up at the monitor on the wall where I could see the first *Cook Around the Clock* of the day being filmed in front of a studio audience. They were recording three programmes, I'd been told by Tracy, the nice young girl assigned to look after me, and I was on the last one. I could have brought a guest but had ended up coming alone, which at least left lots of uninterrupted time for beautiful-young-man-gazing.

Charlotte couldn't get the day off as her boss was away sick and she had to stand in. I'd briefly thought of bringing Stanley and for a moment he'd even looked enthusiastic too, but then his face had dropped again. 'I'd better not,' he said.

'Why not?' I asked. 'I'll write a note and explain'

But Stanley had shaken his head. 'I'll miss stuff,' he said, not looking at me. 'It's difficult if you have a day off.'

'Everything's OK at school now, isn't it? Nobody's being horrible?'

Stanley had shrugged. 'Not really.'

I sometimes thought my mother was right when she periodically reminded me I should have had two children. Stanley wasn't used to the bickering and everyday abuse you got from having a brother or sister. And while St Katherine's, his primary school, had been small and delightfully huggy and happy-clappy, it maybe hadn't equipped him for the rigours of a secondary school with 600 boys and all the jostling and name-calling that was bound to entail.

But he still hadn't revealed any more and Andrew Lazlett had said he seemed fine. What else could I do? I could hardly storm up to the school on the vague possibility that someone was being beastly about my son's name. I had phoned Michelle and now Connor was coming round at the weekend to stay over. Maybe I could find out a bit more about what went on then ...

'Laura?' A girl in her twenties with a brown pony tail and a big smile was in the room. Cal had moved outside into the corridor, still on the phone. 'Hi, I'm Debby – want to come through to make-up?'

I followed her through to a mirrored room like a hair salon. The surfaces were covered with tubes and palettes, sprays and hair straighteners.

'So, what are you cooking?' Debby asked cheerily, as she put a gown around my shoulders and surveyed a huge box of eye shadows. There was a monitor in here too – I could see the chefs – who disappointingly did not include Marco or Gordon or anyone I'd ever heard of – chopping away, helped by two identical grinning blokes who were obviously twins.

'I'm doing *Beat the Chef*,' I said. 'A pudding with meringues and raspberries and a Snickers bar. It's my son's favourite,' I added, not wishing her to think I was an unsophisticated glutton myself.

'Bless him,' said Debby. She put a hand under my chin and tipped my face toward her. 'Do you usually wear a lot of make-up? What sort of colours do you go for on your eyes?'

She chatted away gaily while she blended and brushed and patted. I was turned away from the mirror so couldn't see what she was doing but it felt fairly industrial. I just hoped I wasn't going to come out all orange like Randolph Kendall. She seemed to be putting layers and layers of foundation and blusher on and my eyes took ages too. 'Look down. Look up. Lovely!' she said as she piled on several coats of mascara. 'Open your mouth a little?'

I imagined I must now look like one of those crones on the make-up counters in old-fashioned department stores, whose every wrinkle was filled to capacity with powder and whose lips were drawn in where their own had long disappeared.

'I'm trying to keep you quite natural,' said Debby, as she got out the eyelash curlers.

Another older woman with a deep tan and dark hair tied back in a red scarf came in and gave me the once over. 'Looking good,' she said to Debby.

She smiled at me. 'I'm Marie – I'm wardrobe. We'll have a chat after you're done here.'

Behind her, Cal put his head round the door. 'You OK, Laura? Wow,' he added, coming right up to me. 'You look great.'

Obviously he was being kind. A man like him would have a gorgeous girlfriend of 25 – or younger – or a whole string of them. He would not be really thinking a 42-year-old with three inches of slap all over her crow's feet was anything worth shouting about.

'Thanks,' I mumbled, embarrassed.

Debbie swung my chair back to face the mirror. I stared. For all the masses of gunk she'd put on me, I did look surprisingly natural, but in a whole new, glowing, smoky-eyed way. I had cheekbones I'd never seen before and full, glossy, pouting lips. My skin looked flawless. The bags under my eyes had mysteriously disappeared.

'Gosh,' I said to Debby. 'Can you come and live with me?'

From behind me Cal laughed. 'Can I?' He laughed again to show he was joking. My heart gave a little jolt. *Get real,* I told myself. *You're old enough to be his mother.* Well, almost. I didn't actually know how old he was at all but I was guessing at mid-twenties. Much too young for me, anyway.

'What do you usually do with this?' asked Debby,

indicating my hair.

'Er – well, that's it really.' I'd washed it and dragged a comb through it and tried to fluff it up a bit but there wasn't a lot you *could* do with it. 'I've never been very creative with the blow dryer.'

Debby was plugging in some heated rollers. 'We'll give it a bit more body,' she said kindly. 'Would you mind if I just tidied up your eyebrows?' As she plucked out a few rogue hairs and I tried not to wince too much, I wondered what Marie would have to say about my choice of clothes.

I'd been emailed an even longer list of sartorial do's and don'ts than there'd been last time and instructed to bring at least two outfits while travelling in something else. Currently I was still wearing the latter – one of my floppier pairs of jeans and a T-shirt. The gear I'd brought – the few dispiriting garments I could find that fitted the criteria – had been whisked away from me on arrival.

When Debby had finished and my hair was in pleasing waves, I followed Marie along the corridor to a room with an ironing board and clothes rails. My clothes were hanging up on hooks on one of the walls.

There were the usual black trousers and the grey flouncy skirt as well as a red dress which I'd found lurking in the cupboard in the spare room and which I now hoped they wouldn't like because I wasn't at all sure it would still do up.

Marie looked at them all critically. 'This is OK,' she said, fingering a long-sleeved, stretchy blue top I'd borrowed from Charlotte, 'but I'm just wondering ...' She rummaged along one of the rails and held up an emerald green embroidered smock top. 'This would really bring out your eyes – try it with the trousers.'

She stood watching me as I took off my T-shirt, glad I was in one of my better bras. I looked in the mirror. The smock was nice – it made me look sort of artistic and bohemian – and Marie was right; somehow my eyes did look greener than usual too.

'Now the bottoms,' she instructed. Lucky I wasn't shy, I thought, as I shuffled out of my jeans and Marie openly inspected my thighs. 'Do you do body brushing?' she asked approvingly. I shook my head. 'Well, you're lucky then – you've very little cellulite for a woman of your age. You're really in pretty good shape.'

'Am I?' I paused and looked at my legs myself. They didn't look that clever to me.

'You can always tell the actresses who body brush,' said Marie. 'You should try it – makes a huge difference.'

She pointed in the general direction of my bottom. 'Would just firm up those bits for you. Know that Angel McMullen?'

I nodded, even though I didn't.

'Looks wonderful with her clothes on but you should see her in her knickers – wobbles like a jelly. And she's only young ...'

She surveyed me again once I was dressed. 'Hmm, I like it. Now, what shoes have you got?' She rummaged in the bottom of one of the big sliding cupboards. 'I think there are some green pumps somewhere ...'

They were a bit big but they were comfortable and at least I wouldn't have to worry about tottering around in heels. The only time I'd worn the strappy sandals I'd brought along in case they made me try the dress, I'd almost broken both legs. Marie smiled at me as I stood sideways in front of the mirror – the flowing top was really quite slimming. 'I guess you'll do,' she said.

'You look fantastic,' said Cal, when he came back into the green room where I was nervously picking at the grapes. Tracy had been in to tell me they were halfway through the second programme and to introduce me to Bob and Carol, a husband and wife team who were the contestants just before me.

He was jovial and kept guffawing and saying, 'This is the life, eh?' as he worked his way through the biscuits; she was as white as a sheet and looked as though she might throw up. They'd been taken off to make-up now and I'd been left on my own again, staring at the monitor in increasing trepidation and trying not to chew my lipstick off.

By the look of the clapping from the studio audience, and general shifting about, the second programme had come to an end.

'Claire, our floor manager, is going to come and see you in a moment,' Cal said, 'and then Lucy, our home economist, will run through the recipe. OK? Smile,' he added, shining a huge one of his own on me. 'You're here to enjoy yourself.'

It felt more like waiting for the dentist. My stomach churned as I followed Claire, a vivacious black girl with braided hair and a brilliant red boiler suit that I wished I had the body to wear, down another corridor and through some doors on to the set.

There were tiers of theatre seats, all occupied, and a bright white area down at the front with kitchen units, cameras and lights, and people wandering about with clipboards and saucepans. The chefs were in a little huddle over by the fire escape. I felt the eyes of the studio audience on me as I was shown where I was going to stand.

'OK, so when you get the signal, you come straight down these steps – don't look around you – keep your eyes to the front, come directly to here and you'll meet Bruno, the chef,' instructed Claire. 'He'll shake your hand. But then at the end he'll kiss you on the cheek. OK?' She laughed. 'Try not to crash noses! Austin, the presenter, will ask you a few questions and then we'll start, OK? Now it's recorded as though it's live so we don't stop the camera for anything, all right? Don't look at the camera, just concentrate on what you're doing –'

My head began to whirl – I was never going to remember all this. I glanced sideways at the monitor nearest me. I didn't look bad – not any fatter than usual, and my hair looked better than it had for years. Claire was still talking but I'd missed the last thing she'd said.

'Hey, Austin,' she called now. 'Do you want to come and meet Laura?' Austin was a tall, attractive guy in his thirties with dark curls and amazing teeth.

'Hi Laura!' I noticed he'd changed his shirt again. It had been pink when they were recording the first programme, blue for the second. Now it was red. Together we looked like a Christmas tablecloth. 'Don't sweat, we're gonna have a ball,' he said, fixing me with a brilliant smile. He touched my shoulder. 'I'll see you later.'

He loped off across the studio. 'He's awesome,' said Claire appreciatively. 'Ah – here comes Luce.'

Lucy was a neat, brown-haired 30-year old, wearing a white coat like a lab technician. 'Let's go,' she said briskly. 'We've got all your ingredients ready – now talk me through your recipe ...'

Recipe was going a bit far. Basically you took a packet of shop-bought meringues, a Snickers bar, some tinned or frozen raspberries and a tub of ice-cream. (I imagined Emily Twig's face as she calculated how many calories that little lot came to.) You chopped up the chocolate bar and heated it in a saucepan until it was all melted with the nuts floating, then you crushed up the meringue and added that, and then you put a great wedge of ice-cream in there too and pulverised the lot.

The result was a great melting, crunchy, chocolatey mass which you piled into a bowl, decorated with raspberries so at least there was the odd vitamin in evidence, and devoured as quickly as you could before the ice-cream had totally liquefied.

Stanley loved it – it was standard fare for birthdays and celebrations. Lucy nodded. 'We need to give it a name,' she said dubiously.

'At home we call it Snickers Car Crash. Or Mum's Mess.' I laughed. 'A bit like Eton Mess, but ...

'We'll go for Laura's Raspberry Crush,' said Lucy firmly.

I was introduced to various other people who were doing various other things with cameras and lights, and was miked up with another of those black boxes attached to my waistband. 'Don't worry, it'll be turned off till you come on set – you can go to the loo without fear,' said the grinning boy who fitted it. And then I was taken back to wait in the green room.

There were plates of sandwiches and cheese and biscuits laid out now, but I was too twitchy to eat. I went to the loo down the corridor and then went again. Bob and Carol were on the monitor. The sound was turned down but I could see Bob was still guffawing and waving a wooden spoon around while Carol was gazing at her chef in terror and gripping the edge of the work surface for dear life.

Tracy, my minder, sat down opposite me. 'Would you like another cup of tea?' she asked.

I shook my head, sipping some water and realising my hand was shaking. 'I'm quite nervous now,' I said.

Tina smiled sympathetically. 'You'll be fine once you're on – everyone says it goes really quickly.' The radio thingy on her belt crackled and she pulled it out and listened. 'Got it.' She nodded at me. 'Five minutes,' she said brightly.

After that it was a bit of a blur. I recalled following her to the doors into the studio and coming down the steps to applause, keeping my eyes fixed manically on the spot where I had to end up and my hands trembling so much that I thought I was going to chop one of my fingers off. But afterwards I could hardly remember anything else except the crunch of gristle on bone as Bruno went to kiss me and our noses collided.

'Brilliant!' Back in the green room, Cal kissed me on both cheeks. 'Time for a drink now!' He turned as Bob and Carol came through the door and collected their coats. Cal shook hands with them both warmly. 'Enjoy it?'

'Capital,' said Bob, while Carol, who looked as though she might be suffering from post-traumatic stress, smiled weakly.

'Has Tracy told you your car's waiting?' Cal disappeared out of the room with them. 'Thank you so much for coming,' I could hear him saying as they went off down the corridor. 'We'll send you an email to let you know when it's been scheduled ...'

A skinny bloke came in and got a bottle of mineral water out of the glass-fronted mini-bar. I remembered someone introducing us earlier – Lenny, was it? He was lighting or sound or something. He had long, brown hair pushed back into a pony tail and a tight black T shirt and combat pants. 'Hi again,' he drawled, flopping down opposite me. 'Have a good time?'

'Yes, it was great.'

He nodded. 'You looked good on screen – came across really well.'

'Thank you,' I said, self-consciously. 'That make-up girl –

Debby, I mean – was marvellous.'

Lenny gave a strange laugh. 'It's not the make-up you have to thank, darling'.'

I looked at him quizzically.

Lenny sat up straighter. 'It's all in the lighting. Whatever they put on your face, it's yours truly who decides whether you look good or not.'

'Really?'

'You bet. Why do you think the really old pros carry their own uplighters?'

I shook my head. 'I've no idea. I don't even know what an uplighter is.'

'The secret of all lighting is the source. Think of someone photographed in the harsh sun. It hits the angles and makes deep shadows that accentuate all the wrinkles. Same if you use a small, pop-up flash – makes all the lines on the face sharp and unflattering. That's because the light is hard.' Lenny was leaning forward, quite animated now. 'It's coming from a small source, see?'

He looked at me intently. 'Now,' he said, as if imparting something of great importance, 'compare that with when you bounce the flash off the ceiling– it's all diffused and soft, isn't it?'

I nodded, trying to look intelligent, although I had little idea what he was talking about. 'That sort of light, from a wide source, softens the angles, so lines on your face are smoothed out,'

'Very handy!' I put in encouragingly. 'Could save a fortune on face cream.'

'In a studio photographic shoot,' continued Lenny, undeterred, 'the photographer will shoot the flash into an umbrella, which is basically a reflector. It's the same principle in the studios here. We need the right amount of light to bring your face alive – but not to show every flaw.' He paused and appeared to scrutinise my chins.

'And of course, as you age, the lighting becomes ever more important. That's why the older actresses will always come across and be dead nice to me.' He nodded with satisfaction.

'They know I'm the one who can make or break how they look. The war paint helps, of course, but it's much more about that –'

He pointed at the monitor where the camera in the now-empty studio was trained on a sofa – with various lights grouped around it. 'I was on a shoot the other day. Young girl in her teens – not a line on her face – but the way they wanted to light the guy she was with, it put decades on her.'

'Why did they want the lighting like that, then?' I asked with interest.

'Trying to make him look dodgy,' said Lenny easily. 'You see, you get your angles of light too. Shoot a hard light straight up from the bottom of the face, you'll end up looking like something out of a Hitchcock film; that's how to make things look spooky. Yet with a nice soft light coming from 45 degrees, the modelling effect on your face will be lovely.'

He grinned wolfishly. 'Sometimes they change the light from one to the other. If, for example, you've got a pretty young thing with some randy old goat, you might light her to make her look 15, while you show up every crack and crevice on his face till he looks like her granddad, never mind her father. Seen it done the other way too,' he added with relish.

'There was an actress who'd married a bloke 30 years younger. In fact, she looked great for her age but by the time they'd finished with her on breakfast TV, he only needed a pair of short trousers and she looked ready for her bath chair.'

'That's awful,' I said indignantly. 'If she didn't look like that really.'

Lenny winked. 'It's the way it is. Always remember to be good to your lighting guy. If some old cow's rude to me she'll soon know about it when she sees herself later …'

'I'll remember that.' My fingers went instinctively to my scraggy neck.

'Don't listen to him, Laura,' said Cal from the doorway. 'On this show, we do our best to make everyone look lovely and you looked fabulous.' Cal was carrying a bottle of champagne. Behind him, an unsmiling Tanya had a couple of flutes in each hand.

Cal poured champagne into one of them and handed it to me. 'Want one, Len?'

'Yeah, go on ...'

I watched him fill three more glasses, a little warm glow inside me. I could get used to this, I thought, drinking champagne while people told me how fab I was. I looked at Cal's dark lashes as he bent over the bottle. He was gorgeous and nice with it, with a glamorous job in television. He must have girls falling all over him.

He glanced up and caught me gazing at him. 'You're not in a hurry, are you, Laura?' He gave me a smile and I felt my face colour. I looked at my watch.

'Well – I was wanting to catch the 18.03. I need to be home before eight ...' I had managed to organise Daniel to meet Stanley after school and take him bowling and out to eat by pretending I had an important meeting about work, but I couldn't stay out too late as he'd be wanting to get back to The Twig.

Cal looked at his watch too. 'If we get the car round in half an hour? I just really want to tell you about this project of mine – and Tanya's,' he added, looking toward her. She was sitting close to Lenny, glass in hand, a bored expression on her face.

Cal's brown eyes looked seriously into mine. 'As I explained before, it's about women in their forties and how these days that's a really great place to be. But we'll be looking at the different ways in which different women approach this time in their lives – emotionally, spiritually, sexually ... a holistic approach if you like ...'

Beside him, Lenny put down his empty glass. 'I've gotta split.' Lenny got up and nodded at me. 'See ya.'

Tanya sighed and got up with him. I wondered if they were an item. 'I've got loads to do too. You don't need me, do you, Cal?' It was a statement, not a question. Cal shook his head. 'I'll be off then,' she said flatly, not looking at either of us. 'Come on, Len.'

Cal poured more champagne. 'We're going to be looking at beauty treatments, alternative therapies, fitness regimes, that sort of thing. It's not entirely decided yet – they're still working on the script – but we're probably going to be using three or four women, who have all approached going into their forties in a different way.' He sat back and sipped at his drink.

'One might have lots of kids and has let herself go a bit. Perhaps she thinks she's too old for any of this beauty and fashion stuff any more –the sort of person perhaps your mum used to be when she was 40.'

'My mum was like that when she was 20, believe me!'

He laughed. 'Perhaps she'd like to be in it too, then. We'll have bits of footage showing women a few decades ago in headscarves and slippers etc.'

Hc put the glass down and leant forward, his face animated. 'Then we'll be having another subject who's really fighting the ageing process all the way but with desperation. 'Plastic surgery, short skirts, chasing after younger men …' He gave me a conspiratorial smile. Had I imagined it or had he moved a little closer to me? The distance between our knees seemed to have shortened. 'And then there'd be you, illustrating the balanced approach – showing how you can be fit and attractive at 40 –'

'Actually I'm 42.'

'Perfect! That was exactly the sort of age we were hoping for. Into your forties but still plenty of them left to go.'

I took another gulp of champagne even though it was some hours now since I'd eaten and it was rather going to my head. He was definitely sitting very near to me. I was aware of his breathing.

'So what exactly would I have to do, then?'

'We'd want you to be filmed having some beauty treatments and exercising. Though obviously you're in really good shape already. Would you be prepared to be filmed in a bikini?'

'No, definitely not,' I said, recoiling and nearly choking on my bubbles. 'I couldn't possibly. I mean, I may look OK to you in these clothes but I assure you I'm not up to that close an inspection …'

Cal laughed. 'I bet you are – Marie was most impressed.'

'No, really, I'd be mortified.' I looked at him, embarrassed.

Had they all had a summit meeting on the state of my cellulite?

He stopped laughing and put a hand on my arm. 'Please don't worry – it was just a thought. You wouldn't have to do anything you were uncomfortable with. I was just trying to get a feel for how you viewed yourself.'

He gave my forearm a little squeeze. 'Personally I hate the whole business of women being judged by their bodies and looks – it's what's inside that counts for me. The idea is to make that point.' He looked at me earnestly. 'We're going to show the lengths some women are prepared to go to, with you there to illustrate how you just don't need all that stuff. You'll be showing how you will always be beautiful, vibrant and sexy, however old you are.'

'Well I don't know about that, 'I said, pleased but self-conscious now under his intense gaze. I was also aware of my heart beating. *Don't be ridiculous.*

He leant forward again, our knees almost touching now. 'I do. I really think you'd be good at what I've got in mind ...'

'The thing is,' I said a bit later, trying to sound business-like although I was now feeling quite tipsy. 'It sounds as if it would take up quite a lot of time. And there's my son to think of. And I have to work, of course ...'

'We can fit in around you – we can film in the evenings and weekends – and we can try and do as much as possible at the same time so there's minimum disruption to your routine. You can get a lot done in two or three longish days – if that suits you best. There'd be gaps in filming but from start to finish I should think we could wrap the whole thing up in three to four weeks.'

I hesitated, feeling awkward again. 'Would I be paid?'

'Well, not as such, because it's a matter of ethics again. This is a documentary looking at real women's lives – but you'd get all your expenses and a few extra perks too – some clothes and beauty products maybe. And certainly there'd be treatments and hair appointments; gym membership, maybe a day at a spa. That sort of thing.' He looked at me seriously. 'If it's important, I'll see what I can do – I might be able to work you a small fee …'

He shone the full force of that brilliant, knee-weakening smile on me once more. 'Perhaps you'd like some more time to think about it.'

I thought. Free facials, new clothes and my hair done. Three weeks of being whizzed about by car and followed round by a film crew as if I were a star. All of it in Cal's undeniably gorgeous company. What was it Sarah had said about looking after oneself after the trauma of a marriage break up? Give yourself a few treats?

I smiled back at him. 'Not really,' I said.

Chapter Eighteen

'AGAIN?' STANLEY SAID BELLIGERENTLY. 'You're always going away.'

'It's only for one night. And after that they'll be filming round here. I'm sorry, darling, but it's really important. Just think, I'm going to be in a documentary!' I beamed at him. 'I'll come and get you early on Saturday and Charlotte's going to make you toad in the hole.'

I could see this had scored a couple of points so I swept on. 'And Becky won't even be there – she's on a sleepover with Lauren. So it will just be you and Joe and wall-to-wall PlayStation. Good hey?'

'Why can't Grandma come again?' he said in a half-hearted fashion.

'It's her night for going to the cinema with Betty.' *And I haven't got over last time yet.* I kept smiling. 'And you know you have a good time at Charlotte's – you always say you love her food best of everyone's.'

'I'm on a diet.'

'Stanley, you are not. Don't be so silly – you're growing.'

'I'm fat.' He turned away from me and poked his foot into his school rucksack still lying on the kitchen floor.

'Has somebody said something to you?'

'No.'

'Emily again?'

'*No.* Leave me alone.'

'What's the matter?' I moved round so I was facing him but he turned away once more.

'*You* are!'

*　　*　　*

'Perhaps I shouldn't go,' I said miserably to Charlotte as I sat in her kitchen watching her expertly pipe black icing into spider webs on a rack of cupcakes. 'And look at me, I'm such a shit mother – I hadn't even realised it was Halloween.'

Charlotte straightened up and pointed at the fridge. 'Give yourself a break, for God's sake. And pour me one while you're at it. You know what kids are like – Stanley will be fine.'

She pushed the hair back from her forehead with the back of her hand. 'I've got loads of trick and treat stuff – masks and all sorts – I'll take him and Joe out and there'll be a great time.'

She made a face at the bowl of icing. 'Though why I have to do this lot I don't know – can't any of the other mothers knock up a sponge? I spend my life supplying cakes to that damn PTA.' She wiped her hands on a tea towel and turned to me.

'Look – he's bound to be up and down. Hormones, new school, dad moving out, but he'll survive. You have fun and I'll make sure he's OK. You deserve a few nice things to happen – go and have your crow's feet rubbed or whatever they're going to do and I'll look after Stanley.'

I got up, walked round the table, and put my arms round her. 'I do love you,' I said, emotionally. 'Thank you for everything.'

'I love you too, love. And it's a pleasure. Now, where's that bloody drink?'

I sat on the train and stared unseeingly at the flat Kent fields, still feeling guilty. Stanley had seemed OK when I'd dropped him off at school that morning and had even let me hug him in the car. But he still hadn't been any more forthcoming about what was wrong. Surely he was too young to be hormonal already? He didn't seem to be displaying any other signs of puberty.

I'd phoned the school before I left for the station, hoping for a chat with Andrew Lazlett, but he was away on a training day. The secretary said she'd leave a message. I didn't know what I expected him to do. If it was the other boys' teasing that was getting to Stanley there wasn't much to be done about that, except to hope they'd stop or he'd get used to it.

I decided I'd try to find out more on Saturday when we'd have all day together – Stanley wasn't seeing Daniel till Sunday. Perhaps we'd go for a pizza.

I looked out of the window as we pulled into Bromley South, thinking I'd better start preparing for the day ahead. I dug in my handbag for a mirror and make-up, narrowly avoiding jabbing myself in the eye with an eye shadow brush as the train lumbered off again.

'Do you mind coming by train again?' Cal had sounded apologetic on the phone. 'I think in all honesty it will be quicker at that time of the morning and it does help our budget. Of course we'll get you picked up at Victoria.'

My mobile rang even before we'd got into the station. 'Ms Meredith? I'm your driver today. I'm just outside the Wilton Road entrance ...'

A dark blue BMW was waiting at the kerb, a suited chap in his fifties standing next to it. 'Sorry I couldn't come to the barrier,' he said, as we drove off rapidly. 'We're not really allowed to stop here at all now – not even to drop off.'

As we swung past the back of Buckingham Palace and out on to Grosvenor Place, I looked at the schedule I'd been emailed. First stop an address in W11. *Sally-Ann Le Fern – Rejuvenation Consultant.* I had another look at my saggy face as we drove along Kensington High Street. Ha ha. She'd have her work cut out.

We pulled up outside a tall white house in a tree-lined street. Cal was standing by a white van with three other blokes.

'This is our cameraman, Matt.' A short, dark man in his thirties waved a hand at me. 'Russ is our sound guy –' Taller with blond curls and an earring. 'And –' Cal put his hand on the shoulder of the youngest of the group, a short, fair boy of about 18. 'Gabriel, our Man Friday of the moment.' The boy smiled shyly. 'Gabriel's our runner. Tanya is production on this one but she's going to be joining us later. Right – let's go.'

Inside, the house was stunning with a Mediterranean-type tiled hallway, huge flower arrangement on a polished table, and bright paintings on the white walls. We trooped up the curved staircase to a sort of reception on the first floor – a room with two cream sofas facing each other and a low table with copies of *Vogue* and *Harper's Bazaar*.

I was deposited there with a young, red-headed girl called Leanne who was waiting with a leather trunkful of make-up and a pair of straighteners, while the others disappeared into another part of the house.

Gabriel brought me a glass of water and then he disappeared too.

Leanne didn't say much but dabbed and smudged and patted away while I sat fiddling with my bracelets and wondering exactly what "rejuvenation" was going to involve. Eventually she held up a mirror. I didn't like it quite as much as what Debby had done on the cookery programme – the make-up was much more obvious and my eyes and lips were quite dark – but I looked quite vampish. Cal put his head round the door and nodded approvingly.

Eventually I was taken up another flight of stairs to the consulting room – more cream sofas and magazines – where cameras and lights were set up around a large mahogany desk.

Sally-Ann was a Lycra-clad, tall, blonde American in her fifties with a born-again glow, a brilliant white-toothed smile and a voice a tad on the loud side. She gave my wrinkles the once-over and asked various questions about my general health, diet, how much water I drank and any "afflictions" I had.

When we got to the bit about my PMT she gave me a broad if discomforting smile and swept her eyes over me once again. 'And –' she looked back at her notes, 'you're 42 years old, right?'

Across the room Cal gave me a wink.

Sally-Ann fixed her eyes on mine. 'OK, well, this is a time, honey, when your body is going through *big* changes. Remember the changes you go through as a teenager when all those hormones are bouncing about? Yeah? Well this is about to happen again. You're still menstruating regularly right now, yes?'

I gave a small squirm. 'Yes.'

'Well, the average age that women go through the menopause is currently 51 but some women hit that point *much* earlier. With some women it's all done and dusted at 40. What you have to remember is that you begin to be pre-menopausal five to ten years before the changes start. So you,' she said brightly, 'are probably going through that right now!'

Wonderful.

'In which case we are not so much talking about PMT but about being peri-menopausal.'

'Hurrah!' I said flatly, pulling a face.

Cal grinned.

Sally-Ann frowned. 'If this is so, then your ovaries will have begun to decrease the production of progesterone and oestrogen. Oestrogen redistributes fat but as we age, our body shape changes. We will often notice a thickening of the waist – you know, that roll of fat below the belly button you see on so many middle-aged women?'

I felt my eyes involuntarily drop to my stomach and my spirits plunge in the same direction. I looked resentfully at Cal. *I thought this was supposed to be about being fab at 40, not a lesson in how decrepit I am.* He winked again.

Sally-Ann was becoming animated. 'You will, in fact, become more testosterone-based as your oestrogen and progesterone levels drop and it is this which causes facial hair to appear and bones to start to thin. You may notice your hair thinning too, vaginal dryness, and depleted energy levels. Your sex drive will go and as you get older, skin starts to hang on you more loosely –'

'You're really cheering me up now,' I interrupted gaily. I saw Cal signal to Matt, who moved in closer – presumably to capture the look of unrivalled joy on my face at the news of my impending descent into senility.

'I'm just stating the facts,' Sally-Ann put in disapprovingly. 'If you're aware what you're up against, you can prepare yourself with the tools with which to fight the ageing process. Look at me!' She suddenly sprung from her chair and towered above me. 'How old do you think I am?'

Clearly the answer was going to be "a whole lot older than you look" but I didn't want to offend her unnecessarily even if she was depressing me to hell.

'Er – 48?' I asked, trying not to sound too bitter.

'I am 59!' she cried triumphantly. And I'm telling you that ten years ago I was dying – stiff as a board, burned out, washed up. Now –' I jerked back in alarm as she leapt across the room and performed a handstand up against the wall.

'Yoga has done this for me,' she explained as she dropped back to her knees and wrapped a leg around her neck. 'And it could do it for you too!

'It is all about what you put in and how often you put it there,' she said forcefully once she was mercifully back behind her desk. 'What you eat, what you drink, how often you exercise. What you need to remember is that from now on, you've got to eat less and work out more, just to stay the same.'

Marvellous. Just what I wanted to hear. I could see Cal and Russ grinning at each other while Matt swung the camera round to follow Sally-Ann as once again she rose from her chair. This was obviously making great TV for them even if it was making me want to go home and top myself.

'Give me your arm!' Oh God, what was she going to do now? Sally-Ann grabbed my wrist with one claw-like hand and closed the other one around where my biceps should have been. 'Lift your arm up.'

I lifted.

'Now when I push, resist me,' she instructed. As she pressed against my upper arm, I obligingly pushed up and knocked her hand back.

'Good,' she cried as if I'd done something amazing. 'Now hold this!'

A small glass tube was put into my other hand and my arm was lifted again. 'Now resist me again.' This time she pressed down really hard – she was surprisingly strong – and my arm flopped back against my side.

'*Ah*! I thought so!' She whipped away the glass tube and replaced it with another one and repeated the process. This

157

time she pressed down even harder. 'Yeah!' she cried, as though someone had just scored a winning goal. 'You have a *serious* intolerance here ...'

'Can you explain what you're doing, for the camera?' Cal asked from behind me.

'Sure!' Sally-Ann put yet another glass tube in my hand. 'Kinesiology is the testing of the body's resistance to foods and chemicals using an indicator muscle.' She pushed my arm back down to my side again.

'Intolerances show up as muscle weakness – as each muscle is connected to an organ via a meridian. If I do this –' more shoving of my arm '- I'm testing out any weakness in Laura's stomach. But if we do this –' she repositioned my arm down against my side '- we're testing out the effects of various foods through the meridian to the spleen.

'Resist me,' she said again, grabbing my wrist and pulling my arm outwards. I tried to tug it back.

'Don't turn your shoulder,' she ordered, hauling away. 'Relax!' I went floppy and she held my arm high in the air. 'See?' she cried in triumph.

'Do you suffer from bloating?' Everyone looked at my stomach. 'Are you tired and irritable? Do you get mood swings and bowel problems?' she intoned in a sing-song voice like an old fashioned ad for Anadin.

'Er - no, not really,' I muttered embarrassed. 'Well, sometimes.'

Sally-Ann beamed at me. 'Did you feel how weak you were when you held this, honey?' She waved the small glass phial at the camera. 'You need to stay right away from wheat, lactose, chicken, and onions. You should also cut out alcohol, sugar, and red meat ...'

I gave her a tight smile as the list continued. It was getting better and better. I felt myself glaze over as she began to bang on about the regime of hot water, wheat grass, and royal jelly that had changed her life, suddenly remembering to look fascinated as Matt moved in so close he'd be getting every open pore.

The thought made me put an anxious hand to my upper lip –

what was that cheering comment Stanley had made the other day in the car? 'Mum, you've got a black hair there, like a moustache.' I'd gone straight home for the tweezers but suppose there was another one?

Sally-Ann was talking about wild yam cream and the benefits of a "super-potency soyagen". Her voice drilled into my head. 'A similar molecular structure to progesterone ... Effective in treating hot flushes ... May help with weight loss – increases energy, stamina and sex drive ...' I began to feel like I needed some fresh air.

'There is a theory that it can be even be used as a natural form of birth control,' Sally-Ann said, after she'd finally taken a breath. 'But I wouldn't bank on that one, honey.' Then she laughed loudly. 'Though you're probably infertile now anyway ...'

'Terrific,' I said to Cal as we left, me clutching various packages of powders, pills, and creams and the diet sheet that excluded every single foodstuff I'd ever loved. 'I don't know about rejuvenation – I've never felt so ancient in my entire life. I feel like slitting my bloody throat!'

'She's supposed to be the best in the business,' said Cal. 'Costs a fortune normally – all the Notting Hill set use her. She's got a six-month waiting list.' He nudged me. 'But don't let her get you down. You don't really need her – you look fantastic already. And much younger than 42!'

'Thank you.' I grinned at him, feeling suddenly happier.

He grinned back boyishly, showing lots of very even white teeth. 'And you're going to look even yummier shortly – we're getting your hair done next.'

I wondered if anyone would think about food. It seemed a jolly long time since the muffin I'd eaten on the train that morning. We'd been offered herbal tea in Sally-Ann's and I'd seen Russ eat an apple outside on the pavement between cigarettes. Might lunch be forthcoming at some point?

It seemed not. Cal and I got back in the car while the others carried the equipment away along the pavement. 'Antonio's now, please,' said Cal cheerfully to the driver who put down his newspaper and nodded in the rear mirror. 'Address on your list.'

Antonio's was just off Sloane Square – all mirrors and chrome with fountains running through slate chips and cool black-and-white fittings.

Antonio himself was a smouldering Italian with black curls, beautiful dark eyes, and a sulky expression. 'Who did this to you?' he said, in his heavy accent, picking up a lock of my hair and inspecting it with disdain. 'It is a – how do you say it? A trav-est-y? A dog's breakfast?'

I gave a small snort of laughter.

'It is not good,' he summed up, curling his lip.

'What would you recommend for Laura?' Cal adopted a smooth interviewer's tone as Matt moved in with the camera. 'We're looking for something young and funky.'

In the mirror I saw the skinny Tanya arrive, wearing black leather trousers and a waistcoat. Her hair was spikier than ever, her eyes smoky black, her lips today as purple as her nails. Cal turned and kissed her on the cheek. She didn't smile.

Antonio was still picking at bits of my hair. 'The colour, it is all wrong,' he said. 'There is too much heaviness here –' He flicked his fingers across the top of my head. 'And it is needing something here –' He held up a strand of evening plum at the back of my neck and looked at it pityingly.

'You do whatever you think,' said Cal, smiling at my reflection. 'But we're thinking fun, sexy hair to reflect the modern 40-something woman who's still 19 inside.'

Over his shoulder, I saw Tanya roll her eyes.

Chapter Nineteen

IT TOOK HOURS. CAL and Tanya disappeared somewhere while a smiling girl called Kelly first lightened my hair all over to get rid of the plum and then washed it. Matt filmed me with a towel wrapped round my head, then he and Russ wandered off as well. There was no sign of Gabriel.

They all came back for a while when the colourist, Selena, did her bit, after she'd been in a huddle with Antonio. And then what felt like days later – I was seriously starving by now, despite being given a little wafer biscuit thing with my coffee (nobody seemed to remember what Sally-Ann had also said about caffeine and I wasn't about to remind them) and some grapes – they all regrouped around me once more when Antonio appeared in a flourish of scissors.

As he furiously snipped, Tanya sat on a stool with a clipboard, writing things down and occasionally calling Cal over to look at whatever she'd written. She looked thoroughly bored. Cal seemed as smiling and energised as he had all day.

'You OK?'

He touched my shoulder as Antonio swung my chair round and began chopping away at my fringe. I pulled a face that was supposed to convey the impression I was having the time of my life even if I had no idea what this crazed Mediterranean was doing to me, and Cal laughed.

I now had my back to the mirror so I really did have no idea what Antonio was doing but there seemed to be an awful lot of hair on the floor. God knows what colour it was supposed to be – it just looked wet and brown, though Selena had said she was using four different highlights.

I tried an experimental smile on Tanya. She bent her mouth

into a small grimace in return and went back to her notes. After a while she threw the clipboard on the floor turned her back on everyone and made a very long phone call. I heard her mention "Len" a couple of times, who I remembered was the lighting bloke with the pony tail from *Cook Around the Clock* and – presumably – her boyfriend.

'Hey, Laura, mind if we blindfold you for the last bit?'

'What?' I looked stupidly at Cal, who was smiling down at me.

'We probably won't use it but it might be fun – you know they way they do it in the DIY programmes? We'll unveil the new you and you can scream in joy as you see yourself in the mirror.'

'Or cry,' put in Russ laconically.

There was a bit of general laughter as a scarf was put around my eyes. I hoped it wasn't at whatever had happened to my hair, which was now being dried.

I suddenly wondered guiltily how Stanley was. He must be back at Charlotte's by this time – she'd been going to collect him from the bus stop after she'd got Joe. Charlotte would look after him, I knew, but I hoped he was cheerful and had had a better day at school. I couldn't help feeling that whatever Charlotte said about him growing up and the problems of settling into a new school, really all his anxiety was down to Daniel and I splitting up.

He'd always been a bit of an introvert but it was since Daniel moved out that he'd stopped laughing altogether and started sighing like a little old man. Bloody Daniel …

My hair was being sprayed with something and combed out and I heard the clunk of hair straighteners. That bit went on for some time.

'OK under there?' Cal's voice was close by. 'Round here, Matt. Russ can you …? Thanks. You're looking good, Laura.'

Fingers were twirling and patting – involuntarily I put a hand up to the back of my head. It was firmly removed but not before I'd noticed that there didn't seem to be anything there. How short was my hair?

'OK, shall we take the scarf off?'

'Hang on,' I heard Matt say. 'I need to ...' There was the sound of equipment being moved about.

Leanne seemed to have returned. I felt her pass a big soft brush over my face. 'I'm just going to touch up your lips – can you open your mouth a little?'

Cal's voice was telling Antonio where to stand. 'If you can be the one to undo it –'

I opened my eyes into Antonio's brooding ones. 'You like?' He swung my chair round to face the mirror.

Blimey! I stared at a me I'd never seen before. My hair was shorter, for sure, but there was still quite a lot of it and it was the most amazing shape, with short, spiky bits against long, feathery fronds. It was several shades lighter than before – a sort of dark honey colour with very fine blonde streaks and a single red splash on one side. Even I could see it was a work of art.

But the most amazing thing was what it had done to my face. It looked more heart-shaped – almost elfin. Even though Leanne hadn't done anything further to my eyes, they looked bigger and more luminous, my skin creamier than before. I stared into the mirror, speechless.

I looked sophisticated, expensive, stylish. I looked like someone else.

'You like?' said Antonio again, sounding peeved.

'Oh yes, I love it. Thank you,' I gushed.

He preened and smiled for the first time. 'I am the best,' he said.

'You look fantastic,' said Cal. 'Really great. Can you just smile into the mirror for a couple more minutes? Make sure Matt's got all we need?'

I grinned at myself. No problem. I couldn't wait to show Charlotte. There was no doubt I looked younger. In fact, I couldn't wait to open the door to Daniel on Sunday morning. I'd been dreading facing the slimeball after last time, when he'd dropped his little bombshell about remarrying, but now I loved the idea of him seeing me like this. I could just imagine his double take.

We spent the next ten minutes getting various extra shots –

me nodding and smiling at Antonio, him nodding at me, me looking as though I were listening intently while Antonio explained how to dry my hair and then spike it up with a pot of putty stuff that smelled of apples, and me gazing at myself in the mirror and lovingly twiddling those spikes. I felt fantastic – I felt like a star.

Russ nodded approvingly as he started packing away his mikes. 'It's cool,' he said.

Even Tanya smiled and nodded – she was really quite pretty when she stopped scowling – and then she yawned. 'OK, we're done for today then?'

I looked at my watch. It was nearly seven o clock. My stomach had gone into a cramp from lack of food. Everyone else looked quite relaxed – perhaps they'd all gone off stuffing lunch while I was having my hair done. Though by the look of Tanya she ate about as much as Daniel's Twiglet did. She was at this moment opening a can of Diet Coke. 'Want one?' she said.

'Er - no thanks.' I drank the last of my cold coffee, hoping it would settle my internal rumblings. *Wouldn't mind a proper bloody drink though, and double fish and chips to go with it.*

'Oh, I'm sorry Laura.' Cal seemed to read my mind. 'You must be starving. This all took longer than I thought and I totally forgot – Gabriel was supposed to go out for some sandwiches but he wasn't feeling well and I sent him home. I'm so sorry.'

I smiled. 'No problem – I'm fine,' I assured him, hoping he hadn't heard the noise my stomach had just made.

'There's a wine bar round the corner,' he was saying. 'We can get some food round there. And I want to get a few shots of you relaxing with a glass in your hand. We'll go as soon as we're packed up. '

I read a text from Charlotte saying everything was fine and whizzed off a reply sending Stanley my love and saying I'd call him before he went to bed, then spent another five minutes gazing lovingly at my hair while Cal stood talking to Russ and Matt, who were putting their stuff away. Leanne had long gone. Tanya sat in one of the chairs, reading a magazine and talking on her mobile.

After a bit, Cal came over. 'Come on.'

The wine bar was literally round the corner. Cal and I walked there with Tanya lagging behind, still talking on the phone. We went down to the basement – dark with wooden floors and candles on the tables. 'What would you like?' said Cal.

'Some sort of dry white wine?' I looked at the blackboard behind the bar. 'Pinot Grigio?'

He smiled one of his delicious smiles. 'What would Sally-Ann say?'

I gave a mock shudder. 'Save me from that.'

He got himself a bottled beer and Tanya a Diet Coke and carried them over to a table in the corner. 'You OK here for a few minutes? I've just got to speak to the manager – remind him what we're doing.'

I looked at my phone – there was no signal down here, and I'd have to go back up to the pavement to phone Stanley. Presumably that was why Tanya was still outside. Matt and Russ appeared with their gear and spent a lot of time setting it up around the table. Just as we appeared ready to start, Matt shook his head. 'We're going to need a couple of blondes in here.'

Cal nodded. And then laughed at my raised eyebrows. 'Extra lights,' he said. 'Want another glass of wine?'

I wanted food, really – I'd already had a surreptitious look at the menu on the table and was gearing up for the homemade burger with chunky chips or the chicken fajitas with guacamole and sour cream. I could probably have happily devoured both. But I nodded. Might as well have another drink while I was waiting. Perhaps I'd better have a glass of water too …

Tanya came in and sat opposite me with her Diet Coke. A few more people had come downstairs. I saw them looking curiously at the camera. After what seemed like ages, by which time the second glass had definitely gone to my head and Tanya hadn't said more than two words to me, the chaps all came back and set up the new lights.

At last everyone was in position and Cal sat one side of me

while Russ perched the other holding a furry black microphone.

'How did you feel about being 40, Laura?'

'It was a bit of a shock, really.'

'Great. Could you say that again?'

'It was a bit of a shock, really.'

'Again?'

Really – it was a bit of a shock.'

I shared my amazement and disbelief several more times and did endless nodding, smiling, listening, and being shocked all over again, until I felt like one of those nodding dogs in the backs of cars and my brain was swimming. Someone had brought me another glass of wine but if I didn't get some food soon I was going to have to gnaw the table leg.

A small knot of young people had gathered behind the table and were listening – clearly wondering who I was and if they should recognise me.

'Is she famous then?' a girl of about 18 asked suspiciously, as Russ and Matt began to pack up.

'She will be soon,' said Cal, giving her one of his smiles. The girl gazed at him longingly.

At last, Russ and Matt were gone and it was just the three of us. Finally, Cal picked up the menus. My stomach felt as though it had given up on me and started gnawing itself.

Tanya yawned. 'I'm a bit past the point now. I'll just have another Coke.'

I stared at her in disbelief and Cal turned to me apologetically. 'I'm not really that hungry myself just yet, but hey, Laura, we'll get you something – what would you like?' My heart sank.

'Oh well, if you two aren't …'

'No, I'll have a salad,' said Cal kindly, obviously seeing the desperation on my face. 'Keep you company.'

I looked at these two thin, stylish young people and felt like a block of lard. 'That'll be fine for me too,' I said, hoping the disappointment didn't show.

'You've got to be starting your diet anyway, haven't you?' put in Tanya.

I felt my eyebrows rise. Cheeky cow – was she saying I was fat? I looked from her to Cal but he was looking at the menu.

'Goats' cheese and walnut?' he asked. 'That sounds good, doesn't it?'

'Fine,' I said, not liking to admit that I hated walnuts and wasn't over-struck on goats' cheese either. 'Unless they've got tuna?' I said, adding ironically, 'I'm not supposed to have dairy.'

'I think goats' cheese is all right, actually,' said Cal seriously. He looked at the menu again. 'No, sorry, no tuna.'

'OK, cheese it is then,' I said brightly, trusting it would come with a huge crusty roll I could get down my throat before I fell over.

'No carbs is the best way to shed pounds quickly,' continued Tanya, 'so that's perfect. Just keep eating protein and salad and it will fall off.'

It was the longest sentence she'd managed all day. I stared at her, speechless at her rudeness. What was it with these skeletal types that they thought they could get off on advising everyone else on their nutrition? I looked at Cal again – he was frowning at her.

'Tanya's not meaning to be rude,' he said hastily. 'You're fabulous as you are – you don't need to lose weight. It's just that, actually -' he fingered the bottle of beer in front of him as if feeling awkward '- we wondered whether you would give Sally-Ann's regime a try?' He looked at me appealingly. 'You don't have to go the whole hog.'

'No pun intended,' chipped in Tanya, grinning.

Cal shot her another look. 'I meant – if you could just cut out some of those foods she mentioned from your diet? Eat other things?'

I laughed sourly. 'There isn't much left.' The wine had really got to me now – my lips had that funny tingling feeling.

Cal laughed too. 'Just do your best. You know we've organised you a gym membership and we thought we could do some filming there. There's no need to kill yourself, but I thought if you don't mind having a go at the health and fitness angle ... It's all part of the inner beauty thing – that being fab at 40 is about being well and taking care of yourself.'

I was saved answering by the arrival of the waitress. The salad was tiny – an artfully arranged little stack of leaves and cheese lumps drizzled with balsamic vinegar, which I could have devoured in one mouthful. The only thing there in any quantity was the loathsome walnuts. I made a pile of them at the side of the plate. 'I've got a nut allergy,' I informed Tanya untruthfully.

'Really?' she said, bored. I chewed on my final leaf and looked at my watch. It was 9.30. I still hadn't phoned Stanley. As I hit the air on the pavement upstairs I realised I was really quite drunk and seriously needed either chips or a lie down.

'You sound like you're having a good time,' said Charlotte dryly, after telling me that Stanley was already asleep.

'Give him my love in the morning?' I slurred guiltily. 'It all went on a bit.'

I got a glass of water as soon as I was back inside and drank it straight down. Cal was telling me about next time. I tried to focus.

'So we'll be coming down to you next. We'll cover the gym and maybe get some local shots. We'll want to film the assessment and them giving you your programme. And maybe you starting to exercise. Then we've got some other appointments lined up – we've tried to keep it in your area so you don't have to come to London too much but I will probably need you to …'

He really did have the most amazing eyelashes for a bloke and a lovely face. The way he talked was a disarming mixture of boyishness and assured macho confidence, I thought idly, noting the enthusiasm that lit his eyes, the way his hands moved when he talked.

He could be a male model, really. I could imagine him posing in a pair of Calvin Klein's, hair forward across his eyes as he gazed moodily into the camera, muscles lightly oiled …

Tanya suddenly yawned loudly, bringing me back with a jolt. 'Is that OK?' Cal was saying.

'Oh yes, fine,' I mumbled, looking at my watch, startled to see it was already 10.30 p.m. – where had that last hour gone?

'I'd better get to the station,' I said.

Tanya nodded vigorously. 'Or you'll be stuck here all night,' she said. She yawned again. 'I want to go home too,' she said to Cal.

He looked at me. 'You haven't missed the train, have you?' he asked concerned.

'No.' I felt as though I might fall asleep any minute myself. 'The last one is at midnight, I think.'

'Perhaps I should have organised a car.'

'No really – the train's fine. They sent me a return ticket.' *And I can get something to eat at the station ...*

'I'll come with you to get a cab.'

We gathered our coats and left. It was cold outside. As the three of us walked up to the corner of Sloane Square, I wished I could just close my eyes and be instantly transported back to my bed at home. Instead, I'd have to sit on a train for the best part of two hours with all the old drunks – not a prospect I relished, even if I was one of them.

Cal had managed to conjure up a cab already. 'Victoria station,' he said to the driver. 'Have you got cash?' he said to me. 'Keep all your receipts.'

I nodded, just wanting to slump in the back of the cab. But he had his hand on my arm. 'I'll be in touch,' he said. 'Let you know when we're coming down.' He opened the door and kissed me on both cheeks. 'You've been terrific today – absolutely fantastic.'

'Bye,' said Tanya. She looked as exhausted as I felt, her eyes huge and black in her white face.

Cal waved as the cab moved off. 'I'll call you.'

It was almost 1 a.m. when I was woken up in Ramsgate. I remembered cramming the huge egg and bacon baguette I'd managed to grab before throwing myself on to the 23.07, but the rest of the journey was a blank. I must have fallen asleep almost immediately.

Now, damn it, I had missed my station and by the amused looks I was getting from the grinning bloke opposite had probably spent the journey dribbling or snoring or both. I gave a small start as I saw myself reflected in the dark window of the train – it wasn't just the smudged eye-make-up, it was the alien hair. I'd totally forgotten I now looked like that.

I stumbled up the steps at the station, praying there'd be some taxis on the rank. The one I got smelled of beer but at least it got me home. It was after two by the time I'd wandered about the house in a daze, drunk two pints of water, got my clothes off, and was staring at myself in the bathroom mirror. Not only had the eye make-up spread itself but my whole face had that blowsy, saggy, been-on-the tiles look. Only my hair was holding up.

Could I be arsed to take my make-up off ? Usually in this state, no. But remembering that I was supposed to be being fab at 40, and recalling the state of my face in the mornings when I didn't, I reluctantly pulled my forever-young foaming exfoliating cleanser toward me.

As I finally clambered into bed at 2.40 a.m., putting my mobile on the table beside me, I noticed the text from Charlotte. *Hope u great time. Forgot say got go bloody work after all. Will drop S off on way at 8 get coffee on xx*

I set my alarm for 7.30 a.m. and collapsed into the pillows. I dreamt about Cal.

Chapter Twenty

BEEB DE BEEP DE beep ... Ugh. Yuck. Go away. Shut up!

I groped around for the snooze button for the second time, groaning as the clock showed it was 7.40 a.m. and Charlotte would be arriving with Stanley in 20 minutes.

Despite being so tired when I'd got into bed, I'd woken at 4.30 a.m. and 5.30 a.m., mainly to sit up and look at my hair in the dressing table mirror or stare at the ceiling unbelievingly as I relived my day as TV star. It felt exciting when I looked back on it but deeply unreal.

I'd finally relaxed and got warm and snuggly and ready to sleep for ever at about 6.30 a.m. and had one glorious hour of deepest slumber until I'd been rudely awakened. I dragged myself from under the duvet and staggered toward the bathroom.

I cleaned my teeth and spent ten minutes re-spiking my hair with the putty stuff, until it was pretty much as good as when Antonio had done it.

'*Tra-la*!' I said, opening the door in my dressing gown and giving Charlotte a twirl. 'What do you think?'

'Very nice, love,' said Charlotte.

Stanley's eyes widened. 'Oh – my – God,' he intoned flatly. I kissed him.

'Don't tell me you're embarrassed by having a thoroughly cool and funky mother,' I said triumphantly.

Charlotte nudged him. 'Make her wear a balaclava when she picks you up from school.

'I'd have left Stanley in bed snoring away like the others and you could have got him later,' she said to me. 'But he said he needed to come back to do something with you. Though you look like you should have stayed in bed yourself,' she finished, looking me up and down.

'No, that's fine,' I said, yawning, and remembering that I'd promised Stanley we'd go to see a film or something to make up for my disappearing act. 'We'll have a nice long day together now.'

'He hasn't had any breakfast,' Charlotte informed me. 'I did offer but he said it was too early.'

'That's OK. I'll get him some in a minute. Go and put your stuff upstairs, darling. I'll make you a coffee,' I said, turning back to Charlotte as Stanley trudged off with his rucksack.

'A quick one, then.'

'Are you OK?' I said to her as I poured water into the cafetière. 'You seem a bit distracted.'

'I'll tell you later. Blimey, that looks strong.'

'I'm going to need it to be to stay awake.'

'Good time?'

'It was fantastic. First we went to see this mad American woman ...'

I began to prattle away but I soon got the feeling Charlotte wasn't really listening. 'Is everything all right?' I asked her eventually.

She looked at her fingernails. 'I don't know,' she said thoughtfully.

I felt a frisson of alarm. 'What's wrong with you?'

She looked up and met my eyes. 'Nothing's wrong with me. But I'm rather wondering what Roger's up to.'

'What do you mean?' My stomach was now fluttering anxiously in a way that had nothing to do with my hangover. Was she looking at me particularly hard? 'What's he done?'

'He's just behaving oddly.' Charlotte frowned. 'Becky was waiting for him to take her round to Lauren's for the night and his phone was on the kitchen table and a text came in. Becky picked it up – and when he came into the kitchen and she said, "You've got a text, Dad," he went mad. Grabbed it from her and really told her off – said she should leave people's things alone, that you didn't go reading other people's messages. He was really over the top.'

'Well,' I said carefully, feeling sure the alarm was now showing on my face, 'I suppose that's fair enough. I mean, I get cross when Stanley plays about with my phone – especially when he starts changing the ring tone. Last week, he …'

'I know all that,' interrupted Charlotte impatiently. 'We've brought the kids up to respect each other's things and not read diaries or letters etc. Of course we have – but this was different. She's often told one of us a text is there – she reads mine out to me sometimes. Why shouldn't she? I haven't got anything to hide.' She was still looking at me. 'Have you noticed anything different about him?'

I couldn't hold her gaze. I turned away and pressed down the plunger on the cafetière. 'No, not at all,' I said, feeling dreadful. 'But then I haven't really seen him recently, have I?'

'You were talking to him the other night.'

'Well, yes, but only about ordinary stuff – he seemed just the same to me. Who was the text from, after all that, anyway?'

'Someone from work, he said. About an early meeting on Monday.'

'Well there you are,' I said. 'Perhaps he was just a bit tired and irritable. Friday night, you know.'

'Maybe,' said Charlotte. She picked up her handbag. 'I'd better be going.'

I held out the mug of coffee I'd just poured. 'Aren't you going to have this?'

'Better not. I've got a viewing at nine and I've got to go into the office first.' She took it from me anyway and had a mouthful.

I filled another mug for myself. 'Did you ask Roger why he was like that?'

'Of course. He just got grumpy and said he was sick of the kids always in his things.'

'Well then. I'm sure everything's OK.'

She shook her head. 'But they're not always in his things. And if they are, he's never minded before. And you know something else? He keeps taking Benson out!'

I raised my eyebrows as if I didn't understand.

'Come off it,' said Charlotte irritably. 'You know as well as

173

I do that's not normal. I'm the only one in this house who ever takes that dog anywhere. I have to line them all up against the wall and threaten no food/TV/PlayStation/sex for a week before any of my family will shift their arses to give Benson any exercise.' She snorted. 'But now, suddenly, Roger the Dodger is born again! Lovely long walks along the beach they have, apparently. And the dog does actually come back with sand on him so he's not spending the whole time in the pub.'

'Is he trying to get fit, perhaps?' I asked her lamely.

Charlotte scowled. 'You tell me!'

I didn't get much sleep that night either. Partly because I'd already had two hours by dozing off in the cinema and missing the whole of *Electric War Dog Part Two*. (Fortunately Stanley was so engrossed he didn't notice, and by telling him repeatedly how brilliant I thought it was, I'd managed so far to avoid having to discuss the plot.) And partly because I'd eaten so much stuffed crust pizza (the new regime would begin on Monday) that my stomach was in spasm.

But mostly because my conversation with Charlotte was going round and round in my head. Should I send Roger a text to warn him yet again to stop seeing Hannah?

I hoped he wasn't stupid enough to be meeting her on these long walks on the beach – if so, he'd soon be caught out in a place like Broadstairs, where you only had to stop and discuss the weather with a member of the opposite sex for someone to pop up behind the nearest lamppost and speculate on the state of your marriage – but was simply continuing his counselling by phone (not that that wasn't bad enough, if his wife didn't know about it).

But, dear God, suppose I texted him and Becky picked that up too? And actually read it this time. Or Charlotte did. She'd be furious if she found out I knew something and hadn't told her. I'd have to wait till he was at work on Monday. Then tell him Charlotte was on to him. Though surely he must realise that already if she'd quizzed him about the text business.

Did he have a death wish? Or was he so besotted with this Hannah that he was losing the plot? It would be so much better if I could get to Hannah herself. Tell her in no uncertain terms to sling her hook.

By the time it got to 1 a.m. and my stomach was still protesting and I'd moved on to worrying about the alarmingly long list of work I had to do for Mike over the weekend, having had the whole of Friday away from my desk, I decided to get back up, drink some soothing herbal tea and see if any inspiration might come to me on the gnome front. I still had brochure copy to finish and a set of scintillating ads to produce.

I sat at my computer wrapped in several jumpers and tried to concentrate. But for every sentence I produced on the jaunty angle of a gnome's hat or the quirky irony of his fishing-rod prowess, I spent 10 minutes thinking dreamily of the next filming session with Cal and another 20 fretting over what I was going to do about Roger before his marriage to Charlotte fell apart.

When I was yawning at ten-second intervals and had got seriously cold despite the layers, I decided to give up. It was almost 4 a.m., and I was desperate for sleep. I'd have three or four hours, I thought as I clambered back beneath the duvet, and then start on the gnomes afresh. I'd better do some housework sometime too, and then there was shopping …

I woke with a start to the sound of the doorbell ringing. Confused, I rolled over and looked at the clock – bloody hell, it was 10.05!

Stanley was standing in the doorway in his pyjamas, hair on end. 'I think that's Dad,' he said rubbing his eyes.

I sat up. 'Well, go and open the door. Why didn't you set your alarm?'

'Because I thought you'd wake me – why didn't you set yours?'

'I didn't think I needed to – I always wake up earlier than this!'

The door bell rang again. 'Go and get dressed!' I yelled. I pulled on my dressing gown, stumbled downstairs, and pulled open the front door. Daniel was there, looking irritable.

'Sorry – we overslept,' I said unnecessarily.

'I can see that,' he replied. 'What on earth have you done to yourself?'

I peered in the hall mirror. My hair was standing up on one side, flattened on the other where two days' build-up of hair wax had left it matted in clumps. My eyes were puffy, my face crumpled by the pillow – there was actually a crease right across one eyebrow. I looked horrendous.

'Did you have a lot to drink last night?' he asked disapprovingly, as if a drop of alcohol had never crossed his lips and it was another person entirely who, on his 32nd birthday, had stumbled out of the taxi and been sick in a hedge.

'No, I didn't,' I said, hoping the empty bottle of Macon wasn't visible through the open kitchen door. 'Not that it's anything to do with you.'

'It is when you're taking care of my son,' he said sanctimoniously.

I looked at him with a rush of real dislike. To think I'd been married to this tosser!

'One,' I said, in a low voice so that Stanley wouldn't hear and become even more traumatised, 'he is *our* son. Two, if you had kept your dick in your trousers you'd be looking after him as well, and three,' I finished sweetly, 'whenever did you become such a pompous git?'

Daniel's eyes narrowed but as he opened his mouth to reply we both heard Stanley's feet coming down the stairs.

'Hello, mate,' called Daniel heartily.

'Daddy's here,' I trilled joyfully. 'Are you ready?'

Stanley had on his jeans that were too long and a sweatshirt that was too big. He hadn't combed his hair. He looked at me and frowned.

'Just got to put my trainers on,' he said, going to the cupboard under the stairs. I beamed at Daniel, who was clearly frustrated he'd been prevented from making some peevish reply.

'We'll be back about six,' my husband said heavily when Stanley had shuffled back along the hall.

'Have a lovely day!' I said gaily. 'Love you!'

Stanley frowned again but let me hug him. 'Love you, too,'

he mumbled.

'Bye, bye!' I stood waving madly on the step, seeing Stanley anxiously scanning the street in case any of the neighbours' kids had spied me in my night clothes, until the car had driven away. Then I went into the kitchen and gave Boris an update on the situation. 'That man is a wanker,' I said.

Boris moved aside so I could appreciate the decapitated mouse he'd brought me. He wound himself round my legs and gave one of his special meows that only I could understand. It meant he was agreeing with me. 'A total tosser,' it said.

I looked at my to-do list with something close to despair. After a concerted session of moaning to the cat while eating therapeutic slices of toast and Marmite – this was medicinal – a shower, and an hour trying to make my hair look like it had in the shop – once washed it just looked rather short and rather uneven and no amount of hair gel or wielding the straighteners seemed to change that – it had turned into afternoon and I hadn't even got started on the jobs I'd intended to finish by six.

I looked at the paper in front of me and tried to prioritise.

1) Write copy for gnome ad for Sunday mags. *Urgent* – Mike wants Monday morning.

2) Finish brochure for sodding, boring water coolers – ditto.

3) Look at treatment and proposed script for corporate video for dull, tedious company that Mike wants feedback on.

4) Iron at least one school shirt.

5) Go to supermarket (nothing in house for dinner, let alone nourishing roast with three veg would make if were proper mother, and almost out of cat food too)

6) Get petrol (been on red for two days).

7) Hoover.

8) Contemplate washing basket.

I decided to tackle the list in reverse order of how much brain activity it required, thinking I would start with the mundane and build up to the gnomes and water-coolers once I was fully awake. I collected various garments from Stanley's bedroom floor and carried an armful of washing downstairs wondering how Fab-at-40 Cal would think I was if he could see me now, and, remembering that the next filming session was in the gym, how many days of only hot water and spinach leaves it would take to make my stomach look flat.

Stanley's school jumper had blue paint on it; his trousers were adorned with several lumps of playing field. I noticed his tie wasn't anywhere to be seen and, predicting the usual crisis at 7 a.m., I loaded up the washing machine and went in search of his blazer to see if it was stuffed into a pocket.

I eventually located the blazer screwed up into a small ball inside his school rucksack together with some dog-eared exercise books, an assortment of sweet wrappers and a half-eaten apple. Clearing out the débris I also came across, in various stages of disintegration, an interesting array of letters home that I should clearly have been reading since the beginning of term.

There was one enquiring whether I'd like to join the PTA or stand as a governor (not terribly); another urging me to support the Wine and Wisdom Evening (no problem with one half of it, but sadly lacking in the other); a third informing me of the system of getting appointments for parents' evening (a bit late, now I'd already found my own method of barging in and then bursting into tears), and a stern missive from the headmaster explaining the importance of the school fund which I was evidently meant to be contributing to.

I gathered them into a pile to leave accusingly in Stanley's place at the kitchen table and had a shufty round the outside pockets in case any more treasures lurked. One stiffened rugby sock later, I found a creased white envelope with my name written on the front. It was from Andrew Lazlett.

A brief, friendly, handwritten note told me that he'd had a word with Stanley and they both thought it would be a good idea if Stanley started going to Homework Club which ran from four to five each day and that perhaps if I were picking Stanley up one evening, he, Andrew, could have a quick chat with me to "catch up". Stanley knew all about this and would be talking to me about it.

It was dated over a week earlier – Stanley hadn't said a

word.

'I forgot,' he said blithely, when he returned to find me in a post-housework slump, washing and ironing done, chicken in the oven, car full of petrol but the brochure copy still in its infancy.

'They have a tendency to forget,' said Andrew Lazlett when he returned my phone call the following morning in his break.

'I'd almost forgotten myself,' I admitted, as I joined him that afternoon for the low-down on Stanley's prowess on the homework front.

I'd been deeply immersed in brochure copy all day, fending off Mike's increasingly hysterical phone calls, and it was only when Stanley failed to materialise at 4.30 that I remembered he was staying on at school till 5 and that I was supposed to be there at 4.45 p.m. to see Andrew first.

I was directed to the library where an assortment of boys were dotted about at tables, heads bent over books. I spotted Stanley at the back, chewing his pen. Andrew Lazlett was seated near the door, jacket over the back of his chair, hands behind his head, legs stretched out in front. He got up when he saw me hovering in the corridor.

'Carry on, you lot. I'll be back in a minute – no throwing things.' He nodded sternly at a small, angelic-looking boy with a shock of red hair. 'Especially you, Lewis.'

Andrew Lazlett put his jacket back on. For a moment Stanley looked up, caught sight of me, and looked hastily down again, apparently deep in concentration. Andrew joined me outside and indicated I should follow him. 'I've simply got to have a cigarette – you won't tell, will you?'

We went through a fire door at the end of the corridor and crossed the car park. 'Not cracked it yet then?' I said, as we slid casually behind the bike sheds. They were surprisingly deserted.

'Only because they've all gone home,' Andrew Lazlett said. 'It's a different story at lunchtime –' he pulled a wry face '– when I come round here barking at the sixth formers to put them out and set a good example.' He pulled a packet of Rothmans from his pocket. 'I'm down to two or three a day.' He patted his middle. 'And still paying for it. Even though I'm hardly eating a thing.'

We both considered his midriff. 'I'm bloody starving,' I volunteered supportively. 'I'm on this new regime where I can't have any carbs after 2 p.m. and only boring ones before that. I can't tell you how much I'm looking forward to an evening of hot water and vegetables. I usually live for the moment when I can fall on the wine and crisps.'

'I know,' he said gloomily. 'I'm off the beer too. Maybe we should start a support group.'

'What? For those prevented from eating a single thing they like?'

'Something like that. Though I've joined the gym in the hope I can exercise the weight off instead of dying of malnutrition.'

'I'm joining one tomorrow,' I said. 'The new one up by Tesco?'

'That's where I went. They had a good offer on – hope it's still on for you.'

'Luckily I'm not having to pay for it. I'm on this exercise and diet régime for a TV documentary I'm doing,' I said, feeling a flush of pride as he looked suitably impressed.

'How glamorous,' he said. 'And how's Stanley?'

'I don't know. I think he's OK. How are you finding him?'

'He seems fine. I suggested Homework Club because I thought it would be good for him socially. Some really nice kids come along – they seem to have a laugh together. They'll be chucking things around the room by now.'

'I meant to see if Connor was in there,' I said. 'He was Stanley's friend at primary school but I think he hangs around with other boys now. That's why I worry about Stanley being left on his own.' I felt a lump in my throat at the thought and dug my nails into my palms. I couldn't start that again.

Andrew looked thoughtful. 'Connor French? From 7C? I think he comes sometimes. I'll find out for you.' He drew deeply on his cigarette and smiled at me.

'Thanks for all your help and interest,' I said, humbly. 'You've been so kind – you're very committed ...'

'I love my job,' he said simply. 'I love being with the kids. It feels like a privilege.' I looked at him – he was utterly serious.

'How lovely,' I said, feeling strangely emotional. 'I don't think I've ever felt like that about any job I've done.' I sighed. 'I've always thought there's something very compelling about people who have a real vocation – to have that certainty that you're doing the right thing with your life. I always feel I've wasted half of mine –'

I stopped abruptly. I'd meant to sound flippant but I suddenly felt like crying again. God, he must think me such a flake. I forced a big grin on to my face. 'You know that feeling that you've had your day and somehow you missed it?'

He was looking at me intently. 'What did you do?'

I kept smiling. 'Got married, brought up a child, had a crap copywriting job.'

'And have you enjoyed that child?'

'Oh yes. Having Stanley is the best thing I've ever done.'

'Then nothing's been wasted. Being a good parent is worth more than any career – I think.'

'How many children did you say you had...?' I asked, feeling awkward now.

'Two stepsons. Been with them since they were quite young.' His cigarette was almost finished. He took another long drag on what was left.

'That's nice,' I said feebly.

'And now you're in television?'

'Oh no, not really. I just got involved in this programme through someone I know, it's only – it's nothing much.' I looked at the ground, embarrassed.

He looked at his watch. 'I'd better get back.'

He stubbed out his cigarette and carefully pushed the end underneath the hedge with the toe of his shoe. Then he smiled. 'Perhaps I'll see you in the gym sometime?'

I nodded. 'God help us.'

'And try not to be anxious about Stanley,' he said, as we headed back toward the school. 'It does take them a while to settle in sometimes, but they get there in the end.' His voice was reassuring. 'If you're worried – just give me a call ...'

Chapter Twenty-one

'JUST GIVE ME A call.' That's what Cal had said too after he'd emailed today's filming schedule. *Any problems – just call.* Much as I liked the idea of hearing his voice, I couldn't quite bring myself to ring up to ask what I could possibly wear in the way of gym clothes that wouldn't spell total humiliation.

Charlotte, who regarded the gym with the same disdain she reserved for teetotallers and anyone on a diet, was no help at all, and Stanley just said, 'Oh my God!' again when I told him I was going to be given a work out.

I'd had a quick peer in the sports shop and not only did everything cost a fortune but it was all in that sort of slinky, shiny black Lycra that was guaranteed to make someone like me look even more of a lard arse.

In the end I'd put on my least clapped-out pair of jogging bottoms, a white T-shirt and my heftiest bra.

'You don't want to go getting joggers' nipple, love,' had been Charlotte's idea of support while she was munching her way through my biscuits that morning and laughing as I sipped at my mango juice with raw carrot.

Now, lying on the floor with a series of little pads and wires attached to me, I began to wish I'd started my starvation regime a lot earlier – like about 1986.

'I am going to carry out a bioelectrical impedance analysis,' Nicola, the scary-looking personal trainer, had announced sternly.

'A BIA,' she added importantly, for the benefit of the camera, 'will pass a small electrical charge through your body and will determine how much of you is fat.' Had I imagined it or had she put a particular emphasis on the last word? 'And how much is water, muscles and lean tissue.'

She herself had no breasts and arms like steel cords. 'To do the calculation, we need to programme in your gender, age, and weight. You haven't got a pacemaker, have you?'

The thought of my fat ratio being read out to the entire film crew plus Cal was making me cringe already.

'Does it hurt?' I asked feebly, wondering if I could get out of it by claiming a low pain threshold and then fainting.

Nicola gave a booming laugh. 'Oh, you won't feel a thing. Well, not until I get you doing crunches anyway.' She cackled sadistically and everyone else laughed too.

I looked up at the circle of grinning faces. Being spread-eagled on the floor with a camera hovering above my stomach, a mike close to my nose, and Cal and Russ guffawing in the doorway wasn't exactly what I'd had in mind when I'd signed up to improve my self-image.

'Right!' said Nicola, flexing her biceps. 'We are looking at 29 per cent body fat. This puts you just inside the acceptable limits but is pushing at the boundaries as far as risk assessment is concerned.'

'Could you analyse that for us?' said Cal. 'What does it mean in layman's terms?'

Nicola looked down at me disapprovingly.

'She doesn't want to get any bigger.'

'You will be amazed,' she said, as the crew lugged their equipment across the floor and Matt and Russ began to set up some additional lighting around one of the treadmills, 'how your body will change shape if you follow this programme. I am going to give you a combination of aerobic and resistance exercises so you are both burning calories and building muscle. This, coupled with good nutrition, will bring about an increase of lean tissue and help you burn fat ...'

There was something about her tone that told me it wasn't going to be as easy as that.

'OK, we'll start you off slowly,' she said, with deceptive sweetness, as she pushed me onto the treadmill. 'Head up, arms loosely by your side, nice heel to toe action. Off you go ...'

Ten minutes later the sweat was starting to drip from my forehead, my lungs felt as though they were about to burst, and my legs were two pieces of soggy bread. I grabbed at the handlebar as I stumbled slightly and almost fell off.

'Don't hold on,' barked Nicola. 'I need you to do this for five more minutes, can you manage that?'

No. I do not think I can.

I was allowed about 30 seconds' respite, during which time I mopped my face and drank half a litre of water before being put on the cross-trainer. This was even worse. It felt OK for about the first minute then my legs got that leaden feeling before beginning to seriously ache.

'I–cannot-do-this,' I gasped. Everyone laughed.

The step machine was like an escalator except that instead of carrying you along effortlessly, it went down while you went up so you had to keep trudging or be deposited back on the floor. It was like being in the worst sort of nightmare from the moment it started moving. One of those where you're desperately trying to get somewhere but your legs won't work.

I clung to the handrails, every muscle from calf to thigh screaming in protest. 'I can't,' I said weakly.

'Bit faster,' said Nicola, unmoved.

The second step machine was even more torturous. This time you had to do all the work yourself – a foot on each plate and step up and down. I couldn't even get the plates off the ground. Nicola switched it down several levels, shaking her head.

'This will burn 500 calories per hour if you do it properly,' she said, as I sunk to the floor whimpering. 'And is very good for toning the legs and glutes.'

'Your bum,' explained Tanya helpfully.

I'd given up all idea of replying. I could hardly breathe. My whole body was pulsating. God only knew what I looked like.

'That's probably almost enough for today,' said Nicola. 'I was going to do some weights but I think she needs to get a bit fitter first,' she explained, talking over the top of me as if I was incapable of speech, which was almost true. 'We'll just do a few little sit ups.'

She led me to a curved frame thing and lay down in it herself, sliding her shoulders under the two bars and then gripping them with her hands. 'And then you simply rock forward and sit up,' she said, doing 20 rapid sit-ups while explaining how this would tighten my abs.

'I suggest you start with three sets of twelve,' she said, still propelling herself up and down at alarming speed. She stopped and sprung to her feet, her breathing perfectly normal, cheeks not even flushed. I could feel my hair in clammy tails against the back of my neck, while a glance at the mirrored wall showed my face was a boiled beetroot. 'Now you try.'

I lay down in the frame as she had and allowed her to push and prod me into position.

'Grip here, that's it, and up!' I attempted to heave myself into a sitting position. Nothing happened. 'Up!' she said again.

I heard Tanya snigger. I pushed myself back, feeling the frame roll slightly and made another supreme effort to propel myself upwards.

'Ouch!'

'That's it,' cried Nicola encouragingly.

'Ouch, ouch, oh, my stomach, this seriously hurts,' I squeaked back.

'Three,' cried Nicola. 'Four, five …'

I collapsed in a heap. 'And if I keep doing this, I'll get a flat stomach?' I panted hopefully, thinking that maybe if I could stand it, the pain might be worth having, for the first time in my life, an abdomen that did not resemble a steak and kidney pudding. I prodded the soft layers – my finger sunk inwards for some inches.

Nicola looked at it too. 'It will strengthen the stomach muscles beneath the layer of fat,' she said briskly. 'But if you want to lose the fat itself, you'll have to eat less.'

While I was digesting this inspiring news, the others discussed some sort of 'power plate induction' – whatever that was - but seeing as I could now barely walk, the general consensus of opinion seemed to be that we could call it a day.

'She should incorporate the power plate into her routine, though,' said Nicola. 'It's very effective at toning the muscles and building up strength. Madonna's got one,' she added, as if this clinched it.

'We'll do that when we come back to film the classes,' said Cal.

Classes?

'You've done really well,' he said, shining one of his smiles on me. 'You go ahead and get in the shower and we'll be down to join you shortly.'

'You're not going to film me in there, are you?' I asked in alarm.

Cal grinned. 'Sadly not. We'll get you coming out though – with that virtuous glow, bursting with vim and endorphins.'

It wasn't exactly as I'd have described myself as I looked in the changing room mirror. My face was still scarlet and my T-shirt clung damply to all my bulges. Beside me a long-legged, toned, 20-something was vigorously towelling her naked body. There wasn't an ounce of fat on her tanned body. I stared at her perfectly flat stomach in awe. How long did it take to look like that?

In fact, the two of us together would be a fitness equipment manufacturer's dream. They could photograph both our stomachs for their before and after pictures. The girl saw me staring and smiled uncertainly.

'I was just thinking how good you looked,' I said, still unable to take my eyes off her perfect proportions. 'Has it taken loads of work and dieting?'

She looked embarrassed. 'I um, I sort of look like this generally,' she said. 'Though I do work out, of course.'

Of course. 'Well, you look fantastic – you really are gorgeous,' I said, giving her a big smile.

She smiled back while edging away from me and I suddenly realised she must think I was either deeply weird or chatting her up. I blushed at the thought of either and busied myself with my towels. 'I, um, didn't mean ...' I mumbled.

'That's cool,' she said, edging away a bit further.

They had the camera set up in the corridor when I came out. 'Can you walk jauntily?' Cal said. 'Put a spring in your step, looking pleased with yourself? That's great. That's fabulous –

keep smiling.'

Tanya muttered something to him. 'OK,' he nodded. 'We'll do it both ways.'

He turned back to me. 'And then, Laura, just come out normally – looking a bit knackered maybe.'

'That won't be difficult,' I quipped. When I'd worn out the corridor carpet alternately skipping and trudging up and down it for the benefit of the camera, Cal finally called a halt. 'We could do lunch here,' he said. 'Then we could film that too.'

We all trooped into the café area. At least they were going to feed me today, I thought, as we sat down at one of the plastic tables. I really wanted a panini with ham and cheese and preferably some crisps on the side – I was absolutely starving after all the exercise – but they were all looking at me, so I ordered the tuna salad from the high protein/low fat section of the menu and had an orange juice.

Matt took some footage of me munching, panning in on the lettuce leaf balanced on my fork until I felt like a celebrity rabbit.

Cal laughed when I said this, so I put two fingers up against my head like ears and twitched my nose. He laughed some more.

Tanya swigged at her Diet Coke and spoke dryly. 'You won't be able to do that by next week.'

Chapter Twenty-two

'IT'S ONLY YOUR FOREHEAD you won't be able to move,' said Cal, 'but if you don't fancy it, you don't have to go ahead.'

We were on our way to see someone they referred to as "Mr Botox" and I was trying to decide if I was excited or scared.

'I know it's another long day but then we'll take a couple of weeks off,' Cal said, twisting round in the passenger seat to look at me, while Tanya drove. 'If you can then follow the programme – I think you look fab as you are but it would be good to show you really glowing and how exercise does work – we can film you again, and by then, if you decide to have it, the Botox will have kicked in and you'll be looking all super-smooth too. Is that OK? Are you happy with all that?'

Cal looked into my eyes in a way I half-wished he wouldn't. He probably did it to everyone but it did funny things to my stomach.

'Yes, that's absolutely fine.' I said weakly, although I still wasn't sure about having all those needles in my face. When he'd turned back to the road ahead, I got a small mirror out of my handbag and had a surreptitious look at my wrinkled bits. On the other hand …

The clinic was in Canterbury – not far from Roger's office, I realised, as the van drew up ahead of us in a back street near the cathedral. As I got out of the car I scanned the road in both directions in case I spotted him wrapped around Hannah.

Now, while the others set up their equipment, I sat in a room studying various before and after posters of sagging, blotchy, vein-riddled faces, miraculously transformed. I wondered what it all cost. A lot, no doubt. I was pretty lucky to be getting a go at it for nothing, I told myself.

'Have you had any of this done?' I asked the receptionist – an oriental, line-free beauty of around 30.

She looked offended. 'Not yet,' she replied with a tight smile.

'Of course,' I said hastily, 'you're much too young.'

'I'm 32,' she said. 'We have many women come at this age.'

I wasn't quite sure what this proved so I lapsed into silence and read a leaflet about laser treatments you could have in your lunch hour, until Tanya put her head round the door and said they wanted me upstairs.

Dr Carling was in his late forties with silver hair and an improbably smooth, tight, shiny forehead. He wore a pin-striped suit and a pink shirt and had, I noticed, extremely white teeth – even whiter than Austin's, the *Cook around the Clock* presenter. I wondered if I could suggest teeth-whitening as one of my treatments. Though perhaps not quite that bright. It did look a little unreal. I found I was keeping my mouth closed a bit more than usual as we said hello and shook hands.

'What we'd like you to do,' Cal said to the doctor, 'is to run through the sort of procedures you could offer Laura to make her look younger. Laura, you ask whatever questions you'd ask – how much it costs, how effective the treatment is, how long it lasts and so on. Try to forget we're here. OK, let's go.'

Dr Carling and I surveyed each other across the table.

'Er, how could you make me look younger?' I said lamely. Behind me I heard Tanya sigh.

'Just carry on.' Cal's voice was reassuring. 'We'll do it again at the end.'

Dr Carling leant back in his chair and had gazed at me.

'It all depends, really,' he said eventually, 'what it is you're most unhappy with and what you are trying to achieve.'

'Well just being older and looking younger, I guess,' I said, cheerily, thinking that perhaps it served the film's purpose to state the bleeding obvious. 'You know – I've got these lines and crow's feet and my neck's not what it was. I keep slapping on the old anti-wrinkle cream but it still seems to be downhill all the way ...'

Dr Carling shook his head. 'Collagen creams? Not worth the money. Collagen can't get through the skin. The only way you can get more collagen is by having it injected and that's where the collagen filler comes in. Fillers *can* make a difference to lines and wrinkles by plumping them up from below. Fillers and Botox are our most popular products.'

I nodded intelligently. 'Which is best?' I asked, pleased with my interviewing technique.

'It's a case of horses for courses,' said Dr Carling importantly. 'We would use fillers for deeper lines – those that are really ingrained.' He looked pointedly at my mouth. 'And Botox to soften fine lines, although you can find even quite deep ones disappearing once you can't make the movements that's caused them.' He handed me a mirror.

'Frown,' he said. I duly scowled.

'You see? Doing that has caused *this*.' He directed a manicured finger at the crease between my eyebrows. 'Botox will immobilise those muscles so you can't do that any more. It will take 10 to 14 days to get the full effect but then that should be entirely smoothed out. Show me what else you'd like corrected.'

I looked back at my reflection. 'Where shall I start?' I laughed self-consciously. 'This is new.'

I showed him the line above my upper lip where I screwed my mouth up when I didn't like something. 'Can Botox sort that too? And look at my eyelids. They never used to be hooded like this. Do you know I found a photo of myself when I was 22 – well, my friend Charlotte found it actually – and my eyes were really wide open. Now I look like Old Mother Hubbard.'

Dr Carling looked quizzically at me, while I wondered where on earth that had come from. What did Mother Hubbard look like anyway – was she the one who had all the children in a boot? Or the old crone whose cupboard was bare? That was probably what had brought her to mind – my fridge was a barren wasteland once more. I really must go shopping ...

'Sorry?' I suddenly realised Dr Carling was talking to me.

His eyes twitched in what I imagined would have been a

frown if his forehead had been able to move. 'Lipstick lines,' he said. 'Some people get very strong lipstick lines but your mouth is quite good. Your lips are still full –'

'Thank you,' I said.

'We could probably usefully employ 15 or 16 units of Botox around the forehead down round the eyes, but I wouldn't recommend it around the lips. You have to be very careful there because it could change the agility of the mouth – and if you were a trumpet player or a singer that wouldn't be too good.' He smiled.

'I'm not either of those things, but I do talk a lot,' I said helpfully.

He nodded. 'But we could pop in a little bit of filler there–' He pointed to the corner of my mouth. 'When you're getting a little bit older, the corners of the mouth turn down slightly.' I looked into the mirror – I'd never noticed it before, but so they did. 'If we inject a little filler here, it will lift it slightly.' He leant across the desk and hitched up the side of my mouth with his finger. 'It's a very subtle effect but it can be quite pleasing.'

'Oh yes,' I cried, gazing into the mirror and seeing how instantly and miraculously it took years off me.

He was still prodding my face. 'A bit of hollowing here can pull the cheeks down a bit, so on some women we plump up here too, but I wouldn't say you need that yet. A little work around the forehead, eyes and mouth, that's all.'

I used my own finger to lift my droopy mouth up again. 'How much does it all cost?' I reeled as he told me. 'Really? And how long will it last?'

'Botox – three to six months maximum. Fillers? Depends on which filler you use, but about a year.'

'God that adds up to –' I did a rapid calculation. 'A lot each year!'

Dr Carling nodded unperturbed. 'And my regular clients are more than happy to pay it.' He leant back and locked his hands behind his head. 'It's all about confidence. Others may not notice what exactly has changed in you, they will only know you're different. But you will know, and it will give you greater self-esteem. And that is the most attractive quality of all.'

He waved a hand at a poster on the wall. 'For some women that's brought about by something dramatic like a facelift or a tummy tuck or breast enhancement. For others, it can be something as simple as a new hairstyle. They haven't been changed physically but they look a million dollars because they are happier.' He gave me a big, flashing smile that displayed every one of his dazzling teeth. 'That is why I recommend that the best thing my clients can do is to find someone to fall in love with them.'

'Easier said than done,' I said brightly.

'Not when we have perfected you.' An evangelical note crept into his voice. He leant forward again. 'You will be amazed. I will make you irresistible ...'

Cal interrupted. 'Can we get you looking fascinated, Laura – really hanging on every word?'

I widened my eyes.

'Does it hurt? I'm a bit of a wimp,' I explained. 'Low pain threshold. I take Nurofen when I have my legs waxed.'

Russ laughed. 'So does Cal!'

Dr Carling frowned. 'A slight pricking, that's all – I use a very fine needle. You may get a bit of local swelling, a mild headache – but nothing that paracetamol won't deal with.'

'What about all those toxins, though?'

He shook his head. 'Botox has actually been used medically for years. There is no evidence to suggest there are any harmful effects at all ...'

I was only half listening as he explained its function in treating excessive sweating and stroke victims.

I was asking the questions about safety because I felt it was expected but, really, I was hooked already. I kept thinking about how different my mouth had looked with the corners pulled up, and imagining my newly smoothed brow. I looked sideways at Cal, hoping there was money in the budget for both.

'Fillers can be used in the backs of hands too,' Dr Carling was saying. 'Hands can be very revealing as we get on in years. We carry out a programme of treatment to get rid of age spots and blemishes and then inject tiny bits of filler all over the back of the hand to plump up the surface – particularly between the fingers. We're looking at introducing a foot lift to our treatment list too, probably early next year. '

'A foot lift?' I laughed. 'Are you kidding? That's a step too far, isn't it?' I giggled again.

Dr Carling shook his head. 'Not for some people, not at all. They're becoming very popular in the States. The feeling there is that that wrinkly toes are a big give-away. Women want their feet plumped just as much as their hands.'

I rolled my eyes. 'Give me strength.'

'OK, cut a minute!' Cal was staring at me. 'I am having this brilliant idea', he said slowly. 'I was thinking this would be a fairly straight piece with you. Just a sort of fly on the wall and extended interview about how you felt about the ageing process. But you're really good – you've got so much screen presence, I'm just thinking how we can be a bit more creative.'

'Oh Lordy,' said Russ. 'Not Cal being creative again.'

Matt chuckled. 'Been here before, haven't we, mate?'

Cal ignored them. 'What we can do is maybe contrast different reactions. We'll film your scepticism – that was great, Laura – and then would you be able to do it again as though you were seriously interested? *A foot lift?*'

He said it as though this was a fascinating medical breakthrough that would save the lives of millions. 'Can you give it a go? I can see us showing both – leaving it up to the viewer to see which Laura they identify with. Can you try?'

His face shining with enthusiasm was infectious. I saw Russ and Matt exchange amused glances while Tanya shook her head. Cal looked at me hopefully. I suddenly felt I had to support him.

'A foot lift – that sounds interesting,' I intoned obligingly.

He shook his head. 'You're sounding a bit insincere.'

I smiled at him kindly. 'Because I am insincere – it's a mad idea. Like therapists for dogs and beauty salons for five-year-olds.'

Cal looked disappointed. 'I know you're not a trained actress or anything – maybe I'll have to get someone in. It's just, you know, you've got this presence – this sort of aura about you – I'd really like to use *you*.' His big, brown eyes were fixed on mine. My stomach gave a strange little flip that I hoped was only indigestion. He put a hand on my arm. 'Would you just try one more time?'

I looked from the glossy brochure Dr Carling had put in front of me, to my seriously unmanicured toes. 'A foot lift?' I said wonderingly, trying to sound as though I'd been offered the key to eternal life. 'Wow! How much does that cost?'

Cal clapped his hands. 'Perfect.'

He signalled to Matt. 'Now let's do it one more time – just for luck.'

Matt moved the camera in closer. Tanya tossed her hair about and yawned.

'A foot lift!' I shrieked in ecstasy.

'A foot lift?' I whispered in awe.

'A foot lift,' I murmured with wonder.

Thirty-six elevated feet later, Cal put his arms around me and kissed me joyfully on both cheeks. 'I knew you could do it – you are going to be a star ...'

Doctor Carling was looking thoroughly fed up. We'd filmed our conversation a dozen times and he was beginning to sound rather robotic. Cal was a man on a mission, wanting to get it absolutely right.

'OK, can we just do that one last time? If you could just run through possible side-effects, and Laura – keep nodding but looking as though nothing is going to put you off. Excellent. And now the opposite?'

I was now well into role. 'Botox? Absolutely not! All those toxins going into my face. Who knows what they'll do long term? I don't want to look like a frozen rabbit!'

Tanya sighed. 'Can we lose the rabbit? What is it with you and bunnies?'

Cal frowned at her and then smiled at me. 'Try it again, babe. Shake your head, look concerned, but just stick to the toxins. Maybe say something about Botox being so unnatural.'

I took a deep breath. He sat opposite, fixed his gaze on me

from beneath his floppy curls and gave a slow smile.

'How about Botox?'

I shook my head. 'No, no, I wouldn't feel comfortable with that at all. All those toxins ... Who knows what damage they can do long term.' I adopted a virtuous expression and looked thoughtfully back at Cal in the manner of a woman who (Judi Dench, eat your heart out) was happy to grow old gracefully. 'I am happy for my face to look lived in,' I said gravely.

'I wouldn't be,' said Tanya sourly when we'd finished. 'But thank God I've got years before I have to even think about it. All these old women with shiny faces freak me out.'

'Shut up, Tan,' said Cal good-naturedly. 'Go and have your PMT somewhere else.'

Tanya glared.

'Sorry,' Cal mouthed at me.

I smiled and hugged myself inside.

He called me babe ...

Chapter Twenty-three

'BOTOX!' SAID CHARLOTTE IN disbelief. 'You said you'd never dream of doing anything like that. I thought you hated the idea of poison in your body.'

'That's before it was free,' I replied. 'The doctor says it's completely safe.'

'Well, he would, wouldn't he?' said Charlotte. 'At that price.'

'And Cal says everybody does it these days,' I went on. 'He said it was completely up to me but I thought about it and I thought why not? It only lasts three months or so anyway. He's very considerate of my feelings,' I finished dreamily.

'Probably wants to shag you,' she said dismissively.

'I should be so lucky.'

Charlotte looked at me with interest. 'So you fancy him now, do you?'

I laughed a bit too loudly. 'No, I'm only joking. I'm old enough to be his mother.'

I looked at myself in her kitchen mirror. There was no doubt I didn't look quite so old now the lines around my mouth had been filled out and while I still had to wait for the full effect of the Botox to take hold, my forehead was already looking smoother as well as feeling strangely stiff.

'Hmm,' said Charlotte.

She was still a bit scratchy. I presumed it was about Roger but I didn't want to ask. He was here now, but I'd had no chance to speak to him alone – in fact, he seemed to be avoiding me. Which made me think he was still seeing this Hannah and listening to her tales of woe.

I was still wishing I could find a way to meet her myself but how on earth would I do that, short of waiting outside the office, where Roger would probably come out with her on the way to their evening sojourn?

I didn't know her other name and I couldn't even be sure I would recognise her again. So how could I ever get to speak to her?

In the end it was much easier than I thought.

'Ugh,' said Charlotte that weekend as she was tidying piles of paper on her kitchen table. She scanned the piece of card in her hand. 'Another of Roger's firm's bloody ghastly social dos. God save us.'

'What's that, then?' I said, casually.

Charlotte looked at the card again. 'Senior partner's retirement drinks. Yuck. Standing around for three hours, drinking mediocre wine, being forced to make polite chit-chat with people I've nothing in common with, while they count how many glasses I've had and exchange looks every time I go for a fag.' She pulled a face. 'And then tell Roger what a *character* I am.'

'Could I come?' I said.

Charlotte looked at me in astonishment. 'Er – why?'

'I don't know. Just fancy it.'

Charlotte gave a disbelieving snort. 'You fancy spending an evening with Jeremy who thinks he's God's gift to women and will try to chat you up, or Gordon who only ever talks about his composting club while his droopy wife – wears white cardigans, say no more – sits there simpering? Or you can be bored to death by Alan the other senior partner – short, fat, bald, halitosis – or *his* wife who's built like a tank and wears very tight satin dresses and too much blue eye shadow?' She reached for her cigarettes.

'Then there's the secretary who always, always drinks too much and ends up in the ladies', sobbing, from which I am usually the one to retrieve her and tell her to buck up, as all the other wives are completely useless and just flap round her making sympathetic noises.' Charlotte shook her head witheringly and lit up.

I wondered if this secretary could be Hannah. 'Well, if I

came, I could do that instead,' I said helpfully.

'But why would you want to?'

'Just sounds amusing. And,' I said, inspiration hitting me at last, 'because Mike wants me to put together a dummy in-house magazine for a big law firm in the city. It's supposed to be something they can take home that will appeal to their families too. You know, a bit of corporate bonding – get the wife on side etc – and I need to know the sort of people I'm dealing with. This party could be really useful.'

Charlotte shrugged. 'Why didn't you say so? Of course you can come. I'll tell Roger when he comes back.

'Will he mind?'

'He'll be thrilled.'

Roger hid his feelings of delight well.

'Really?' he said, when he and Benson got back from their walk. He looked at me dubiously. 'What do you want to do that for?'

'She's got to write an outline for a magazine for some big law firm,' said Charlotte. 'Thinks meeting your lot and all their old trouts will be good research.'

'I can't see how,' said Roger, giving me a look. 'We're only a small provincial set-up.'

'Well, she can come,' said Charlotte decisively. 'It will give me someone decent to talk to at least.'

'Fine,' said Roger, with what was clearly a forced smile. 'Yes, of course you can.'

He sat at the end of the table, ostensibly reading the paper, but I could feel the tension radiating off him. Once I glanced down the table to find him looking up at me, a watchful expression on his face. Was he worried about me meeting Hannah?

Charlotte seemed oblivious, chatting on about the rigours of having to have Roger's mother for Sunday lunch the following day. 'And I can't do pork because crackling plays havoc with her teeth; she still goes on about mad cow disease if I give her beef – bit late for her to worry – and then she says, "Oh it's chicken again – we had this last time, dear."'

She nodded down the table at Roger who was still reading. 'And who goes down the pub the minute she arrives? Comes back just long enough to eat and then disappears in front of the television the moment we've finished? Ugh, Benson!' Charlotte stepped backward as the Labrador shook himself vigorously, sending grains of sand in all directions.

'And now the kids are bigger,' she went on, 'they're as bad. I'm the one trapped here with her. Becky will talk to her for a little while but she soon gets fed up because of the way the old dragon argues about everything ...'

There was a thump overhead. As if on cue, Becky burst into the kitchen.

'Mum, those boys are so annoying. Can you go and tell them to keep out of my bedroom?'

Charlotte rolled her eyes. I stood up.

'I'll go and sort them out. Sorry Becky. I must take Stanley home now anyway – he's got his friend Connor coming to stay.'

I felt Roger's eyes on me as I walked past him to the door.

Chapter Twenty-four

TEN MINUTES AT GRADIENT five, ten minutes at gradient seven, moving up to ten minutes at ...

I hit the stop button. My God, I'd only done five minutes. I clung to the bars of the treadmill, heart pounding.

I'd got up early, determined to really go for my new regime. Namely an hour in the gym every morning, working through my programme, leaving home as soon as Stanley had gone to school. Followed by a protein breakfast of poached eggs and maybe grilled tomatoes (absolutely no toast) and then a hard day's work for Mike, to get well ahead of myself in preparation for the further filming we were doing in two weeks' time.

A time by which my new silhouette would be starting to emerge and the Botox would have worked its full magic. Fuelled by visions of myself leaner, firmer, and looking at least a decade younger, I strode through the doors of the gym at 8.15 a.m. with a resolute heart.

Now I stared hopelessly at the sheet in front of me, feeling the sweat running down behind my ears, my fat bits aquiver.

'Why do we do it, eh?' A small, rotund man in his sixties grinned at me as he walked past. I shook my head in wordless empathy and took another swig from my water bottle.

'He doesn't,' said a voice from behind me. 'All I've ever seen him do is wander about with that towel over his arm.'

I swung round to see a short, stocky girl in her early thirties, brown hair back in a pony tail, wearing a pink T-shirt and tracksuit bottoms, with a pair of headphones slung round her neck. She smiled.

'It's torture, isn't it?' she said. 'I'm absolutely bloody knackered and I've still got another 300 calories to go.' She climbed onto a cross-trainer. 'Christ, I can't tell you how much I hate this ...'

Her name was Clara, and – I found out as I heaved myself onto a machine beside her – she had five weeks left to fit into a bridesmaid dress that was three sizes too small.

'A bloody bridesmaid,' she puffed, arms and legs pumping wildly beside me. 'I'm too old to be trailing down the aisle in cerise silk, not to mention much too fat.'

'You're not fat,' I puffed back, every muscle in my legs already screaming. 'Can't you just get a bigger dress?'

Clara shook her head. 'It was the only one left. It's by some up-and-coming Italian designer, hideously expensive. Vicky got them all as a package. She's got about six of us – a couple of cute three-year-olds, two eight-year-olds, her nineteen-year-old sister – and me!'

She turned to look at me, legs still going up and down. 'Everyone else got the right size but the one they had for me was a size eight. Eight! Haven't been that small since I was about seven. And all Vicky said was, "Well, you'll want to lose weight for the big day anyway, won't you ..."'

She came to a stop, breathing heavily. 'I can't talk at the same time as doing this.'

I stopped too and looked at my card. 'Oh blimey, I'm supposed to do 20 minutes.' I looked back at the dial. 'I've only done six.'

'It's a bit much,' I said, slumping against the screen, waiting for my heart to slow to normal. 'It's her big day, not yours. How can she expect you to drop three dress sizes for her?'

Clara shrugged. 'Everything's got to be totally perfect – she's always been like that. She's really tall and a size eight herself. We look like Little and Large,' she said ruefully. 'I've lost six pounds so far. When I first put the dress on, I couldn't close the zip at all – now I can get it up about an inch. But that's taken me weeks. The more I come to the gym, the more I want to eat!'

I suddenly realised I was starving myself. 'How much longer have you got to go today?' I asked.

I had lemon and ginger tea instead of coffee and one slice of brown toast with Marmite – this was an emergency, I didn't think I could get home without fainting – and Clara had a smoothie and a cereal bar. Everyone on the tables around us seemed to be eating bacon.

'I did read an article,' said Clara glumly, 'saying that research has shown people who go to the gym actually consume a third more calories after each session than they would usually.' She sighed. 'And the smell of cooked breakfast doesn't help. Who's going to have the low-fat fruit and muesli bowl when you can have two fried eggs and a sausage? Look at this,' she said, breaking off the end of her oat and nut bar and glaring at it. 'It's like cardboard. I do want to lose weight obviously but I really can't … Oh hi!' She broke off as an enormous bloke in jogging bottoms and a rugby shirt came into the café area. 'How you doing?'

He stopped by our table, towering over us. He had dark hair and amazing blue eyes. Clara gave him a big smile. 'This is Laura – a new recruit to the torture chamber. Laura, this is Alfie. And hey! You look like you've shifted a few more pounds.'

He grinned. 'Can almost touch my toes now. Still can't see them, mind you.'

'He was a lot bigger before,' said Clara, as Alfie went off, swinging his kit bag. 'He really was absolutely vast. The doctors told him it was getting dangerous and there was talk of him having a gastric band fitted but he's been coming here and he's on this special diet – one of those awful ones where you drink nasty soups all day. He's lost about three stone. He's got another five to go, I think.'

'Bloody hell,' I said. 'I want to shift ten pounds and that seems hard enough.'

'You don't even look like you need to lose that much,' said Clara supportively. She rolled up her sleeves. 'This is what I need to work on.' She grasped her upper arm with the other hand and shook it. 'And this,' she added, patting her midriff. 'Just got to stop drinking wine, keep eating this crap –' she poked the half eaten cereal bar '- and keep coming here. Up for it tomorrow?'

Clara, it turned out, was a radiographer at Margate hospital where she worked shifts. This week, she told me, she was "on lates", so was coming early each morning when she finished work, before going home to bed.

'It's supposed to be easier with a gym buddy,' she said optimistically. 'If we do half an hour on the treadmill, half an hour on the cross-trainer and then some weights and power plate, it will fall off.'

'I haven't had my induction session on the power plate yet,' I said. 'I suppose I could ask …'

'I'll show you tomorrow,' said Clara. 'And bring your iPod.'

I'd have to wrestle it off Stanley first, I thought, as I drove home.

'Music is what you need,' Clara had said. 'Get your son to put on some good dancing stuff – then you just think of the treadmill as five songs. If they're four minutes each, that's twenty minutes gone. And if you get into the beat, it goes in no time.'

But Stanley was surprisingly amenable to spending his evening on the computer with my credit card and the iPod Nano he and Daniel had bought for me the previous Christmas and that he had used almost exclusively since. Especially when I agreed he could download five songs of his own choice too.

'The new iPhone is so cool,' he said longingly, between mouse clicks. 'If I had one of those I could put all my music on it and wouldn't have to use yours. Can I have one for my birthday?'

'We'll have to see,' I said, although I'd already decided he could. I might have come back from the cookery programme with a hamper full of high-class soups and dried truffles instead of hard cash, but the work Mike was piling on me daily would pay for it, and Stanley deserved something lovely.

I'd already told Daniel I'd stump up for the phone if he paid for the contract each month. To my amazement, he'd agreed without argument – obviously realising that a) it was the least he could do and b) it would save him a shopping trip and give him more time to stay home eating tofu and nutritious seed mix with The Twig instead.

'There you are,' said my son proudly, handing me the iPod an hour later. 'I've made you a special playlist called *Gym Songs for Mum*. I've put the songs you wanted on, and some other good ones I think you might like. They might be a bit young for you,' he added doubtfully, 'but they should be all right to jog to.'

'I'm not sure I'm going to be jogging just yet,' I said. 'I'm doing fast walking uphill at the moment. But thank you very much.' I kissed him. 'I'm going to go every morning this week.'

'Right,' he said, looking at me cynically. Then he grinned. 'Bet you don't.'

'Oh yes, I will!'

I dropped the corkscrew into a drawer and shut it, taking another sip of my delightfully fat-free water. If Clara had already lost six pounds and the cheery Alfie a whole three stone, then what was stopping me doing it too …

I didn't feel quite as enthusiastic as I dragged myself from bed the next morning, and I was positively exhausted after Clara not only put us through our paces on treadmill and cross-trainer but insisted we did five minutes on the more punishing of the two step machines.

'Sadist,' I gasped as I tottered across the floor to the water fountain.

'Power plate now!' she said, undeterred. 'You'll love this.'

It was a strange-looking machine shaped like old-fashioned weighing scales with a vibrating platform that you stood on to perform various squats and stretches.

'The idea is,' said Clara, as if reciting from the brochure, 'that the vibrations cause your muscles to contract zillions of times a minute and that tones them up. They say ten minutes on here is worth an hour of ordinary press-ups and stuff. Here – try.'

She pressed the start button on mine and leapt onto the

machine next to me. 'Like this,' she said, thrusting her backside outwards like a pregnant duck and bending her knees. 'Feel the vibrations?' I nodded mutely as I juddered from head to foot. 'Hold that for a minute and you'll be toning your buttocks and inner thighs. Or–' she said wickedly, when we'd come to a merciful halt '- you can forget all that and just sit on it. It's a step up from the washing machine.'

I buckled gratefully at my weak knees, plonked myself down on the plate, and pressed the repeat button. 'Mmm – it's got definite possibilities …'

We collapsed in giggles.

'Hey, you're not supposed to be enjoying yourselves.' Alfie loomed over us, a towel around his shoulders. 'I daren't get on that – not sure it would take my weight.'

I looked at him as he chatted. He was quite good-looking under all the extra flesh. He had a nice face and those lovely bright blue eyes.

'He's doing ever so well,' said Clara, as he headed off to other machines. 'He's here every morning without fail.'

And so would I be. I did two more mornings with Clara till her shifts changed and then made myself go alone. She was right about the music. Listening to The Proclaimers declare that they would walk 500 miles, I could stride along quite happily myself on the treadmill, while a spot of Take That was brilliant on the cross-trainer.

I had Stanley put some more Madonna on the iPod for me too, and a selection of my favourite Oasis songs. 'It makes all the difference,' I told him. 'Do you think I'm looking thinner yet?'

Stanley screwed up his nose. 'I can't really tell,' he said, 'but I told them at school you let me use your credit card and they thought it was cool.'

'Oh good.'

'I've told them you're going to be on TV too.'

'Really – what did they say?'

'They thought that was cool too. Danny said did that mean we were really rich? I said no, we weren't, but that I thought I might get the new iPhone for my birthday.' He looked at me hopefully.

'No promises,' I said. 'They're a lot of money.'

'Not if you go on a contract – then the phone isn't so much or it's even free sometimes.'

'Nothing is free – if you don't pay for the phone, you have to pay loads for the contract and you wouldn't use the minutes, so it would be a waste.'

'I could phone you and phone Connor and I could have all my music on it and it's got really cool apps.' Stanley looked more animated than I'd seen him for a long time.

'We'll see. So is everything OK at school now – better than it was?'

'It's OK.'

'Shall we have Connor round again soon?'

'OK.' Stanley suddenly remembered. 'And Mr Lazlett asked how you were and if you were going to the gym. He went this morning before school.'

'Oh – I didn't see him.'

'He says he's got to get thin too, or his wife will be cross with him.'

There was no danger of me being cross – well, not visibly anyway. The Botox had taken a grip and I could no longer frown or raise my eyebrows. It felt very odd at first and there was something different about my expression – I was somehow wider-eyed and my eyebrows were higher, which was strange.

But for the first time, I could understand people who had shedloads of money spending it on their faces. The fillers worked too. The corners of my mouth had plumped out and the tram lines coming down from either side of my nose were now hardly visible. I was beginning to wonder what I'd look like with an eye lift. And my wrinkly knees – shame I couldn't do something for them.

Really, I needed to win the lottery or marry somebody hugely rich, so I could be one of those ladies who lunch, and spend my days having treatments, and seeing my personal trainer. There was one at the gym called Marco, Eastern

European with dark eyes and a moody expression. Clara spent a considerable amount of time watching his bum as he stalked about the floor, and bemoaning the fact that she couldn't afford a one-to one with him.

'He's supposed to be a complete slave driver,' she said dreamily.

'You're a complete slave driver,' I grumbled back. 'Can we stop now?'

'Two more of these.' Clara sat on the power plate with her knees tucked up toward her chest, wobbling precariously, an agonised expression on her face. 'Hit start,' she gasped.

'Is it working? I enquired when her minute was over and she was rolling on the floor, clutching her abdomen.

'It had better be.' Clara prodded herself in the stomach. I think it's all a bit firmer than it was.'

'I think mine is too,' I said, poking myself. 'But I don't seem to be that much smaller – I want to lose weight as well as firming up.'

'Not too much, though,' said Clara. 'Look at her!'

She nodded over to where an incredibly skinny woman was running on the treadmill, ear phones clamped to her ears, weights on her wrists.

'She does it for hours,' whispered Clara, 'until she's pouring sweat and seems about to pass out. It can't be good for her. And she doesn't even look nice.'

We both stared at her. Her arms and legs were like sticks and she had a minute bottom. With a shock I realised it was the woman I'd seen in the changing room the first time I came to the gym. The one with the fabulous body. She seemed to have lost about two stone since then and it wasn't an improvement.

'You can definitely be too thin,' I agreed.

'Not that we have to worry about that just yet,' said Clara wryly. 'She has training sessions with Marco,' she went on in the same low voice. 'I think she's got a few quid – I've seen her getting into a Merc outside and her clothes are fab. But she's totally obsessed. I was talking to her in the changing room one day and she tests her urine every morning to make sure she's in ketosis and burning fat. She told me she has an egg white omelette for breakfast and another one for lunch. That's it. Chicken and salad in the evenings. I suppose she's on one of these missions to get to a size zero. She's already got the horrible breath.'

'Blimey,' I whispered back. 'Isn't she starving?'

Clara shook her head knowledgably. 'Apparently once you're in ketosis you stop feeling hungry. Alfie said that too – he's only on about 600 calories a day, and endless litres of water.'

Lucky old them, I thought. My appetite was showing no particular signs of abating.

'Neither's mine,' said Andrew Lazlett a couple of days later, after we'd almost crashed into each other as I stumbled sleepily into the gym and he swung his way through the turnstile on the way out.

'Goodness, what time did you get here?' I said, looking at the clock.

He pulled a face. 'Six a.m. when they opened. Only way I could fit it in. I really need to be in school by eight – lots to do.' He sighed. 'And I could do with being earlier than that. I think I might have to start coming at six in the evening instead.'

'Ooh no,' I said, 'that's glass of wine time.'

'I know,' he said with feeling. 'Beer time for me. But I'm still off it.' He pulled another face. 'I'm on water only.'

'Well, so am I actually,' I admitted. 'Well, in theory anyway …'

I was trying to cut down on alcohol and eat only good things. Forcing down Sally-Ann's vitamin protein shakes when I could bear it and attempting to remember to rub her pungent creams into various parts of me morning and night. This was a complex procedure dependent on recalling whether you did your breasts yesterday or this morning and if it was the turn of your upper arms or inner thighs to smell peculiar.

I hadn't noticed any particular enhancement in my cleavage yet – one of the benefits promised in the extensive leaflet that came with the product – but from the dreams I'd been having, causing me to wake up flushed and strangely embarrassed, it seemed to be doing something to my sex drive. Or perhaps that was just all the exercise which, Clara informed me, done properly produced as many endorphins as a "stinker of an orgasm".

'I can barely remember,' I told her.

But whatever it was doing to me, I realised one morning I was actually looking forward to the gym. There was something about being on the cross-trainer, hot and sweaty, legs aching, short of breath yet with the music pounding away in my ears, my legs and arms moving to the rhythm, that felt good and uplifting. It was nice to go with Clara if she was around, but equally OK to go on my own.

Sometimes I did forgo the wine totally and went early evening if Stanley was elsewhere. I even took myself down there on a Sunday morning once Daniel had picked him up, instead of taking up my default weekend position of staying in my pyjamas and eating crisps.

'It's exhilarating,' I explained to Charlotte.

She looked deeply unimpressed. 'Doesn't turn me on, love.'

'That,' said Becky, 'is because you're sad. If you exercised a bit more, and gave up smoking ...'

'Now you're *both* boring me,' said Charlotte.

'Do you understand?' I asked Andrew, with whom I'd fallen into the habit of having a freshly squeezed orange juice if we happened to coincide in our sessions and then catch each other's eyes across the top of the chest press.

'I don't think I'm quite there yet,' he said. 'I come because I know it's doing me good – I am beginning to feel my abs again – and because I do like the feeling of being in shape. I know it's hard to believe, but I used to play football for The Flying Duck when I lived in Southampton.' He grinned at me. 'And I ran a marathon for Cancer Research when I was in my first year of teaching. And up until just a year ago I used to cycle everywhere. I was really quite fit – I know it doesn't look like it now.'

'No, I can believe it,' I said. Looking at him afresh, he did have that look of the former athlete about him. Something about the way he moved, the easy rhythm of his running. The way he caught an exercise ball lobbed at him from across the floor by Alfie.

He waved at Alfie now. 'He's a great guy,' Andrew said. 'I can't believe how much weight he's shifted, he's so focused.'

I waved at Alfie too. His once-great girth appeared to have shrunk a bit further every time I saw him. He seemed taller as a result and his face had more definition.

'And he always looks so cheerful with it,' I said.

'He does. I'd like to enjoy it more. But I'm not getting the high out of it just yet. Still kicking myself for everything I can't do. Hey, do you play tennis?' Andrew asked.

'Er - no, not really. I mean I have done, but badly.'

'Well, perhaps you could try again. Maybe we could play in the spring?'

'Yes, maybe.'

We lapsed into silence.

'How's the diet anyway?' I asked after a while.

'Boring,' he said. 'I've never eaten so much bloody cheese in my life. I'm sure it must be sending my cholesterol sky high and I'm about to keel over with heart disease and furred-up arteries, but Elaine says it's only short term and it's the quickest way to shift all this lard. But, frankly, if I don't get a piece of toast soon ... Hey,' he said again, looking round the café area, 'can you stay for breakfast?'

I shook my head. I'd been feeling comfortable sitting talking to him but at the mention of his wife, I felt myself withdraw. Andrew was a nice bloke who'd been really kind, always asking after Stanley and checking how we were, and I liked him. But it while it was very well passing the time of day with him, I'd just been forcibly reminded that he was married and having breakfast together seemed a bit more intimate than just chatting over an orange juice. I didn't want to be any sort of Hannah figure, especially after I'd been so vociferous about her.

I was no closer to getting to the bottom of exactly where Roger was with all that, but I'd be going to his works do soon

210

and I was determined to find out then. I'd only popped into Charlotte's a couple of times recently and he hadn't been there either time, but I'd gathered via a casual comment from Charlotte that Roger went for a drink most nights after work, so I assumed he was still in Hannah's thrall.

'That's a pity,' said Andrew now, smiling. 'While it's the weekend and I can. Another time perhaps?'

I smiled back but shook my head again. 'I'm really busy at the moment,' I said.

Chapter Twenty-five

IT WASN'T UNTRUE. MIKE was giving me more work than ever before and what with going to the gym and looking after Stanley and needing to concentrate on not eating too much, it was a constant battle to keep up.

Whereas once I was delighted to be interrupted by Charlotte at any hour of the day, now my heart sank slightly if the doorbell rang, knowing I would have to abandon my brochure-writing for an hour - the latest deadline was getting scarily close and there were still pages to go – and that she'd also expect me to eat biscuits.

I'd tried not having any in the house but Stanley had been mutinous and Charlotte, upon finding the cupboard was bare, simply turned straight round again and went out and bought some.

This afternoon she'd brought them with her, not trusting me to have a decent supply, and was morosely eating her seventh garibaldi, while I stared into middle distance, reliving the delicious conversation I'd just had with Cal.

'Things are really tough out there,' she was saying. 'I mean, I know there's a bloody credit crunch on but I was still sure I'd sell that place in Harbour Street quickly. It is seriously fabulous inside and he's knocked almost a hundred grand off the price. I'd bloody buy it myself if I had the money. I even asked Roger if we could get a loan. But he's still being very peculiar of course. Wouldn't even discuss it!'

She looked at me expectantly and I dragged myself back to the present. 'I didn't think there were any loans,' I said vaguely. *Cal's coming down tomorrow to do some more filming. He said he's really looking forward to it ...*

'I'm sure there are if you know where to go,' said Charlotte crossly. 'I've decided it's definitely a mid-life crisis. You know, he's reading some very odd books at the moment …'

He's been thinking about me a lot and there's something special he wants to discuss with me …

'Like what?' I said.

'Oh, I don't know what it was called but I read the back cover, and it was some poncy-sounding "relationships" effort. You know the sort of thing–' She pulled a comic face and adopted a faux intellectual tone. 'This deeply complex novel examines the frailty of modern liaisons, challenging at the deepest levels our common perceptions of love and marriage with a unique insight into the human psyche that is both uplifting and disturbing …' Charlotte gave a loud and magnificent snort. 'This is a man who reads wall-to-wall Jeffery Archer or James Patterson and used to take the piss out of me for liking Joanna Trollope. He said someone at work recommended it.'

I snapped out of the daydream where the "something special" was Cal's overwhelming desire to take me away to a deserted island in the Bahamas for two weeks, and gaped at her. 'Really? Who?'

'I don't know,' said Charlotte impatiently. 'You know how weird they all are. Well, you don't, but you'll see for yourself next week.' She suddenly looked at me hard. 'It's not just Roger – there's something funny about you too. You've got a really odd expression on your face – and it's not just because your eyebrows are three inches too high. Have you shagged this Cal bloke and neglected to tell me?'

I gave myself a shake. 'No, of course I haven't. I wouldn't mind though …' I said, in a lame attempt at humour. 'But as I've told you before, I'm old enough to be his mother. Well, not quite …'

Charlotte was still scrutinising me keenly. 'So how old is he again?'

'Twenty-eight.'

'Oh well, that's OK, then. Older women are all the rage now – I was reading about it. He should be bloody grateful a gorgeous woman like you might want to teach him a thing or two.' She wasn't smiling.

'Come off it,' I said, embarrassed.

'But,' said Charlotte, with sudden fervour, 'you can do better than some shallow youth from a TV company. Bet he spends more time looking at himself in the mirror than at you.'

'No,' I said at once. 'He's not like that at all. He's really sweet and not shallow either – he's terribly clever. He was telling me on the phone this afternoon about this production of *King Lear* he worked on when he was a student and how it totally turned all the preconceptions about false love and vanity on their heads and made him realise that, in fact –'

I stopped as Charlotte put down her coffee cup and stood up. 'Hmm, very interesting I'm sure.'

'Anyway,' I burbled, 'they're coming to do the next lot of filming tomorrow and I'm supposed to have lost weight. Do you think my arms look better?' I held them up for her inspection.

Charlotte picked up her handbag. 'Sorry, love, they just look like arms to me.'

Clara understood.

'Ha! Another pound gone,' I cried triumphantly, as I jumped off the gym scales and braced myself for what we now termed "the nasty steps".

'I'm not weighing myself till the weekend,' said Clara, wiping at her face with a towel. 'And it had better be good when I do. I haven't had any alcohol for ten days, no biscuits, no chocolate, no cocktail pork pies. If I haven't lost at least half a stone, I am going to seriously consider killing myself.'

'You look visibly smaller to me,' I said encouragingly. 'You really do – that T-shirt is much looser than it was when I first met you.'

'You look thinner too,' said Clara. 'Especially on your upper arms.'

We both examined them. 'After all the bloody weights I've lifted I should think so.'

I turned sideways so she could assess how much my

stomach was sticking out. 'I'm still not what you would call skinny, am I?'

'No,' admitted Clara, 'but would you really want to be? Do you want to look like that?' We both turned to gaze at the now *really* skinny woman, running as usual on the treadmill, who Clara had found out was called Annabel. 'She's getting that lollipop look,' said Clara. 'I'm sure she's anorexic.' We both sniffed.

'Do I really look a bit thinner all over, though?' I said anxiously. 'They're filming me here again tonight and I'm supposed to look as though "the regime" has started to work.'

'Yes, you do and ooh, what time? Perhaps I can pop in on my way to work.' Clara beamed. 'I want to see this sexy young director of yours.'

I shook my head, trying to pretend I wasn't longing to as well. 'He's not mine, unfortunately. Though he is lovely.'

'Well, get in there, then.'

I laughed a bit too loudly. 'He's a bit young ...' I pushed away the memory of his smile, and the way he'd called me "babe".

'It's all the rage to have a toy boy,' said Clara.

'I don't think he sees me like that,' I said firmly. 'It's purely professional.'

Though, if anything, Cal seemed even more affectionate this time – he gave me a big hug when he arrived and draped an arm around my shoulders as we went up the stairs to the studios.

'I've had a word with them at reception,' he said, 'and they're happy for us to film you doing a little bit of each class. There's yoga at six, and a step class at the same time and then afterwards there's "On the Ball" and a dance group. So if you can join in for about 15 or 20 minutes of each – and change your top in between? Did you remember to bring some different gym clothes?'

I nodded, and he squeezed my shoulder. 'Well done. You're so great to work with. And later,' he added, with a melting smile. 'I'm taking you out to dinner.'

A collection of women in leotards and yoga trousers looked at me curiously as the cameras were set up around my mat. Cal smiled at them all. 'Thank you so much, ladies, and my apologies for any disturbance. Please try to ignore us and enjoy your class.'

I watched them wilt under his charms as we waited for the instructor to arrive. He was small and dark with a soft, sing-song voice that I could barely hear.

As we all lay down and began waving our arms around, I kept my eyes firmly on the woman next to me, so I could see what I was supposed to be doing, trying to ignore the fact that there was a large microphone by my left ear and a camera hovering above me.

'Lift your left leg uuuuppppp ...'

The small man's own limbs looked as though they were made of rubber. He sat in a lotus position in front of us, his feet curled in impossible balls, while instructing us how to breathe deeply with one finger against the side of our nose.

I was beginning to feel a bit twitchy, rather than chilled out and relaxed. The bloke's voice was getting on my nerves and breathing through only one nostril was making me tense. 'And-the-other-oooonnnneee ...'

I closed the other nostril and breathed a bit more.

'Now put your fingers in both ears, and ...'

I took my fingers out again. What?

'Buzz like a bee,' hissed the woman next to me. I looked about. All around me the women were making a strange humming sound deep in their throats. Our bendy little instructor was the loudest of them all.

I closed my eyes and made a noise too – it resonated around my head and vibrated down my neck in a not unpleasant way. After a while I stopped and opened my eyes. Everyone else was still going.

The room was full of droning hums. The woman next to me was rocking and buzzing, her eyes screwed tight shut, her head rolling – obviously well into whatever it was supposed to be doing for her.

I shut my eyes again and buzzed a bit more. The noise filled my head and was strangely relaxing. I felt my shoulders drop, as the noise rose up from my chest in soothing waves. I wondered where Cal and I would go for dinner. Did he mean just me and him or would everyone come? Matt and Russ were here, of course. And Tanya. Being her usual cheery self ...

Buzzzzzzzzzzzz. I could almost curl up on this mat and go to sleep now but it was probably time to open my eyes again –

I looked up. Everyone else had stopped and was sitting on their mat, watching me. There was a camera about six inches from my nose – Matt grinning behind it. I gazed wildly around the room at a series of amused expressions. Oh God, how long had I been buzzing on my own?

As I sat there, scarlet, our teacher went into a set of praying, bowing movements and they all began flapping their arms up and down. Cal nodded at me to do it too so I stretched my arms out until my forehead was on the floor, glad to hide my hot face.

He put an arm around my shoulders once I'd got up. 'That was great,' he said, obviously struggling to keep his features under control, while Russ and Matt stood openly grinning. 'Very good.'

I cringed. 'I feel a complete prune.'

'You were fine.'

'What, buzzing away on my own like a demented wasp?'

Cal smiled. 'We probably won't use it – we do all this filming but only a tiny proportion actually ends up in the programme. And it doesn't matter – shows how you were really receptive to what you were doing. It was great – honestly. Now, the step class is full, so have a breather and we'll go into "On the Ball". Looks like fun. You don't have to do all of it,' he said soothingly as I groaned. 'Just give us a taste.'

The class was run by Marlena, a dramatic-looking 40-year old with a tight Lycra top, bright red lipstick, and very shiny black hair. 'Are we ready to have fun?' she cried through her microphone, nearly taking my ear drums out. 'Are we ready to work?' She darted across the room and hit a switch on the CD player. 'We're going to work!

'Grab those balls, ladies,' she yelled like a manic redcoat. 'And gentleman,' she added with a high, cackling laugh in the direction of the lone man in the room – a round faced bloke in his fifties with thinning hair and a T-shirt saying *Not Out, Still Scoring*.

Most of the big, squashy balls were blue. I took the only orange one. 'Beryl usually has that,' said a voice in my ear. Beryl also clearly had the place in the middle of the room right in front of Marlena, with her two blonde-rinsed, pearl-earringed, neat-tracksuited friends either side. The three of them – looking like the Broadstairs answer to the Golden Girls – glared when Cal directed me into a similar position. And exchanged nods of satisfaction when I sat on my ball and promptly fell off it.

Sitting was the easy bit. By the time we'd bounced up and down on the ball, laid on the floor and pushed it up and down between our legs, done press-ups, sit-ups and something excruciating involving one of the Beryls squatting on my ankles, I was unable to move, let alone speak.

Cal seemed to have disappeared. Matt and Russ were packing up all the camera gear.

The music was still blaring. 'On your feet,' cried Marlena. 'And it's jack jumps!' As the room propelled themselves upwards, arms flailing, I hobbled toward the door, glancing at myself in the mirrored wall as I went.

My hair was flattened to my head. The make-up I'd carefully layered on earlier in order to look cool and alluring was smudged and streaked. I was red, sweaty, and exhausted.

Outside in the corridor, Tanya had arrived and was on the phone. She nodded hello, giving me an amused look. 'Yeah, doing this gym stuff,' I heard her say to whoever was on the line. 'It's hysterical.'

Glad you find it so entertaining, I thought sourly, as I sat in the changing room, towel wrapped round me, trying to do something with the gym hairdryer and without Antonio's magic clay stuff that I'd forgotten. I wondered what Tanya actually did to contribute to anything – so far all I'd ever seen her do was make phone calls and drink Diet Coke.

She was nowhere to be seen when I'd finally changed into jeans and my most slimming stretchy black top and joined Cal and the others in the café area for the "feedback" session.

'We just want you to talk about how you're feeling about your new exercise plan,' said Cal. 'And then we'd like some extra shots of you speaking to your personal coach about it.'

I was by now an old hand. As the camera was set up around one of the tables I held forth about my new-found enthusiasm for the cross-trainer, listened to some advice from Nicola about increasing the amount of time I spent in cardio-vascular activity to enhance fat-burning and then engaged in some fervent "noddies" – the extra bits of film they used for cutaways, whereby I nodded at Nicola as if she were talking to me and then she did the same to me, feeling suitably proud and film star-like as various gym-goers watched from afar. I was now able to look dismayed/fascinated/disbelieving/joyful on cue.

'I really can feel a difference,' I proclaimed for the third time, sounding like a TV ad.

'OK, we're done!' Cal kissed me on both cheeks. 'You're a natural.'

I went to collect my stuff from the changing room and put some more make-up on. When I came back, Tanya, Russ, and Matt were outside smoking. I could see the glow of their cigarette ends in the darkness. Cal was waiting for me inside the glass doors, wearing a soft grey jacket over his open-necked white shirt and jeans. His hair was a bit longer than last time, I noticed now. It curled against his collar.

He gave me a big smile. 'So can you recommend somewhere good to eat?'

Tanya came back through the doors as he said it. 'You coming with us?' he asked her.

She ran a hand through her spiky hair and shook her head. 'I'm going back to town with the guys,' she said sharply. 'I'm hitting Kay's party later with Len.'

For a moment I thought Cal looked irritated then he shrugged. 'OK. Have a good time.'

Tanya turned on her heel and strode back outside again.

'Is she OK?' I asked.

'Yes, she's fine.' Cal smiled again. 'Just having one of her strops.'

Probably because she never ate anything, I thought, as I got into Cal's dark blue BMW. Low blood sugar could make you bad-tempered. Stanley was the same – when he was a small child I'd carried biscuits in my handbag in case he threw a tantrum and I needed to get him in a half-nelson and ram one of them into his mouth. I grinned at the memory of how he would be instantly wreathed in smiles.

'You look happy.' Cal swung out of the gym car park. 'And I must say you look amazing too. I can't believe how much weight you've lost.'

'It's only a few pounds,' I said self-consciously.

'Well, the effect's terrific.'

I might lose even more at this rate. I was strangely un-hungry myself despite not having eaten for hours. Finally being all alone with Cal had left my stomach ridiculously fluttery and I couldn't think of a single thing to say.

Fortunately, he talked. By the time we reached the bottom of Broadstairs High Street I knew he'd read English with Film Studies at Warwick, had a garden flat in Clapham and an older brother who was a photographer. He'd briefly worked as a production assistant on *Big Brother* but found it "very manipulative" and had high hopes of our film giving him a name in the industry and leading on to greater things.

'Who knows, maybe we'll do something together again one day,' he said casually, as we turned into Albion Street. 'Where do I park?'

I'd suggested we went to Greens because it was the first place that came into my head and because at least I could just have something snacky like hummus and pitta bread – except that I'd have to demonstrate my eschewal of all things carbohydrate so it would be hummus and hummus – and the wine bar was friendly and relaxed and a bit more trendy than some of the other proper restaurants and, if I were totally honest, I wanted to show Cal off to Sarah.

She didn't disappoint me. 'Mmm,' she said under her breath as I went to the bar for menus, leaving Cal at the table in the window. 'Where did you get him from?' I told her about the documentary and she raised her eyebrows in admiration. 'Lucky you! I must say you're looking ever so well – I love your hair – and very slim!'

I patted my stomach. 'I'm wearing those jeans that hold it all in. But yes, I have lost a bit – been sweating it out in the gym.'

'I keep thinking I should do that,' said Sarah. 'But then I get all the exercise I need in this place running up and down the bloody stairs to the kitchen.' She laughed. 'You could crack nuts between my thighs!'

There was a pop as she uncorked a bottle of Macon Blanc Villages.

'How's Stanley now?' said Sarah, putting two glasses in front of me. 'Has he settled down?'

'I think so,' I said. 'Although he does get anxious – especially about his weight. I mean he is a bit chubby I suppose, but he's hardly obese ...'

Sarah shook her head. 'You really shouldn't worry. He's only 11 isn't he?'

'Nearly 12.'

'He's only young – it will sort itself out. Luke was always like that. He'd keep growing outwards and then just as I was thinking I'd better do something, he'd suddenly shoot up and it would fall off again. Look at him now!' Her eldest son was a head taller than her and like a beanpole.

'Anyway,' Sarah continued, 'I should leave him be. Better they're a bit plump than get an eating disorder. My cousin's boy got anorexia when he was 14. It was awful – he ended up in hospital.'

'Oh,, I don't say a word. It's the twiglet who lives with my husband who goes on about it. She's obsessed.' I picked up the bottle and tucked two menus under my arm.

Sarah laughed. 'Well, tell her to put a sock in it. There's some specials on the blackboard,' she added. 'We've got a great seafood linguini.'

'Not doing carbs,' I said.

Sarah pulled a face. 'Don't get obsessed yourself, eh?'

'That's what Charlotte says,' I told Cal as he poured me more wine. 'She thinks I've become obsessive too.'

'Maybe she's jealous?' suggested Cal. 'Because you're looking so good?'

I nibbled on a bit of grilled halloumi. 'Oh no, Charlotte's not like that at all. I mean, she's being very supportive. Stanley's round there now – she said she'd have him to stay so I could do all this. It's just that she isn't into dieting and exercise and doesn't understand.'

'When people make radical changes to their lifestyle, it can be quite challenging for those around them,' said Cal thoughtfully. He cut into his steak. 'There was a documentary on Channel Four last year – *The Women Who Lost Forty Stone* – did you see it?'

I shook my head. He put a small piece of tomato onto his fork and speared a cube of fillet. I found myself watching his mouth as he chewed.

'Well,' he said, when he'd swallowed. 'These eight women had lost over forty stone between them. They looked totally different, all of them, years younger, full of confidence. But what was interesting was that by the end of the programme, five of them had split up with their partners!'

'Oh well, no worries there,' I chortled. 'Mine buggered off while I was still fat.'

'You weren't at all,' said Cal at once. 'I thought you looked great as you were, actually. But you do look very yummy now.' His eyes lingered over me and I was suddenly glad I was wearing my new uplift, cleavage-enhancing bra. The wine had mellowed me nicely and I felt suddenly warm and sexy.

'Thank you,' I said coyly. I looked at his hands on the table; the long fingers, the clean, manicured nails.

'Are you pleased with your face?' Cal was saying. 'It's very subtle – you mostly just look very fresh and healthy but you do definitely look younger too.'

I glanced sideways into the mirror on the wall next to us. Sarah had lit the candle on our table and in the shadowy light of the flickering flame I did look OK.

Suddenly I was, indeed, still young and firm, the contours of my face clearly defined, my eyes large and shining. I remembered Tanya's Lenny telling me how lighting was everything. I turned my face slightly to get an even better angle.

'Thank you,' I said again, feeling a thrill of excitement run through me. Perhaps if spent the rest of my life just sat here in the half dark I could still pass for 35 …

'So, in three weeks, we're going to do one last session with you,' Cal was saying. 'We've found a really fabulous new boutique hotel in Clerkenwell where they're thrilled for us to film – I think they're really going to push the boat out – and they've got a pool and Jacuzzi, steam room and sauna. So – bring your swim suit.'

He topped up my glass and crinkled his nose at me in a way that made my stomach flip. 'Unless, of course, I can persuade you into a bikini after all, as you're going to be in such wonderful shape?'

'Oh no, I don't think so. I won't be in that sort of shape,' I said, flustered and taking a larger swallow of wine than I'd intended.

He smiled. 'No pressure,' he said lightly. 'I'm just indulging my fantasies.' I swallowed again.

Cal was still talking. 'They got a terrific write-up in *Heat*,' he said easily. 'The restaurant and the cocktail bar has been attracting the A-list already. I think we're going to have a fab night whatever we do.'

I held up the almost empty bottle, not knowing what else to say. 'Don't you want some more wine?'

'I'd love some but I can't – I'm driving. You have it.' He put his hand on mine. 'I've got some really exciting ideas for our final session and I know you're going to be fantastic. And listen, La, I know your role has really expanded, so I'm getting you a fee sorted from the budget. It will only be a few hundred quid but the point is you'll have the beginnings of a show reel with the DVD of this programme and you might be able to get some other TV work on the strength of it.'

My head was reeling – not just from the thought of being on television as "work" but from him calling me "La". Charlotte called me "Lu", but I'd known Charlotte for ever. Shortened names like that were intimate – were for people you felt close to.

He was looking at me intently, his head lowered, his hair flopping. I wanted to run my hands through it.

'Really?' I squeaked.

'Really.'

He leant over and kissed me very gently on the corner of my mouth. 'It's been a great evening and I'm really looking forward to next time. We can celebrate the end of the filming.'

He kissed me once more – so lightly it was like a feather brushing my lips.

'I won't be driving then …'

Chapter Twenty-six

'READY FOR YOUR HOT night out?' Charlotte stood on my doorstep looking lovely in a long black skirt and fuchsia top, and big chunky silver and black beads. Her usually wild mass of blonde curls was held back from her face in two silver clips. 'Speaking for myself,' she said, 'I can hardly contain my excitement.'

She waited while I gathered up my handbag and shouted goodbye to Stanley and Ashley – the 16-year-old from down the road who was performing his début as a babysitter.

'He seems very sensible,' I said to Charlotte as we walked back down the path. 'I don't think they'll burn the house down.'

'Roger's got a face on,' she said breezily as we reached the car.

'Oh, why?'

'Doesn't want to go and I'm making him drive. As I said to him, how does he think I feel? I think I'm a pretty brilliant wife to spend an evening with all those bores – I'm certainly not staying sober while I do it.

'Just telling Laura you've got a face on, love,' she said, as I opened the back door of the car.

'Hi Roger!' I enthused. 'Thanks for this.'

He greeted me back and then lapsed into silence. I wondered whether Charlotte was right about his mood. Or was he sweating, not only about his wife and Hannah being in the same room, but me there too, watching it all?

Part of me felt guilty and interfering but another stronger part said if there was nothing going on, there was nothing for him to worry about. Charlotte was no fool anyway – if this

Hannah was hanging about, she'd soon pick up on it. Hopefully that might be enough for Roger to send her packing.

'Where is this do, anyway?' I asked brightly. 'In the offices?'

'Upstairs room of the Conservative Club,' Charlotte informed me. 'Pictures of Thatcher and Queenie everywhere. Lots of old farts in blazers. Usual curly sandwiches and sausage rolls.'

'You said the food was lovely last time,' said Roger mildly.

'I said the food was the best thing about it,' Charlotte replied briskly. 'Which is not the same thing at all. I'm always amazed how many people have no idea how to put on a decent buffet.'

For the rest of the journey Charlotte treated us to a diatribe entitled *The Worst Party Food I've Ever Eaten*, with sound effects, so that I was feeling suitably nauseous by the time we made our way up the blue-carpeted stairs of the Conservative Club. At the top, I followed her and Roger into a dark panelled room with a bar at one end.

A waitress in uniform held a tray with white and red wine or small glasses of sherry.

'Bet it's not cold enough,' muttered Charlotte, taking a glass of white.

'Think I'll get a beer,' said Roger heavily, heading for the bar.

Clumps of people stood about talking, the men mostly in dark suits, the women in dresses and skirts. I scanned the room for anyone who looked even vaguely like the woman I'd seen Roger with.

'Which is the one who always cries?' I asked.

Charlotte surveyed the room too. 'Can't see her – perhaps they've got rid of her – but, oh God, here we go.'

A large woman in bright blue chiffon was bearing down on us.

'Ah Charlotte, how lovely.' She kissed Charlotte loudly on both cheeks before swinging round to bestow a bountiful smile on me. 'And this is?'

'This is my friend, Laura,' Charlotte said. 'Laura is carrying out some research into the families of lawyers – their perceptions of their role in the furthering of the corporate whole and its values.' Mrs Chiffon looked slightly glazed. 'She's come along to see how we do things at Hammond and Barnes. Laura, this is Sheila Hammond – wife of Alan, the longest-standing of the senior partners. Alan's the one retiring.'

I tried to keep a straight face as I held out my hand. Sheila pressed the tips of my fingers with hers. 'How fascinating,' she said, looking round the room. 'Have you spoken to Ellen, yet?' she asked Charlotte, lowering her voice. 'She's still getting over the operation ...'

While they were talking, I checked out where Roger was. He was standing near the end of the bar with three other men in their fifties. I couldn't see anyone who looked remotely as I remembered Hannah. She must be coming. Charlotte had said that the practice were very hot on every single employee and their partner turning out for these do's and if she was a senior partner's secretary she'd surely have to be here – especially if it was the one who was leaving.

'A face I don't recognise!' Beside me, a tall man in an expensive-looking suit was holding out his hand. 'I'm Jeremy, one of the partners.'

'Oh hi – Laura,' I said. 'I've come with Charlotte and Roger.'

'Splendid! We could do with a bit of fresh blood at these things.' He laughed. Charlotte looked over her shoulder and winked at me.

'Hello, Jeremy,' she said dryly.

'Hello, darling,' Jeremy gave her a long, lingering kiss on the cheek, which made Sheila Hammond raise her eyebrows.

'Do behave yourself, Jeremy,' she said, as he swept toward her.

'You just want one too, I know,' he declared, planting a kiss on her cheek as well.

'Don't be silly.' Sheila gave a girlish giggle.

'So what do you do, Laura?' Jeremy turned back to me and raised one eyebrow in what he clearly thought was a rakish manner. 'Fill me in.'

I gave him the line about the research and the in-house magazine, deliberately doing so with lowered lashes and an admiring look on my face. I glanced back quickly. Charlotte had moved away slightly. She and Sheila were now talking to a tall woman with grey hair and a stick.

'Maybe,' I said coquettishly, 'you could fill me in on the gossip. Any good office scandals erupted lately? Romances? Affairs?' I kept my eyes on his.

'Oh well,' he said, moving in closer and putting a hand under my elbow. 'Let me see now, we could always start one ...'

He was quite attractive in a self-congratulatory sort of way and quite amusing to talk to if you didn't mind the size of his ego. He didn't have any beans to spill about anyone else but I stood nodding and smiling as he regaled me with tales of the long line of secretaries who had fallen so uncontrollably in love with him they'd been unable to do their jobs, and the High Court judge who was always asking him to visit her in chambers.

While he was talking I kept one eye on Roger in the corner and the other roving around the room for any sign of the Bunny Boiler. Jeremy probably thought I had a squint.

We'd just got to the point in Jeremy's story where he'd been invited back for a nightcap but had been warned by the male PA that it might be a threesome that was on the menu, so was considering his options, when I suddenly saw her over his shoulder.

It was the same woman for sure. I recognised the way she held her head, slightly to one side as if shy. She was wearing a calf-length, dark green jersey dress over boots, and several strings of beads with little dangly bits. Her hair, this time, was blow-dried in a big cloud around her face and, apart from lipstick, she didn't seem to have much make-up on which made her appear quite pale and fragile. Probably quite deliberately, I thought crossly, as I watched her slide up and nonchalantly join Roger's group.

I saw him turn and give her a brief smile, the other two men nodding to her too. But it was Roger she positioned herself next to. As I watched, their arms were almost touching.

I spun around in alarm to see where Charlotte was. She was still talking to the grey-haired woman. Sheila Hammond seemed to have disappeared.

'So I thought – ha ha,' Jeremy was saying, 'discretion being the better part of valour and all that …'

'Yes, quite!' I chortled too, though I hadn't got a clue where we'd got to in the saga. I darted another glance over to where Roger's group were still talking, catching Charlotte's eye accidentally as I did so. She gave me a little wave and mouthed something. I wondered how I could get to talk to Hannah. I guessed I'd just have to wait till she went to the loo and follow. I looked again. She had a glass in her hand now, though by the look of it, it was only water.

Let's hope that wasn't all she was going to drink and she didn't have a cast-iron bladder that would last till she got home.

'I hope you're looking after my friend, Jeremy.' Charlotte had appeared by my side. 'And not leading her astray.'

'Unfortunately not,' said Jeremy, with an expression of mock regret. 'But we are having a delightful time. How are you darling?'

'A little wine-depleted,' said Charlotte, holding up her empty glass. 'And it looks as though Laura is too. Would you be a star …?'

She grinned as Jeremy headed for the bar. 'He's all right, really,' she said. 'If you don't mind all his bullshit. I notice he's on his own tonight so I think we can safely assume the latest woman has very sensibly dumped him. They never last very long. Can't think why.'

'He's quite funny,' I said absent-mindedly, still looking at Roger. Was it my imagination or was that woman actually brushing against his sleeve now?

'What's the matter? What are you staring at Roger for?' Charlotte asked suddenly.

'I'm not!' I said quickly. 'Actually, I was looking at that guy he's talking to – he, er, looks familiar – who is he? The one in the pink tie?'

'Dunno,' said Charlotte dismissively. 'Haven't seen him before. The other bloke is Tom their finance guy – he and Roger get on well.'

'Is that his wife?' I asked innocently.

Charlotte shrugged. 'No, Linda's over there. Don't know who she is either. One of the secretaries, I expect. They always seem to have a few new ones knocking about. Jeremy frightens the old ones off!' she added, as Jeremy returned carrying two white wines.

He laughed. 'I can't help it if they all get the hots for me and fade away with unrequited desire,' he said smugly.

'In your dreams.' Charlotte laughed too. They began reminiscing about the previous year's Christmas party and someone called Jeanette who'd dressed up as a reindeer and done something Jeremy had never fully recovered from when she'd got him behind the photocopier after too many Tia Marias.

'Don't give me that! You couldn't believe your bloody luck,' Charlotte was saying. 'Apparently she needed her stomach pumping ...'

A waitress appeared with a tray of cheesy pastry squares and I took one. More people seemed to have arrived and there were now a large couple blocking my view of Roger and his gang. I craned my neck to see if they were all still there and caught sight of the back of Hannah's head. Damn it, I'd need a pee myself soon and I couldn't keep going. Still, it would be as well to find out where the loo was, so I was prepared.

I asked Charlotte, left her and Jeremy still running through past episodes of drunken debauchery, and went out of the room and along the corridor to the ladies.

It was empty. As I was washing my hands, the door opened and I braced myself, wondering what I would say if it were *her*. But another woman of about my age came in, smiled, and went into one of the cubicles. I put some more lipstick on in the big mirror and stuck a bit more gel on the spiky bits of my hair, which, miraculously, had gone into quite a pleasing shape tonight, and was just about to go out when the door opened again. It was Charlotte.

'Wondered where you'd got to. You bored witless yet?'

'No, not at all. I'm having a good time.'

Charlotte pulled a face. 'You're easily pleased.'

She went into one of the cubicles. I waited, fiddling with my hair a bit more. It would be just my luck if Hannah came in now while Charlotte was in earshot. Though quite what I was going to say to her, I didn't know. *Leave my mate Roger alone or I'll scratch your eyes out?*

'I hope they bring out something a bit more substantial to eat soon,' Charlotte called, over the sound of flushing. 'I've had all this wine and I'm starving. Still, at least Roger won't want to stay very late,' she said, as she came out and went to the basin. 'Not if he's had to cuddle the same pint all night.'

As long as that's all he's cuddling, I thought darkly.

As we went back into the party room, I suddenly felt apprehensive. What *was* I going to say to Hannah? A waitress came up to us with a bottle in each hand.

'Sorry,' I looked around. 'I don't know where my glass is.'

As Charlotte went across the room to where some filled ones were still on a tray, I looked for Roger once more. Now there was only him and the guy Charlotte had said was Tom, leaning against the bar. Hannah had disappeared. *Shit.*

'Here you go.' Charlotte put a glass in my hand. 'Now, where's the bloody food?'

I searched the room as if looking for it. I couldn't see Hannah anywhere.

'I think I've left my lipstick in the loo,' I said. 'I'll just go back and look.'

Charlotte nodded. 'I'm going downstairs for a fag. Can't wait any longer. Linda!' She waved at a dark woman in a red dress. 'Ciggie break?'

'You be OK?' she asked me.

'Yes, sure.'

'Rog is over there, if you need him,' said Charlotte. 'He'll look after you. Ah, here's someone for you to talk to.' I sighed inwardly as she pulled a smiley girl with long brown hair toward us. 'This is Anji Perkins – she's one of us. Likes her wine and wants something decent to eat with it.'

Anji was very friendly, but I was only half listening to her as she regaled me with what a great cook Charlotte was and how, having spent nine years in Asia, she, Anji, even though she said it herself, made a mean curry …

Usually I'd have been fascinated – I like a good Jalfrezi myself – but I was twitching to locate Hannah before Charlotte returned.

'I'm so sorry,' I blurted out after a few minutes, 'I've just got to …'

I beetled back down the corridor and flung open the loo door. Two of the cubicle doors were closed. She must be in one of them. I needed whoever was in the other to come out quick and sod off.

But neither of the women who emerged was Hannah. One was a woman I hadn't seen before and the other was Sheila Hammond, with whom I was forced to have a tedious exchange about what a marvellous time I was having and how friendly a company it was and how she and Alan would miss it when Alan had retired, except that, knowing Alan, he wouldn't really retire because he just wouldn't be able to keep away …

I had been grunting in an interested fashion for several minutes and was just hoping we were drawing to some sort of conclusion when the main door opened again and, in she walked!

She didn't look at either of us but went straight into one of the cubicles. My heart began to beat harder. Sheila was showing no signs of letting up – we were now going over Alan's obsession with the work ethic for the second time – and if she didn't belt up and bugger off soon, Hannah would be out and off again while I was still trapped.

But as the flush eventually sounded, Shelia abruptly stopped speaking and swung round. 'Ah, Hannah, dear, there you are. How's life treating you?'

I could hardly join in the conversation, so I got out my make-up bag and began to reapply eye shadow very slowly, hoping Hannah might linger to do a bit of the same if Sheila ever slung her hook.

But she was busily giving Hannah much the same speech as

she'd just given me and Hannah was murmuring politely. I started layering on mascara and waited, afraid they'd leave together and my chance would be lost. Or, worse, Sheila would go and Charlotte would reappear!

Instead, praise the heavens, someone else arrived. A much younger girl, that I'd seen earlier, popped her dark head round the door and saved the day by announcing cheerily to Sheila that people were waiting for her.

'Excuse me, Mrs Hammond – they'd like to start the presentation soon.'

Sheila whipped out a bright pink lipstick, pursed her lips in the mirror, and scuttled after her. I started painting my own mouth, watching Hannah in the mirror as she stood alongside me washing her hands, and wondering how to begin. When I couldn't find another square inch of my face to make up, I took a deep breath and turned toward her.

'So – you're Hannah.'

She looked at me uncertainly. 'Yes, I am.'

'I'm Laura,' I said boldly. 'I'm a very good friend of Roger's wife.'

I'd thought she might look embarrassed, or try to brush it all off by being terribly friendly as if she and Roger were entirely above board, but she did neither. She gave a tiny smile, brushed some hair from her eyes in an irritating, little girl way, and looked at me calmly.

'Oh yes,' she said. 'He's told me about you.'

For a moment I was lost for words, shocked that Roger would have spoken to her about our conversation. Then I felt annoyed.

'It was me who answered the phone when you rang up,' I said coldly, taking a chance. I couldn't actually be sure if it was the same voice or not – she wasn't being particularly breathy now – but she had a light, girlish, slightly soppy tone that could easily have sounded that way if she'd wanted it to.

She didn't reply to this – just went on looking at me.

'We didn't choose it to happen,' she said eventually, sounding like a bad film. 'It just did.'

'What did?' I said, heart beating hard. 'You've had a few

drinks together, that's all – he feels sorry for you.'

'Is that what he's told you?' She gave another small secretive smile and I wanted to slap her.

'Yes,' I said. 'He told me you've been bleating on about your boyfriend dumping you and, as you obviously seem unable to cope with life, he's tried to be kind to you.'

I saw her flinch and for a moment regretted being so nasty – suppose in fact Roger *was* just being kind and she really was having a terrible time. But then again …

Her eyes narrowed. 'He's been a bit more than that.'

'Have you slept with him?' I asked in alarm, before I could help myself.

She smiled again, and her tone took on a triumphant note. 'What do you think?'

'I don't know what to think,' I said. 'Except that you must be very sad and desperate to deliberately go after a married man and attempt to break up his family.'

'I didn't,' she said curtly.

'What was that phone call about then?'

'I don't know what you're talking about.'

I looked at her with contempt. 'Right.

'Charlotte and Roger have a really happy marriage,' I went on, cold at the thought of Roger being stupid enough to risk it with this destructive creature and praying she was making it up about them going to bed together, 'so why can't you–'

'It doesn't sound that way to me,' she interrupted. 'That's why he needs someone to talk to. We talk all the time, and when we can't talk, we text. He says I'm his soul mate.'

I snorted. 'He's got Charlotte to talk to.'

Hannah looked defiant. 'He says nobody listens to him at home. He is really unhappy and unfulfilled.'

'He is not!' I said exasperated. 'And I've never noticed him not being listened to.' Even as I said it, I knew that wasn't strictly true, but he and Charlotte were still friends, they were comfortable with each other. Up until this woman had come on to the scene I would have said they had the happiest marriage I knew …

'What we have is very strong and we will be together in the

end. He needs me. We have a bond,' Hannah said, a mad, dreamy look in her eyes.

'He's got a bond with his wife,' I snapped. 'It's called two children and a mortgage.'

We stood staring at each other for a few seconds. And I began to feel a real sense of unease. This woman could be about to wreak absolute havoc and Roger - what the hell was Roger doing?

'Don't you bloody dare –' I began, but she suddenly leapt toward the door, opened it and shot through it, leaving it swinging back in my face as I tried to shoot after her.

By the time I got outside, she was already further down the corridor, mobile phone in hand, looking as if she was about to text someone. Roger, presumably, to tell him I'd just harangued her in the loo. As I strode toward her, she put the phone back in her bag and scuttled back into the room where the party was. I caught up with her at the doorway and followed her through.

But as we got back inside, it had all gone quiet. Everyone was standing still and up at the front a man with a rather red face, grey hair, and a moustache was holding forth. Next to him, Sheila and a short, bald man with a visibly sweating pate, smiled stiffly.

'We are so grateful to Alan for his years of dedicated service,' Red Face was saying. 'It is through his hard work and commitment – '

Hannah had sidled away from me past the knots of people and was standing near the window. Her face looked pinched and calculating. *What was she going to say to Roger?*

'So fortunate that he has agreed to remain a consultant –' Red Face was still going. 'And Sheila for all her loyalty and support ...'

Or God forbid, to Charlotte. Supposing Hannah announced all that to her! Whatever happened, I must keep my friend away from that woman so she didn't get the chance ...

'See them at many more splendid gatherings such as this one ...'

Roger had to tell Charlotte first. He'd have to say this

deranged woman was coming on to him. That he'd only been trying to help ...

'We will be calling on his expertise. So it's not goodbye, Alan, but rather *au revoir –*' Red Face had paused for the appreciative titters and a smattering of applause.

I watched Hannah – she was creeping along the wall opposite, obviously trying to get back to Roger's side before I did. I stood on tiptoe trying to see where he was – over by the bar, still standing with Tom, eyes turned toward the speaker. I began to edge slowly through the bodies.

'So sorry,' I whispered, sliding past the woman with the stick and a couple of youngish girls. I couldn't see Charlotte anywhere but knowing her, once she'd got a whiff the speeches were starting she'd have grabbed a fresh drink and gone back downstairs for another fag. I hoped she'd stay there for a while.

Across the room, Hannah was still making her way round the edge of all the listeners. She would be at the bar any minute and be able to whisper her poison to Roger before I got there. If she told him I'd tackled her in the loo and warned her off, he'd probably be furious with me. But if I could get to him first and warn him that she was hell bent on breaking up his family ...

Red Face had started again. 'In the meantime, as a token of the esteem in which we hold you both and our deep affection ...' I saw Hannah stop and begin to clap along with everyone else as Alan waddled forward and began what I could tell was going to be a long speech himself. The couple in front of me had ignored my whispered excuse-me, so I stopped too.

Sheila had moved forward, smiling around the room like a duchess as Alan droned on about his joy in watching the firm blossom. I kept my eyes firmly on Hannah. The moment she moved, I was going to as well. Never mind whether the couple in front of me wanted to shift aside or not.

'And my much-valued secretary – Hannah!' I started as I heard her name. There was an outburst of clapping and Hannah smiled coyly. The people in front of her moved back to let her through. Tossing back her hair, affecting a wide-eyed expression of surprise, she walked up to Alan, head on one side again, as if embarrassed by the limelight.

At that moment I knew exactly what sort of woman she was. I could bet she didn't have a single girlfriend to call her own. I could just hear her ridiculous, girly voice talking about how "I get on better with men, really" and the way she'd simper and act helpless when any of them talked to her.

There was no way she was going to fuck up Charlotte's life.

As Hannah took the flowers with a nauseating mixture of pseudo self-deprecation and smug complacency, I turned toward Roger.

He was smiling broadly and clapping. Oh God, surely he didn't really think she was his soul mate? Why were men so simple sometimes? You only had to look at her to see she was barking and bloody dangerous to boot.

She was holding the flowers against her chest, modestly listening to Alan with lowered eyes as he listed her finer points.

I wanted to shake her.

At last the speeches seemed to be coming to an end. Hannah had kissed Alan's sweaty cheek and he'd said something about more drinks for everyone and how we must enjoy the rest of the evening and then I saw her break through the gathering at the front, heading for Roger.

'Excuse me,' I said again to the couple in front of me. The woman sighed and let me past. People were still bunched together beyond that, crowded around Alan and Sheila, who was now receiving people with a gracious nod as though she were Queen.

Seeing Hannah held up for a moment by someone admiring her bouquet, I executed one final almighty shove with my elbow, broke through and reached Roger's side seconds before she did. Tucking my arm through his, I grinned up at him manically.

'How are you doing Roger?' I said loudly. 'I think Charlotte would like to go home.'

Chapter Twenty-seven

'I NEED TO SPEAK to you urgently,' I said, without preamble, the minute Roger answered his mobile.

'I'm at work,' he said plaintively.

'Well, leave early and see me on the way home. This is serious, Roger.'

'Yes,' he said flatly. 'Hannah told me what you said to her.'

'I wonder if she told you what *she* said to *me*! You need to hear this Roger. No – not at my house. We can't risk Charlotte popping by. In the town somewhere. Before Stanley gets home. Roger – I am seriously worried about you both. You have got to promise me not to listen to anything Hannah says or go anywhere with her until you've spoken to me. Just keep away from her today. And don't sigh like that.'

'She's off work this week,' he said, when I eventually drew breath. 'Alan has left, of course, and we've got a new woman starting who Hannah's going to work for but she doesn't get here for another fortnight. So Hannah's taken some leave. She's going to see her mother in Northampton for a couple of days and then …'

'I don't need the details,' I snapped. 'Just meet me somewhere – I've got to tell you what happened.'

'I know what happened. Hannah phoned me this morning.'

'Well there's a surprise,' I said. 'Just bloody get over here.'

We met in *Peeps* – the new café bar on the seafront. Roger was already sitting at a table in the window when I got there. He looked awkward; I felt like throttling him.

'Let's move back a bit,' I said crossly. 'Just in case Charlotte drives past.'

'She wouldn't see us anyway,' he said. 'I've had to run into the road and throw myself in front of the car to get her to notice me before now.'

'Well, I shouldn't do that if she finds out about Hannah,' I said grimly. 'She's likely to put her foot down and flatten you.'

He looked at me, troubled. 'What do you want?' he said, getting to his feet.

I studied his back as he waited at the bar for my coffee. He looked big and solid and dependable. Six week ago, I'd have said those words summed him up perfectly. I want, I thought, feeling upset, for you to see sense before it's too late.

As soon as he sat back down, I told him what Hannah had said. 'It's exactly as I feared,' I finished. 'She's determined to have you for herself and she doesn't care who she hurts along the way. And Roger – really – is she worth throwing your whole marriage away for?'

'I'm not going to do anything like that,' he said defensively. 'It's not like that at all.'

'So what is it like?'

'We – we talk and discuss things. She's just a friend.'

'Oh, come off it, Roger! You go for a drink with her every night, you text all the time – that's not just a friend. If she was just a friend, you'd tell Charlotte all about her. If she's just a friend then why don't you invite her home for a drink so she can meet your wife?'

Roger looked irritated. 'She's not my wife's type. Charlotte wouldn't like her.'

'Too bloody right she wouldn't!' I exploded. 'Charlotte would take one look at her and know exactly what she was up to. Charlotte hates women like that and so do I.'

'Like what?'

'Women who home in on other women's husbands because they can't find one of their own.'

Roger shook his head. 'She really isn't like that. She's been through a very hard time, she's very ...'

'Calculating?'

'I was going to say caring.'

'The only person Hannah cares about is herself.'

I could see, satisfying as it might be (this was Day Ten, which was always dodgy on the self control front), I wasn't going to get anywhere by shouting, so I started again.

'Roger,' I began, in my best counselling tones, 'I think the problem here is that while you may regard you and Hannah as just work mates, Hannah herself is seeing it rather differently. You think you are being kind and supportive; she is seeing your natural colleague-type concern as sexual interest. You want a bit of a drink and a chat after work, she wants you to be her life partner.'

He shook his head.

'Roger,' I said, my voice rising despite my best efforts. 'She is a woman on a mission. She's saying you're going to end up with her!'

Roger shook his head again. 'That's not going to happen,' he said. 'But –' he twisted his cup in his hands, uncomfortably. 'I do – get something from her.'

With great force of will, I kept my mouth shut and waited for him to tell me what.

'I don't want to leave Charlotte, of course I don't,' he went on. 'I love her and you know I wouldn't do anything to hurt my kids. But, you know, we've been married a long time. It's comfortable but it's not always –' he frowned as he searched for the right word '- stimulating. Charlotte has a lot going on – she's taken up with the kids and the dog and work and her friends. We don't really talk about what we think about things any more – she says she loves me but she doesn't think I'm particularly clever or exciting. You know how it is when you meet someone new – make a new friend,' he corrected himself hastily. 'You get the chance to talk about who you are. I haven't done that for a long time.'

He turned the cup round and round in its saucer. 'Hannah is so – so *interested.*'

I shook my head in despair. Hannah knew exactly what to do and it had worked a treat.

'Do you understand?' Roger gave me a beseeching look.

I glared back. 'Yeah, I understand. I understand that your ego has had the best massage it can remember in years. And if it carries on, you will hurt Charlotte whether you want to or not, and then she'll get you by the balls and twist them off.'

Roger winced.

But for all my words, I felt a sudden flush of discomfort. Because I did know what he meant. It *was* nice, after years of being in the same relationship, to have someone pay you real attention, to want to know what you thought, what kind of person you were.

It was all very well for me to take the moral high ground, but if all this TV stuff had happened while I was living with Daniel, wouldn't I have still been flattered by Cal flirting with me? I was pretty sure I wouldn't have gone any further, not that "further" was necessarily on offer. Here I paused to relive, for the thousandth time, the memory of his mouth on mine. The delicious, feathery brushing of his soft lips. The way it had sent a tingle right up my spine. And into a few other places …

I shook myself back to the present to consider the matter in hand. Could I honestly say that if I were still married I wouldn't have wanted to go for a drink with Cal, wouldn't have been taken and tempted by *his* interest?

Roger was looking at me miserably. I softened my voice again. 'I'm sorry,' I said. 'But look, Rog, if you want to talk about who you are, take Charlotte out more. Life doesn't have to be humdrum – you don't have to only discuss the dog and the kids. Do all that stuff they tell you to do on the problem pages. Make a date with her – take her away for a dirty weekend. Go for dinner, just the two of you, and start a better conversation. Who knows? She may want to tell you how *she* is too. I do think you two have something pretty good together – I mean you're still friends, you still like each other.'

'Oh yes,' said Roger. 'We are friends, of course. But Charlotte's not always easy, you know.'

'Easy?' I squawked, freshly outraged. 'Of course she's not easy. She's passionate and intelligent and sexy and has given you two beautiful children and a wonderful home life and loves you to bits. What do you fucking want?'

'I know, I know,' Roger said awkwardly. 'I love Charlotte, you know I do.'

'And would you like it if she was going out with one of *her* colleagues every single night and texting him when she got home?'

'No, probably not.'

'So what are you bloody doing?' I asked, realising we'd come full circle and got precisely nowhere.

'I don't know. Obviously ... Well the thing is, I mean ... Well, I can't just dump Hannah. She needs me at the moment – she's fragile.'

I looked at him hopelessly. 'Oh pur-lease. She's playing you. Being all needy – I can't stand women who do that.'

'She's not playing me,' said Roger. 'But she does need me, I think. She is depending on my friendship. I suppose she has got a bit–' he hesitated '–attached to me. It's probably my fault.'

I stared at him. 'Have you slept with her?'

'No! Not really.'

'What do you mean "not really"? You either have or you haven't.'

'She wanted to, we got close to it, but I didn't.'

'Why not?'

Roger looked embarrassed. 'We didn't have any contraceptives,' he said uncomfortably.

'So you would have done, if you had?' I demanded.

'No – well, I don't know. She was upset and I ... I wasn't going to but we got a bit carried away ... And I think she just needed some affection. She was really quite distressed. But I didn't, that's the main thing.' He'd started on the napkin now and was twisting it tightly round and round into a spiral in his fingers.

I shook my head in disbelief. 'But she still wanted to, didn't she? She was still going to sleep with you whether you had a condom or not. Jesus!'

'I don't know really – she wasn't thinking straight – she'd had too much to drink. Her ex had called her and she–'

'See?' I cried agitated. 'See what she's doing? Roger, please promise me you won't ever touch her again. Even if you had a condom she'd probably make a hole in it. Are you *mad*?'

Roger shook his head silently, looking wretched. I gripped his arm in frustration.

'Look at me. She's trying to trap you – she wants to turn up on your doorstep pregnant. What would Charlotte say then?'

Roger shuddered. 'She was crying. I felt a bastard.'

'I bet she bloody was,' I said grimly. 'I bet emotional blackmail's right up her street.'

Roger shook his head. 'I don't think she's doing it deliberately,' he said slowly, 'but I do think she's maybe a bit disturbed emotionally at the moment. To be honest, I did feel worried this morning when she phoned me. Even before you rang, I was thinking: what have I got into and how am I going to detach myself? I know it's getting heavier than I ever intended and I don't know what to do. It was only meant to be platonic ...'

'But these things never really are, are they?' I said wearily. 'Not really. Not unless the other person's as ugly as sin and totally sexless to boot.'

'Well, look at us – we are,' Roger said, with a weak smile. 'And I'm dead handsome and you look OK in the right light.'

'Thank you,' I said. 'Very funny. We're platonic because we're like family. We've known each other a long time, watched the kids grow up together, seen the worst of each other. Generally, seriously, it doesn't happen often, does it? There's usually a frisson – a little something if a heterosexual woman is spending time alone frequently with a heterosexual man – and even if they don't remotely fancy each other, it's still different from two women or two men, isn't it? The sex thing is always there – even if it's totally buried and nobody thinks about it.'

'I guess so.' He looked at me appealingly. 'What am I going to do?'

'You are going to accept that she's bad news and stop the whole thing in its tracks right now. You don't have to be a bastard. You simply tell her that you love your wife and kids and that while you're sorry for her and about all her troubles, you can't risk hurting them. Give her all that crap about what a special person she is, how she deserves a proper relationship of her own – with someone better than you.'

I gave him a hard look. 'And then you stick to it. No drinks, no texts, no phone calls. Tell her it's the best way for both of you – so you can both get over it. It doesn't really matter what you say as long as you mean it and don't give in.'

Roger nodded, suddenly resolute. 'I will.' He grabbed my hands. 'Thank you, Laura. *Thank you.*'

Chapter Twenty-eight

I HAD A BRIEF text from Roger telling me he'd "done it"; that Hannah had been very upset but he was holding firm.

Thank God for that, I thought, as I swung my gym bag over my shoulder and left the changing room, looking sideways into the large mirror to check my newly toned arms.

I was definitely beginning to see a difference all over now. My upper arms had the beginnings of a shape to them – even my stomach didn't wobble as much as it had done. I'd been on the treadmill for half an hour, spent 45 minutes on the cross-trainer – Clara had been right, it was just a case of building up and with the right music I could keep going almost indefinitely now – done some weights and a few squats on the power plate to finish off.

Clara herself was "on earlies" that week so I wasn't able to have an in-depth analysis with her of pounds lost and muscle tone gained – nor could I borrow the tape measure she carried in her handbag to check on the progress of our midriffs, but I felt firmer and my tracksuit bottoms were looser than they had been.

I walked through reception, waving to the girl behind the desk and feeling pretty pleased with myself, loving the thought of Cal seeing how I'd changed even more in the last two weeks. I paused in the car park to send Clara a text update – I missed having her to compare notes with.

So I was quite pleased to find Charlotte on my doorstep when I got back. Even though she'd be bored in seconds, at least it was someone to show off my triceps to.

'You not at work today?' I asked cheerily, as I stuck my key in the lock, noticing that my friend had on a pair of old jeans and a sweatshirt, and sported a distinct lack of make-up.

'No,' she said shortly.

'Are you OK?' I looked at her more carefully. Her blonde curls were scraped back into a scrunchie. She looked tired, her eyes small. She might even have been crying.

'No,' she said again.

'What's the matter?' I asked carefully, as I threw my jacket over the newel post and walked ahead of her down the hall to the kitchen, dreading looking at her. Surely that bloody Hannah hadn't phoned her and told her all, just as Roger had finally done the decent thing.

I filled the kettle and got mugs out of the cupboard. When I turned round, Charlotte hadn't sat down at the table as she usually would, but was just standing looking at me. 'What's the matter?' I said again.

Charlotte stared at me. 'It seems Roger's been seeing someone else.'

I swallowed, feeling awful. 'No. Really?' I squeaked. 'Are you sure?' Even to me it sounded unconvincing.

'Yes I'm quite sure.' Charlotte had a strange expression on her face I'd never seen before. 'Becky saw you.'

'What?' My mind was racing. What had Becky seen? Me talking to Roger? But she wouldn't have known what we were talking about.

'What do you mean?' I asked stupidly.

'Becky saw Roger – her father – hidden away down the town with you. Holding hands.'

'No!'

'Yes – she saw you, Laura. She's been worrying about it for two days. I found her crying this morning. She hasn't gone to school – she's at home crying now. And I hate you for that even more than I hate you for going behind my back and having an affair with my husband!'

I had a horrible nauseous feeling in my solar plexus. My heart was thumping in my chest.

'*No*, Charlotte, listen, you've got it all wrong. I'm not having an affair with Roger. Charlotte, I wouldn't – how can you think that?' My hands were shaking.

'Oh quite easily, really,' said Charlotte, still in the same flat, remote voice. 'It's all making sense now. I noticed you couldn't take your eyes off him at his bloody boring drinks do that you were so keen to come to. Why was that then? So you could be close to him? Oh yes, it's all falling into place. The way you've been whispering together, the way you've been behaving as though you have a secret, the way you've been losing weight and dolling yourself up like a teenager.' She looked at me with disdain. 'I thought you were having a mid-life crisis, trying to make yourself feel better about Daniel. I didn't know you were just after my husband.'

'I wasn't! I'm not.'

'And the really stupid thing is that, as you know, I'd convinced myself that *he* was having one too. So I'd stopped worrying about him disappearing off and being funny about his phone and buying new shirts. And all the time, he was doing it all for you. I bet you were both having a good laugh at me, weren't you?'

'No, no, no. Charlotte, please believe me – you've got this all wrong.'

'Have I?' she said furiously. 'What were you doing holding hands then? Why were you in a bar in town together?'

'We weren't holding hands – we were just talking.'

'So my daughter is a liar?'

'No, of course not. I think I put my hand on his – you know, for emphasis – and Becky must have seen me do it and got the wrong idea. Honestly Charlotte, we were just talking ...'

'What about? And why, if you had such pressing things to say to my husband, didn't you come round to our house to talk to him. Openly – in front of me?'

My heart was pounding even harder now. Roger had promised me it was over – that he'd told Hannah and would get everything back to normal. I couldn't drop him in it now. I looked frantically at Charlotte. She looked utterly miserable, her eyes full of pain and confusion.

I took a deep breath. 'We were talking about you.'

Charlotte continued to look at me.

'Look,' I said in a rush. 'You're not supposed to know

about it but he's taking you away on a special weekend. Somewhere lovely. And I –' I took another deep breath, my brain in overdrive, desperately trying to come up with something plausible. 'I am having the children.'

Charlotte looked at me in disbelief. 'Now I know you're lying,' she said coldly. 'Roger has never taken me anywhere as a surprise in twenty years. Why start now? He doesn't do that stuff. It would never occur to him.'

'It was my idea,' I said desperately. 'You know that night when you came in and we were talking and you said what are you two looking so intense about?'

'Yes,' said Charlotte sourly. 'I know now, don't I?'

'No, no, you don't. He'd had a bit to drink and he was saying how much he loved you and how he knew he didn't really do enough to show it, and I said, because I was drunk too, and I was feeling all emotional, you know –'

I looked at her appealingly; she stared stonily back. 'I said he should show it because it was awful when my marriage ended and a strong marriage like yours should be nurtured and appreciated.'

I stopped and took another deep breath. 'I said you should do something special. And then a few days later, I saw this ad for a romantic weekend away and I thought he could take you on it, so I phoned and said would he meet me and I suggested it and said I'd stay at your house and look after Benson and all the children.' I stopped, feeling close to tears.

'Where?' Charlotte was still glaring.

'Paris,' I improvised.

'And when is it?'

'I'm not entirely sure – he went off to book it. Um – end of the month, I think.'

I could see Charlotte was weakening and I felt a mixture of relief and a horrible, sickening guilt that I was still lying to her. I turned away, suddenly unable to meet her eyes and started spooning coffee into mugs. 'He was going to let me know when it was confirmed.' I spun round, in sudden panic. 'You haven't said anything to him yet, have you?'

Charlotte sounded sad. 'No. He'd already gone to work

when Becky told me. I thought I'd come here first and find out what was going on. Kick him out later.'

'Don't do that!' I tried to laugh. 'This really is all a terrible mistake.' I poured water and opened the fridge for milk, my heart still hammering. Charlotte had at least sat down now. I put a mug in front of her and sat down too.

'I'm really sorry – it's all my fault. I should have just talked to him about it on the phone. I only suggested we meet because it seemed easier. I never meant to cause all this. Never thought for a moment anyone would think ...'

I knew I was gabbling but didn't seem able to stop. 'I think he squeezed my hand when he said thank you, that's all. I'm so sorry Becky is upset. It never occurred to me that anyone would see us And even if they did, I never dreamt you'd think ...' I put my hand on her arm. 'I'm so sorry.'

Charlotte looked at me miserably. 'I want to believe you but it doesn't feel right.'

I dragged up a smile, knowing it sat half-heartedly on my treacherous face. 'It's true. Look, please don't say anything to Roger because it's a surprise and he said himself that he's never given you a surprise before and he really wants to see your expression when he shows you the tickets.'

My insides contracted painfully at the now-fluent lies that were tumbling out of my mouth to my oldest, dearest friend.

Charlotte put her head in her hands. 'I don't know,' she muttered.

'Charlotte,' I said, desperately, feeling close to crying. 'How could you think I would do anything with Roger? I mean, I love Roger but he's like a sort of brother or how I imagine a brother could be – not like Anthony, of course, who's a bit of a dick. And he's *your* husband. Charlotte, I wouldn't, I couldn't ...'

Charlotte raised her head. There were tears in her eyes too.

'Jesus Christ,' she said.

Chapter Twenty-nine

NEVER MIND THE ATKINS, the Dukan or the GI Index, if you want to lose weight, have a trauma.

Until I knew Roger had booked a weekend in Paris and safely presented the tickets to Charlotte, I could barely sleep or eat, so big was the knot of anxiety in my stomach.

I hated the fact that there would now be this huge, unspoken issue between me and my best friend. Things could never be the same again. She might think everything was OK but I would always know I hadn't told her the truth and neither had Roger, and we were complicit in that. It felt like betrayal.

As I said to Roger, there are many more ways of being unfaithful than getting in the sack.

Charlotte had been sheepish the next time I saw her and I'd felt even worse.

'I'm really sorry I thought that,' she said. 'I don't know what came over me.'

'It's OK,' I said, feeling as guilty as hell because her instincts were right even if she'd got the wrong woman. I remembered saying it myself after Daniel – the worst bit of the whole business was the way he'd let me think I was paranoid. I didn't want that for Charlotte.

'I want you to tell her,' I'd said to Roger when he'd phoned to say the weekend was sorted. 'I want you to pick your moment and tell her that you're sorry if you've been a bit odd lately but there was a girl at work coming on to you and you were worrying about it. That you've now told her it has to stop.

'Quite aside from the moral aspect,' I added, 'it would be a good safety blanket. Suppose Hannah does one of her heavy breathing acts down the phone again?'

I noticed he no longer tried to deny that it had been her who'd been making the anonymous phone calls.

'I'm so sorry Becky was upset,' I said to Charlotte now. 'I hate the thought of her in tears because of me.'

'Oh, she's hormonal,' Charlotte said, trying to make light of it and failing. 'She's always in tears about something.'

I gave her a hug. 'I love you,' I said, a lump in my own throat. 'I wouldn't do anything, ever, to hurt you.'

Charlotte hugged me back hard and then pushed me away. 'Don't start me off too.'

I wouldn't have chosen the method but the extra, unexpected weight loss from two days of not eating was handy. The final shoot was in ten days' time, just after Charlotte's weekend away, and Cal was hoping there would be a real visible difference in me they could capture on film. I was spending every spare minute at the gym and trying to live on cheese and tomatoes. I was also trying not to dwell on the fact that we were going to be staying in the hotel overnight ...

Cal had phoned several times since I'd seen him, with arrangements for the final session and once, he said, just to see how I was. It was probably, in fact, to check I hadn't been detained under the Mental Health Act, since he'd managed to catch me the time before, still shrieking manically at Stanley while picking up the phone. 'Sorry,' I said, shamefaced, 'hormones are raging.'

He gave a low, sexy chuckle. 'That's OK – I wouldn't mind getting you on film doing that,' he joked. 'Just to show your human side – viewers like a bit of raw female passion.'

The words had sent a jolt through me. 'You've got to be joking,' I'd said hastily, thinking it would probably rather suit me as well ...

'So are you up for it, Laura?'

'Sorry?' I came back to the present to find Clara speaking to me. It was Sunday morning and we were having an après-gym juice with Alfie and Andrew but I had no idea what she was talking about. She winked. 'That's if you've got any energy left after all these hot dates with your toy boy.'

A slightly odd expression crossed Andrew's face. A kind of disapproval or distaste. I flushed, anxiously hoping he wouldn't say anything to Stanley and then pulled myself up short. Of course he wouldn't – he was a teacher and would be responsible and ethical. Anything said to him in the gym was confidential, surely.

'He's not my toy boy,' I said quickly.

'Come off it,' smirked Clara. 'I saw you together the other night, remember. And I must say I don't blame you one bit ...'

'Anyway,' said Alfie. 'Are we a team?' He'd lost even more weight now and was really beginning to look good – his face was more chiselled and his eyes seemed bluer than ever.

'I'm game,' said Andrew.

'What do we have to do again?' asked Clara.

Alfie looked at the paper in his hand. 'A 1km row, 2km run on the treadmill, 1km on the cross-trainer, 50 lengths of the pool, 2km on the bike and 50 press ups. Mixed teams of four – fastest times win.'

'Press-ups?' I groaned. 'Can barely do five of the bloody things, let alone fifty.'

'It will be a challenge,' said Andrew firmly. He patted his middle. 'Right – when can we all get together for a team training session? I for one need some incentive to carry on – it's only seeing your three bright, cheery faces that keeps me going.'

'He's lovely, isn't he?' said Clara fondly, after Andrew had taken all our mobile numbers and promised to text us our team training schedule. 'You can always tell a teacher,' said Clara. 'And he's quite yummy in his way, isn't he?'

'He's married.' My voice was sharper than I'd meant it to be.

'Aren't they always?' Clara smiled.

'I'm not,' said Alfie.

'Well I don't know why,' said Clara, grinning now, ''cos you're yummy too!'

'I've always been a bit too much to handle,' he quipped back.

'How much have you lost now?' I asked him. 'You look really different.'

'I'm down four and a half stone,' he said proudly.

'Christ, I wish I was,' said Clara gloomily. 'I'm supposed to be meeting Vicky tonight but I'm going to have to cancel. She's bound to ask if I can get into the dress yet – and last time I sort of implied it was just a bit tight. The truth is that I still can't get the zip up; it's nearly there but still not all the way, and even if I could fasten it, it would look terrible – I bulge out of it everywhere.' She looked at us both in despair. 'It's just too small.'

Alfie patted her arm. 'I think you look terrific as you are,' he said loyally.

'Can you really not get it taken out?' I asked.

Clara shrugged. 'I don't think so – I've looked at the seams. And they'd never match the fabric if they tried to put panels in and Vicky would notice, and God help us all if it didn't match everyone else's exactly, and oh my God, the wedding's in 13 days. I'm going to have to be on hot water and enemas from now on to have a fighting chance of even getting it on properly. I'll still look like a barrage balloon.'

'Can't you just tell her?' I said. 'Can't you be a maid of honour instead and wear something different?'

Clara shook her head. 'I shouldn't think so. When Vicky has a vision, that's it. Just the thought of seeing her makes me just want to go home, hide under the duvet, and eat chips.'

And she's your best friend, I said silently, suddenly suffused with emotion at the thought of Charlotte, who was mine. I'd never be in that situation with her – we had a real closeness, a bond, and I was now appreciating how rare and special it was.

Bloody Roger for jeopardising it. Bloody Hannah. Bloody hell.

What have I done?

'Thanks for all you've done.' Charlotte hugged me as Roger put their luggage into the boot. 'I've left you lots of food and lists of what the kids are doing and the Aga is stoked right up – you should be OK.'

'We're only going for the weekend,' said Roger, 'and we really must hurry or we'll miss the ferry.'

I thought he looked anxious and I knew it wasn't just about getting to Dover on time.

'She keeps texting,' he'd said worriedly, while Charlotte was upstairs. 'She says she needs to see me and talk to me or she doesn't know what she'll do. Says she's desperate. I haven't answered the last three, but I feel terrible – suppose she kills herself?'

'She won't,' I said, in what I hoped was a reassuring manner. 'I know it's hard but she'll get over it and meet someone else. But for God's sake, tell Charlotte – you don't have to go into every last detail. Just say a girl at the office is getting a bit disturbed about you. Just to prepare her – in case she comes home to find Benson simmering gently on the hob! Oh my God, I'm sorry,' I said, clapping my hand to my mouth as Roger looked stricken. 'Really bad, tasteless joke, I'm sorry. Didn't mean it. Look, it will be OK and if she keeps on, just turn your phone off.'

Roger shook his head. 'Can't do that – not until the end of the day anyway – I'm expecting work to call. I'll just ignore her. Or shall I text her once more and say I'm sorry but I can't see her?'

'No – I don't think –' I stopped as Charlotte came into the room.

'Got everything?' I smiled brightly. 'Don't worry about a thing here.'

Stanley hadn't been over-enthusiastic about the idea of a whole weekend at Becky's but it made sense to uproot one child rather than two. Especially as there was also Benson to consider and Becky had an inset day today and would be bored left to her own devices in my house.

Also I'd need entertainment for both boys, and Charlotte's house was where the PlayStation was, which clinched it. So I'd loaded Boris's dishes with food and asked Rosie, my next-door neighbour, to come in and out and had brought my laptop and anything else I might need to last me till Monday.

Though as I said to Stanley, who seemed to have packed an inordinate amount of goodness-knows-what for three nights, we only lived two miles away – we could always pop back.

When Charlotte and Roger had driven off, I left Becky, still in her dressing gown, sprawled on the sofa in front of Jeremy Kyle, made a coffee and set my laptop up on the kitchen table. With no distractions to hand, I was hoping to finish the current brochure copy – patio heaters and braziers one can't live without – and start tackling a video script Mike had given me to "polish up", which I knew from experience might be a lengthy process.

After an hour or so, I thought I'd better check how Becky was doing. She'd moved on to *My American Dream* – a vile-looking programme about 16-year-old girls in Florida who had nose and boob jobs and their own life coaches – and looked set in for the day.

'Do you want a cup of tea or something, Bex?'

She nodded at me. 'Toast?' she asked hopefully.

'Sure.'

Oh God, how much I could do with some toast myself. With Marmite, or peanut butter, or maybe both. I went back to the kitchen and sawed at the large brown loaf Charlotte had left. Maybe just a tiny end bit for me – it was a four-slice toaster after all. Shame to waste all that power ...

It had just popped up when the phone rang and Becky wandered into the room. 'I'll get it,' she said, fishing the handset out of Benson's bed.

I got plates from the cupboard and started buttering.

'No, sorry she's not here,' Becky was saying. 'No – he's not here either – they've gone away. Yes. Paris. No, on the ferry – Mum doesn't like tunnels. About an hour ago. No, I'm sorry I don't know. Um, yes, of course, just a minute –'

As I heard her start to give out Charlotte's mobile number, a sudden alarm bell rang. I threw down the butter knife.

'Becky!'

She had wandered into the hallway with the phone against her cheek, still talking. 'OK. Bye.'

'Who was that?'

Becky shrugged. 'Don't know. Someone for Mum – said she needed to talk to her.'

'Did she give a name?'

'No.'

'Here, let me have that a moment.' I took the phone from her and dialled 1471. Number withheld.

'What did she sound like?' I asked, trying to sound calm.

Becky shrugged again.' Dunno. Normal.'

Which was precisely what she wasn't if it was Hannah, which I suddenly felt sure it was. It was all those questions. Oh God, what if it was her and she was about to phone Charlotte before Roger had a chance to break the news?

Suppose she drove to Dover and declared her undying love in the middle of Departures. Informed the whole queue at passport control that Roger had been within a condom's reach of having her? Oh my God, again.

I wondered what to do. If I texted Roger he might ignore it – he'd think it was Hannah and wouldn't want to start reading texts in front of Charlotte. I'd have to phone him – then he'd answer in case it was work. But then he might look at the display and say, 'Oh, it's Laura phoning,' and put me on to Charlotte and then Charlotte would wonder why I was phoning him and not her and we'd be back to square one.

My head whirled.

I could phone from their home line so he thought it was Becky. But no – same problem. He might hand it to Charlotte if he was driving or in the middle of sorting the tickets or something.

In the end, I took a deep breath and withheld the number. It rang and rang and then went to voicemail. Shit – he must think it's Hannah.

I'd just have to risk it – if Charlotte answered, I'd have to pretend it was to do with the hotel booking or something – say there'd been a call about it. Christ, how I hated all this subterfuge. With stomach churning, I dialled again, letting my number show. Roger answered immediately. There was a lot of background noise, with people talking and some sort of announcement coming over a Tannoy. I spoke as quickly as I could.

'Roger, it's me but pretend it's work. I think Hannah might have phoned here – a woman called and asked Becky a lot of questions. She knows where you are now and Bex gave her Charlotte's mobile number. You must tell Charlotte at once – in case she turns up there or phones her.'

Roger answered briskly. 'OK, got that – thank you for calling. We're just about to sail but I'll deal with it later.'

I put down the phone in relief. At least if they were about to leave there'd be no time for any dramatic scenes and once they were in French waters Charlotte probably wouldn't answer the phone anyway.

I'd been on holiday with Charlotte often enough to know that her general philosophy when one had to pay to receive calls, and she was busy sunning herself, was to look at the number and if she didn't recognise it or there wasn't one, to say, 'I can't be arsed,' and turn it off.

I just hoped Roger would take my advice a bit more quickly than he had last time and tell her about Hannah as soon as possible since it didn't look as though the mad shrew was going to give up on him any time soon. Charlotte needed to be in the picture by the time she got back on Monday. In the meantime, if Hannah phoned here again, I was going to give her very short shrift indeed.

I was so distracted by planning exactly what I'd say, that I ate two slices of toast and Marmite.

In an effort to burn off these careless calories, I took Benson for a walk on the beach before I left to pick up Joe from St Mary's, and then scooped up Stanley from the bus stop on the way back.

The exercise and fresh air left me invigorated, and seeing the kids all safe and sound round the table, eating the lasagne Charlotte had left us, filled me with such pleasure and relief that I almost began to feel sorry for Hannah.

It must be awful to be home on your own, feeling desperate and deranged over a man you couldn't have. It was why I was trying very hard not to think about Cal 24/7 even though a thrill of anticipation ran through me every time I pictured the next filming session. And the lingering way he'd kissed me goodbye ...

I decided, as I passed the bowl of salad around the table, knowing only Becky would even look at it, that if Hannah did phone again, I would be calm and kind to her. I'd tell her that Roger loved Charlotte and that she, Hannah, must concentrate her energies on finding someone else – someone who was single and available.

So once the boys had headed for the PlayStation and Becky had gone off for a shower, I was glad I was still in the kitchen stacking the dishwasher when the phone rang, so I could grab it before any of the kids.

'Hello?'

'You cow.'

I was speechless for a moment – taken aback by the ferocity in her voice. 'Charlotte? What are you talking about?'

'I've just been through my husband's phone – this is what you have driven me to, thank you so much – and it was you calling him earlier, when he told me very specifically it was someone from the office. What's the problem? Were you missing him already?'

I had no idea what to say. As it happened, Charlotte wasn't going to let me get a word in anyway. She sounded furious and bitter.

'To think I apologised to you! I am going to sit him down now and make him tell me all the gory details – just so I can fully understand how stupid I've been – and then we'll use the peace and quiet to thrash out the details of the divorce. My feeling so far is that I get the house, the kids and the money. And Roger gets to go to hell.'

I felt sick. I could hear Roger in the background giving a sort of groan. 'Charlotte,' I heard him call out. 'Please don't, it's not her fault.'

'Oh, how sweet! He's defending you.' Charlotte's voice was laced with sarcasm. 'Are my children all right?'

'Yes, of course. We've not long eaten and they're ...'

'Just you look after them!' The phone went dead.

I stood staring at it in my hand. God almighty, how much

worse could this get? Hannah must have contacted Charlotte and said something about Roger. Charlotte wouldn't have been looking in his phone otherwise – they were fine this morning. I did some deep breathing and tried to get a grip.

Roger would sort it now. He'd tell Charlotte about Hannah and she would realise, once and for all, there was nothing going on with me. I knew that and knew Charlotte would calm down once she got the truth, but I still felt shaken. I had never heard Charlotte so angry – and she'd certainly never spoken to me like that before.

I wondered whether to send her a text, but decided it was better to keep my head down and leave it to her and Roger. She'd probably phone back later anyway – she'd want to say goodnight to the kids.

She did, but she clearly didn't want to speak to me because an hour later she phoned Becky on her mobile and chatted to Joe on that too.

She even sent her love to Stanley but I wasn't called to the phone.

'Mum all right?' I asked Becky casually, when the boys were having one last go on their football game and she was back on the sofa in front of Jonathan Ross. She hardly looked up from the TV.

'Yeah, think so.'

I wondered if Roger was …

I was up early the next morning despite not having slept well. It wasn't just the unfamiliar bed and Charlotte's noisy heating pipes that disturbed me, it was the jumbled dreams about Cal and Roger and Charlotte and Hannah and – oddly – Alfie, that startled me awake and left me staring at the ceiling, wondering what exactly was going on in Paris.

I hoped Hannah hadn't called Charlotte – I dreaded to think what sort of reception she might have got if she had – and it could only make it worse for Roger. Though perhaps he had told Charlotte the whole story by now and everything was OK.

'I'll take you for a walk later,' I said to Benson as he reappeared from the garden. At the word "walk" he flung himself at me and then charged into the utility room where Charlotte kept his lead and throw-the-ball thingy. I heard his tail swishing wildly against the wall.

'No, not yet,' I said, as he came back out with his lead in his mouth and threw himself against me again. 'We've got to do some other stuff first.'

I consulted Charlotte's list. Joe had football club at 10.30 a.m. till 12 p.m. and Becky quite often went to Lauren's on a Saturday afternoon, but then again Lauren might come here if I didn't mind one more.

I ought to do some work if there was an opportunity and also needed to get Stanley some more school trousers, but since I wouldn't get to the gym this weekend, I wanted to keep my promise to the dog and fit in a decent tramp along the beach.

I made some coffee and waited for the kids to appear. Only Joe did, already dressed in his kit. I went to look at the other two while Joe ate his cereal. Stanley was sprawled across Joe's bottom bunk, Becky was curled up in the middle of a huge pile of duvet. Both were out cold. And they still were when it was time to leave. I gently shook Becky.

'You OK left here with Stanley while I drop Joe at football? Does Mum leave you on your own?'

Becky nodded sleepily. 'Yeah, no problem.'

'Call me on my mobile if you need me. Stanley knows the number, but I'll leave it on the kitchen table.'

I felt on hyper-alert being in charge while Charlotte was so far away – and already so furious – but if Stanley's weekend routines were anything to go by both kids would probably still be snoring when I got back.

In fact, once I thought about it sensibly, I remembered that Charlotte often left the kids on their own for short periods during the day, while she walked the dog or went to buy something.

So, having deposited Joe at the school playing fields where dozens of small boys were already charging about in circles, I decided to whizz up to the shopping centre at Westwood Cross and buy Stanley's trousers before it got too busy. Then I could relax and spend the rest of the day with the kids. Perhaps we'd *all* walk the dog – that would please and amaze Charlotte if I could tell her I got them all out for a couple of hours' exercise.

The traffic was already heavy and it was nearly 11 a.m. by the time I'd parked near Marks and Spencer and heading rapidly for 12 p.m. by the time I'd discovered that they had every size in black school trousers apart from Stanley's, and had queued up for some considerable time to order a pair which might be in on Tuesday.

I was just getting seriously anxious and abusive at the third roundabout hold-up on the way back to get Joe – imagining him standing forlornly on his own at the school gates – and shrieking, 'Come on, move, you bugger!' at the car in front - when my mobile rang. It was Becky.

'Joe's going home for lunch with Michael,' she said. 'Yes, yes, it's fine. He does it all the time. His mum said you can pick him up about five.'

Relieved, I drove back to Charlotte's to find Becky's friend Lauren installed in her bedroom and Stanley in front of a computer game. 'How about a nice walk on the beach with me?' I enquired.

'How about lunch,' he said grumpily. 'I haven't had breakfast yet and I'm starving.'

'Come and help me make it, then.'

'You OK?' I enquired, as he buttered bread with bad grace.

'Yeah.'

I left the three children sitting round a heap of sandwiches and grabbed Benson's lead before I weakened and tucked in myself, putting an apple and a banana in my pockets instead. It was incredibly cold on the beach – the wind coming off North Foreland was biting – but Benson, throwing himself joyfully into the rock pools, and then shaking himself all over me, didn't seem to care.

'You're so lucky to live here,' Cal had said wistfully when we'd had dinner. 'I'd love to have the sea at my doorstep.'

He was right – I was lucky, I thought, looking at the broad sweep of Botany Bay, the gulls squawking high up in the recesses in the cliffs. Even when the sky was grey and raw it was still beautiful. I ought to appreciate the simple things like that more. As I shouted for Benson and we made our way back up the steps to the green at the bottom of Charlotte's road, I suddenly felt better about everything.

Charlotte and Roger would work things out. I'd be seeing Cal again soon. I didn't have to clap eyes on Daniel's slimy face this weekend and I'd managed not to eat any bread yet today. Stanley was healthy and Charlotte had left me two bottles of Pinot Grigio in the fridge. The only downside to the situation I could see so far was that I was bloody starving and if I had a glass of wine I'd cave in and eat everything in the house.

Not that I could drink just yet because there was still Joe to fetch.

'Where does Michael live?' I asked Becky, once Lauren had been collected and it was almost 4.30 p.m.

Becky looked at me blankly. 'I don't know.'

Chapter Thirty

I TRIED TO KEEP calm. Becky, it transpired, did not only not know where Joe was, but she didn't have a number for Michael's parents or know what their surname was.

'I think she said her name was Julie. Or something like that.'

'But you know her, don't you?'

'No.'

'But you said Joe went there all the time.'

'No, I didn't – I said he goes to play with people all the time. And Mum never minds.'

'But Charlotte does know this Julie?'

'I don't know.'

Alarm was radiating through my chest. I tried to stay rational.

'But Michael's a friend of Joe's?' I persisted.

'Yeah, I think so.'

'And so he's been there before?'

'I don't know – I can't remember.'

My voice rose in exasperation. 'Try to think!'

Christ, supposing it was Hannah – suppose she really was a lunatic and had taken Joe as a way of getting to Roger. But surely Joe wouldn't just go with a stranger? Then again, she was a woman and looked normal enough and she'd probably have told him she was a friend of mine or Charlotte's. She'd be able to talk about how his mum had gone to Paris. The bitch ...

Becky was still gazing at me vacantly.

'What did this woman say exactly?' I asked sharply.

'She just said was it OK if Joe came home with them for lunch and I said OK.'

'Without even asking where they lived? For Christ's sake, Becky. Didn't you think at all?'

Becky put both hands to her head and tugged at her hair. 'Stop going on at me,' she suddenly shrieked. 'It's not my fault!' She burst into tears.

'Oh Becky, I'm sorry,' I said, stricken, putting out my arms to her. She backed away from me.

'Why are you being like this?' she wailed. 'Mum said you'd gone all funny.'

I stared at her, feeling terrible. 'Oh darling, I'm sorry – I haven't gone all funny. I'm just worrying because I'm supposed to be looking after you both. Come on, Bex, you know I love you – I've known you all your life – you're like my family. Please don't cry.' She let me hug her this time and I felt close to tears myself as I stroked her hair.

Stanley came into the kitchen in his socks, took one look at Becky sobbing and hastily backed out again.

'Look,' I said, trying to sound brighter than I felt. 'Let's give your mum a quick ring. She'll know where Michael lives.'

And if she doesn't, and she's never heard of Michael or Julie then I'll really start to panic.

'You give her a ring, Becky, and I'll make us some tea.'

As I put the kettle on the Aga hotplate, Becky fetched her mobile phone. After a few moments she held it away from her ear. 'She's switched off.'

'Try your Dad.'

He was switched off too. It was 4.55 p.m. I felt sick. 'Oh well,' I said with forced cheer, 'when nobody comes to get Joe, Michael's mum will phone again. Then I'll ask where they live and go and get him.'

Becky took her mug of tea and nodded. 'I'm going to wash my hair,' she said. 'Before *X Factor*.'

'OK!' I beamed at her. 'You do that and I'll get us all some dinner once Joe's home.'

As soon as she'd gone upstairs, I stared anxiously at the clock. Then at the phone. What the hell was I going to do if nobody called?

Nobody had by 5.15 p.m. But Julie – if she existed – was

probably still waiting for someone to arrive. She might not think to phone for another half an hour yet. At what point did I give in to hysteria and call the police? By 5.30 p.m. I was pacing the kitchen.

What would I say to the police if I did call? *Yes, that's right. I'm in charge of this seven-year-old boy who has gone off to the house of someone whose name and address I don't know but who may in fact be a mad woman called Hannah whose surname also eludes me and I have no idea where she lives either.*

I'd have to do something if I hadn't heard by six. I had the handset on the table right in front of me next to my third cup of tea and was glaring at it, willing it to ring.

At 5.50 p.m. my mobile burst into life instead. I snatched it up from the work surface. It wasn't a number I knew.

'Yes?' I squawked.

'Laura? Is that you?' The voice at the other end sounded uncertain. 'Thought I'd got the wrong number for a minute.'

It was Andrew, trying to organise a training session with Clara and Alfie for the next morning. 'Nine a.m.?' he was saying. 'Or is that too early for a Sunday? We need to start getting our act together if we're going to be the dream team in this challenge.' He gave a groan. 'Not that I quite see myself in that role ...'

Eventually, I stuttered something incoherent back.

'Laura,' he said, 'are you all right there?'

I'd had no idea he lived in Kingsgate too. Within ten minutes of me weeping down the phone, he was in Charlotte's kitchen, patting me on my heaving shoulder.

'I don't generally burst into tears every five minutes,' I assured him shakily, before sitting down at the kitchen table and doing just that.

When we'd put the kettle back on and I'd mopped at my face with some kitchen roll, Andrew assessed the situation. 'They'll phone eventually,' he surmised. 'They won't keep someone else's child all night.'

'But suppose it wasn't really Michael's mother who phoned?' I wailed. 'Suppose it's a set-up and someone's taken him?'

Andrew spoke calmly. 'In my experience, people do not go pinching small boys in Broadstairs and if they did, they wouldn't phone up to warn you first.'

I told him about Hannah. He listened carefully.

'Even so,' he said, when I'd finished, 'it's one thing to get hung up over a bloke, it's quite another to kidnap his child.' He gave my arm a small squeeze. 'I'm quite sure it's all OK.' He cupped his chin in one hand, thoughtfully. 'Who organises the football club? They'll have a list of all the kids involved.'

'I don't know. I did ask Becky but ...' I shrugged, glancing anxiously at the clock. It was 6.30.

He looked round the room. 'Have you got a computer here?' I fetched my lap top from the chair in the corner.

'Let's see if we can find out,' he said, opening it up. 'What school was it at?'

I put my head in hands. 'What will Charlotte say? The last thing she said was that I had to look after her children. Now I've lost one, traumatised the other, and I haven't even fed them yet.'

As if on cue, Stanley appeared in the doorway, looking suitably famished. His eyes widened with horror at the sight of his form tutor sitting at the table while I sniffed.

'Doesn't matter,' he muttered, leaving again.

I watched Andrew tapping away at the keyboard.

'I was supposed to collect Joe at five – it's now an hour and a half later,' I said. 'Do you think I should call the police?'

He stopped and looked at me. 'Well, if you're really worried ...'

And then the doorbell rang. I flew out into the hall. Joe was on the doorstep wearing an unfamiliar tracksuit, with another boy of about the same age and a large, smiling woman of about 35 with a mop of dark curls. She stuck out her hand.

'Hi, I'm Judy – sorry if we're late. I didn't realise the time and then when I did, I wasn't sure if you thought I was bringing him home or you were just running late yourself.' She laughed. 'I know what it's like. I did try phoning but your line's engaged. Kept going straight to answerphone. Lucky old

Charlotte, eh? Being whisked off to Paris. When's she back? Do you need any help with the school run?'

I leant on the doorpost, weak with relief as she rattled on. 'Do you want to come in?' I asked eventually

'No, must go – I've left the dinner on.' She handed me a carrier bag. 'Joe's kit. He was covered in mud so I popped him into something of Mikey's. Tell Charlotte no rush to get it back.'

'Thank you. Thank you so much for bringing him home.'

I shut the door and hugged Joe hard. 'Stanley's upstairs somewhere, sweetheart,' I told him as he squirmed. 'Shall I come and run you a bath?'

Joe screwed up his nose and shook his head.

Becky appeared in her dressing gown. She smiled at me. 'Back then!'

'She was called Judy,' I said.

'Oh, was she?' said Becky vaguely, adding, 'Oh, yeah, I think I've heard Mum mention her.'

Andrew was on his feet when I went back into the kitchen, teeth firmly clamped to my tongue.

'All's well that ends well, eh?'

'She'd been phoning,' I said, pulling a face. 'Becky must have been on the line upstairs ...'

'Oh well,' Andrew shrugged. 'No harm done.'

We looked at each other for a moment. 'It was so kind of you to come,' I said awkwardly.

'No problem.'

'Would you like a glass of wine?'

He hesitated. 'Um. Yes, why not.'

'Oh – unless – will your wife mind? Do you need to get back?'

'She's not there. Taken the boys to visit her sister.'

'Oh.'

I handed him a drink and dug about in the freezer for something to feed the children. When I'd filled a baking tray with sausages and put it dubiously in the Aga – with little idea how long it would take to cook – I sat down opposite him with my own glass.

'How old are your kids?'

They were his stepsons, he reminded me, and they were 13 and 15. He'd married Elaine eight years ago, so they'd been through a lot together. 'They're great lads,' he said. 'How's Stanley now?'

As usual, he was easy to talk to. We had a second glass of wine and before I knew it, I'd given him the full low down on Daniel and The Twig and how upset Stanley had been the day Daniel had finally packed his bags.

'I felt such a failure,' I said, the words surprising myself because I'd not analysed it before. 'It's not that I want him back – especially now he's got really boring about everything. But it felt as if I wasn't good enough to be able to keep my husband. Though how could I compete? Emily is 20-something, naturally blonde – well unnaturally, probably,' I added bitchily, 'and her whole body is about the size of one of my thighs.'

Andrew grinned.

'And there was a time,' I went on, 'when Daniel used to talk about women being too thin and how he liked nothing better than a steak and kidney pudding.'

'Certainly nothing to feel a failure about then,' said Andrew. 'If Daniel hadn't left you, and gone off with this young, skinny, blonde girl, you'd be feeling fine about yourself, wouldn't you?'

I looked at him quizzically. 'Well, maybe, but the point is, he did.'

'And the point is – it's him who's changed, not you. Mad fool, I say. You're lovely.'

I looked at him, startled, suddenly acutely aware he was not only Stanley's teacher but married to boot. Should he be paying me compliments like that? 'Will you tell your wife what you've been doing?' I blurted out, unable to stop myself.

Andrew looked surprised. 'Probably,' he said. 'If she's interested. The thing is -' he began, stopping as Becky came into the room.

'Is it food soon, Laura?' she asked beseechingly. 'We're starving.'

I jumped up. 'Yep, sorry – just coming.'

Andrew got up too. 'I'll leave you to it. I'll call you tomorrow about the gym.'

I felt exhausted by the time the kids had eaten a mountain of sausage, chips, and beans (I'd fill them up with vegetables tomorrow) and were collapsed in front of the TV. I had a last mouthful of wine, ate a stray sausage myself, and went upstairs for a long shower, thinking that then I'd attempt to shepherd everyone into bed and have an early night.

As the hot water drummed down on my back I thought about the days ahead. This time next week I'd be doing the final filming with Cal – we'd be in the hotel now. Before that I had Stanley's birthday to think about – the new iPhone had already arrived and was safely hidden away, but I hadn't organised anything else – and in the meantime I had heaps of work to get through for Mike. What with the Joe fiasco I hadn't looked at any of that today. I should be thinking of ad ideas for water coolers …

But I was really tired now and my mind slipped away from all these issues (except for a delicious vision of Cal's lips touching mine, possibly while he had no shirt on) and refused to concentrate. I turned off the water and gave up trying. I'd be better after a good night's sleep.

I came downstairs in my dressing gown, rubbing my hair with a towel. The boys had gone back to the PlayStation, but Becky was still curled up on the sofa, a bowl of crisps beside her. 'Mum called,' she said.

'Oh good. How did she sound?'

Becky shrugged. 'Fine. Like Mum.'

I nodded. However many domestics Charlotte was having in Paris, she'd sound fine to the kids – it didn't mean a thing.

'Are they having a nice time?'

'Suppose so – she didn't really say. Just wanted to know if we were all OK.' She gave me sudden smile. 'I didn't tell her about Joe. Though she'd only have laughed if I had.'

I tried to smile back. I wouldn't bet on it, I thought.

'Did you speak to your dad?' I asked casually.

'No, he was in the shower too.'

'Oh, OK. So no message?'

'No,' said Becky, turning back to *The X Factor*. 'Mum just asked what you were doing and I told her you were upstairs.' She settled herself down among the cushions. 'Then she wanted to speak to Joe.'

But she didn't want to speak to me ...

Despite my unease about Charlotte, I slept better than I had done the night before. We spent the morning drifting about in our pyjamas and then I insisted on a mass exodus into the outside world to walk the dog which, with the exception of Joe getting a Wellington boot full of sea water and Benson losing two more rubber balls, passed without incident.

Late afternoon, I made a heroic effort to do what Charlotte would have done and cook them all a roast dinner, under the questionable supervision of Becky, who provided tuition on how to use the Aga.

The chicken seemed to cook in a flash but by the time I came to do the potatoes the oven didn't seem hot enough and they took forever to brown. Meanwhile the chipolatas (Joe had begged for more sausages) were wizened. It was all two hours later than planned but it tasted all right and the kids shoved it down happily enough.

By the time I'd got Joe into bed, prised Becky away from Facebook, surgically removed the PlayStation from Stanley's sweaty grasp and sent Benson to his basket for the night, I had the sense of having almost completed a survival course.

Once all the kids had been safely despatched or delivered to school the next morning, I heaved a sigh of relief that echoed round Charlotte's eerily quiet kitchen.

Benson and I walked to the corner shop and bought some fresh milk to leave in the fridge and I did the last bit of washing-up. Roger and Charlotte would be back in time to pick Joe up and be home for when Becky got in.

I picked up a piece of paper to write a note. What should I say?

Hope all OK?

Hope the Bunny Boiler didn't phone?

Trust Roger has explained all, and the divorce has been shelved?

In the end I decided it was a matter of least said, and simply wrote *Welcome Home*.

Then I called Benson in from the garden, checked his water was topped up, gave him a biscuit, and patted him on the head.

'Thank you for being a good dog and not chewing anything this time,' I said, carefully shutting the kitchen door so he couldn't have a relapse the moment I left. He jumped up at me eagerly – clearly thinking we were going for another walk.

I pushed him down. 'Not now. One of them will take you out when they get back.'

I put on my coat and gathered up my overnight bag and Stanley's, suddenly feeling that strange blend of homesickness and nostalgia and regret you can feel when you are leaving a place where you've been happy and now realise you will never go back to.

'I'll see you soon,' I said firmly to Benson, to dispel this depressing thought. 'Oh, and Benson,' I added, catching sight of the huge pot Charlotte used when she was making curry for the masses. 'Watch your back.'

Chapter Thirty-one

I WAS GOING TO have to watch mine too. Mike was on the warpath, wanting to know how quickly I could get the script I was working on, back to him. It was for a sales video designed to extol the virtues of the Home Water Coolers range to various gatherings of supermarket and department store buyers. As suspected, it was so thoroughly turgid and dire that "give it a polish" basically meant starting again.

Meanwhile, Mike was jumping from foot to foot because the recording studio had been booked for the voice-over and they couldn't finish the final edit until they'd got the soundtrack.

'Time's money, Laura,' he said for the 16th time.

'I know, and I'm doing my best,' I snapped back. 'If you could just leave me in peace I might be able to get a decent run at it.'

I could almost hear him twitching at the end of the phone. 'End of the day?'

'End of the day.'

Which at this rate might have to be defined as midnight, I thought, as I made yet another cup of coffee and girded my mental loins. I hadn't heard from Charlotte since she'd got back yesterday except for a brief text saying thanks. So I was pretty much of a twitch myself, waiting to find out if she had sorted it all out with Roger and I was now finally and irrevocably, in the clear.

The doorbell rang at midday. Charlotte was carrying a large bag and had a suit on, which meant she was at least back at work, but her face was serious.

'Hello you,' she said.

I stepped forward and hugged her. She hugged me back half-heartedly – her arms stiff. I swallowed as she followed me down the hall to the kitchen. I'd known Charlotte for 30-odd years and I'd never felt awkward with her like this.

'Good time?' I asked, glad to see she was at least sitting down this time.

'Terrific,' she said flatly. There was a silence.

'Are you OK?' I tried, as I re-filled the kettle.

Behind me, Charlotte sighed. 'I don't know, really. I'm pretty disappointed, I guess. Roger's told me all about it. About Hannah and your efforts to warn him of the error of his ways. I'm obviously sorry I doubted you. I know that was madness I do know you wouldn't do anything with Roger. But for God's sake, Lu,' she burst out, suddenly emotional, 'why the hell didn't you tell me?'

I sat down opposite her. 'I'm really sorry,' I said, taking my bracelets off and turning them round in my hands. 'I didn't know what to do. I could see she might be trouble but Roger hadn't actually done anything wrong–'

I looked at Charlotte, wondering exactly how much detail Roger had gone into but she just looked steadily back so I went on. 'And I didn't want to make trouble. I didn't know if Roger … I would have told you if he hadn't managed to get rid of her.'

'Well, he didn't manage to, did he?' said Charlotte, exasperated. 'You should have told me right away. Roger said she phoned our house.'

'Yes, she did.'

'And you sat there and said nothing!'

I hooked one open-ended bangle around another. 'I wasn't sure if it was anything to worry about. It might have been a wrong number. I wanted to find out from Roger first, rather than upset you for nothing.'

Charlotte gave a hiss of annoyance. 'But if you'd told me – that very evening – I'd have interrogated him, forced the truth out of him there and then, and put a stop to it. We would have been saved all this.'

'I'm sorry, I said again, miserably. 'I was shocked. I was

273

trying to do the right thing.'

'It was utterly the wrong thing,' Charlotte said crossly.

I got up and opened the coffee cupboard. 'Look, Charlotte,' I said, trying to be reasonable. 'If you'd found out about Daniel and The Twig before I did – would you have told me straight away? Wouldn't you have checked you were right first?'

'No. Well, yes. Maybe. I may have spoken to him first, got him by the balls, and demanded to know what was going on but then–'

'That's what I tried to do.'

'Well, you didn't do it hard enough.'

'I'm sorry,' I said again. 'I don't know what else to say.'

'So am I,' she said wearily, but she wasn't looking at me. 'I've - um - got a present here for Stanley.' She rummaged in the bag and produced a parcel and card. 'Give him a hug from us, eh?'

I stared at her, stricken. Usually she'd come round for tea on Stanley's birthday – they all would. I nodded silently, afraid I would cry.

Charlotte looked uncomfortable. 'Listen, Lu – thanks for looking after the kids. At least I got a weekend in Paris. But I'm feeling a bit let down by both of you, to be honest. It's bad enough Roger doing that to me. Bloody hell, it's like Benson getting up and biting me.' She suddenly looked upset. 'I don't know what they got up to, he said they never actually … But who knows?'

'I'm sure they didn't,' I put in hastily. 'He told me nothing had happened – it was all in her mind. Just her warped fantasy.'

Charlotte's expression had hardened. 'Yes, and what's that all about? *You* telling *me* about my marriage! He shouldn't be telling you these things. I should have known. If he had some mad shrew after his body, he should have come to *me*. But no, he didn't come to me, I went after him. I asked him what was going on and he denied there was anything wrong.'

'I know, he told me,' I said tactlessly, before I could stop myself. Charlotte glared.

'The thing is,' she went on. 'I'm upset with Roger, I feel hurt by Roger, I'm bloody furious with him. I feel he's made a fool of me. You know – we used to sit and watch those TV dramas where some bloke has an affair and it all blows up in his face and Roger would say, "What an idiot." Well, who's the bloody idiot now?'

I tried to speak calmly although my heart was beating hard. 'I don't think he meant to. It was her. Playing on his sympathy–'

Charlotte shook her head despairingly. 'Yes, well, I have to believe that, even though you and I both know it always takes two, because that's the only way I can deal with it. But what I was trying to say is that however angry with him I am, I tell myself Roger's a bloke – we know they're stupid, only half-formed at times. But *you*–' She stopped and took a deep breath. 'You're supposed to be my best friend. You should have told me. I hate the thought of you two discussing this whole bloody business, shutting me out. Putting me through all that pain when I thought it was *you* after my husband. Do you know how that felt?'

'I can imagine,' I said quietly. 'But Charlotte, you should have known I wouldn't …'

'That's easy to say now, but at the time …' She shook her head again. 'Look at it from where I was standing. You're behaving strangely, he's behaving strangely. I ask both of you about the other and neither of you can look me in the eye.' She slapped her hand hard down on the table. 'What the hell was I supposed to think?'

She picked up her bag. 'You let me down, love. And I'm pretty pissed off about it.'

I put out a hand and touched her arm. 'I'm so sorry, Charlotte. You know I love you and appreciate you. I'd never do anything to hurt you and I'm sorry I got it wrong but I didn't know if I was overreacting. I mean, in the beginning he was just trying to help her – it wasn't his fault she turned out to be a bunny boiler – and I didn't know what to do. I meant well – I did, really …' I was in tears now.

'I know,' she said briskly. 'I know that and I'll get over it. Look, I'll see you soon but right now I need to get my head round it all. Just give me a bit of time, OK?'

I nodded blindly.

'When's the rest of the filming?'

'Saturday.'

'I hope it goes well, and when's the programme?' She was talking to me in the polite tones she'd use to someone she didn't know very well.

'Um, the following weekend. I think it's 9 p.m. on Saturday – I can't remember if it's BBC 3 or 4 ...'

'OK – well, we'll be watching it, of course.'

'OK.'

'And I hope Stanley has a lovely birthday. I'll phone him.'

I stood staring at Stanley's parcel, feeling wretched. I'd never had a row with Charlotte before. We'd got impatient maybe, snapped at each other a bit if our PMT coincided, but nothing like this.

I went upstairs and looked at my computer screen, totally overwhelmed by the task in hand. I couldn't think of a single sentence to describe water coolers that I hadn't used a dozen times already. I looked at the pile of bills and bank statements on the corner of the desk and realised I should have paid my credit card by now.

I wandered along the landing and looked into Stanley's room with its usual medley of discarded clothes and gadget magazines and CDs and empty crisp packets and trainers and I felt that familiar feeling of tension and despair rise up in me – everywhere I looked there were things to do.

Boris, winding himself round my legs, loudly reminded me we were down to the last tin of cat food again. A look in the fridge revealed a total lack of sandwich fillings for Stanley, while the ironing pile made me want to burst into tears.

I made a cup of coffee and did some deep breathing, thinking how odd it was that I wasn't diving into the chocolate biscuits. I just felt sick.

I had a look in my diary. Day 20. Usually I'd be halfway down a packet of HobNobs by now. Perhaps there was something in all this protein and hot water and heaps of exercise malarkey after all.

Unable to make any sort of decision about what to do next at home, I decided to get some fresh air and go to the supermarket, hoping that the exercise of at least crossing the car park and striding up the aisles would calm me down. If I was back by two, I'd have three hours to get the rest of the script done before I went to collect Stanley from homework club – I could email it to Mike at five, just before I left.

Then, I thought, as I put tomatoes and garlic and mushrooms in my trolley, I'd cook Spaghetti Bolognese – all that stirring and chopping would be soothing – and do the ironing in front of *EastEnders*. Once Stanley was in bed I'd spend a calm hour sorting all the bills and post and rubbish on my desk and at the weekend Stanley and I could tidy his bedroom together …

'Do you need bags?' The dull-eyed young man at the check-out looked bored.

'Er – yes, please.' I had about 35 Bags for Life stuffed into the bottom of my kitchen cupboard at the last count – if ever I remembered to bring them back to the supermarket, I could keep the whole queue and their grandchildren going.

He dumped a small pile of carriers into the packing area and started the conveyor belt, not waiting for me to finish unpacking the trolley.

By the time I'd hastily off-loaded all my goods – including things I didn't even remember picking up, I'd been in such a trance – my shopping was piling up at the other end. I shoved the trolley down there and tried to open one of the bags.

A large can of beans had squashed itself into the tomatoes. Bread was flattened under cat food. I felt myself grow hot and flustered as five kilos of potatoes piled on top of that. I pulled the tomatoes away and put them to one side with the eggs, still struggling to separate the thin, slippery plastic.

The conveyer belt came relentlessly on toward me. Down came a large bottle of olive oil which careered into a ripe avocado. The jam doughnuts I'd lovingly selected for Stanley, were being slowly pulverised by a large jar of mayonnaise and I still couldn't get the bags open.

Still the shopping came. I could see Stanley's birthday cake heading my way, followed by a large bag of onions. I pulled furiously at the top of the bag in my hands. It split in my fingers. My nerve ends jangled.

'Can you stop!' I shrieked. The youth looked at me uncomprehendingly, lower lip jutting.

'Sorry,' he mumbled eventually as the conveyer belt ground to a halt. He frowned at my shopping.

'I can't open these fucking bags,' I snarled. I heard loud tutting from the queue behind me as my bottles of wine rolled down and dented the broccoli quiche. The youth picked up one of the bags and rubbed it between his thumb and forefinger – it opened instantly.

'Thank you,' I said furiously, feeling like punching him in the throat.

Then someone chuckled and I heard a familiar voice behind me. 'Would you like some help with your packing, madam?'

'Do you live in here?' I asked ungraciously, when my shopping was safely stowed in my trolley and I was composing myself on the bench beside the taxi phone. At the check-out, the old lady who'd been tutting glared at me as she paid for her cheese scones.

'I think this is the second time we've met like this,' Andrew said mildly beside me. 'I do have to eat.'

'Shouldn't you be at school?'

'It's the lunch hour – even teachers are allowed out sometimes. Do I gather you are having a bad day?'

I put my head in my hands. 'Sorry. That seems to be my word of the day.' I told him the latest about Charlotte, trying very hard not to cry so that he didn't think me an even bigger flake than he must do already.

He patted my arm. 'She'll come round. She's stinging from it all now but from what you've told me about your friendship, it'll work out. Give her a day or two.'

I nodded, still upset.

'Are you going to be OK?'

I blew my nose. 'Yep. As you said, just having a bad day. Another one,' I added, before he could think it. 'How come you always pop up and help me?'

He laughed. 'I just happened to be doing the shopping. Trying to be a new man – my wife's not keen on the old one!'

I felt myself instantly stiffen again. What was it with these bloody blokes bleating about on their marriages? Did he think I was going to start being sympathetic after we'd had this whole conversation about Roger and Hannah and the way taking confidantes wrecks relationships?

'I'm sure she is, really,' I said tightly, standing up. 'Anyway I'd better go. Thanks for your help.'

He stood up too. 'See you at the gym soon? We've still got that challenge to do.'

'I don't know, I'm busy. I've got a lot of work to catch up on and the last bit of filming to do and um –'

'Oh yes, Stanley was telling me – it's on TV soon, isn't it?'

'Yes, it is,' I said, the thought no longer giving me any pleasure at all.

I still felt unaccountably tearful as I drove home. Thoughts of work, Charlotte, Stanley, Roger, and whether I'd been too abrupt with Andrew who, after all, was only trying to be kind, all swirled about my head with an ever-growing list of things to do that pressed in on me until I could feel the panic rising in my throat.

I had to finish the script, give Stanley a lovely birthday on Thursday and clear up the house when all I felt like doing was going to bed. And oh my God, I really would have to clear up too – my mother would be coming round …

At the thought of her, my father came vividly to mind. Tomorrow he would have been dead for 12 years. It felt preposterous. I still wanted to talk to him. He would have spoken calmly.

'One thing at a time,' he'd have said. 'Start with one small task.' I could almost hear his voice. Soothing, yet brisk. Amusement laced with sympathy. 'Take a deep breath, lovey. Get that work done – that's what's earning you the money. Do the stuff that keeps a roof over your head … You'll feel better when you get going.'

It's all a mess, Dad. My home's a mess, I'm a mess, I've

messed up with Charlotte.

'It'll work out. It's never as bad as you think it is.' He shook his head, a small reproving smile. 'Not worth getting in a state about.'

Hormones, I told myself. *Only hormones.*

But as I put the shopping on the kitchen table, there was Charlotte's parcel for Stanley. *You never saw him, Dad. I so want you to see him.*

I looked at my friend's familiar, large, looping handwriting; the beautifully tied ribbon. *Happy Birthday, Stanley darling ...*

And I cried all over again.

Chapter Thirty-two

STANLEY WAS TOUCHINGLY THRILLED with his iPhone and didn't appear to notice that Charlotte and her family hadn't put in an appearance. I heard him thanking her on the phone for his sweatshirt and PSP game – "really cool" – and also saying "yes, she's fine", so I assumed Charlotte was checking I was still alive while obviously not wanting to actually speak to me.

Instead, I had the joy of my mother, who had barely drawn breath since she'd arrived. She was here for the duration both to celebrate Stanley's birthday today and keep him in her tender care when I went off to do the filming tomorrow. She watched disapprovingly as he and Connor ate delivered pizzas the size of dustbin lids with various weird and wonderful "extras" and some lurid-looking ice cream with enough E numbers to run the national grid.

She brought her own brand of *joie de vivre* to the proceedings by engaging in her most favoured leisure pursuit: reminiscing about my dead father's shortcomings and highlighting my ineptitude in allowing my own husband to slip through my fingers.

'Boys need fathers,' she announced, when we'd completed the birthday cake ritual and Stanley and Connor had finally retired to watch a DVD. I went to the fridge and poured a very large glass of white wine while deep breathing. My PMT was still ferocious – so much for Sally-Ann and her funny-smelling creams – and I needed to keep a lid on the tide of emotion that was already fermenting inside me nicely.

I held the bottle up to my mother and bent my mouth into a smile. 'Would you like one?'

'All right, then,' she said, as though helping me out.

I don't think it was entirely my fault. I did try. I twittered on about how Stanley seemed to be getting on better at school and the beauty of the Thanet coastline I had so appreciated on my bracing walks with Benson. I shared with her the difficulty of producing a full Sunday roast in Charlotte's Aga and offered the opening speech in a debate entitled *But Does It Make Nicer-Tasting Chicken?* Thus giving her the cue to launch into one of her own favourite diatribes: *Why Things Don't Taste Like They Used To.*

I asked after her friend Betty's gastric reflux problem and even, in desperation, enquired whether she had spoken to my hallowed brother lately, not flinching when she mentioned the dreaded C word. (I had been studiously ignoring the fact that Christmas was looming – not only had I been dreading it since July but now things were the way they were with Charlotte, the thought of not going to her house but remaining here, staring at my mother's sour features, was a vision too horrendous to contemplate.)

But apart from a brief respite while she gazed lovingly into the middle distance and ran through Anthony's sterling qualities, gifts, and achievements, she was not to be deterred.

'In our day we stayed,' she said, putting down her empty wine glass and waiting for me to refill it. 'We didn't run at the first sign of trouble. You got married for life and it meant life, no matter how much of a dance they led you.'

'I stayed,' I said. 'Daniel was the one who left.'

My mother's eyes narrowed. 'You know what I mean. You made him. You threw him out.'

'He was having an affair,' I said, realising too late the sort of ground I was stepping onto.

'Lots of men have affairs,' said my mother, drinking her wine with uncharacteristic speed. 'It's what they're like.'

'Well, I couldn't cope with it,' I said tightly, hoping we weren't going where I feared we might be.

'It's all very well for you, what about him?' she said, jerking her head in the direction of the sitting room from where we could hear the muffled sounds of gunfire. 'What about Stanley?'

'Daniel didn't want to be with me. It would have been different,' I added meaningfully, 'if he had.'

My mother gave one of her more dramatic snorts.

'I know what your father got up to,' she said, nastily. 'But I still put you and Anthony first.'

'You never let anyone hear the end of it, though, did you?' I bit my lip. Too late, it was said. I'd had enough wine to say it but was still, unfortunately, sober enough to know I'd pay.

She glowered. 'I made sacrifices. I kept the family together. Put up with him being weak and swanning about with his fancy woman, so that you and your brother would have a stable home.'

I looked at her with disbelief. 'Anthony was at university, Mum, and I'd already left.'

'But you had somewhere to come back to, if you wanted to.'

But we didn't want to, Mother. Because you filled every room with resentment and your bitterness soured the air. Because you interrogated our father every time he left the house, because you totally refused to let him go and because, he, good man that he was, keeping his marriage vows, stayed to look after you, even though he was quietly dying, weighed down by his guilt and your relentless contempt ...

I pulled a large piece of black and green icing from Stanley's football cake. 'You could have gone if it was that bad.'

'Huh! And let that strumpet have him!'

'You didn't want him, Mum. You hadn't shown him any love or affection for years.' *Not since Anthony was born ...*

'Is that what he told you?'

'He didn't need to tell me. I was there, I saw it.' *And I felt it. You went off me too ...*

My mother stood up, filled the kettle and sat down again. 'You don't know what you're talking about. We had a perfectly normal marriage until that floozy came along and got her claws into him.'

I took another mouthful of wine. 'Jenny wasn't a floozy. She was an ordinary, decent woman. She was devastated when Dad died.'

There was a sharp intake of breath. 'You saw her?'

I felt myself recoil. My mother was looking at me with something close to hatred. But, recklessly, I was on a mission now. I wanted it all said, all out in the open and done with.

'Yes, I went to see her. I'd met her before. She was nice. Just a straightforward, middle-aged woman – not glamorous or scheming. No claws. Not a strumpet or a tart or a floozy – just warm and kind and interested.' As I said it, I had a sudden pang about Roger. I pushed it away.

'Jenny really loved Dad. And he loved her. But he loved you too – enough to stay and look after you because he knew that's what you wanted.'

I'd seen her flinch when I'd used Jenny's name but she spoke with venom.

'He wanted,' my mother said, with quiet fury, 'what they all want. A bit of extra jam on his bread.'

'*No.*' I tried to speak calmly. 'He wanted someone to cherish him. To appreciate and value him, not constantly criticise and put him down. He just wanted a wife who would treat him like the nice, decent human being he was – who would be his friend. Who would *listen* …'

For a moment my mother was quite still, her features rigid with rage. Then she gave a peculiar little smile. She leant across the table and brought her face close up to mine.

'Perhaps,' she sneered, 'that's how Daniel felt too.'

I held it together while I shepherded Stanley and Connor to bed, reminding them gaily that it was – birthday or no birthday – school tomorrow and that they must get some sleep.

And while I watched my mother weave her way, somewhat unsteadily, up the stairs.

It was when I got back to the kitchen and sat alone, shaken by her cold anger and the memories we'd raked up, that I stared at the cyclamen on my window sill and wept.

I've had it for years, that cyclamen. I only water it when I remember; it hasn't been fed or ever re-potted. Yet despite me, it valiantly flowers on. Sends up endless curling buds, opening into creamy white flowers. The more I neglect it, the more it blooms again.

I would have done anything to keep my father alive just a little bit longer – just long enough. He had nurses there, he was wired up to drips and tubes; he had every possible care and he was trying his best, but he just couldn't hang on any more. Why are some things robust while others die so easily? I've had other cyclamens that have expired within days; that have rotted away or shrivelled up. This one just keeps on going.

It's him who's changed, not you. That's what Andrew said about my husband. Daniel was good back then when Dad died. He stroked my shoulder as I sobbed and sobbed. I sometimes wonder if that is why Stanley has the weight of the world on his shoulders - because he was born when I had such a burden of misery on mine.

I tried to imagine what my father would say to me if I told him about this now. But I couldn't even conjure up his voice any more. *Dad, can you hear me?*

I looked at the kitchen walls, the flower on the window sill, the teacup on the table, imprinted with lipstick from my mother's acid mouth.

Dad?

Only silence bounced from the empty walls.

Chapter Thirty-three

I WOKE UP PUFFY and piggy-eyed, with a headache and a feeling of doom. For the first time I wasn't looking forward to the filming at all. I just wanted to put my head back under the covers and stay there. If it hadn't been for the thought of seeing Cal, I'd have phoned in sick.

I went down to the kitchen where my mother was already wielding the oven cleaner. 'Oh dear, look at you,' she said with satisfaction. 'You look *terrible*.'

'Thank you,' I said, going back to the hall mirror to confirm this truth for myself.

'Well if you will get yourself in such a state.' My mother gave one of her sniffs and then a few more for good measure. 'I've made Stanley's rolls – he likes the way I do them with cheese *and* ham – and when I've got this oven into a decent condition, I'm going to do him a nice casserole with proper vegetables. Not much goodness in all that rubbish they put away last night. I offered that other boy rolls too, but he says he has school dinners.' Her tone suggested she didn't believe him.

'His name's Connor,' I said. 'Have they had breakfast?'

'Yes. You look like you could do with some too.'

Food was the last thing I wanted. I felt tired and miserable as I drove the boys to school.

'Thanks for having me,' said Connor, as I pulled up on the zigzag lines.

'Mum – you're not supposed to stop here,' said Stanley anxiously. 'Look, Mr Longmead is coming – he's seen you!'

'Jump out then and I'll go,' I said, as a rotund figure in a raincoat came waddling toward us at surprising speed. 'Have a nice time with Grandma tonight and I'll see you tomorrow. I'll be back in the afternoon.'

'OK.' Stanley got hastily out of the car before I could attempt to kiss him. Connor was already on the pavement. Keeping my eyes on the rear-view mirror, I watched them both scuttle into school, the backs of their blazers disappearing just as Mr Longmead bore down on me, wagging his finger.

Unable to cope with anything more of that ilk from my mother, I went straight upstairs when I got back and embarked on a serious repair job on my face, involving industrial amounts of concealer and big dollops of camomile and peppermint eye rescue mask that promised to dispel bags but just made me smell like a polo mint.

Hopefully, by the time I'd sat on the train for an hour and a half and then in a cab for a bit longer (the car and driver seemed to be a thing of the past but at least they weren't making me get the tube) my puffy bits would have settled down. And at least the filming was in the evening, where the lights might be dim.

Cal had been vague about what I was actually going to do, simply saying he wanted some last odds and ends and that as we were staying overnight in the hotel where we were shooting, we could use some of the facilities when it was quiet. 'And we'll have a few drinks to celebrate it being finished,' he'd added. 'You've been really great.'

He was the only person left standing who seemed to think so, I reflected, as the train pulled into Victoria. I felt the tears at the back of my throat whenever I thought about Charlotte. My mother had simply looked me up and down and sniffed again when I said goodbye and even Andrew had seen what an old bag I could be after the supermarket scene.

Which was perhaps just as well – he was married, after all, and what with everything Roger had been through, I certainly didn't want to be too much on the receiving end of his sympathy. It was highly unlikely we'd have a third supermarket encounter but I shuddered at the thought of his wife popping up one day behind the baked beans and thinking I was Hannah Mark Two.

By the time the taxi stopped outside the hotel in Clerkenwell, I was feeling thoroughly sorry for myself and a quick look at my face just before I paid the driver, showed that still looked in a pretty sad way too. When Cal saw me he'd be thinking twice about the "fab" bit. Fed up at 40 was nearer the mark.

But he beamed at me as brightly as ever when he bounded into reception minutes later.

'You all right, babe?' He wrapped both arms around me in a big, jubilant hug. 'Final session tonight. Let's get you checked in and we'll have a drink and go through it all.'

He picked up my overnight bag and swung it easily over his shoulder. 'Did you remember to bring something sexy? No? No problem – the girls at the office have borrowed some fab dresses for you. They've all been dying to try them on themselves ...'

He chatted on gaily and I began to feel better. My room was lovely. Someone had put fruit and mineral water and half a bottle of dry white on a tray next to the flat-screen TV, and the bathroom had a massive shower and huge fluffy white towels.

'Come back down and have a glass of wine first,' Cal had said. 'And then you can get yourself glammed up.'

'Am I doing my own make-up, then?' I asked, when I joined him in the bar. I forced a laugh. 'I was rather hoping for some expert help – I know I'm looking a bit rough.'

'I thought how stunning you looked when you walked in,' said Cal smiling. 'You've lost loads more weight. I think you're looking really good. You've really thrown yourself into this – it's going to make terrific TV.'

He gave our order to the waiter and turned back to me. 'We've gone over budget a bit so I didn't bring make-up in today – but I really don't think you need it. Just put a bit on yourself – dark sultry, eyes perhaps, plenty of lipstick ... You know the sort of thing – you always look great anyway.'

I smiled at him gratefully, beginning to relax a little. He was so lovely the way he always tried to make me feel a million dollars. The very opposite of how Daniel had set out to portray me in the last six months we'd lived together. Which was flabby at 40 and barking mad.

The moment I started drinking wine I realised I was really hungry. I hadn't had anything to eat yet today. The waiter bought a small dish of nuts and cheesy biscuits but I didn't like to eat too many of them since I was supposed to be behaving in a slim and sophisticated manner, not cramming food down my throat the first chance I got.

I thought fondly of Charlotte, who would have emptied the bowl in one hit and sent the waiter for a refill without turning a hair. Cal didn't touch the nibbles at all and neither, of course, did Tanya, who had now joined us and was drinking her usual Diet Coke.

I looked at her, leaning back on one of the long leather seats, texting, and wondered afresh what she actually did as "producer" of this film. I'd still only ever seen her make endless calls on her mobile and sit around looking murderous. She'd given Cal a desultory kiss when she came in and nodded at me. Since then she hadn't said a word.

'Have you brought the clothes for Laura?' Cal asked now.

She gave him a bored look. 'The office should have sent them over earlier – they're probably out there.' She nodded her head toward reception.

Cal smiled at her but I detected a bit of tension between them. 'Do you think you could go and check?' he asked with exaggerated patience.

She sighed and got up, pausing to address me with a sardonic smile. 'I've got you some fuck-me shoes too – just in case you get lucky with one of the saddos tonight.' As she sauntered out, Cal looked annoyed.

'What's she talking about?' I asked him, noticing two women on the next table gazing at Cal appreciatively, clearly glad that Tanya had gone and hoping I'd follow soon.

'Don't take any notice of her.' Cal shook his head. 'She's a strange girl sometimes. The thing is,' he said, shining his smile back on me and then hesitating, looking for a moment like a little boy, 'the thing is – I've had a bit of a last minute idea. Turns out they've got this do on here tonight – one of these speed dating parties? And I thought maybe you …'

Any good feelings I'd begun to build up, evaporated.

'Speed dating? You're joking.'

He looked at me appealingly. 'It would just be for laughs. I think it would really work – you all confident and looking fab. You don't have to take it seriously. Just chat to a few of the guys – see if there's anyone worth flirting with.' He laughed, showing his white teeth. 'We'll have you in a really great dress –'

I shook my head. 'Oh no, I don't think I could – I wouldn't know what to say.'

Cal leant forward. 'You don't have to say anything – they'll be flocking round you. Just smile and answer their questions. I've found out about it – you only talk to each one for three minutes and then you fill in a little card with anyone you like. There'll be loads of champagne and I'll be right there with you.'

He was looking into my eyes in a way I found very hard to resist. 'I don't know ...' I faltered.

'You can try out one or two or them to get the hang of it and then we'll find a couple of guys happy to be filmed chatting to you. One of the guys organising it is up for it anyway so he'll pose for us if nobody else wants to be on TV, but in my experience –' he grinned at me '- once they've got a few drinks inside them, we'll have plenty of willing candidates.'

He put his hand on mine. 'Are you OK with that?'

'I don't know,' I said again, something inside me cringing at the thought of having to make small talk with a stranger on film. I was bound to say something inane.

'See how you feel when you've changed. I think you'll enjoy it – all those men after you. I think it could be empowering.' He was still holding my hand. 'But I wouldn't want you to do anything you felt uncomfortable with. You're in charge.'

His eyes held mine for a long moment and I felt a shock of real desire that thrilled and alarmed me in equal measure. I saw him notice it too. His fingers tightened.

He started to say something, then abruptly sat back and let go of my hand as Tanya stalked back in and flopped back down on the long leather seat opposite.

'Are they here?' Cal said.

She scowled. 'Yeah.'

Cal was suddenly business-like. 'So, Laura, if you go up and have a shower or whatever you want to do, and get your make-up on, we'll wait here for the guys and then Tanya can come up and help you choose a dress. OK?'

Tanya in my room was the last thing I wanted but I didn't like to say so. I nodded dumbly and got up, brushing past Cal, shaken by the electricity that had just passed between us.

I'd much rather you helped me get dressed, I thought as I shampooed my hair. *Or undressed, even* ... I giggled. The wine on another empty stomach had definitely had its effect. The two shortbread biscuits that were on the tray with the tea and coffee making stuff had helped a bit, but I definitely needed some proper food if I was going to have much more to drink. Or I'd be anybody's!

I soaped my body slowly, thinking about Cal and the way he'd looked at me. I hadn't imagined it.

Nor was I imagining the warm, tingling sensation suffusing my body that had nothing to with the powerful jets of hot water hammering down on my back. A feeling I'd all but forgotten. There was no doubt about it. I was horny.

I was just wondering where the nearest Ann Summers shop was, while picturing Cal, bare-chested, slowly running his hands down my body, when I was rudely interrupted by a series of loud bangs on the door.

Hurriedly wrapping a towel around my head, I pulled on the white, fluffy robe hanging on the back of the bathroom door, and opened up, harbouring a hopeless fantasy that it might be Cal come to ravish me. Tanya stood there with an armful of clothes and a cross expression.

She walked in without comment and dumped the garments on the bed. Then she opened the mini-bar, took out a Diet Coke and sat in the chair in the corner. There was a hiss as she pulled at the ring pull. 'Gonna try some stuff on, then?' she asked flatly.

'Yes, sure,' I said, flustered. 'I won't be a minute.'

I grabbed clean underwear from my case and went back in the bathroom to rub at my hair. When I came back out, with the robe wrapped round me again, Tanya had separated out the dresses. There were four of them: a silver glittery affair; two black ones, and a short red taffeta thing. I could see at once that the silver one was too small.

'What size are these?' I asked, thinking how embarrassing it would be if I couldn't cram my lardy self into any of them.

Tanya shrugged. 'Dunno. Try them on.'

I took the two black ones back into the bathroom. The shorter one was tight and shiny; even before I'd zipped it up, I was a black pudding. The other one was long and strappy with a built-in bra bit that gave amazing cleavage without being too revealing. It was soft and draped and flattering. I turned sideways – my stomach, always so ready to pop forth, looked pleasingly flat.

I must keep this weight off, I thought. That half stone or so I'd shed made all the difference in the world. I came out to show Tanya, feeling pleased.

'I really like this one,' I said. I gave a little twirl. 'Once I've got my make-up on and maybe if I clip my hair back a bit – ' I held it away from my face.

Tanya looked at me strangely. 'Try the red one as well,' she said. 'Red would be a better colour.'

I reluctantly took the black dress off and pulled the red one over my head. It was tighter and shorter. It also gave me a cleavage but one more reminiscent of Barbara Windsor in her heyday. And I definitely looked heavier.

'There are shoes,' said Tanya, rummaging in a bag and pulling out a pair of perilous-looking scarlet heels.

'I don't think …' I began.

'Just try them,' said Tanya.

I put them on and looked in the mirror. They did something for my calves, for sure, but seeing so much of my legs generally, after a decade of jeans and long, droopy skirts was disconcerting.

'Yep, that's good,' said Tanya, a note of enthusiasm finally creeping into her voice. 'You look much better in that.'

'Do you think so?' I asked, looking doubtfully at my middle. 'Don't you think it's a bit tight?'

'No, it looks fine,' said Tanya, already losing interest again. She looked at her watch. 'We ought to be getting downstairs, so you'd better do your make-up. Put plenty on or you'll look washed out.'

'I don't think short dresses suit me,' I said anxiously. 'I think I look better in the black one.'

'You really didn't – that one is exactly right.'

I looked at her. She stared back, her face challenging. I hesitated. It was ridiculous to feel intimidated by her – she was young enough to be my daughter.

'Shall we ask Cal?' I said at last.

'No,' Tanya almost snapped. 'Well, not now, we need to get started. Get made-up first and dry your hair. Come downstairs like that and we can see what *Cal –*' she enunciated his name with a studied scorn '– thinks then.'

I wondered why they so obviously didn't get on. Professional rivalry presumably, though if she was jealous it was her own fault. Cal was evidently so committed to his job and getting the film just right and Tanya didn't seem to give a toss.

I took a deep breath and tried once more. 'I really think I'd rather wear the black one,' I said, but Tanya was already gathering the rest of the dresses up and heading for the door.

'You look much better like that,' she said firmly. 'You're supposed to be partying.'

Partying! I did my make-up but looked neither glamorous or sultry – just rather raddled – and my hair was a disaster. I realised to my horror I'd forgotten to bring my straighteners or the right hair gel, so had to go for a messy just-out-of-bed look that didn't quite come off. I was still tugging at it hopelessly when Tanya rang the room and told me to hurry up.

I teetered down the corridor in my heels and looked at myself in the lift mirror with despair. I could hear my mother's voice: *mutton dressed as lamb*.

The lipstick looked garish in the harsh light and my skin

293

blotchy. My hair, that was supposed to appear wild and shaggy in an edgy kind of way, just looked unbrushed. I determined to go down and tell Cal I wanted to get changed into the other dress and I needed more time to do my hair. Perhaps the hotel would have straighteners. At least Cal cared about how I felt – he wouldn't railroad me like Tanya had done!

He was waiting in the foyer with Matt and Russ. 'Hey, you look terrific!' He came forward and kissed me, then stood back and surveyed me from head to toe. He sighed appreciatively. 'Fabulous.'

'Actually, I'm not really very happy in this dress,' I told him. 'There was another one – a black one – I felt much more comfortable in. It was more sophisticated, you know, this one feels a bit – well, a bit tarty.'

'Nothing wrong with that,' put in Russ, behind me. He and Matt guffawed.

'No really,' I said, rattled. 'And I can't walk in these shoes and my hair hasn't gone right –' I stopped as, over his shoulder, I saw Tanya give a sort of smirk. I swallowed. 'I think I look terrible,' I said, suddenly feeling tearful. I stopped again, afraid now I would make a fool of myself and cry.

Cal put an arm round me and led me away from the others. 'What's really the matter?' He looked at me, his brown eyes full of concern.

'I just feel very fat in this dress,' I said, biting my lip. 'I'm sorry I've got really bad PMT and I've had an awful week. It's been the anniversary of my father's death and my friend Charlotte –' My eyes filled with tears and I scrabbled in my handbag for a tissue, feeling a complete idiot.

Cal touched my face gently with one finger and spoke in a low voice. 'Honestly, babe, you look fantastic. Not fat at all – just really sexy. I'm really sorry you've had a bad time. As soon as we've done this bit, we'll sit down and have a drink and you can tell me all about it. The thing is –' he looked worried '- we need to get on and film this speed dating thing right now if we're going to do it, and as I've sweet-talked the organisers and the hotel management into letting us, I feel we should. I said we'd be discreet – get in there and do it quickly and get out again, so it won't take long.' He glanced at his watch in the same way Tanya had done. 'I'm really sorry but–' He looked at me appealingly. 'Are you sure you're OK?'

I dabbed at my eyes and nodded.

'Look, just do this,' he said. 'I'll get it wrapped up as soon as I can and then you can go and get changed if you like for the next session, but I, for one, think you look wonderful.'

He trailed a finger across the top of my arm, lowered his voice, and gave me a slow wink. 'I almost wish I was doing a bit of dating myself ...'

Chapter Thirty-four

I GAZED AT HIS back as he walked away to the others. He really was flirting with me now – not just being nice. But he was genuinely kind, too – he always went out of his way to make me feel better about myself.

I went to the loo to repair my make-up, having one more go at my hair with the last squidge from an ancient tube of leave-in conditioner I found in the bottom of my handbag and managing to create a couple of spikes, and putting on lots more lipstick.

I still looked a bit grim, I thought, but the lights in ladies' loos were notorious for that – presumably they'd be turned down a lot lower in the speed-dating gathering to give the dodgy-looking a fighting chance. Cal had seemed to genuinely think I looked OK, so perhaps it was just me being hormonal.

The speed-dating affair was held in a large room a bit like a seventies nightclub, with a small dance floor in the middle and a bar running down one side. It was all rather retro with plush red banquettes and black walls with mirrored pillars and a huge metallic disco ball slowly revolving from the ceiling.

Clumps of men and women stood near the bar with glasses in their hands. I noticed a lot of the women had on short, cocktail-type dresses like mine. I also noticed they were a lot younger than me.

'I feel a prune,' I said to Cal, as Russ and Matt set up the camera and mikes.

He grinned. 'Have some champagne. I always find it cheers one up.'

I took a glass from the tray proffered and looked around the room. There were stools in twos against the narrow bar that ran around the walls and more pairs of seats dotted about the high round tables surrounding the dance floor.

A young guy in tight black trousers and white shirt handed me a black card like a menu, embossed with silver hearts, and a silver and black pen. 'Inside are the numbers of each position,' he said briskly. 'As you move on round, you give a tick against any of the guys you feel you'd like to talk to again later.'

I glanced sideways into one of the mirrors – I didn't look quite so bad in here, but I still felt daft.

'Just start doing it,' said Cal, 'and we'll get some general shots of you, then we'll come in close for the conversation in a while.' He grinned and nodded at my glass. 'Keep knocking it back. You'll be fine.'

I was directed to one of the tables near the dance floor. Number Six was an earnest-looking bloke of about forty with a beard.

'Is this your first time doing one of these?' he asked. I nodded. He was studying political science as a mature student, he told me, and liked Genesis and "radical theatre". I told him I was a copywriter and he asked me what I thought about the toxicity of global consumerism. I said it made me want another drink. It was hardly a match made in heaven.

'Brilliant,' said Cal, grinning some more as I moved on to number 28.

'He's too young,' I hissed as I tried to climb elegantly on to the bar stool opposite a boy with spots.

'Just play along with it,' Cal murmured back. 'It's good to see some variety.'

'How old are you?' I asked bluntly.

'Twenty-three,' said the juvenile dubiously, clearly wondering who this old woman was.

'Can you look a bit more interested, La?' Cal whispered in my ear. I felt a little flicker of pleasure at the special name, but I still frowned.

'I'm going to look like a paedophile,' I muttered back. 'I'll be interested in someone older.'

Cal put an arm around my shoulders as everyone moved round again. 'Lots of younger men really fancy older women,' he said casually. 'I could see it written all over that guy's face

– he'd have jumped at the chance. I don't think you realise how attractive you are …'

He grabbed another drink from a passing girl with a tray and pressed it into my hand. 'Here, have another one – tell yourself you're fabulous. Never fails with me.' He laughed. 'Champagne makes everything better.'

He was right. By the time I'd had my third glass, I was feeling very much improved. I found I could walk in the heels, after all, and even the dress felt a bit looser now I'd been wearing it a while.

'I think we've nearly got enough now,' said Cal, after I'd sat through three minutes in the company of a bloke with a twitch and overpowering garlic-breath, 'but maybe just a couple more. I know it's excruciating for you but –' he gave me a wink. 'Just pretend.

'I'll make it up to you later,' he added softly, his hand trailing down my bare arm. I felt a delicious shock go right up my spine and could still feel the glow of his finger tips as I went on to the next table.

Number 17 was quite good-looking and probably about my age. He chatted easily about his job as a software engineer and his recent divorce (there was always something). I leant forward and tried to look fascinated, thinking that if I were doing this for real, he'd be one I might have put a tick against. 'Oh, and I'm a vegan,' he finished. Perhaps not then.

The last contender I spoke to was the organiser, posing as one of the punters. He was one of these open shirt, hairy chest, too much aftershave, too-tight trousers types – the only thing missing was the medallion.

He gave me the full low-down on his attributes, including the flash penthouse and sports car, and offered plenty of innuendo about his prowess in the sack. He grinned into the camera frequently, evidently thinking that since he was totally irresistible, women all over the country would flock to his speed-dating parties in the hope of tracking him down.

Thoroughly into role now, I pouted and made eyes at him while trying not to snort out loud.

'Oh my God, save me from any more,' I giggled to Cal,

now feeling pleasingly tipsy after my fourth glass of champagne. I fluffed my hair up a bit more in front of one of the mirrors and tugged up my dress – my cleavage now looked in danger of escaping altogether. I didn't look too bad at all now. Though I really needed to eat.

Cal signalled to Matt. 'Yeah – come on, let's get out of here. OK, it's a wrap.'

He put his hand on my waist and led me out of the room. Hot date Number Six was still sat at his table, introducing himself to a girl in a bright pink T-shirt and jeans, using the same sparkling opener he'd used on me. 'Is this your first time doing one of these …?'

'We're nearly done now,' Cal was saying. 'We just want to get a little bit more of you talking to camera. We may not use it, but just in case …' He led me into another bar. 'We've done quite a lot of that with the other two subjects and we might need a bit more from you for balance. Is that OK? It won't take long.'

He sat me a table in the corner. As usual I could see people glancing toward us as Matt and Russ set up. Cal had got me yet another glass of champagne. I pulled a face at him. 'This is going straight to my head – I haven't really eaten today.'

'We'll have dinner afterwards,' he promised, sitting down opposite me and giving me one of his slow smiles that made my toes tingle.

'OK. We're just going to talk about how you feel. I'll be asking you questions off screen, but basically it's going to be you talking to camera.' His eyes fixed on mine and he gave me that look again. Something inside me went soft and squidgy. His voice was low and sensual.

'How do you feel about being in your forties, now?'

'Well,' I said. 'I'm feeling better about it. I know I'm a bit dodgy today – I've got shocking PMT -' I paused to laugh, to show that this didn't mean I was about to start chewing on small children '- but generally I have been feeling pretty good. You know, with all the exercise and stuff – the going to the gym, the new haircut. I feel good about having lost some weight.'

I wasn't slurring but I had that sense of my words becoming a bit treacly. Cal didn't seem to notice. He was nodding encouragingly. 'How did you feel before then?'

'Well – I was pretty horrified at actually turning 40. You don't really think it will happen to you. I didn't put any of my cards up – I felt really weird all day – and it took me six months to actually say the F word. But I sort of got over that –'

Cal was leaning across the table. He'd taken my hand again. 'Go on,' he said softly. 'Can you tell us about your marriage break-up?' His thumb moved gently across my palm. It sent shivers right up my arm.

'But what really set me back was my husband, Daniel, leaving me for a 28-year-old. Then I really did feel old and unattractive with that sense that life had passed me by. I started to look around me and everyone else was young. And young people seem to do so much more with their lives than we ever did. Though I suppose one still could … I mean, even Daniel, with his younger woman, is getting new trainers and eating tofu –'

I clapped a hand to my mouth. 'Actually, I don't want to say that – not about Daniel – I don't want to give him the satisfaction. Not on TV.' I looked at Cal, agitated. He squeezed my fingers.

'No problem. We won't use more than a few seconds of this. Probably just the stuff about you feeling good.'

'I need to stop for a minute, anyway,' said Matt from behind his camera. 'Bloody desperate for a pee. Be right back.'

'I'm going to get a beer,' said Russ. 'You want anything?'

I shook my head.

'I'll have one too,' said Cal. 'Where's Tan?'

Russ shrugged. 'Dunno, mate.'

'Are you feeling better now?' asked Cal, when they'd all moved away. 'You said you'd had a difficult week?'

He listened sympathetically while I explained about my father and relived the hoo-hah with my mother that had ended with me in floods of tears.

His own father, he told me, squeezing my hand, had left his mother when he, Cal, was seven and his mother had been very bitter for the rest of his childhood. 'She can still be quite difficult,' he said with feeling. 'Needy, clinging. I'm sure you know what I mean.'

He pushed the floppy bit of hair away from his forehead, looking like a young Hugh Grant. 'And what's happened with Charlotte?'

I gave him a brief recap, not going into any of the personal details as far as Roger was concerned, but explaining the misunderstanding.

'Wow,' said Cal. 'Tangled webs. But if you're good friends then she'll get over it, surely?'

'We'd got a bit strained before that to be honest,' I said sadly. 'I don't think she really liked the new me. She's not into all that losing weight and exercise stuff.'

'I told you before,' said Cal. 'She's envious because you're looking so fabulous. And maybe she's let herself go a bit?'

I shook my head. 'Oh no, I wouldn't say that – Charlotte's really attractive. I mean, she is bigger than me but she's beautiful and she's very comfortable with herself and she's happily married – well, usually – and that's worth a lot.'

I took a mouthful from the new glass of champagne that had appeared by my side. 'Charlotte says she quite likes getting older 'cos she doesn't have to try so hard any more –' I giggled. 'She says she's looking forward to elastic-waisted trousers and no longer having to hold her stomach in.'

'Yuck,' said Tanya, who seemed to have reappeared behind me.

Cal kept his eyes on mine. 'But you don't feel like that?'

I shuddered. 'Oh no, I hate it when I feel fat. I don't like it at all when I catch sight of myself in the mirror and my bum looks big.' I grinned at him. 'I don't want to look like an elephant.' I put a hand to my mouth again. I was still managing not to slur, but even to myself, I sounded as though I'd been drinking.

'Is my voice all right?' I said to Cal, who was nodding to Matt who was back behind the camera. 'Can we stop now?'

'Your voice is fine,' Cal said smiling at me. 'And we can stop. We'll go and get something to eat. But just to finish on an

301

uplifting note – what would your advice be to any woman who's in her forties and feels as though she's getting on and is past being sexy and wearing great clothes and having fun?' He moved back to let Russ bring the big mike closer to me. 'Maybe you could say something encouraging about being in your prime – remember the programme is going to be called *Prime Time* – and we could perhaps end with you saying that?'

The more I said it, the less convincing I sounded.

'You're in your prime. This is your prime time …'

'Just once more,' said Cal.

'It's prime time – you're in your prime …'

'And again? What's the best thing about being 40?'

'This is the time when you're in your prime.'

'Can you look as though you're thinking about it first?'

A little knot of people had gathered to watch and, once again, I suddenly felt all film star-ish. I rolled my eyes heavenwards as if considering life's mysteries and then faced the camera. 'You are in your *prime*. This is *prime time.*'

Cal clapped his hands. 'Terrific! I can't believe how you've taken to this.'

For the first time in my life I actually knew what it was like to go past the point of wanting to eat. By the time, we sat down in the restaurant I could quite easily have curled up and gone to sleep, but Cal seemed as energised as ever and was happily scanning the menu, making suggestions for me.

Russ and Matt had disappeared somewhere, Tanya was at the table with us, with a massive face on.

'Nothing,' she said coldly, when Cal asked her what she wanted.

She sat drinking Coke and texting while I picked at rocket leaves with parmesan and pine nuts and watched Cal devour a chicken Caesar. I wished she'd go and leave us on our own together. I wanted him gazing into my eyes again. I wanted him all to myself …

And when I came back from the loo a bit later, it seemed I might have got my wish. Tanya was standing in the foyer, her coat over her arm, obviously arguing with Cal. He waved to me as I went back into the restaurant.

'I'll be with you in a minute,' he called.

'You need to let me do it my way,' I heard him say to her.

I didn't catch her reply but it sounded suspiciously as if it included the word "bastard".

By craning my neck and shifting my chair along a bit I could just about still see them, through the open doors. Tanya's arms were waving about and Cal was standing with his hands stretched out, as if trying to appease her.

Then she disappeared from view and a few minutes later he came back in and sat down beside me, sighing.

'Everything OK?' I asked, throwing wheat-free caution to the winds and eating a bit of bread roll.

Cal shook his head wearily. 'We're disagreeing on a few technical issues,' he said. 'Tanya's gone home.'

'Oh dear,' I said, gravely, thinking it might not be tactful to toss my napkin in the air and begin whooping.

'Well, we've more or less finished,' said Cal. 'She doesn't need to be here.'

'Are you still going to stay?' I asked casually.

'Oh yes,' he said, suddenly looking more cheerful. 'I'm all booked in – why not? It's great here, isn't it?' He poured some more wine into my glass.

I buttered the rest of the roll.

'I'm very excited about this project,' he told me, as we drank the coffee I'd thought it prudent to order. 'It's a big thing for me. OK, so it's not on a major channel but it's on a Saturday night. So it will get noticed. Who knows one of the big boys might pick it up. Someone might pick you up!'

'Do you really think so?' I said, hopefully.

'Yes, I do.' His face was serious. 'You're a natural.'

'Will I be able to see it before it goes on TV?'

Cal shook his head. 'I doubt it. We're going to be cutting it pretty fine with the edit – we've only got a few days. And I'm not really allowed to give out DVDs before it goes on air.' He took my hand again. 'But I shall really look forward to hearing what you think of it.'

We sat for a moment, gazing at each other. Then he gently let go of my hand, slowly unwrapped one of the chocolate mints, and pushed it against my mouth, watching intently as my lips parted.

'Mmm,' I said, unable to take my eyes away from his. Was this really happening? Was I sitting in a posh London hotel being fed chocolate by a gorgeous young hunk, who'd just put his hand back in mine and was looking at me as if I were beautiful?

'You're beautiful,' he said. 'Want to go swimming?'

What?

'The pool closes at ten,' Cal was saying, 'but if I tell the management we need to film in there, they'll let us use it as late as we want. They've been absolutely fantastic – given us all the rooms and everything, for a credit.'

'I haven't got any swimming stuff.'

He smiled slowly. 'Doesn't bother me … No, I'm only joking. They've some gear for sale up there – we'll get you a bikini.'

I looked at him suspiciously. 'I don't want to be filmed in it!'

'You don't have to be – though I don't know why not. You've got a fabulous body.' He stood up and gave me a boyish grin. 'Come on. I love swimming – it's such a great way to unwind.'

I vaguely wondered if leaping into water was a good idea when we'd both had so much alcohol, but I obediently got in the lift with him to the top floor and 15 minutes later, the sight of Cal in a pair of swimming shorts banished all thoughts of health and safety. His body was smooth and muscular, lightly tanned even in December. I looked at his long limbs and strong chest and my heart gave a little skip.

He walked to the far end of the pool, did a perfect dive and swam a length under water, coming up in front of me – still perched on the side in a red and white polka dot bikini – and putting his hands on my knees.

'Come in, it's wonderful. So warm!' His hair was plastered against his head – his blonde streak standing out against the

304

darkness of the rest, his muscles glistening. I slid into the water. His hands went around my waist. Suddenly I really wanted him. Wanted to put my arms around him, put my hands up and pull his face down onto mine …

He kissed me briefly and slid back under the water again, emerging at the far end of the pool. 'Swim,' he called. 'It's fabulous!'

I swam slowly down after him, stretching out my fingers and toes in the balmy water, enjoying the sensation of weightlessness. 'It's ages since I did this,' I said, when I reached the other end. 'It's lovely.'

He nodded. 'Shame it's not the Caribbean, but still …' He suddenly submerged himself again, coming up behind me, kissing the top of my neck and sending ripples all the way down my back. I turned over and floated, feeling relaxed and sensual. Cal cupped the water, sending a stream across my stomach, and I flipped back again, watching him glide along with long, languid strokes till he too spun over and drifted, lazily supine, hands trailing beside him.

I forgot all sense of time as we circled each other, turning and revolving in the oily warmth, my body light and free beside his, mind empty except for the lapping of the water against us, the soft splashes as we broke the surface. I felt as though we were suspended there for ever, until movement at the side of the pool caught my eye.

I came abruptly out of my dreamlike state to see Matt and Russ in the far corner, the camera trained on the water.

'Cal – you said you wouldn't!' I cried, but I couldn't be cross. My body was heavy and warm. I smiled at him.

He held out his hands in contrition. 'Just a bit of you swimming – that's all, babe. They're packing up now.'

He swam right up to me and put his arms around me. 'Unless you'll just walk along the side for me? Just from here to the steam room?'

I shook my head, embarrassed. 'No thank you. I'm too old for that sort of thing. I don't want the whole world seeing my bottom.'

'But what a very lovely bottom it is.' He ran his hands

lightly down the sides of my waist, resting his fingers on my hips. Sending shoots of desire right through me. 'Please, Lala?'

I looked at him helplessly.

'Just for me,' he was saying. 'Just a few metres. It will be so empowering – other women will see you being bold and unashamed and will feel inspired. Look at how Helen Mirren went down a storm. She's much older than you.'

'She's also got a much better body than me.'

'She hasn't!' said Cal vehemently. 'I've been looking at you under water and you have an amazing body and I'm not even going to add that insulting tag – for your age. You look great, babe. I think you're fantastic.'

His hands were still on my hips. He was so close to me, I could feel his breath steamy on my face. I was melting inside.

'Go for it,' he murmured. 'Show them all how beautiful you are …'

I wanted to please him – I wanted to feel wild and high. I wanted him to touch me all over …

'OK.'

Cal threw up a jubilant hand and put a thumb up toward Matt. 'Just one take of Laura and then pack up, OK? You can go and get some beers.'

'It will only take seconds,' he said to me. 'Go up the steps, look across at Matt and then walk down to the steam room and go in.' He lowered his voice. 'And then I'll join you …'

I swam up to the steps and got out of the pool, telling myself I was that beautiful, confident woman Cal had described. I could still feel his hands. As I stood up straight, I felt suddenly lighter and slimmer than usual. I glanced back at Cal who was smiling from the middle of the water.

He blew me a kiss. For a moment I hesitated. Then I blew him one back. And, filled with reckless abandon, I tossed back my wet hair, beamed at the camera, and sauntered down the side of the pool, even giving a small, triumphant wiggle of my hips as I opened the door to the steam room.

Moments later Cal sat down on the wooden bench beside me as the steam swirled around us, sending streams down my chest. Droplets ran down his face as he took me in his arms, murmuring as his mouth found mine, 'La, I want you …I want you now.'

The rest was a blur. I could only remember him unhooking my bikini top, stepping out of his shorts, his body hard and urgent against mine in the rising steam.

And later, in my hotel room, my legs wrapped around his waist while he filled me up, holding me tightly to him, as we rocked together in the centre of the huge bed, lost in pleasure.

And his mouth on my face, feathering it with tiny, fervent kisses while he groaned over and over. 'You're amazing, Lala. You're fantastic. Oh God – La. Oh *yes* …'

I woke in the early hours, head pounding. I saw Cal's shape in the darkness – at the end of the bed, putting on clothes. As I sat up, he leant over me and kissed my mouth. 'I'm sorry – I've got to go, babe.'

I looked at the clock – it was only 5.30.

'We've got to start the edit today to get the film put together in time,' said Cal in apology. 'They're expecting me at the studio first thing. And I need to go home first.' He began to button his shirt. 'I'll see you really soon though.'

'How about the weekend?' I said impulsively.

He nodded. 'We'll work something out.'

'My son is away with his father next Saturday night. If you came down to Broadstairs, I could cook you dinner.'

I held my breath, waiting for him to make an excuse, telling myself not to feel crushed. But he put a hand out and touched my face. 'I'd like that.'

'We can watch the programme together?'

He nodded. 'That'll be great.'

I hugged him, feeling suddenly bereft as he gently disengaged himself and picked up his jacket from the floor. 'I'm sorry, La – I really do have to go.'

I hugged my knees instead. 'I'll see you next Saturday then.'

He bent down again and softly kissed my cheek. 'I can't wait.'

Chapter Thirty-five

'I CAN'T WAIT!'

Mike, in full heart-attack mode, was speaking in a voice several octaves higher than usual. 'I've promised their MD that I'll deliver by tomorrow lunchtime. You cannot let me down, Laura, the entire campaign depends on it. And I need to see it first. I can't hold on till the morning.'

'Well you're just going to bloody well have to,' I said cheerfully. 'Why do you make these ridiculous promises? I'm doing my best but, quite honestly, with the dog's breakfast you sent me, you're lucky I can do it at all in this tight time scale.'

A time scale, I thought, as Mike hyperventilated, that would be not quite so tight if I hadn't spent the previous weekend in London with Cal but I wasn't going to let Mike know that.

My skin still leapt with delectable little shocks every time I thought about Cal's hands touching me. The way he had looked at me before he left. I'd gone back to sleep until late morning and it had taken several ibuprofen tablets to get me in a fit state to hail a cab to the station, but I'd texted him when I'd got home, telling him how wonderful it had been and had got two kisses back.

I hadn't heard anything from him since, but he'd told me he'd be required in the editing suite almost 24/7 till they delivered later today, Thursday, so I assumed he was too busy for anything else.

I was in much the same position myself. Some of this work had come through from Mike a couple of days before Stanley's birthday but what with that, and Charlotte, and my bloody mother, and then the filming – pause for the luscious memory of Cal's fingers moving up the inside of my thigh – I hadn't even looked at it. Hadn't even remembered, in fact, that the deadline was this Friday morning.

Now, in addition to another dreadful script to rewrite and some brochure copy, Mike also wanted me to come up with a series of ad captions and was screaming for the whole lot to be ready by five tonight. No chance.

'I will keep going until it's done,' I told Mike soothingly, thinking that if I didn't have any wine and just sat here, doggedly ploughing my way through, I could probably get it done by late evening. 'And I'll email it tonight so it will be waiting for you by the time you get to the office tomorrow. Then you'll have all morning to print it up and get copies made.'

When he'd finally rung off I got the wretched video script up on my screen. This was intended as a sales tool with which to persuade every DIY store and garden centre in the land they should be stocking large quantities of Paradise Gardens' unique range of gnomes, and had been written by Martin, the Paradise Gardens' Gnomes Sales Manager I'd met weeks back in Ashford.

A sales manager who, unfortunately, might be good at flogging diminutive outdoor figures with rods, on a face-to-face basis, but who couldn't write for toffee. I would have expected Stanley to come up with more original phraseology and certainly better spelling.

As morning slipped into afternoon and I read of yet another gnome described as "unique and witty"', just to ring the changes from "original and witty" or Martin's ground-breaking "witty and original", I began to realise it could be a long night.

My progress wasn't helped by the way my brain would keep sliding away from the job in hand and back to Cal. I wondered if he was thinking about me too. He'd been so passionate on Saturday night – he'd really made me feel beautiful and sexy and even though I'd had a mega-hangover, the endorphins had still been surging through me the next morning. Even now, I felt a rush of pleasure every time I thought about it.

It was amazing, I thought, that a man like him could feel

like that about a woman like me, and gratifying too. So Daniel wasn't the only one who could pull a younger model, after all!

I wanted to text Cal but didn't know whether I should or not. He was up against a deadline too and might not appreciate being interrupted. On the other hand, I'd left him alone all week and I wanted to be sure he was still on for Saturday. I'd have to go shopping tomorrow if I was going to cook dinner for him.

I wanted to show I was thinking of him without being pushy or needy. I tried out various word combinations before finally settling on *Looking forward to cu Sat. What time you get here? Hope edit go well xx*

That should do it – not too heavy, not demanding, but a question in there so he would answer at some point. Or should I demonstrate an appreciation of the time pressure he was under too – he'd said he might be up all night. Show that I knew how busy he was and that he couldn't just drop everything to text me?

I vaguely remembered him making an impromptu speech in praise of older women when we were back in my hotel bedroom, devouring each other. Hadn't he said that older women were easier company because they were more laid back, more accommodating? I inserted *no rush to reply* and pressed *send* before I could change my mind.

By the time Stanley got home from school I was beginning to see a glimmer of light at the end of the video script tunnel. 'I can't stop now, darling,' I said as my son appeared in the doorway. 'Let me just finish this.'

In the end, it took another two hours and we had to have a thrown-together supper of eggs, bacon, beans, and toast, which got Stanley's seal of approval but left me fretting about his five portions.

'Please eat an apple,' I said, as I made my way back to the computer with a cup of coffee. 'And perhaps you'd better bring me one too.'

Three a.m., when your eyes are gritty from lack of sleep and your limbs are twitching from caffeine overload, is not the best time to be creative with gnomes.

Some bright spark at the agency had come up with the brilliant idea of a series of magazine ads which would feature a full-colour photograph of gnome in amusing position, with amusing play on words beneath it. Mike, naturally, thought this was pure genius. Guess who had to come up with the words?

So far I'd managed *Gnome Sweet Gnome* (gnome standing outside chocolate-box style cottage with roses round door) and *Gnome on the Range* (gnome perched on top of bucking bronco; gnome in dust cloud behind herd of rampaging cattle) and was just considering *Honey Gnome* (gnome standing proudly by beehive) and wondering if that was a tad obscure, while questioning how much longer I could keep my eyes open.

Yawning, I went down to the kitchen for my 17th coffee of the evening and looked for the umpteenth time at my mobile phone. No word from Cal. Perhaps he was up against the clock too. 'What else rhymes with bloody gnome?' I asked Boris, who was yowling about my feet.

He didn't know. Just yowled a bit more.

'You are not hungry,' I told him. 'You are supposed to be asleep. Or out hunting or something.' He looked at me appealingly. I gave him some fishy-shaped, vitamin-enhanced cat biscuits. At least someone in the family might be properly nourished.

It was 6.20 a.m. when I emailed off the final gnome witticism – *When in Gnome?* (gnome standing at the foot of the Spanish Steps). Mike phoned five minutes later, sounding as if were finally having that coronary.

'What does number five mean?' he shrieked. '*London Gnome*?'

'He's standing outside the O2 Centre,' I explained patiently. 'It used to be called the London Dome, didn't it?'

'No, it didn't,' said Mike tetchily, 'It was the Millennium Dome. You're thinking of the London Eye.'

'OK, well, we'll call it *Millennium Gnome* then.

Mike's hiss of exasperation reverberated around my left ear. 'I don't think so! That was over a decade ago. It's got to be now – happening – this year's must-have! Not something associated with the turn of the century.'

'OK, I'll think on.'

'Yes, do that – I've had everyone up all night working on this presentation and they'll be flat out till the client gets here.'

I forbore to say I hadn't exactly had any sleep myself and if he didn't promise everything yesterday, they wouldn't have to. I knew it would only elicit the "this-is-what-puts-us-apart-from-the-crowd" speech, about fast turnarounds and lightning response being what clients wanted in our uncertain, credit-crunched world.

Instead I ran a bath, poured large quantities of invigorating foaming bath essence into it, and lay there struggling to stay awake. *Gnome Bath*? I thought as the bubbles rose up around my neck.

That would work. A gnome's hat appearing above a sea of bubbles in a sumptuous bathroom. Right up Mike's street …

I was still thinking as I made Stanley's toast in a trance, barely hearing what he was saying to me, and waved him off to the bus stop. *Dome, Rome, foam, comb, tome* … By this time, I was so bloody tired I was barely functioning.

Still, oddly, I didn't feel like going to bed. I was in that strung-out, slightly manic state, on a curious, shivery high from lack of sleep, with my brain running in strange circles. Cal still hadn't replied to my text – maybe he'd been up all night too – and, as I tried to get my head round what I needed to do today – apart from come up with some inspirational word play about gnomes in the next 10 minutes – I felt oddly in limbo.

I don't know whether the words or the image came first but I grabbed the phone, feeling that rush of excitement I used to feel in my twenties when I was working with Mike in the office, and all-night sessions at the desk, propped up with thick, syrupy coffee and endless cigarettes, were regular events.

Mike answered immediately. 'Gnome standing on desolate wasteland, with barbed wire behind him,' I cried. '*Gnome man's land*.'

'Genius!' shrieked Mike. 'Provocative, controversial, edgy.

I love it!' He sighed happily. 'Soldiers in the distance. Maybe some blood. This could be our Benetton ad – I'm thinking shock factor.'

I listened while he shouted the good news round the office – smiling as I imagined the sheer joy of those faced with producing more lightning artwork when they'd already been up all night – then said goodbye before he could think of anything else to pile on me.

The day passed in a bit of a haze. I drove carefully to the supermarket thinking I may as well assume Cal was coming tomorrow – he was too considerate not to have let me know if he wasn't – and shop for that as well as find something for Stanley and me to eat tonight.

I then carried out a series of mundane and mindless tasks involving the washing machine and the iron, while drinking lots of coffee and slapping myself regularly around the face so I would stay conscious long enough to greet and feed my son and then fall into bed the moment *EastEnders* was over. Which was pretty much what I did.

Waking in a fog 12 hours later, I staggered downstairs, fed Boris, drank several cups of tea while listening to the latest gloom and doom on the radio news and then, seeing the clock creeping its way round to 10 a.m., made my way back upstairs to see what my son was up to.

Stanley was sitting on the edge of his bed, still in pyjamas, his hair uncombed. 'What are you doing?' I asked unnecessarily.

Stanley did not look up. 'Nothing.'

'Have you packed your bag to go to your father's?'

'No.'

'Well, you'd better get a move on – he'll be here soon. You need to get your school uniform ready and your books for Monday if you're staying with him on Sunday night as well.'

Daniel was taking Stanley to a football match and had suggested that as he hadn't seen him on his birthday, they made a longer weekend of it than usual. Stanley had seemed pleased with this arrangement at the time.

'Emily's going away,' he'd told me, 'so Dad says it's just him and me.' He'd lowered his voice, 'We're going to have pizzas.'

'How lovely,' I'd trilled, thinking it was all rather fortuitous too, what with the romantic weekend I had planned.

Now, though, Stanley stared miserably at the wallpaper and I felt a frisson of foreboding. 'What's the matter?' I asked cautiously.

'I don't want to go to school.'

'Well, darling, it's only Saturday and you're not going to school till Monday so don't think about it now. Think about the lovely time you're going to have with Dad.'

'I've still got to go after.'

'Well, yes,' I conceded, 'but we all have to go to school. It's never that bad when you get there, is it?'

'It is,' said Stanley mutinously. 'I hate it.'

I felt my phone vibrate against my thigh through my dressing gown pocket. Cal – it must be Cal. 'Hold on, darling.'

I fished it out just as it burst into song, anxiously scanning the screen for the number calling.

It was Clara, talking about our gym challenge and wondering when she was next going to see me. I walked into my office and shut the door so I could whisper to her about Cal's impending visit. She was suitably agog.

'You lucky thing,' she said. 'That will burn off heaps of calories. I've got a week left and I still can't do the bloody zip up. In fact I was so worried about it last night that I ate a whole packet of tortilla chips and then a tub of Ben and Jerry's. And I've got to see Vicky tonight – I can't put her off again.' Her voice rose to a wail. 'What am I going to *do*?'

By the time I'd calmed her down by promising that I'd join her in a three-day starvation diet of hot water and lemon and would accompany her on the body wrap offer she'd found – buy one, take your fat friend for half price – on which she was pinning her final hopes, Stanley had at least got dressed and was throwing things into a bag.

'Got everything?' I asked cheerily.

'What do you care?'

I looked at him, shocked. 'Don't be like that! Of course I care. What's the problem?'

'I've told you. Except you never listen.'

'I do listen, that's not fair.'

'No, you don't – I tried to talk to you yesterday and you just went to bed.'

'I'm sorry, but I'd been working all night, darling. You know that.'

Stanley glared. 'You're always working – and if you're not, you're off *filming.*'

'Well, that's all finished now.' I glanced at his bedside clock. Daniel was due in five minutes 'Talk to me now,' I said firmly. 'What's the matter at school?'

Stanley continued to glower at me.

'Has someone been teasing you again?'

'No.'

'Why are you upset then?'

'I've still got a stupid name and I'm fat.'

I sighed. 'Oh Stanley, not this again! It's a lovely name and you're lovely. You're not fat at all and, anyway, weight really doesn't matter.'

Stanley kicked at his overnight bag in sudden fury. 'Why have you become completely obsessed with yours then?'

I stared at him, startled. 'I haven't,' I said lamely. 'I've just been getting fit for the TV programme.

'You've gone really funny.'

My heart was beating harder. I thought of Becky saying the same thing. 'I haven't really. I'm just the same – I've just been busy.'

'You keep going away.'

'I'm sorry. It's finished now. I'll be here from now on.' I put out of my head any thoughts of how I was going to deal with my relationship with Cal – presumably I'd have to go to London some of the time, but perhaps he could come here at weekends. I hoped Stanley would like him. But now was not the time to mention it …

'And you still haven't even been on TV,' Stanley was saying. 'And it's ages since I told them at school that you

315

would be and now nobody believes me and they're being even more horrible.'

'What do you mean?' I asked anxiously. 'Even more? I thought it had all been fine …'

'No, it hasn't.'

'But Mr Lazlett said everything was OK …'

'They wouldn't do it in front of *him*, would they?' Stanley was shouting now.

I tried to keep my own voice calm. 'Look, Stanley, darling, kids do tease each other, don't they? Do you think you're just a bit tired? Things always seem worse then – they do to me too. You'll feel better after the weekend. And come Monday, the programme will have been on and they'll know you were telling the truth and it's not *all* the boys is it? You've got Connor there and didn't you say Jamie was a nice boy?'

'Yes,' said Stanley grudgingly. 'it's not him.'

'Who is it?'

There was no reply.

'Is it one person in particular?'

Stanley gave a tiny nod.

'Who is it, Stanley?'

He turned away from me and muttered something.

'Who? Did you say Bobby?'

'Robbie.'

'I haven't heard you mention him before.'

'He's new.'

I moved round so I could see Stanley's face. 'Ah, well, that's probably why he's being difficult – because he needs time to settle down. You know how hard it is when you first change schools.'

'It isn't that – he's just horrible anyway.'

'What's he been saying?'

'That I'm fat and ugly and stupid,' said Stanley hotly. 'And he said if you were really going to be on the TV you'd be on Google and he looked you up when we were in IT and you weren't there so he told everyone I made it up because I'm sad.'

Stanley's face had gone very red. He turned away from me

316

again. I patted his arm. 'And tomorrow night they'll know you didn't make it up. Look, try not to think about it today. You're going to have a nice weekend with Dad, aren't you? Seeing Chelsea play? Wow. You can take the programme in on Monday and show them all that too.'

'I might as well go and live with Dad.'

A stab of alarm went through me. 'You know you don't mean that. You live here with me. How would you go to school if you lived with Dad?'

'I hate my school. I could go to another one.'

We'd gone full circle. 'Now, come on,' I chivvied, conscious that Daniel was due to arrive any moment. 'I'll speak to Mr Lazlett again and ask him ...'

'*No.*'

'Well you couldn't live with Dad anyway, because I'd miss you too much.'

Stanley was silent.

I sat down next to him and wrapped him in a big hug. He didn't protest. 'I promise I'll sort it,' I said. 'I love you, Stanley.'

I felt him mumble against my shoulder. 'Love you too.'

While our son was searching for his second trainer, I managed to convey to Daniel that he was suffering some school-related angst and might need a bit of jollying along.

Daniel, for once, was quite nice, and didn't blame me in any way but promised to look after Stanley and take the opportunity to have a fatherly chat. He didn't comment on the fact that I was still in my dressing gown with my hair unwashed, but even wished me a good weekend.

Blimey, I thought, as I closed the door. Emily should go away more often – perhaps it was the thought of being able to eat pizza instead of steamed mung beans that had made him a bit more human.

I made a coffee and considered the best way to get everything done before Cal got here. I still wasn't sure quite when that would be because he still hadn't answered my text, but I'd said dinner so presumably he would be here by about

317

seven. And I'd better get everything ready well before in case he left early and arrived at six.

On the other hand, he'd also said how he loved to walk along the beach when he got anywhere near the sea, so maybe he'd decide to get here while it was still light – like about three.

And I hadn't even plucked my eyebrows.

Or would we walk on the beach in the morning? He hadn't actually said he was staying the night but I'd sort of presumed - well, hoped. I'd already stripped the bed and put on my best duvet cover.

I'd dithered for ages over what to cook, a decision not helped by the fact that I'd rarely seen Cal eat anything at all. I didn't know whether to do a proper meal with two courses and set the table with linen and candles, which seemed a bit formal and might feel embarrassing, or just get lots of delicious nibbly bits we could have with chilled wine in front of the TV.

Or champagne. He'd said we'd be celebrating. In the end I'd decided on a halfway house and had bought half a crispy duck with pancakes and hoisin sauce and got lots of other Chinese-style starter things like spring rolls and prawns in batter which we could eat in our hands in a suggestive way with lots of finger-licking. They would stop me drinking on an empty stomach but wouldn't fill me up so much that I fell asleep at the big moment. Presuming there was going to be one.

By the time I'd spent three hours preparing my body for this eventuality, changing tops and cleavage-enhancing bras three times and trying on several different pairs of trousers before ending up in the same pair of sparkly jeans – think young, think funky – I'd started with, I already felt like a drink but didn't dare have one as I didn't know if he was driving or coming by train. He could need picking up at the station.

I looked around the kitchen – all the dim sum bits and pieces were laid out neatly on foil-lined baking trays ready for the oven and the duck was already in. I knew from experience it needed twice as long as it said on the box if it was to be really crispy and fall apart, and it could easily be kept warm if he was late.

By 6.30 p.m. I decided that if he needed a lift, he was going to have to get a cab. I poured a large glass of the Chablis I'd chilled and emptied the hand-fried crisps into a bowl. By 6.45 p.m. they were half gone and I was on tenterhooks by seven.

The documentary was at nine. Was he just going to roll up? If I sent another text and he didn't answer, I'd be none the wiser. I'd have to phone. I felt ridiculously nervous and spoke to myself sternly.

For God's sake, we had slept together. He had talked in the future tense and he was much too nice to just not turn up – there must be something wrong. I went and plumped up the cushions on the sofa one more time and lit another scented candle.

Then I pressed his number.

The phone rang and rang but just as I was bracing myself for the answerphone to cut in, he answered, sounding stressed.

'Laura! Listen, I'm just with someone. Can I call you back in five minutes?'

So he hadn't even left yet. It was nearly 7.15 p.m. I had another drink. Five minutes passed, then ten. He obviously wasn't coming. Disappointment welled up from the pit of my stomach. I felt like I had, aged 14, when Darren from the fifth year had failed to materialise outside the St Peter's Fish Bar. 'You bastard,' I said without conviction.

But Cal wasn't a bastard – he was sweet and kind and thoughtful. Why was he doing this? I felt ridiculously close to tears and swallowed down some more wine.

After 20 long minutes, my mobile rang. I snatched it up, forgetting to play it cool.

Cal sounded upset. 'Laura, I am so sorry. I can't make it this evening. I should have let you know before but –'

I was barely listening. I realised I'd been hoping he'd say he was simply running late. His voice ran on about a problem with an edit and having been called into an unexpected production meeting. There were voices in the background; I could hear laughter. Someone's mobile was ringing.

'Are you still there, Laura?'

'Yes,' I said, trying to keep the dismay from my voice,

trying to be matter of fact. 'I'm still here,' I added as brightly as I could muster, knowing I sounded as if I'd just had both legs amputated.

'I'm really sorry,' he was saying. 'I wish I could be there, watching with you, I really do, but let's see each other soon – come up in the week and we'll go out for lunch and celebrate. I'll phone you Monday and we'll sort something out.'

Not tonight? You won't phone me tonight when the programme's over? Or tomorrow? You won't come to Broadstairs and walk along the beach with me, hand in hand ...

My solar plexus was a tight ball of misery.

'OK then. Well, I'm looking forward to seeing the programme, anyway.'

He laughed. 'Yes, you're a star! I hope you didn't go to any trouble for me.'

'Oh no,' I said loudly, as if I wasn't looking at enough fried rice to keep Shanghai going. 'Not at all.'

I sat my waxed, manicured, scrubbed, plucked, perfumed self down in front of prawn toasts for the five thousand and ate all the rest of the crisps in a state of numbness.

A star, huh? Sat on her own on a Saturday night. I suddenly missed Charlotte with a crushing intensity. She should be here now – waving a champagne bottle about and making rude comments. Someone should be here. Even Stanley – though he'd be rolling his eyes in embarrassment – would be better than sitting on my own.

If I'd known, I could have invited someone – Clara maybe, or Sarah. But Sarah would be working in the wine bar, of course, and Clara had already said she'd have to video it because she was out with Vicki. Anyway, it was too late to call anyone now.

I got the duck out of the oven and pulled at a bit of it half-heartedly. I didn't feel hungry any more. By the time 9.00 came, I just felt sick. I'd taken my clothes off and put on an old pair of pyjamas and my dressing gown and curled up on the sofa with the last drops of the wine and a hollow feeling in my stomach.

My big moment, my first serious TV début – the shrieking on *Rise up With Randolph* didn't count – and I had nobody to share it with. I'd thought that Charlotte might relent and send a good luck text, but my phone was silent. As the opening music began and *Prime Time* flashed in big letters across the screen, I felt suddenly nervous.

I found myself clutching a cushion as a young, female presenter – not a line on her face, fiercely upstanding breasts – explained the psychological ramifications of turning 40.

A bit of background ensued (cut to footage of care-worn woman in droopy cardigan and slippers, lowering herself wearily into fireside chair) with an overview of how things had begun to change (Madonna throwing herself across the stage with two cones strapped to her chest) and then, with lowered voice and dramatic movement of eyebrows (no Botox for her yet), Miss Presenter posed the question: How do women feel about being in their forties *now?*

First up was a pleasant-looking woman, looking nearer 50 than 40, with a couple of grandchildren sprawled across her lap. 'I am very happy with where I am,' she said. 'I am 49 and comfortable with myself.' Clips of her and husband strolling into an upmarket restaurant. 'These days, I no longer worry about what anyone thinks about the way I live my life …'

More film of woman and her husband going to the theatre. Her and small children frolicking in garden, her and daughter shopping for baby clothes. Her at reading group, explaining to fellow members how much she lives for the next Joanna Trollope. It all seemed a very long way away from anything I had done with Cal.

'I am content with the skin I have,' the woman said, as the camera panned in on her crow's feet. Where was the Botox and the keeping fit and looking fabulous? Where was I?

And then, suddenly, there I was.

Oh Christ …

Chapter Thirty-six

I GRADUALLY SANK INTO the corner of the sofa, holding the cushion protectively against me, just daring to peep over the top of it, as a cold clammy horror crept up my back.

'Laura,' the voiceover chirpily informed us, 'is fighting 40 all the way.' And there was the first shot of me, leaning across the table, in the tight red dress, unflattering bulges under my arms, explaining how "horrified" I'd been at the big birthday and how I couldn't even say the F word. I seemed to be having difficulty saying anything at all. I looked and sounded drunk.

Now here I was again, red-cheeked and sweaty, pounding up and down on the cross-trainer; and there with needles being stuck in my face. I watched numbly as I hauled myself into agonising-looking sit-ups, sat in Sally-Ann's office with peculiarly dark lips and heavy eye make-up, looking stricken, and again as I twittered excitedly to the doctor over the idea of having my feet pumped up to look younger.

Any shots of me looking fit and fabulous had obviously hit the cutting room floor. When the presenter announced I'd just completed two weeks of my "rejuvenation régime", I didn't look glowing or youthful or even particularly thin – I just looked exhausted.

When we got to the dating scene, my whole body went into such a deep cringe it sent my back into spasm. I clutched the cushion ever more tightly, and as soon as I'd caught the first sight of myself leaning lecherously across the table at the bloke with his chest hair on display, I buried my face in it.

Too horrified too watch, too scared not to, I screwed up my eyes and my courage to raise my eyes again, just in time to see myself sashaying down the side of the pool in my bikini, cringing all over again as I wiggled my hips and droopy bottom as though I thought I were 17.

I sat frozen as frame after frame showed me alternately hyper and morose. One minute I was gushing in a strange, high, false voice that sounded nothing like me about facial treatments that might change my life, the next I was slurring across a table, droning on about how awful it was to be old.

I didn't even remember saying half of it. My face burned as I heard myself talk about Charlotte. 'She's bigger than me,' I announced, my face hard, lipstick too bright on my pursed mouth. Hadn't I said how beautiful she was too? That wasn't there.

It was one long, alcohol-fuelled whine. The only time I was seen showing any enthusiasm for anything was when Dr Carling got his needles out. It was so awful I felt numb. Perhaps it would turn out to be one of those weird dreams where it's so realistic you wake up and think it really happened.

Perhaps this was a horrible figment of my imagination brought on by too much wine and not enough sleep and eating crisps instead of vegetables.

I stared unseeing as the credits went up. I'd worked on enough video scripts to know what a judicious edit can do. I should have remembered they had the power to take only the words they wanted. I recalled instead, that day I'd looked at myself in the mirror – in the soft light – in the wine bar with Cal, and had kidded myself I was still young and sexy.

And I remembered too all that Tanya's Lenny had said in the green room at the very beginning. Lighting could turn the Madonna into a monster.

This film was my worst nightmare. I'd been stripped away, revealed for what I was – a sad, ageing woman, clawing at her receding youth, desperate to hang on to any last vestiges she could still grab. One who sounded unbalanced and looked totally mad. I pointed the remote control at the TV and snapped it off.

What was Cal going to say now? You were fantastic, babe? You looked great? He wasn't going to say a word. My phone lay silent on the kitchen table. He'd known what he was doing all along.

I jumped as the land line rang out in the hall. But it wasn't him. It was Charlotte's number flashing up on the caller display. I backed away from it. She would be even more disappointed with me now. There'd be no point telling her they'd edited the nice bits out. I'd betrayed her all over again. I sat on the bottom stair and put my head in my hands. What a bloody mess.

I don't know how long I sat there but when the doorbell rang, it made me jump all over again. Strangely, for a moment it was hope that jolted through my veins. Even though he'd made a fool of me, I still half wanted Cal to turn up after all. To bound in and make it OK again. To tell me that it was the disappointment of him not coming that had made me see the film with a jaundiced eye. That really, I'd been brilliant …

As I began to get up, there was a clatter as a small piece of card came through the letterbox and landed on the rug. I bent to pick it up – would it say *sorry I'm late?* Was it his idea of a surprise? I couldn't decide if I'd fall into his arms or punch his lights out. The writing looked vaguely familiar.

Do you fancy a drink?

I opened the door, remembering too late I was in my dressing gown. It was Andrew. 'What the hell are you doing here?' I snapped.

He held up a bottle of red wine, unfazed. 'Stanley happened to mention he was with his dad this weekend. And I thought you might need a glass of something.'

I glared at him. 'Why's that then?'

'I just saw the programme,' he said quietly.

I was immediately deflated. And dangerously close to tears. At the mention of Stanley I felt even worse. What would the boys at school say to him now? What had I done to him? I'd promised him I'd sort it but instead I'd failed him in the worst possible way. I tried to make my voice light and failed. 'Was it that bad?'

'It wasn't very kind,' Andrew said.

I stood back so he could come in, swallowing hard. 'It's a

nightmare,' I said. 'I looked so horrific.'

'They lit you badly. You don't look anything like that.'

I looked at him, surprised.

'I used to do a lot of photography,' he said. 'Had my own darkroom and all that caper. People say the camera never lies, but it does. If you take someone with a wide-angled lens, they look wide. If you take them in harsh light, they look harsh.' He gave a small, rueful smile. 'They didn't do well by you.'

I had a rush of emotion at his words. A disturbing blend of anger and embarrassment and disappointment.

'It's my fault,' I said. 'I should have known.'

I should have known I'd already had enough to drink too, but I still went to the kitchen for clean glasses.

'Oh,' said Andrew, hesitating in the doorway, looking at the table with its two empty plates and trays of uneaten food.

'I was expecting a friend,' I said, embarrassed to expand any further. 'He couldn't come.'

'Right.' Andrew looked uncomfortable. I felt him glance again at my attire but couldn't bring myself to explain.

'Are you hungry?' I said instead, trying not to sound bitter. 'There's lots to eat.'

Andrew shook his head, taking the corkscrew from me and opening the wine. 'I should have phoned first,' he said. 'But I thought you'd either not answer or say you were all right even if you weren't.' He looked at me. 'And I thought you might need someone to talk to.'

I nodded. 'That was kind of you,' I said stiffly. He was being very kind but I still wanted to curl up and disappear. I sat down at the table, taking the glass he held out to me.

'Things any better with Charlotte?' he asked.

I shook my head and took a large mouthful of wine. 'They'll be even worse now,' I said miserably. 'I didn't just say she was big, I said she was really attractive, but they cut that bit out.'

'She'll understand if you explain.'

'I wouldn't bet on it.' I felt my chin wobble.

'How's Stanley?' said Andrew brightly, obviously trying to divert me.

It didn't work. At the thought of my son I dissolved into tears. 'He's going to be so embarrassed – now they'll all tease him even more. He's already having a terrible time.' I stumbled out what he'd told me about Robbie.

Andrew brought his chair close to mine and put a hand on my arm. 'It will be OK. I'll make sure he's OK.'

'How can you?' I sniffed, fumbling in my dressing gown pocket for an ancient tissue. 'He says they do it when you're not there.'

'I'll have a word,' he said. 'I'll deal with it.'

'I can't believe I've been such a fool,' I wailed. 'I got carried away. I believed all their hype. I thought I was going to look fabulous.'

'You usually do,' Andrew said matter-of-factly.

I jerked away from him. 'No I don't. I've been deluding myself – I am the wrong side of 40, with wrinkles and too much body fat. And all I've done is made myself look ridiculous trying to be something else.'

'It will soon be forgotten,' he said soothingly.

'No, no, it won't. I won't forget it. Every time I think about that film I'll remember how old and decrepit I am.'

'Come off it – you're not 80.'

'I'm middle-aged. It's all Daniel's fault,' I burst out. 'He made me feel old and past it and then the film people –' I couldn't bring myself to say Cal's name '- made me feel young and attractive again.'

'You are.'

'Not like I was in my twenties,' I cried, anguished.

'Well, no, none of us are.'

'They made me think I could turn the clock back and I fell for it.'

'We have to be realistic.'

He had put his hand back on my arm and now he rubbed it up and down through the towelling of my robe. It felt warm and comforting. Suddenly I felt child-like and pathetic and wished he'd give me a really big hug. I looked into his face. His eyes were a dark green colour - I'd never noticed before - and they were fixed on mine, full of concern.

'Seriously,' he said quietly, 'you're a very attractive woman. You don't look old. You look sexy and curvaceous, and if I might say so –' He stopped and laughed. 'Still crumpet!'

I smiled in spite of myself.

'Haven't heard that word for a long time.'

He pulled a face and gave my arm a squeeze. 'It's a great expression, I think. Sums up the situation perfectly. Although if my wife, Elaine, could hear me, she'd be furious at me for being so un-PC –'

At the mention of his wife, I jerked away from him again and stood up, knocking a foil container of noodles onto the floor. For a moment, in my upset, wine-befuddled state, I'd forgotten he was married. I felt as though I'd been slapped for the second time that night.

'You shouldn't be talking to me like that,' I said, agitated. 'You've got to go.'

'Sorry,' he said quickly. 'I've gathered you've got someone already. I wasn't trying to ...'

'It's not about *me*,' I squawked. 'It's you – you're married. What are you doing here when you've got a wife? What would she think if she could hear you?'

'She wouldn't much care. I've tried to tell you ...'

'Don't!' I shrieked. 'Don't start doing that stuff. You'll be telling me she doesn't understand you next.'

He gave a grin. 'She doesn't.'

'Get out!' Enraged, I pushed him away from me across the kitchen, just stopping myself from delivering a hard slap while I was about it.

He put his hands up. 'Let me explain.'

'Just go!' I stalked past him down the hall and yanked the front door open. 'Now.'

He picked up his jacket from the banister and turned to look at me.

'My wife and I have been having problems for some time,' he said calmly, 'and now –'

'I don't want to know!' I yelled. 'I am so sick of men never being satisfied with what they've got. First sign of things not being absolutely perfect and they think it's fine to come on to some other woman. Well, not this one. I don't do that stuff.'

Even as I said it, the heat flooded my face. Hadn't I, just moments ago, been thinking how nice it would feel if Andrew put his arms round me?

Guilt made me angrier than ever. 'If you're looking for a bit on the side, you're looking in the wrong place. So sod off.'

I slammed the door after him. The letterbox opened. 'I am not trying to have an affair with you,' he called.

'Go away.'

I sank back down onto the bottom stair where I'd started. Bloody men. All the bloody same. You couldn't rely on any of them. Roger, Cal, Daniel, now even kind, reliable Andrew wasn't the loyal, faithful sort I'd imagined. I'd make sure my lovely Stanley didn't grow up like that.

At the thought of Stanley and how I'd let him down, the sickness and anxiety swept through my body again, from my solar plexus, right down to my fingertips. I curled up, clutching myself, engulfed in a dark, bottomless, miserable despair.

I was never, ever going to recover from this.

Chapter Thirty-seven

I FELT EVEN WORSE in the morning, shame and humiliation compounded by a horrible hangover. I staggered around the kitchen, dropping things and averting my gaze from the congealing Chinese until I felt up to the task of disposing of it.

I couldn't decide whether my clumsiness was down to the DTs or more PMT. In theory I should be in my manic, positive phase now, but these days I seemed to spend every day of my life teetering on an emotional knife edge. Perhaps Sally-Ann was right and I was menopausal instead. What a cheering fucking thought that was.

I pushed the dishes to one end of the table and sat down with my third very strong coffee, adding the possible shrivelling of my ovaries to the mental list of issues of joy on which to congratulate myself.

1) Have made a total prat of myself with a younger man who was evidently stringing me along just so that he could make an even bigger prat of me in a film which, for a portrait of just how bad older women could look with too much lipstick and the wrong dress on, rivals *What Ever Happened to Baby Jane?*

2) Have lost my best friend, who might have had some sensible, grounding things to say on the matter and who I should have listened to in the first place.

3) Have been beastly to the only person who *has* tried to be nice. Here I grew hot-faced as I recalled shrieking at Andrew to get out of my house. The details were a bit of a blur now but I could remember shoving him and him protesting through the letterbox. Of course he wasn't trying to have an affair with me at all – who on earth would want to? – but was paying me

compliments to try to make me feel better about going out on national television looking like Bette Davis.

4) Have provided enough WIT points to keep Stanley in therapy for an extra decade.

Every time I thought of my son, my eyes filled with tears. He was already upset and now I'd done this to him. I prayed that the kids at school had been so disbelieving they hadn't bothered to check the telly or had forgotten when it was on. Better Stanley was thought to be a fantasist than the spawn of a mad, drunken, hormonally ravaged mother like me.

Had Stanley even seen it himself? Hopefully he'd been too busy eating pizzas. I prayed Daniel had taken him out to eat instead.

I wished I could find out. Then I could say the video machine hadn't worked here and he might never need see it. My phone was still quiet. We didn't usually have contact when Stanley was with Daniel unless he phoned to say he'd be late back or something, but now he had the new mobile I thought he might have sent me a text.

I wondered whether to send him one. I wouldn't mention the film in case it reminded him. In case Daniel had set his video after all, and Stanley asked to watch it. I would just gauge his mood.

Hi darling hope u having good time with dad. Love you very much xxxx

As a sudden afterthought, I sent one to Andrew too. *Sorry.*

I pressed *send*. Then when I'd stared at it for 20 minutes and nothing had come back, I put the phone down and made a supreme effort to get up and throw all the food out of the back door where it was instantly attacked by a hoard of screeching gulls. I watched as one got another's head in its beak as they fought over the last pancake roll.

5) Have wasted money and become one of those people who throws away a quarter of their food uneaten.

6) And also the sort of person who spends the day in bed.

Because having fucked up so royally on every count, there was nothing I could begin to contemplate doing now except climbing back under the duvet with painkillers.

I looked at myself in the hall mirror as I made for the stairs. Yesterday's make-up was still smeared around my face, which was blotchy from crying. My hair stood up in clumps, sticky with old hair gel. My eyes were creased and baggy. I looked about ninety.

Cal, eat your heart out.

I was at least up and showered and dressed when Daniel came banging on the door the next morning, although I still felt like shit and the sight of his sanctimonious face did nothing to improve things.

'I've taken Stanley to school,' he said pompously. 'And how do you think he's going to feel when all his friends have seen his mother looking like *that?'*

I felt instantly sick. 'What did he say?'

'He was embarrassed – what do you think? Luckily for you, I turned it off before he could see too much.' Daniel looked at me scathingly. 'But we saw enough.'

I swallowed.

'I'm wondering if, in the circumstances, I should pick him up from school again tonight,' Daniel went on in the same contemptuous tone. 'And take him back with me.'

'No,' I said at once. 'He's been with you two nights already. He's coming home now.'

Daniel looked me up and down. 'I've already told Stanley to phone me if he'd prefer not to. So perhaps I should take some more clothes with me in case.'

'How dare you!' I cried hotly. 'He lives here. How dare you suggest he might not want to be with me?'

'Well can you blame him? Making a spectacle of yourself like that. What were you thinking of?'

'You sound like my mother.'

'A pity you don't. You sounded drunk.'

Daniel took my silence as an opportunity to stick the knife in a bit more. 'You're not really setting a very good example, are you? It's hardly surprising that Stanley is anxious about school. It's what's going on here. He says you've been away a lot. I think maybe he should be spending more time with me if

331

you can't cope ...'

I shook my head, not trusting myself to speak. Normally I would have been yelling at him by now but I just felt like crying.

'I can cope,' I said eventually.

'Well, I don't think you can and I want to be a lot more involved. I want him to spend half the Christmas holidays with me.' The thought of Christmas, about which I had done precisely nothing, and that we wouldn't now be spending with Charlotte, made me want to cry even more.

'How does Emily feel about that?' I asked tightly.

For a moment there was a flicker of discomfort across his face.

'Stanley is my son and she will always welcome him, of course,' he said stiffly.

'Yeah, right. So she can go on badgering him about his calorie consumption.'

Daniel stood up straighter. 'I don't think you are in any position to criticise Emily.'

I was suddenly weary. 'Oh bugger off, Daniel.' I tried to shut the door. 'I've got work to do.'

Daniel remained in my way. 'I'll call Stanley later to see how he is,' he said ominously. 'And I'll come and get him if he needs me.'

After he'd gone, I tried hard not to burst into tears. Stanley hadn't answered my text yesterday and I had absolutely no idea what he was going through at school. Daniel was right – I was a terrible mother. I'd been totally carried away with the film and, all that time, Stanley was worrying about this revolting child, Robbie, and feeling awful about himself and I'd done nothing to help. I felt hot with shame.

The phone started ringing. I glanced at it as I walked past; it was Mike. I couldn't face talking to him now. Whatever new deadline he'd just created would have to wait.

I wondered whether to text Stanley again, but if his phone started beeping in the middle of a class it would be confiscated and that would stress him even more. If only Charlotte would get in touch. All of a sudden I remembered seeing her number flashing up on Saturday night and rushed to the phone to see if she'd left a message. She'd know what to do now. Even if it only involved a large glass of wine and a doughnut. I pressed buttons and listened to the robotic voice. *You have no messages.*

She must still be deeply upset with me. I cringed all over again at the thought of what I'd said about her on the film.

I spent the afternoon pacing and twitching and failing to come to a decision. I toyed with the idea of either meeting Stanley from school – shuddering at the thought of coming face to face with Andrew – or waiting by the bus stop. But decided that if the kids were really teasing him about me, that would make it all worse.

When the phone rang again about half an hour before he was due home, I nearly ignored it, imaging it would be Mike again, who'd been alternately trying the landline and my mobile and no doubt leaving increasingly tetchy messages if only I could be bothered to listen. But something made me go and look at the display and I snatched it up in panic.

'Stanley?'

He sounded normal, cheery even. 'Can I stay the night with Connor, mum? He's got the new Pro Evo soccer and his mum says it's OK. And he's got some stuff on his iPod I can put on my phone. If I come home now and get some clothes, his mum will pick me up at five. Mum, is that OK?'

I was swallowing, trying to make my own voice light. 'Yes, yes, it's fine. Are you OK?

'Yeah, gotta go – the bus is coming.'

'But Stanley, what about –'

The phone had gone dead.

He came in looking the same as he always did. Hair on end, muddy trousers, overflowing rucksack trailing beside him. I wanted to hug him for ever. He wriggled away from me.

I followed him round as he gathered up more clothes, games, CDs, and school books, handing him clean uniform, making him a drink, waiting …

At ten to five, I couldn't stand it any longer. 'Stanley,' I said, voice bright and brittle, praying I could hold it together.

'What happened about the film? Did the other boys at school see it?'

Stanley didn't look at me. 'Oh yeah, it was cool. They said a few things but I told them you were an actress and so you had to take on all sorts of roles and in this film it was one of an unhinged woman with ageing issues. I said you were pretending because that's what an actress has to do – pretend.'

He turned and smiled. 'I told them they put special make-up on you and had a special lighting man to make you look so horrible.'

I stared at him wordlessly, both horrified and impressed. 'That's really clever of you.' I managed eventually. 'How did you think of saying that?'

Stanley shrugged. 'Mr Lazlett told me to.'

While I was digesting this startling information, Stanley dug around in his rucksack and thrust some papers into my hand. 'There's stuff from school and I need a costume for the play.'

'Play?' I asked weakly.

'Yeah. I'm in it.' He gave a huge grin now. 'Mr Lazlett said as I've got acting in my blood I should have the lead. I'm the Chief Inspector and I get to question all the suspects. Everyone else is well jealous. But Robbie wants to come round and do lines with me. He's my sergeant.'

I felt the tears well in my eyes. Dear, kind, thoughtful Andrew.

Stanley frowned. 'Why are you crying?'

I sniffed and made myself beam. 'I'm just so proud of you.'

I kissed him goodbye at the door, waving to Michelle, who was parked in front of the gate. 'I love you, Stanley. I'll see you tomorrow.'

He swung his rucksack on to his back and picked up the bulging carrier bag at his feet. 'Yeah.'

I watched him walk away looking taller, somehow more grown up, than he had done on Saturday morning. Halfway down the path he paused and turned.

'You OK, Mum?' he called.

'Yes, darling, I'm fine.'

334

Chapter Thirty-eight

I DIDN'T ACTUALLY KNOW what I was. I was relieved Andrew had saved Stanley from embarrassment, mortified that he'd had to, disappointed in myself for being so blind and stupid and – a feeling that was gaining in intensity the more I thought about it – absolutely enraged with Cal.

I went through the papers Stanley had given me from school, thinking there might be a note from Andrew but it was all about the Christmas Fayre and the second-hand uniform shop and a skiing trip in February.

I shook my head. Andrew hadn't replied to my text apology – why should he decide to write to me now? He'd been kind enough to get Stanley out of a hole by giving him the lines to explain how "horrible" I'd looked, but he probably wanted nothing more to do with me. And anyway he was married to this woman who didn't understand him.

I squirmed again at the way I'd reacted to that. It was none of my business if he was the sort of bloke who liked to whinge about his wife and how presumptuous I'd been to assume it meant he was after me!

Presumably Cal was no longer after me either. He'd said he'd call today. Part of me never wanted to speak to him again, seeing what he'd done to me on film; the other part of me remembered our passion that Saturday night, the way he had of fixing his brown eyes on mine and making me feel a million dollars. Had I imagined it all?

I felt wound up, cross and hormonal. I knew even as I picked up the phone I shouldn't do it. That I should just maintain a dignified silence and see if he ever got in contact again. But I wanted to understand. Wanted to know what had made him pretend to like me, or if he had been pretending. It seemed extraordinary lengths to go to, just to get a bit of film footage. But if he did feel anything for me, why hadn't he phoned ...

He answered at once. 'Hello, it's Cal!' He sounded brisk and business-like. My heart plummeted. 'Can you just hold a minute?'

I could hear other voices. I waited silently until he came back. 'Hello?' he said again.

'It's Laura.'

'Hold on,' said Cal. There was the sound of a door closing and it all went quiet. 'Laura?' His voice was much closer now. 'How are you?' His tone was as warm as ever. 'Sorry I haven't called.'

'It doesn't matter,' I said dully.

'And sorry again about Saturday. I'd have loved to see you again. And we will have that lunch sometime –'

The "sometime" landed hard in stomach. 'That's OK,' I said, my voice still sounding strange and flat. 'Don't worry about it. I know you're busy.'

'No Laura, I am sorry, really – you've been such a good sport. It's not you, honestly.' I stiffened. *Oh God, please don't say "it's me". I shall throw up. A good sport? I thought you were making love to me* ...

He was still talking. 'I'd have liked to watch the programme with you ...' *Liar! After the way you made me look?* 'But the thing is –' He lowered his voice. 'It's Tanya – she was quite upset about Saturday night.'

I frowned, not expecting that. 'I don't understand.'

'I said we just got a bit carried away – my fault. All that champagne. When you –' He gave a small chuckle. 'Well, I just couldn't resist you and I've been in the dog house ever since. When she's calmed down a bit, you know, we can maybe do something – but at the moment she'd throw one if I saw you.' I heard him sigh. 'It was Ross and Matt. They carried on with the witticisms until it was bloody obvious what I'd been up to. So I had to tell her something. They're sods, really.'

For a moment I was speechless, feeling sick and cold. Wasn't Tanya with Lenny? Was Cal telling me that, in fact ...? I forced my mouth open. 'I didn't realise you and she were –'

'Yes,' he laughed easily. 'Supposed to be moving in together. I don't know, to be honest, if it will work out but –'

'Well, good luck!' I interrupted, trembling with pain and fury. 'I'd better be going.'

'Oh yes, and you,' he said warmly. 'Someone will be in touch from the office about any outstanding expenses. You really were terrific – '

''Bye, Cal.' I pressed my thumb hard against the red button on my phone. *Go boil your dick.*

I sat quite still on the kitchen chair. It was odd how it was always my first instinct when bad news came to stay motionless. It was illogical but it was though I believed that if I didn't move at all, I could suspend everything, that I wouldn't feel. I knew once I stood up, if I even stretched out a hand for my cold cup of tea, that the waves of wretchedness would come crashing in.

I'd imagined us cuddled up on my sofa, walking along the beach in the morning, hand in hand. Now it turned out I'd just been a drunken shag. The temporary other woman in his long-term relationship with his young girlfriend. He'd just been flirting with me to get me to do what he wanted. No wonder Tanya had always been in such a foul mood.

I pictured those soulful brown eyes I'd been so taken in by. Remembered us locked together on my hotel bed. Never had I felt worse about myself. My errors of judgement were piled high, one upon another. Cal, Charlotte, Andrew. How many more situations could I misread?

How could I ever have thought Cal would really be interested? I should have known it was too good to be true. I was in my forties. Sagging and past it. Of course he would want some firm, youthful beauty – not me.

Every time I thought of myself staring drunkenly into the camera I was washed over afresh with waves of hot shame then cold dread, and something peculiar happened around my knees. It was so deeply cringe-inducing it made me feel the way I had when Daniel's mother had insisted on sharing with me the lurid details of how one of her operations had gone wrong. However often I'd said, 'Please don't, I'm feeling squeamish,' she'd carried on until I'd had to sit on the floor and put my head between my ankles.

Except this time, I wanted to put my entire body into a very deep, dark hole and leave it there.

Keeping still wasn't working. I sat squirming with humiliation and hurt, and the sickening knowledge that I had been breathtakingly, awe-inspiringly stupid.

Out in the hall, the phone was ringing again. *Fuck off, Mike, and leave me alone.* I grabbed my bag and keys and ran out of the house.

I drove to the gym without thinking. Perhaps it was wanting to lose myself. I had my iPod in my handbag. I pulled into the car park thinking maybe if I could exhaust myself on the treadmill, with the music up really loud, I could block out the thoughts that ran round and round my head. Calm myself as I'd been able to at other times. I felt shivery and sick, my heart was pounding as if I'd already been running.

'I saw you on the telly!' As I walked toward the big glass entrance doors, a short, dark-haired woman who looked vaguely familiar was coming out, swinging a gym bag. She stopped and laughed. 'I recognised you at once. I said to my husband – I've seen her up at the gym.'

I nodded. 'I was brilliant, wasn't I? What did you think of my bingo wings?'

The woman looked startled.

'Sorry,' I muttered, as the doors opened. 'Having a bad day.'

As I came through the turnstile, my heart sank as I saw Clara and Alfie at a table in front of me, next to the huge twinkling Christmas tree. It was too late to do anything but say hello.

Clara looked radiant. In front of her was a panini and a glass of red wine, some carrot cake and a large flapjack. 'I told Vicki to shove it,' she said happily.

338

'Oh.' I made myself smile back.

'She was so awful on Saturday night. Said I'd let her down by not losing more weight. I was terribly upset but then, as Alfie said, I realised real friends accept you as you are, so I told her.'

She looked lovingly at Alfie beside her, who, I noticed, was even thinner and more good-looking and was gazing back at her equally adoringly.

'I said, stuff your bridesmaid's dress. Alfie likes me just as I am.' She took his hand.

'Good for you,' I said, a huge lump in my throat, feeling touched and overwhelmed, terrified I'd cry and spoil their happy moment. 'That's lovely. Well, I must go – not got long and I need to get on that cross-trainer!'

Clara looked surprised. 'Aren't you going to stay and see Andrew about the gym challenge? I thought I'd still do it anyway as Alfie is. He sent us all a text. Didn't you get it?'

I shook my head. 'He didn't send it to me. He doesn't want me involved any more.'

Clara frowned. 'I'm sure he does. Are you OK, Laura? Listen, I'm really sorry I haven't seen the film yet. I videoed it but ...' She smiled at Alfie again.

'You haven't missed a thing,' I said quickly. 'It's rubbish.'

Alfie stood up. 'Let me get you a coffee or something,' he said kindly. 'Andrew will be here in a minute – his text to you must have got lost.'

'No!' I took a deep breath. 'No, sorry. I must get on.'

Clara stood up too, and took my arm. She looked concerned. 'You seem upset. Has something happened with Cal?'

I shook my head. 'There was no Cal. I've got to go. Please, Clara, please don't tell Andrew I'm here.' I almost ran through the doors to the changing room.

It was deserted. I shoved my handbag in a locker and dragged off my sweatshirt, finding I was trembling. The thought of coming face to face with Andrew had filled me with unspeakable panic. Grabbing my iPod, I was just about to leave, when I heard a wail of anguish from behind me, followed by loud sobbing.

I peered round the corner to see a girl crying hysterically into a towel.

As I hesitated, I recognised her as the once-gorgeous, now emaciated, fitness obsessive that Clara and I had seen running endlessly with weights. Annabel, was it? She looked thinner than ever. I looked from her to the door. I was anxious to get into the gym before Clara could come after me, but I felt bad walking away from someone this state.

I walked tentatively toward her.

'Are you all right?' I asked, even though she clearly wasn't. Obviously she must have just received terrible news. Clara had said she was rich – perhaps her entire fortune had just been lost in a banking crisis. Or every living relative had died in an earthquake and she was now all alone in the world.

I patted her gingerly on the shoulder, looking to see if she was clutching a phone beneath the towel. Instead she held up what looked like a Coke can and burst into a fresh torrent of tears.

I put my arm around her skinny frame and she immediately clung to me, gulping out something I couldn't understand. I caught the words "wrong" and "mistake" in between great, racking convulsions.

I could hardly leave her now so I led her to a bench and made her sit down. 'I'm sorry, you'll have to say it again,' I said, praying that she hadn't just been told she only had six weeks to live and was clinging to the hope that the hospital had mixed up the results, because I wouldn't know what to say. Perhaps I could call someone for her. I tried to remember if my mobile was in my handbag.

She took a huge breath and held up the drink can again. 'It's got sugar in it,' she howled. 'I picked up the wrong one.'

I stared at her. 'Well, never mind. I'm sure one sweet drink won't hurt you – you're so thin already.' I took the can from her. 'Look, it's only got 85 calories in it – that won't make any difference.'

'It's sugar!' she wailed again. 'I won't be in ketosis!'

I frowned. 'Well, I don't mean to be rude but someone like

340

you shouldn't be. It makes your breath smell and when you're as skinny as you are, it makes the body start eating up its lean tissue – your heart and liver and things will begin to disappear.'

This made her cry even harder and I immediately regretted what I'd said – especially as I wasn't over-sure of my science but was just regurgitating something Clara had said to justify having a digestive biscuit with her orange juice. I decided to rephrase it.

'You don't need to lose weight,' I said, more gently. 'When I first saw you, I was so envious because you had such a perfect body. And honestly,' I added truthfully, 'you looked much better then.'

Annabel continued to weep loudly. 'My – husband – didn't – think – so,' she gulped between sobs.

'Has he left you or something? Try to take some deep breaths,' I advised, as she buried her head in my shoulder and howled some more and I made "I'm dealing with it" faces at two women who'd just come in and were hovering nearby.

Her husband, Annabel told me, when she'd recovered herself sufficiently to speak, and the two women had disappeared in the direction of the swimming pool, had indeed left her. For a girl with the improbable name of Jiggy, who was a size four.

In explaining why he felt moved to pack his bags and take up residence in Jiggy's loft apartment in Hoxton when he had a beautiful home here in Broadstairs and had only been married for 18 months, he had made much of the fact that not only did Jiggy have her own political PR company, but that she was very small. 'He kept saying,' Annabel sniffed, 'how tiny she was.'

She gazed at the can she was still turning around in her hands. 'And it made me feel,' she went on brokenly, 'for the first time in my life – fat.'

I knew exactly how she had felt.

'Men are such bastards,' I said. 'He didn't leave you because you were too fat – you looked absolutely beautiful that first day I saw you. He left you because he's an inadequate shit who has problems with commitment and loyalty and is one of those men who thinks there's always something better going on elsewhere.

'I can just imagine this Jiggy,' I continued. 'She's probably one of these high-powered women who secretly longs to be at home in a pinny. She probably over-compensates for her sterile existence by acting as his sex slave or something. When he gets fed up with her hip bones sticking into him, he'll move on again.'

Annabel nodded, seeming to find this analysis of someone I had never met and knew absolutely nothing about, of some comfort.

I tried to reassure her further. 'They make up a reason that turns everything into our fault because they don't want to admit that they're half-formed, unweaned, dick-led cretins,' I said, warming to my theme. 'My husband said he was leaving me because of my PMT and mood swings!'

Annabel was wide-eyed. 'And you didn't have them?'

'Well, I did, but it was still just an excuse.'

Her husband, it seemed, was even more adept at making excuses than mine. One of the reasons he'd given for dumping Annabel was that she'd once eaten a portion of black cherry cheesecake in bed and left crumbs on his pillow.

'He didn't care about things like that on our honeymoon,' she said sadly.

I was still making sympathetic noises but getting increasingly agitated inside. Clara had poked her head round the changing room door at the height of Annabel's distress, raising her eyebrows. I'd waved her away but I was afraid she'd come back any minute and I really couldn't bear to discuss anything that had happened. I wanted to stay out of the way until they'd all gone.

'I've got to go,' I told Annabel. 'But you've got to eat or you'll make yourself ill and no man's worth that. Next time we'll have a coffee and some cake.' As I said it, I realised that I hadn't eaten today either. I had that strange, light-headed feeling but I wasn't hungry at all. Perhaps I was in ketosis too and had breath like stale cabbage.

'You'll meet someone else,' I said, trying to sound cheery,

although my throat was now tight with tears as well. 'You get yourself back to normal and they'll be queuing round the block.'

I left her sitting on a bench, still holding the can, staring ahead with the hopeless eyes of a famine victim. 'I'll see you soon,' I said. She smiled weakly.

The irony of our conversation wasn't lost on me as I hurried upstairs. It would be easy to mock Annabel, to think her reaction to the break-up of her marriage and her hysteria over her diet extreme if not downright deranged, but I wasn't so very different. I was too weak-willed to lose any significant amount of weight – though post-traumatic stress was turning out to be a good diet aid – but look at what I'd done instead.

I shuddered as I got on the treadmill and pressed start. I'd allowed myself to be made a total fool of on television, by believing in the charms of a younger man who, if I'd stopped to think about it for a minute, was never likely to be attracted to someone who was the same generation as his mum.

I pushed the gradient up 15 per cent and set the speed to a brisk walk.

He'd conned and manipulated me and I'd fallen for it every step of the way. Obviously he'd never had any intention of watching the film with me and had been stringing me along from the beginning. He and Tanya probably used to lie in bed at night, laughing together at how gullible I was.

I turned my iPod on, increasing the volume as Oasis began to play.

I recalled yet again what Lenny had had to say – presumably Tanya was hanging out with him to get her own back on Cal for flirting with me – about the power of lighting and how it could make or break you on TV. Why hadn't I thought about that earlier?

I pushed the lever on the treadmill to make it go faster.

And with a horrible sick jolt, I remembered the argument between Tanya and Cal that final night at the hotel, and Cal saying, 'Let me do it my way.'

They weren't talking about the artistic nuances of the film, they were planning the best way to get a shot of my massive arse in a bikini. The most effective method of getting me to look really sad. Which was for Cal to pretend he wanted to go to bed with me.

I thought of giving that wiggle as I walked to the steam room and moaned out loud in embarrassment.

I pushed the lever on the treadmill again. Noel Gallagher was advising me *Don't look back in anger*. Ha, ha, ha.

I was up to 7.5 kilometres per hour now and had to break into a run. I turned the music up louder and pushed the treadmill further uphill too, wanting my legs to ache, wanting to hurt physically so I could focus on that instead of the terrible sick feeling I had inside.

What did Andrew think of me now? What would Clara and Alfie think when they saw the video? Thank God I'd responded to my mother's lack of interest by not telling her it was on.

Had Charlotte been upset watching it? I missed Charlotte. But Charlotte obviously didn't care about me at all and who could blame her. She was right – I'd been a rotten friend, fucking up the whole Roger-Hannah scenario like I fucked everything up …

I ran on, pushing the speed up to ten, my breath rasping in my chest, legs hurting, T-shirt sticking to me, wanting to flee it all, wanting to empty my head of everything but the throb of the music.

But instead a film reel ran relentlessly on in my mind, as clearly as if it were on a screen in front of me. Me, with my newly raised eyebrows, leering drunkenly at the camera, me slurring my way through a mortifying accolade to my own fading youth. Me in too-short dresses and ridiculous heels. *I'm in my prime? This is my prime time.* Who was I kidding?

I'd told Annabel the blokes would be queuing up for her and they would, but nobody was ever going to want me again. Men were always going to be either nice but married or unmarried because they were tossers or unmarried because they were too young for me with equally young girlfriends who were going to move in with them.

Who was going to look at a washed up 42-year-old who'd let it all hang out on prime-time TV?

I was still running, my limbs weakening, muscles sore. The monitor was flashing, warning me I had a high heart rate but still I kept going, feet pounding one after the other, gasping for breath, realising that I was crying too, the tears mixing with the sweat that was running down my face and chest, running and running, afraid to stop …

Until suddenly, I felt my legs lose their rhythm as the treadmill slowed right up and the gradient lessened and I saw the hand that had come across in front of me and reached out for the big red button to turn the machine off.

'Stop now,' Andrew said. 'It's enough.'

As the platform came to a halt, he took my damp hand and pulled me from it on to the floor beside him. I tugged half-heartedly away from him. He held on.

He was wearing dark shorts and a white T-shirt. I couldn't look up to meet his eyes but I felt the soft, dry fabric and breathed in the scent of fresh air and soap laced with the faintest warm, smoky tones of tobacco as his arms went round me and I pressed my wet cheeks into his chest.

Chapter Thirty-nine

HE WAS WAITING FOR me when I came out of the changing room. I'd taken off my sticky T-shirt and underwear and showered but had had to put the same tracksuit bottoms back on and was wearing nothing under my sweatshirt.

'I need to go home,' I protested, when he offered to take me out for dinner. 'I can't go out like this and even if I got changed, suppose someone sees me who saw the programme? And I'm not really that hungry and anyway, I know you're being very kind to me, but –' I took a deep breath and looked him straight in the eyes now. 'What about your wife?'

He sighed. 'You can't hide away for ever. You need to eat. And if you'll finally let me finish without interrupting or hitting me, I will tell you about Elaine.'

He put his arm through mine as I hesitated. 'We'll compromise. I'll go and get us fish and chips. You go home and get the plates out.'

I shook my head. 'I'm not supposed to be eating carbohydrates and there's about a thousand calories and God knows how much fat in cod and chips.'

He nodded. 'Exactly. I'll get you a large one.'

'We separated eight months ago,' he said, once we were sat at my kitchen table in front of two heaped plates, the scent of vinegar rising in the steam. 'Mainly because we could no longer stand living in the same house. She got a transfer and moved back to Woking, where her parents live, taking the boys with her, of course, and terrifying a different set of clerks in the bought ledger department of CGH Building Supplies where her ability to get blood out of a financial stone is legendary.' He gave me a wry smile. 'We are very different people.'

I nodded, my mouth full of fish. I'd become suddenly ravenous as soon as I'd unwrapped the warm, fragrant parcels and was glad he was talking so I could keep on eating.

'And that was fine for us,' he continued, a hand cupped beneath his chin, green eyes serious, 'except that the boys really missed me. Even though I'm not their father I've been around since they were small and I have to say I missed them too. We stayed in touch by phone but the house seemed very big and quiet and I was lonely. Elaine was having trouble with the kids not settling, suddenly she and I were talking a lot, far more than we ever did when we were together.' He took a mouthful of wine. 'And I guess the doubts set in. We were getting on so well, we decided to have one more go. She took some extended leave and got the boys out of school and into one down here and came back to see if we could make it work this time.'

He stopped to spear a chip with his fork. I waited while he chewed.

'Except we couldn't. Within days, we remembered why we'd split up. She finds me too messy and sentimental and weak-willed. She was furious that I'd started smoking again once they'd left. I found her too rigid and controlling and judgemental. The final straw came for both of us when she made a chart with colour coded stickers, informing me what I could and couldn't eat, and I cried in front of her at the end of a re-run of *Chariots of Fire*.'

I couldn't help giggling. 'She doesn't like men showing their feminine side, then?'

He ate another chip. 'My wife doesn't believe in emotional displays of any kind. That's why when you sat in front of me at parents' evening and burst into tears, I was instantly smitten.'

I examined my plate, embarrassed. 'You were?'

'I was. I thought you were beautiful. Even with watery eyes and a red nose.'

I began cutting my cod into small pieces, unable to look at him.

'I was really disappointed when Clara said you were seeing

the director chap. But do I gather that's finished?'

'It never started,' I said. 'Only in my head.' I told him the sorry tale. Andrew touched my hand.

'I'd never defend anyone who works in reality TV,' he said. 'I think all those programmes are awful. But I bet you, even if he was piling on the charm to keep you sweet for the film, he enjoyed every minute of it. That's why his girlfriend was so upset, because she knew he fancied you rotten – just like I do – and he had the perfect excuse to indulge himself.' Andrew leant over and squeezed my shoulder. 'He behaved badly, but you shouldn't feel bad about it.'

I cut my food up a bit more. 'Thank you,' I said awkwardly.

'Anyway, it was when I saw you losing it in the supermarket that I really fell for you,' he continued easily. 'I loved the fact that you were so volatile. Even though your eyebrows were a bit scary by then, I was drawn to all that passion. I sometimes used to wonder just what it would take to make Elaine lose control. I've still never discovered the answer to that one.'

'I had PMT,' I said self-consciously. 'Were my eyebrows really scary?'

'Yes, they were quite. What did you tell me you said to Annabel in the changing room? You looked better before?'

'It's nice being a bit thinner.'

'You're crumpet however much you weigh – am I allowed to say that now? And as for the night the programme had been on, you looked so lovely and you got *so* cross. When you started shouting, I just knew I was going to have to win you round.' He grinned.

'Why didn't you answer my text then? When I said sorry.'

He looked at me, still smiling. 'I did. I kept sending texts. You were the one who didn't answer. I assumed you were still in a strop.'

'I didn't get them. I haven't had any texts at all.' I got up and dug in my handbag for my phone and handed it to him. 'See?'

He looked at it and smiled some more. 'Excellent. You are dippy and un-technical as well as given to emotional outbursts.

Perfect!'

I peered over his shoulder. 'There aren't any texts on there. It hasn't beeped or anything.'

'No – because the phone's full of them.' He pointed to a tiny flashing envelope in the corner of the screen. 'When did you last delete any?'

'Not sure I ever have.'

He made coffee while I scanned through weeks of messages, noting before I pushed the button that would erase them all, how many were from Cal. *Can't wait to see you.* I bet you bloody couldn't, I thought.

'So what's happening now with Elaine?' I asked as a series of beeps told me the backlog of texts was finally coming in.

'She's gone back to her job and rented house in Woking,' Andrew said. 'We're going to sort things out properly so she can buy somewhere. And I'm going to have the boys to stay regularly – and go up there for Christmas. I think it's a relief for both of us. Now we know it's really over, we'll be able to be civilised – maybe even be friends, who knows.'

I nodded, but I was only half-listening. The thought of Christmas, about which I'd done nothing, and being here on my own with Stanley, had sent a stab of pain through me. 'We were supposed to be going to Charlotte's,' I said miserably.

'You still might be.' Andrew pointed to my phone where the screen was filling up. It read *12 messages received.* 'Only about six of them are from me,' he said.

When he'd gone into the garden for his post-dinner cigarette, having refused my offer of having one indoors on the grounds that he wanted it all to be as difficult as possible so he finally did give up, I sat and read all the texts, my eyes filling with tears.

There was one from Andrew sent the night I'd thrown him out, saying not to worry about anything and would I let him explain about his wife, please? And one a little later the same evening from Charlotte which simply read *call me, you silly cow.*

This progressed to *answer the phone, you silly moo*, when I would have been lying in bed the next day, ignoring the incessant ringing, and *still love you daft bat text me back* this morning and finally, when I'd have been on the treadmill thinking about how much I missed her, *Miss you sorry for everything. Let's stop this now. Call me or else.*

'Oh my God,' I said, as Andrew came through the back door. 'She thinks *I've* been ignoring *her.*'

'I know how she feels.'

I looked at the next one. *You're still gorgeous.*

'I don't feel gorgeous,' I said, my chin wobbling all over again.

'Well, you are.'

I shook my head. 'I feel and old and unattractive and I've made an idiot of myself in front of thousands of people.

'You are gorgeous. And you always were. You were badly lit in a TV programme that hardly anyone watched. And most of those who did, don't even know you. As the kids would say: get over it.'

'And I sounded stupid.'

'You were unfairly edited. It's a lesson for next time. You'll have to get over that too.'

I shuddered. 'There is never going to be a next time.'

'So let's concentrate on now.' He reached out a hand and drew me toward him, bringing his dark, curly head close to mine, his green eyes gleaming. I gazed back at him. Part of me wanted to fall into his arms, to feel their warmth around me, to be hugged again, to believe I could be attractive. But the rest of me was still mortified. I remembered the way I'd gazed into Cal's eyes and fallen so readily for his insubstantial charms. Andrew was a lovely man and he was being very kind to me but ...

'But you're Stanley's teacher,' I said lamely, stepping back from him.

'We can deal with that – I'm not going to snog you in the middle of the classroom.'

'And you've got all this to sort out with your wife ...'

He dropped my hand. 'I've told you it's sorted. Aren't you just making excuses, Laura?' He looked at me sadly. 'Isn't it more that you're still hung up on your director chap? Or of course,' he went on flatly, 'it could be that you just don't fancy me. Perhaps I'm rather jumping the gun here ...'

His eyes were searching mine and I suddenly felt miserable and defeated. I wanted to say something nice, to explain, to let him put his arms around me but all I could see was him watching me on TV and I felt awkward and embarrassed and washed over by shame all over again. I looked away from him.

'I'm sorry,' I said. 'I just can't.'

Chapter Forty

MY GREATEST FEAR IS that PMT doesn't exist and this is my true personality.

I turned the wooden plaque over in my hands. 'Thank you,' I said. 'How thoughtful.'

Charlotte laughed loudly. 'Knew you'd like it. You can put it up in your kitchen. And look what else I've got!' She opened her fridge to reveal two bottles of pink champagne. 'I thought we'd have a bit of a party!'

'Why?' I asked suspiciously, my PMT, as it happened, bubbling away nicely and making me scratchy. 'Presents, inviting us for dinner, champagne … Why are you being so nice to me?'

Charlotte snorted. 'Cheeky moo. I'm always lovely to you and you spend half your life eating round here. But if you must know,' she went on, 'I am getting sick of the sight of your miserable face. I thought if I could get you half-cut on fizz, you might cheer up.'

'I'm sorry,' I said, glumly.

'It's about time you snapped out of it,' continued Charlotte, removing the foil from one of the bottles. 'That wretched TV programme was weeks ago and everyone has completely forgotten about it. So I really think it's time you stopped walking around like someone's died.'

'I am mourning my lost youth.'

'You're being a pain in the arse.' Charlotte covered the top of the first bottle with a tea-towel and twisted. There was a loud pop. 'Glasses! Quick!'

'We could ask Alfie and Clara round if you like,' she said, as she poured. 'I've got a massive piece of beef.'

'They're in Rome,' I said. 'Alfie booked a weekend trip for Clara's birthday.'

'Lucky buggers. I'd like to go there – or Milan. My New Year's resolution,' she added, as Roger appeared in the doorway, 'was for my husband to take me away more.' Charlotte gave him a mock-severe look. 'Off his own bat!' She raised her glass cheerily. 'Come and get a drink, love.'

She didn't look at me as she filled a glass for Roger. 'How about inviting Andrew, then?' she said slyly.

I put my drink down in irritation. 'For God's sake, you never give up, do you? Andrew is not interested in me. I haven't heard a word from him.'

Charlotte took a large swig of champagne. 'What did you expect? He declared his passion for you and you turned him down – you can't expect the poor bloke to keep coming back for more after that. It's down to you. I bet if you called him now and said we're having a little celebration, he'd be round here like a long dog.'

'What are we celebrating?' I asked moodily.

'Wait and see!'

I looked at her as she opened a bag of peanuts. She was smiling to herself and I felt a deep sense of foreboding. The last time she'd looked like that had been my 21st birthday, when she'd had the bright idea of rounding up my previous boyfriends to join in the fun and I'd been forced to dance with Kevin Gornley, last seen aged 15, whose spots and foot odour had only intensified in the meantime.

Stanley and I'd been round for Sunday lunch plenty of times before but at this point it was usually her and me and a glass of Pinot Grigio at the kitchen table while she peeled vegetables and Roger watched the sports channel. This felt different.

And I knew why as soon as the doorbell sounded. I glared at Charlotte as Roger went into the hallway and I heard a familiar voice floating toward us.

'How could you?' I hissed furiously. 'I asked you not to interfere. I don't want to see him.'

Charlotte was unrepentant. 'Never mind what you want,

love. It's Sunday afternoon and I'm in the mood to party. The more the merrier. Can you get those crisps open?'

'I'm sorry – you know what she's like,' murmured Roger, winking at me as he passed on the way to the fridge, carrying cans of beer. I looked up unwillingly. Andrew stood just inside the door, wearing jeans and a soft blue shirt. Charlotte was beaming at him. 'Glass of champagne? We won't be eating till about four so do have some nuts ...'

'Hello Laura.' Andrew gave me a polite smile. I cringed inside as I muttered back a greeting. What the hell was Charlotte doing? He didn't want to be here like this any more than I did.

Roger was making jolly conversation. 'How are things? Good Christmas?'

Charlotte pulled a face. 'That was ages ago. And best forgotten. If ever the Americans want to develop a new torture I've got one – eight hours listening to your mother at the same time as Laura's. Thank God for the numbing effects of alcohol.'

Too right, I thought, knocking back all the rest of the champagne in my glass and wishing I could go home. I couldn't believe Charlotte had gone to such lengths to do something so utterly crass. She hadn't even put the meat in the oven yet – we were going to be stuck together for hours. What would we all talk about?

The answer was nothing, it seemed. 'Let's all go and watch television,' Charlotte said brightly. I stared at her. This was the woman who used to berate Roger for hiding behind the remote control if she had friends round.

'Call the kids, Roger!' she instructed. She looked up at the clock. 'Come on – we've got five minutes.'

She refilled my glass and held out the bottle toward Andrew. 'Have a top-up,' she said, picking up the crisp bowl with her other hand. 'Bring the peanuts, Lu.'

I trailed behind her and the others into her sitting room, wondering what on earth she was up to, feeling suddenly sick as a horrible possibility occurred to me. Surely not ...

'You weren't going to tell me, were you?' Charlotte was

saying, pressing buttons on the remote. 'Lucky I still had Alicia's number, she was very helpful. She told me that your cookery programme–' Charlotte turned round to look hard at me '–went out on Thursday.'

I heaved a small sigh of relief. 'Did it?' I asked casually. 'Oh, I didn't know …'

'Alicia said you'd have been sent an email,' said Charlotte accusingly. 'She did it in the end with one of her friends – they pretended to be cousins, I gather – and she got an email weeks ago with the dates. Why didn't you tell me?'

'I deleted it,' I said shortly. 'I didn't want to know.'

'Well, I did,' said Charlotte. 'And guess what?'

Please don't tell me you've got a recording …

'It's repeated today!' she cried triumphantly. Charlotte grinned at me. 'It's being shown on Foodies UK and we're all going to watch it right now.' She threw back her head and yelled, '*Boys!*' before looking at Roger. 'Thought you'd called them?'

'I did,' he said.

'We'll record it too.' Charlotte seemed oblivious my horror. 'Bex will be furious if she can't see it. I told her to watch it at Lauren's but she says they might be shopping. For a change!'

I felt sick to my boots. 'Charlotte, please …' I began shakily, stopping as Joe and Stanley came reluctantly into the room, my son looking suitably askance to find his form tutor there.

'We were in the middle of a game,' Stanley said to me plaintively. I shrugged helplessly.

'Well, this is much more exciting,' said Charlotte. 'We're going to watch your mother being a television star!'

I stared at the carpet, hating her. Why was she doing this? Surely she could imagine what it was doing to me.

'I'll tell you what,' I heard Andrew say. 'Stanley's fantastic in the play we're doing at school. Quite the star himself – got his mother's acting ability, all right.'

I bit my lip as I felt tears of humiliation tingling at the back of my nose. That was all I needed – him taking the piss. Bastard. Why had he come? Just to laugh at me with everyone else?

Then suddenly the opening music started and I shrunk back into the sofa as the red and green lettering of the *Cook Around the Clock* logo bounced across the screen. 'Oh my God ...'

Andrew was somehow next to me. 'You're going to be great,' he said brightly.

Yeah, right – like I was last time?

'Entertaining, anyway,' added Charlotte with a grin. She beamed at me across the room. I scowled back, feeling like crying and longing to run from the room.

'Embarrassing, more like,' said Stanley glumly from the carpet, where he was sprawled next to a giggling Joe.

I stared mutely at the screen as the couple I remembered as Bob and Carol appeared in front of me.

'And now we have Bob and Carol!' cried Austin the presenter, flashing his improbable white teeth. 'Are we excited?' he cried.

'She was terrified,' I snapped.

'She looks it,' said Roger.

'He looks a right dick,' said Charlotte. 'Told you,' she continued triumphantly, when Bob had finished regaling the audience with his prowess in the kitchen and special flair for making sausage and apricot curry.

'No, I can't cook at all,' said his wife Carol faintly, looking as though she might collapse.

'Probably doesn't want to go in the kitchen if that prat's in there,' said Charlotte.

'Stop talking,' said Roger. 'You're worse than the kids.'

Stanley and Joe were too busy hoovering up the nibbles to say anything much. but both looked suitably bored as Bruno the chef led a quaking Carol off to one side of the studio and Bob made a show of putting his chef's hat on and striding off to the other. My hands clutched each other, nails digging into my palms. My stomach was churning.

I could feel Andrew breathing beside me as we watched Bob guffawing his way through the creation of a chicken and leek pie while Carol gripped a large knife in frozen terror before eventually managing to chop some broccoli. I slumped in relief as Austin grinned manically at the camera and the music played.

'Let's get the next bottle open,' said Charlotte getting up and prodding Roger as the adverts came on.

'Can we go back upstairs now?' asked Stanley.

'No,' said Charlotte. 'Your mother's on next.'

Stanley sighed.

'Got a football? I'll stand in goal for two minutes,' offered Andrew. 'That OK?' he said to Charlotte. He didn't look at me.

'Good idea. I'll come and watch,' said Charlotte at once, delving into her handbag for her cigarettes.

'She's supposed to be giving up,' said Roger, as they all disappeared through the back door and I stood uncomfortably in the kitchen while he got champagne out of the fridge.

'Well, she's got a nicotine ally out there in Andrew,' I said. 'Unless he's stopped again by now.'

'Charlotte says she's cut down,' said Roger, pulling a disbelieving face. 'Though I can't say I've seen much evidence of it.'

'Is everything all right now?' I asked awkwardly. We hadn't spoken about Hannah since Charlotte and I had made up. She and Roger seemed happy enough, but I wanted to make sure.

'Yes, it's good,' said Roger. 'After I told Charlotte everything, we said we'd put it behind us. Well, I told her nearly everything,' he added, slightly shamefaced. 'I didn't go into detail ...'

'You told her enough,' I reassured him.

He nodded. 'Yeah. Thank you.'

'And Hannah's not being a problem any more?' I held out my glass to be topped up.

Roger poured. 'I've been waiting for a chance to tell you. She's left the company. Got a job in Ashford. It was a huge relief when she went.'

'And you've told Charlotte?'

He gave a wry smile. 'It was Charlotte's idea.'

A fresh wave of nausea came over me as the programme re-started. I'd tried to hide in the bathroom but Charlotte, an iron grip on my arm, had marched me back to the sofa, where I now sat clutching a cushion to my face with clammy hands.

'Oh hey – you look fab, love.' Charlotte gave a sudden squeal. I peered around the edge of the cushion to see myself running down the steps of the studio and shaking hands with Bruno. 'Lovely top!'

'So, Laura,' Austin was saying, 'what are you going to make for us today?'

I stared at myself on screen. I appeared remarkably composed as I smiled back at the presenter and explained about the pulverised Snickers bars in my special dessert. My voice sounded odd – not like me at all – but I looked much slimmer than I expected to, with the green top flowing around me.

I'd forgotten what my hair was like before it was cut. I preferred it shorter and funkier, but it looked pretty sophisticated the way they'd done it, and my make-up was brilliant. My skin looked flawless, my eyes really large and shining.

Beside me, Andrew gave me a tiny nudge and murmured something I couldn't hear. I didn't dare look at him.

'You look fantastic,' shrieked Charlotte.

'Lovely,' said Roger.

Even Stanley smiled. 'Not bad, Mum,' he said, before groaning, 'Oh no,' as I mentioned that the pudding was his favourite.

'Now you're famous too,' Andrew told him.

I breathed out in stunned disbelief as we watched me stirring a saucepanful of chopped chocolate, me chatting with Austin as I spooned ice cream into a large bowl, laughing with Bruno as we compared desserts at the end. I seemed very confident and assured in a way I couldn't remember feeling at the time.

It was OK! It had been as beautifully filmed as the other had been awful. Somehow they'd edited it so that you couldn't even see the way our noses had crunched together when Bruno and I kissed goodbye.

As I gazed at myself it felt like a dream. It all seemed so

very long ago now and this witty, smiling Laura, who looked glowing and even youngish, was a person I'd never seen before.

'Congratulations, love,' said Charlotte as the credits went up. 'To Laura!'

They all raised their glasses.

'Now can we go back upstairs?' said Stanley.

'Aren't you going to answer that?' said Charlotte as, back in the kitchen, my mobile began to ring.

Still in a daze, I glanced at the display and shook my head. 'It's Alicia. She keeps phoning. She's trying to get me to go on *Round-up With Randolph* with her. You know, this programme where they show all the highlights of the last series. I've already told her no.' I pushed the phone away from me across the table. Charlotte pounced on it.

'Hello Alicia, how are you, love? Yes, we saw it. She was excellent, wasn't she? Yeah, we're all celebrating.' Charlotte winked at me. 'Really? That sounds good – tell me more. Uh huh. Yep, brilliant, yes I'm sure she'd love to. Sure. Well she's a bit busy now, but don't you worry, I'll persuade her and get her to give you a call. Yes, absolutely. Oh, OK. Hang on!'

She cupped her hand over the phone and looked at me. I shook my head. 'You are not going to persuade me,' I said firmly. 'There is no way I am going back to see that creep Randolph Kendall or watch myself screaming like a banshee. She can go on her own.'

Charlotte looked smug. 'It's not Rudolph – this is something else.'

'I'm not doing it,' I said.

Charlotte continued. 'Alicia's agent has put her up for some sort of magazine show on – oh I don't know, some little-known channel. They haven't got many viewers yet anyway, so it's nothing to worry about. They're having an advice slot where there's a phone-in and the viewer with the problem gets tips from three generations. She's doing the twenties and she's putting her gran up for the oldie and she wants you for the woman in the middle. They need someone in her forties.'

'You're joking,' I said. 'No way.'

'She says it will be loads of fun, you'll get paid, and why don't you at least go for the audition?'

'No,' I repeated. 'Never again. I'm not getting involved in anything to do with being middle-aged. Or anything on TV at all.'

Charlotte put the phone back to her ear. 'She'll give it a whirl, love. Email her all the gen.'

'Just go and do the audition,' she said calmly when I'd spluttered my protests. 'It will do you good. What did our riding instructress used to say when we fell off? Get straight back on again.'

'You only went once,' I said. 'And you never did fall off because you were too scared to go any faster than a walk.'

'When *you* fell off, then,' said Charlotte unmoved. 'Now, I'd better get that beef in the oven or we won't be eating till midnight.' She looked from Andrew to me. 'You two wouldn't give Benson a quick walk for me, would you, while I do the spuds?' she said. 'He's been cooped up all day – just take him for a run on the beach before it gets dark?'

'Of course.' Andrew smiled at her as my heart sank. Would she never leave it alone? This was going to be so embarrassing.

'Maybe the kids would like to go …' I said.

'I doubt it,' said Charlotte. 'They're spot-welded to that PlayStation again.'

She pulled open a cupboard and loaded Andrew up with a ball thrower and poop scoop, handing me Benson's lead, as the Labrador threw himself against me, tail thrashing excitably. Then she gave a large, unsubtle wink. 'No rush. Take your time …'

'She's incorrigible,' I said with an awkward laugh, as we went off down the path, Benson tugging madly at my arm.

'She's a good friend to you,' said Andrew.

'I know.' We fell back into silence as our feet tramped along the road toward the cliffs. It was cold. I zipped my jacket up a little higher, wishing I'd borrowed Charlotte's gloves. I felt ill at ease, wishing I was anywhere else and wondering what Andrew was thinking.

Was he remembering the last time we'd been together, leaving my house, looking hurt and uncomfortable, while I stood powerless – wanting to call him back, wanting to put it right again, but paralysed, feeling too wretched to speak. I knew I should try to explain.

'I'm sorry,' I began. 'Last time I …'

But he cut across me. 'You looked great on the TV today.'

'Thank you,' I mumbled.

'I'm glad Charlotte tracked me down and I was able to see it.'

'How did she get hold of you?' I asked.

'Phoned the school. We had a very long chat,' he said meaningfully.

I squirmed, wondering what exactly she'd said. I hoped it wasn't that I'd admitted I found him quite attractive and wished I hadn't pushed him away – I'd told her that in confidence, and only because I'd had too much sherry on Boxing Day. I didn't mean it.

'Were you pleased with the cookery show?' he continued, as we got to the grassy seafront and Benson began to leap toward the path down through the chalk to the beach. 'Has it made you feel better?'

'Yes, I suppose so,' I said, bending down to undo Benson's lead, trying to hide my discomfort. The dog bounded away from us in joy. We followed him down on to the sand.

'Good,' said Andrew, swinging back the ball-thrower and sending the ball whizzing off into the distance. He looked back at me as Benson galloped after it. 'I hope it's taken the bad taste away from what that little prick did.'

I smiled at him. 'That's not very teacher-like!'

'Well, don't tell Stanley.' He smiled back. 'But really, I thought you were terrific on that programme – a real natural.'

'Now you're sounding like the little prick.'

'Ah but when I say it, it's true. And it would have been true when he said it if he hadn't presented you so badly.' He looked at me, his green eyes serious. 'Today was the real you,' he said. 'That's the one to remember.'

'How's things with your life?' I asked, turning my face

away, embarrassed by the intensity of his gaze, wanting to change the subject. 'Are you and Elaine still apart?'

'Yes, of course. She's in the middle of buying a new house and our old one's on the market. It's too big for me; I'm going to look for somewhere smaller nearer town ...'

I stole a sideways look at him as he went on talking. The wind was blowing his dark curls about in the same way as it was whipping my own hair across my face. He looked tall and strong and ruggedly sexy and I suddenly wished he would hold my hand. But that wasn't very likely after last time. I'd blown it.

We stood a metre apart, watching as Benson bounded back and forth. The tide was coming in and the grey sea crashed against the rocks. The sky was darkening, the horizon smudged purple. Gulls screamed above me and I could feel the spray on my face and stinging my eyes. It was really bitter now – I put a hand up to my cold nose.

'Perhaps we'd better get back,' I said. 'It'll be dark soon.'

He nodded. 'Last one,' he said to Benson, who was panting at his feet. He flung the ball away from him again, smiling as Benson hurled himself after it.

'You know, perhaps Charlotte's right,' said Andrew casually. He turned and faced me. 'About getting back on the horse.'

I rolled my eyes. 'Charlotte doesn't know one end of a horse from another.'

He laughed. 'I mean perhaps you should give this advice thing a go? Now you've had a positive TV experience, why not let something good come out of the whole thing – it might be fun, as she says.' His green eyes were fixed on mine. 'Because you know Laura, if there's one thing I've learned over the years it's that sometimes you have to know when to try again.'

Andrew looked down the beach where Benson was trotting along at the water's edge as if looking for something. His words were almost drowned in the sound of the wind and waves and I could only just make them out.

'Even if you've been knocked back before.'

He whistled. Benson looked up briefly and went back to

examining the rock pools. Andrew turned back to me. 'You look freezing. Here, come out of the wind.' He pulled me back into a recess in the cliff.

'Because it seems to me,' he was saying, 'that you did that whole TV thing to feel better about yourself. Wasn't that the idea? To show you were still strong and young and beautiful?'

'Not really,' I muttered.

'Well, it's how you looked today, anyhow,' he went on. 'And that's how you'd look if you did this advice programme. I tell you what -' He was still looking at me intently. 'Let's try you out.'

He leant back against the chalk, eyes upwards as if thinking.

'What would you say to an ageing 48-year-old with a spare tyre since he tried to give up smoking, who thinks he might be in love with a mad, hormone-ravaged female who throws wobblers in the supermarket?'

My stomach gave a small somersault. 'I'd tell him to get a grip.'

Andrew's arms tightened around me. 'Just what I was thinking ...'

His hand felt surprisingly warm around my cold fingers as we made our way back up the path, Benson trotting ahead of us.

'You really are lovely, you know,' he said. 'On TV, off TV – you're beautiful and you've got a great body.' He nudged me as we walked. 'So feel good about yourself, now, eh?'

'I'll try. It's just that on that bloody documentary ...'

He stopped beneath the street light outside Charlotte's house and put a hand beneath my chin and a finger across my lips. 'Forget it! Hold on to how you looked today. How you look to me now ...' His eyes shone in the light as he wrapped his arms around me. 'Now we've dealt with that and I've explained about my impending divorce and you know that I wasn't just being nice, and that in fact I fancy you rotten, can I kiss you again?'

'What about Stanley?' I asked. 'He collected enough WIT points last year to last him a decade of therapy. My New Year's resolution was to give him as normal an upbringing as I can manage. Will he be traumatised if he thinks I'm snuggled up to his teacher?'

Andrew looked up at one of Charlotte's brightly lit windows. 'He might already have a bit of an idea …'

We both watched the two small faces rapidly disappear behind the curtain.

'I won't always be teaching him,' said Andrew. 'And in the meantime, he'll cope.' He bent his head toward me. 'Of course, they always think it's fairly gross when old people do things like this …'

'Old people?' I echoed, outraged. 'Speak for yourself! I'll have you know,' I declared, adopting a Scottish accent supposed to be reminiscent of Miss Jean Brodie, but sounding rather more Irish and as if I'd had too much champagne, 'that I -' I ducked away, laughing, struggling to finish the sentence before his mouth closed over mine. 'I am in my *prime* …'

The End